About the Author

Diane Gaston's dream job had always been to write romance novels. One day she dared to pursue that dream and has never looked back. Her books have won Romance's highest honours: the RITA® Award, the National Readers Choice Award, Holt Medallion, Golden Quill, and Golden Heart. She lives in Virginia with her husband and three very ordinary house cats. Diane loves to hear from readers and friends. Visit her website at: http://dianegaston.com

Regency Scandals

Regency Scandal:

Unsuitable Marriages

DIANE GASTON

MILLS & BOON

First Published in Great Britain 2020
By Mills & Boon, an imprint of HarperCollins*Publishers*
1 London Bridge Street, London, SE1 9GF

www.harpercollins.co.uk

HarperCollins*Publishers*
1st Floor, Watermarque Building, Ringsend Road
Dublin 4, Ireland

REGENCY SCANDAL: UNSUITABLE MARRIAGES
© 2020 Harlequin Books S.A.

Bound by a Scandalous Secret © 2016 Diane Perkins
Born to Scandal © 2012 Diane Perkins

ISBN: 978-0-263-28196-5

MIX
Paper from
responsible sources
FSC™ C007454

This book is produced from independently certified FSC™ paper to ensure responsible forest management.

For more information visit: www.harpercollins.co.uk/green

Printed and bound in Great Britain
by CPI Group (UK) Ltd, Croydon, CR0 4YY

BOUND BY A
SCANDALOUS
SECRET

To the memory of my Aunt Gerry who was endlessly energetic, efficient, and, it seemed to me, could do just about anything.

Chapter One

Lincolnshire—December 1815

Genna Summerfield first glimpsed him out of the corner of her eye, a distant horseman galloping across the land, all power and grace and heedless abandon. A thrilling sight. Beautiful grey steed, its rider in a topcoat of matching grey billowing behind him. Horse and rider looked as if they had been created from the clouds that were now covering the sky. Could she capture it on paper? She grabbed her sketchpad and charcoal and quickly drew.

It was no use. He disappeared in a dip in the hill.

She put down the sketchpad and charcoal and turned back to painting the scene in the valley below, her reason for sitting upon this hill in this cold December air. How she wished she could also paint the galloping horse and rider. What a challenge it would be to paint all those shades of grey, at the same time conveying all the power and movement.

The roar of galloping startled her. She turned. Man and horse thundered towards her.

Drat! Was he coming to oust her from the property? To chase her from this perfect vantage point?

Not now! She was almost finished. She needed but a few minutes more. Besides, she had to return soon before someone questioned her absence—

The image of the horse and rider interrupted her thoughts. Her brush rose in the air as she tried to memorise the sight, the movement, the lights and darks—

Goodness! He galloped straight for her. Genna backed away, knocking over her stool.

The rider pulled the horse to a halt mere inches away.

'I did not mean to alarm you,' the rider said.

'I thought you would run me down!' She threw her paint-brush into her jug of water and wiped her hands on the apron she wore over her dress.

He was a gentleman judging by the sheer fineness of his topcoat and tall hat and the way he sat in the saddle, as if it were his due to be above everyone else.

Please do not let this gentleman be her distant cousin, the man who'd inherited this land that she once—and still—called home.

'My apologies.' He dismounted. 'I came to see if you needed assistance, but now I see you intended to be seated on this hill.'

'Yes.' She shaded her eyes with her hand. 'As you can see I am painting the scene below.'

'It is near freezing out,' he said. 'This cold cannot be good for you.'

She showed him her hands. 'I am wearing gloves.' Of course, her gloves were fingerless. 'And my cloak is warm enough.'

She looked into his face. A strong face, long, but not thin, with a straight nose that perfectly suited him, and thick dark brows. His hair, just visible beneath his hat was also dark. His eyes were a spellbinding caramel, flecked with darker brown. She would love to paint such a memorable face.

He extended his hand. 'Allow me to introduce myself. I am Rossdale.'

Not her cousin, then. She breathed a sigh of relief. Some other aristocrat.

She placed her hand in his. 'Miss Summerfield.'

'Summerfield?' His brows rose. 'My host, Lord Penford, is Dell Summerfield. A relation, perhaps?'

She knew Lord Penford was her cousin, but that was about all she knew of him. Just her luck. This man was his guest.

'A distant relation.' She lifted her chin. 'I'm one of the scandalous Summerfields. You've heard of us, no doubt.'

The smile on his face froze and she had her answer. Of course he'd heard of her family. Of her late father, Sir Hollis Summerfield of Yardney, who'd lost his fortune in a series of foolish investments. And her mother, who was legendary for having many lovers, including the one with whom she'd eloped when Genna was almost too little to remember her. Who in society had not heard of the scandalous Summerfields?

'Then you used to live at Summerfield House.' He gestured to the house down below.

'That is why I am painting it,' she responded. 'And I would be obliged if you would not mention to Lord Penford that I trespassed on his land. I have disturbed nothing and only wished to come here this one time to paint this view.'

He waved a dismissive hand. 'I am certain he would not mind.'

Genna was not so certain. After her father's death, Lord Penford had been eager for Genna and her two sisters to leave the house.

She stood and started to pack up her paints. 'In any event, I will leave now.'

He put his hand on her easel. 'No need. Please continue.'

She shook her head. The magic was gone; the spell broken. She'd been reminded the house was no longer her home. 'I must be getting back. It is a bit of a walk.'

'Where are you bound?' he asked.

Surely he knew *all* the scandals. 'To Tinmore Hall.' She gave him a defiant look. 'Or did you forget that my sister Lorene married Lord Tinmore?'

He glanced away and dipped his head. 'I did forget.'

Genna's oldest sister married the ancient Lord Tinmore

for his money so Genna and her sister Tess and half-brother Edmund would not be plunged into poverty. So they, unlike Lorene, could make respectable marriages and marry for love.

Genna had not forgiven Lorene for doing such a thing—sacrificing her own happiness like that, chaining herself to that old, disagreeable man. And for what? Genna did not believe in her sister's romantic notions of love and happily ever after. Did not love ultimately wind up hurting oneself and others?

The wind picked up, rippling her painting.

Rossdale put his fingers on the edge of it to keep it from blowing away. His brow furrowed. 'You have captured the house, certainly, but the rest of it looks nothing like this day...'

She unfastened the paper from the easel and carefully placed a sheet of tissue over it. She slipped it in a leather envelope. 'I painted a memory, you might say.' Or the emotion of a memory.

The wind gusted again. She turned away from it and packed up hurriedly, folding the easel and her stool, closing her paints, pouring out her jug of water and wrapping her brushes in a rag. She placed them all in a huge canvas satchel.

'How far to your home?' Rossdale asked.

Her *home* was right below them, she wanted to say. 'To Tinmore Hall, you mean? No more than five miles.'

'Five miles!' He looked surprised. 'Are you here alone?'

She pinched her lips together. 'I require no chaperon on the land where I was born.'

He nodded in a conciliatory manner. 'I thought perhaps you had a companion, maybe someone with a carriage visiting the house. May I convey you to Tinmore Hall, then?' He glanced towards the clouds. 'The sky looks ominous and you have quite a walk ahead of you.'

She almost laughed. Did he not know what could happen if a Summerfield sister was caught in a storm with a man?

Although Genna would never let matters go so far, not like her sister Tess who'd wound up married to a man after being caught in a storm. Why not risk a ride with Rossdale?

She widened her smile. 'How kind of you. A ride would be most appreciated.'

Ross secured her satchel behind the saddle and mounted Spirit, his favourite gelding, raised from a pony at his father's breeding stables. He reached down for Miss Summerfield and pulled her up to sit side-saddle in front of him.

She turned and looked him full in the face. 'Thank you.'

She was lovely enough. Pale, flawless skin, eyes as blue as sea water, full pink lips, a peek of blonde hair from beneath her bonnet. Her only flaw was a nose slightly too large for her face. It made her face more interesting, though, a cut above merely being beautiful. She was not bold; neither was she bashful or flirtatious.

Unafraid described her better.

She spoke without apology about being one of the scandalous Summerfields. And certainly was not contrite about trespassing. He liked that she was comfortable with herself and took him as he was.

Possibly because she did not know who he was. People behaved differently when they knew. How refreshing to meet a young woman who had not memorised Debrett's.

'Which way?' he asked.

She pointed and they started off.

'How long have you been a guest of Lord Penford?' she asked.

'Two days. I'm to stay through Twelfth Night.' Which did not please his father overmuch.

'Is Lord Penford having guests for Christmas?' She sounded disapproving.

He laughed. 'One guest.'

'You?'

'Only me,' he responded.

She was quiet and still for a long time. 'How—how do you find the house?' she finally asked.

He did not know what she meant. 'It is comfortable,' he ventured.

She turned to look at him. 'I mean, has Lord Penford made many changes?'

Ah, it had been her home. She was curious about it, naturally.

'I cannot say,' he responded. 'I do know he plans repairs.'

She turned away again. 'Goodness knows it needed plenty of repairs.'

'Have you not seen the house since leaving it?' he asked.

She glanced back at him and shook her head.

The grey clouds rolled in quickly. He quickened Spirit's pace. 'I think it will snow.'

As if his words brought it on, the flakes began to fall, here and there, then faster and thicker until they could not see more than two feet ahead of them.

'Turn here,' she said. 'We can take shelter.'

Through a path overgrown with shrubbery they came to a folly built in the Classical style, though half covered with vines. Its floor was strewn with twigs and leaves.

'I see Lord Penford did not tend to all of the gardens,' Miss Summerfield said.

'Perhaps he did not know it was here.' Ross dismounted. 'It is well hidden.'

'Hidden now,' she said. 'It was not always so.'

He helped her down and led Spirit up the stairs into the shelter. There was plenty of room. She sat on a bench at the folly's centre and wrapped her cloak around her.

He sat next to her. 'Are you cold?'

Her cheeks were tinged a delightful shade of pink and her lashes glistened from melted snowflakes. 'Not very.'

He liked that she did not complain. He glanced around. 'This folly has seen better days?'

She nodded, a nostalgic look on her face. 'It was once one of our favourite places to play.'

'You have two sisters. Am I correct?'

She swung her feet below the bench, much like she must have done when a girl. 'And a half-brother.' She slid him a glance. 'My bastard brother, you know.'

Did she enjoy speaking aloud what others preferred to hide?

'He was raised with you, I think?' It was said Sir Hollis tried to flaunt his love child in front of his wife.

'Yes. We all got on famously.'

She seemed to anticipate unspoken questions and answered them defiantly.

'Where is your brother now?' he asked.

'Would you believe he is a sheep farmer in the Lake District?' she scoffed.

'Why would I not believe it?' Almost everyone he knew could be considered a farmer when you got right down to it.

'Well, if you knew him you'd be shocked that he wound up raising sheep. He was an officer in the Twenty-Eighth Regiment. He was wounded at Waterloo.' She waved a hand. 'Oh, I am making him sound too grand. He was a mere lieutenant, but he *was* wounded.'

'He must have recovered?' Or he would not be raising sheep.

'Oh, yes.'

'And your other sister?' He might as well get the whole family story, since she seemed inclined to tell it.

'Tess?' She giggled but tried to stop herself.

'What amuses you?'

'Tess is married.' She strained not to laugh. 'But wait until I tell you how it was she came to be married! She and Marc Glenville were caught together in a storm. A rainstorm. Lord Tinmore forced them to marry.'

How ghastly. Nothing funny about a forced marriage. 'I am somehow missing the joke.'

She rolled her eyes. '*We* are caught in a storm. *You* could be trapped into marrying me.' She wagged a finger at him. 'So you had better hope we are not discovered.' Then an idea seemed to dawn on her face. 'Unless you are already married. In that case, only I suffer the scandal.' She made it sound as if suffering scandal was part of the joke.

'I am not married.'

She grinned. 'We had better hope Lord Tinmore or his minions do not come riding by, then.'

No one would find this place unless they already knew its location, even if they were foolish enough to venture out in a snowstorm. If they did find them, though, Ross had no worries about Lord Tinmore. Tinmore's power would be a trifle compared to what Ross could bring to bear.

She took a breath and sighed and seemed to have conquered her fit of giggles.

'I am acquainted with Glenville,' he remarked. 'A good man.'

'Glenville *is* a good man,' she agreed.

He could not speak of why he knew Glenville, though.

He'd sailed Glenville across the Channel in the family yacht several times during the war when Glenville pursued clandestine activities for the Crown. Braving the Channel's waters was about the only danger Ross could allow himself during the war, even if he made himself available to sail whenever needed. This service had been meagre in his eyes, certainly a trifle compared to what his friend Dell had accomplished. And what others had suffered. He'd seen what the war cost some of the soldiers. Limbs. Eyes. Sanity. Why should those worthy men have had to pay the price rather than he?

He forced his mind away from painful thoughts. 'I had not heard Glenville's marriage had been forced.'

'Had you not?' She glanced at him in surprise. 'Goodness. I thought everyone knew. I should say they seem very happy about it now, so it has all worked out. For the time being, that is.'

'For the time being?'

She shrugged. 'One never knows, does one?'

'You sound a bit cynical.' Indeed, she seemed to cycle emotions across her face with great rapidity.

Her expression sobered. 'Of course I am cynical. Marriage can bring terrible unhappiness. My parents' marriage certainly did.'

'One out of many,' he countered, although he knew several friends who were miserable and making their spouses even more so. His parents' marriage had been happy—until his mother died. In his father's present marriage happiness was not an issue. That marriage was a political partnership.

'My sister Lorene's marriage to Lord Tinmore is another example.' She glanced away and lowered her voice as if speaking to herself and not to him. 'She is wasting herself with him.'

'Has it been so bad? She brought him out of his hermitage, they say. He'd been a recluse, they say.'

'I am sure *he* thinks it a grand union.' She huffed. 'He now has people he can order about.'

'You?' Clearly she resented Tinmore. 'Does he order you about?'

'He tries. He thinks he can force me to—' She stopped herself. 'Never mind. My tongue runs away with me sometimes.'

She fell silent and stilled her legs and became lost in her own thoughts, which excluded him. He'd been enjoying their conversation. They'd been talking like equals, neither of them trying to impress or avoid.

He wanted more of it. 'Tell me about your painting.'

She looked at him suspiciously. 'What about it?'

'I did not understand it.'

She sat up straighter. 'You mean because the sky was

purple and pink and the grassy hills, blue, and it looked nothing like December in Lincolnshire?'

'Obviously you were not painting the landscape as it was today. You said you painted a memory, but surely you never saw the scene that way.' The painting was a riot of colour, an exaggeration of reality.

She turned away. 'It was a memory of those bright childhood days, when things could be what you imagined them to be, when you could create your own world in play and your world could be anything you wanted.'

'The sky and the grass could be anything you wanted, as well. I quite comprehend.' He smiled at her. 'I once spent an entire summer as a virtuous knight. You should have seen all the dragons I slew and all the damsels in distress I rescued.'

Her blue eyes sparkled. 'I was always Boadicea fighting the Romans.' She stood and raised an arm. *'"When the British Warrior queen, Bleeding from the Roman rods..."'* She sat down again. 'I was much influenced by Cowper.'

'My father had an old copy of Spencer's *The Faerie Queene*.' It had been over two hundred years old. 'I read it over and over. I sought to recreate it in my imagination.'

She sighed. 'Life seemed so simple then.'

They fell silent again.

'Do you miss this place?' he asked. 'I don't mean this folly. Do you miss Summerfield House where you grew up?'

Her expression turned wistful. 'I do miss it. All the familiar rooms. The familiar paintings and furniture. We could not take much with us.' Her chin set and her eyes hardened. 'I do not want you to think we blame Lord Penford. He was under no obligation to us. We knew he inherited many problems my father created.' She stood again and walked to the edge of the folly. Placing her hand on one of the columns, she leaned out. 'The snow seems to be abating.'

He was not happy to see the flakes stop. 'Shall we venture out in it again?'

'I think we must,' she said. 'I do not want to return late and cause any questions about where I've been.'

'Is that what happens?' he asked.

'Yes.' Her eyes changed from resentment to amusement. 'Although I do not always answer such questions truthfully.'

'I would wager you do not.'

Rossdale again pulled Genna up to sit in front of him on his beautiful horse. How ironic. It was the most intimate she had ever been with a man.

She liked him. She could not think of any other gentleman of her acquaintance who she liked so well and with whom she wanted to spend more time. Usually she was eager to leave a man's company, especially when the flattery started. Especially when she suspected they were more enamoured of the generous sum Lord Tinmore would provide for her dowry than they were of her. No such avaricious gleam reached Rossdale's eyes. She had the impression the subject of her dowry had not once crossed Rossdale's mind.

They rode without talking, except for Genna's directions. She led him through the fields, the shortest way to Tinmore Hall and also the way they were least likely to encounter any other person. The snow had turned the landscape a lovely white, as if it had been scrubbed clean. There was no sound but the crunch of the horse's hooves on the snow and the huff of the animal's breathing.

They came to the stream. The only way to cross was at the bridge, the bridge that had been flooded that fateful night Tess had been caught in the storm.

'Leave me at the bridge,' she said. No one was in sight, but if anyone would happen by, it would be on the road to the bridge. 'I'll walk the rest of the way.'

'So we are not seen together?' he correctly guessed.

She could not help but giggle. 'Unless you want a forced marriage.'

He raised his hands in mock horror. 'Anything but that.'

'Here is fine.' She slid from the saddle.

He unfastened her satchel and handed it to her. 'It has been a pleasure, Miss Summerfield.'

'I am indebted to you, sir,' she countered. 'But if you dare say so to anyone, I'll have to unfurl my wrath.'

He smiled down at her and again she had the sense that she liked him.

'It will be our secret,' he murmured.

She nodded a farewell and hurried across the bridge. When she reached the other side, she turned.

He was still there watching her.

She waved to him and turned away, and walked quickly. She was later than she'd planned to be.

She approached the house through the formal garden behind the Hall and entered through the garden door, removing her half-boots which were soaked through and caked with snow. One of the servants would take care of them. She did not dare clean them herself as she'd been accustomed to do at Summerfield. If Lord Tinmore heard of it, she'd have to endure yet another lecture on the proper behaviour of a lady, which did not include cleaning boots.

What an ungrateful wretch she was. Most young ladies would love having a servant clean her boots. Genna simply was used to doing for herself, since her father had cut back on the number of servants at Summerfield House.

She hung her damp cloak on a hook and carried her satchel up to her room. The maid assigned to her helped her change her clothes, but Genna waited until the girl left before unpacking her satchel. She left her painting on a table, unsure whether to work on it more or not.

She covered it with tissue again and put it in a drawer. She would not work on it now. Of that she was certain. Instead she hurried down to the library, opening the door cautiously and peeking in. No one was there, thank goodness, although it would have been quite easy to come up with a plausible excuse for coming to the library.

She searched the shelves until she found the volume she sought—*Debrett's Peerage & Baronetage*. She pulled it out and turned first to the title names, riffling the pages until she came to the Rs.

'Rossdale. Rossdale. Rossdale,' she murmured as she scanned the pages.

The title name was not there.

She turned to the front of the book again and found the pages listing second titles usually borne by the eldest sons of peers. She ran her finger down the list.

Rossdale.

There it was! And next to the name Rossdale was *Kessington d.* D for Duke.

She had been in the company of the eldest son of the Duke of Kessington. The heir of the Duke of Kessington. And she had been chatting with him as if he were a mere friend of her brother's. Worse, she had hung all the family's dirty laundry out to dry in front of him, her defiant defence over anticipated censure or sympathy. He'd seen her wild painting and witnessed her nonsense about Boadicea.

She turned back to the listing of the Duke of Kessington. There were two pages of accolades and honours bestowed upon the Dukes of Kessington since the sixteen hundreds. She read that Rossdale's mother was deceased. Rossdale's given name was John and he had no brothers or sisters. He bore his father's second title by courtesy—the Marquess of Rossdale.

She groaned.

The heir of the Duke of Kessington.

Chapter Two

Ross sipped claret as he waited for Dell in the drawing room. The dinner hour had passed forty minutes ago, not that he'd worked up any great appetite or even that he was in any great need of company. He was quite content to contemplate his meeting with Miss Summerfield. He'd been charmed by her.

How long had it been since a young woman simply conversed with him, about herself and her family skeletons, no less? Whenever he attended a society entertainment these days all he saw was calculation in marriageable young ladies' eyes and those of their mamas. All he'd seen in Miss Summerfield's eyes was friendliness.

Would that change? Obviously she'd not known the name Rossdale or its significance, but he'd guess she'd soon learn it. Would she join the ranks of calculating females then?

He was curious to know.

The door opened.

'So sorry, Ross.' Dell came charging in. 'I had no idea this estate business would take so long. I've alerted the kitchen. Dinner should be ready in minutes.'

Ross lifted the decanter of claret. 'Do you care for some?'

Dell nodded. 'I've a great thirst.'

Ross poured him a glass and handed it to him.

'First there is the problem of dry rot. Next the cow barn, which seems to be crumbling, but the worst is the condition of the tenant cottages. One after the other have leaking roofs, damaged masonry, broken windows. I could go on.' He took a swig of his wine.

'Sounds expensive,' Ross remarked with genuine sympathy.

How many estates did Ross's family own? Five, at least, not counting the hunting lodges and the town house in Bath. There were problems enough simply maintaining them. Think of how it would be if any were allowed to go into disrepair. This was all new to Dell, as well. He'd just arrived in Brussels with his regiment when he'd been called back to claim the title. His parents, older brother and younger sister had been killed in a horrific fire. Ross had delivered the news to him and brought him home.

A few weeks later Dell's regiment fought at Waterloo.

'A drain on the finances, for certain,' Dell said. 'Curse Sir Hollis for neglecting his property.'

'Do you have sufficient funds?' Ross asked.

His friends never asked, but when Ross knew they were in need he was happy to offer a loan or a gift.

Dell lifted a hand, 'I can manage. It simply rankles to see how little has been maintained.' He shook his head. 'The poor tenants. They have put up with a great deal and more now with this nasty weather.'

The butler appeared at the door. 'Dinner is served, sir.'

Dell stood. 'At least food is plentiful. And I've no doubt Cook has made us a feast.'

They walked to the dining room, its long table set for two adjacent to each other to make it easier for conversing and passing food dishes. The cook indeed had not disappointed. There were partridges, squash and parsnips. Ross's appetite made a resurgence.

'I hope your day was not a bore,' Dell said. 'Did you find some way to amuse yourself?'

'I did remarkably well,' Ross answered, spearing a piece of buttered parsnips with his fork. 'I rode into the village and explored your property.'

'And that amused you?' Dell looked sceptical.

'The villagers were talkative.' He pointed his fork at Dell. 'You are considered a prime catch, you know.'

Dell laughed. 'I take it you did not say who *you* were.'

Not in the village, he hadn't. 'I introduced myself simply as John Gordon.'

'That explains why there are no matchmaking mamas parked on the entry stairs.'

Ross smiled. 'I do believe tactics were being discussed to contrive an introduction to you.'

Dell shrugged. 'They waste their time. How can I marry? These properties of mine are taking up all my time.'

How many did he have? Three?

'I'm not certain your actual presence was considered important.' To so many young women, marrying a title was more important than actually being a peer's wife. 'In any event, it would not hurt to socialise with some of your more important neighbours, you know.'

'Who?' he asked unenthusiastically.

Ross took a bite of food, chewed and swallowed it before he answered. 'They said in the village that Lord Tinmore was in the country.'

'That prosy old fellow?' Dell cried.

'He's influential in Parliament,' Ross reminded him. 'It won't hurt at all to entertain him a bit. He might be a help to you when you take your seat.'

'Your father will help me.'

'My father certainly will help you, but it will not hurt to be acquainted with Tinmore, as well.' Ross tore off some meat from his partridge. 'You are related to Tinmore's wife and her sisters, I was told.'

'They are my distant cousins, I believe,' Dell said. 'The ones who grew up in this house.'

'Perhaps they would like to visit the house again.' Ross knew Genna would desire it, at least.

Dell frowned. 'More likely they would resent the invitation. I learned today that, not only was the estate left in near shambles, but the daughters were left with virtually nothing. My father turned them out within months of their father's death. That is why the eldest daughter married Tinmore. For his money.'

'Seems you learned a great deal.' No wonder Genna Summerfield sounded bitter.

Dell gave a dry laugh. 'The estate manager was talkative, as well.'

'Perhaps it would be a good idea to make amends.' And it would not hurt for Dell to be in company a little.

Dell expelled a long breath. 'I suppose I must try.'

Ross swirled the wine in his glass. 'I would not recommend risking offending Lord Tinmore.'

Dell peered at him. 'For someone with an aversion to politics, you certainly are cognizant of its workings.'

'How could I not be? My father talks of nothing else.' Ross refilled Dell's glass. 'I would not say I have an aversion, though. I simply know it will eventually consume my life and I am in no hurry for that to happen.'

Dell gulped down his wine and spoke beneath his breath. 'I never wanted this title.'

Ross reached over and placed his hand on Dell's shoulder. 'I know.'

They finished the course in silence and were served small cakes for dessert.

When that too was taken away and the decanter of brandy set on the table, Dell filled both their glasses. 'Oh, very well,' he said. 'I will invite them to dinner.'

Ross lifted his glass and nodded approvingly.

Dell looked him in the eye. 'Be warned, though. The youngest sister is not yet married.'

Ross grinned. 'I am so warned.'

Two days later, Genna joined her sister and Lord Tinmore at breakfast. Sometimes if she showed up early enough to share the morning meal and acted cheerful, she could count on being left to her own devices until almost dinner time. Besides, she liked to see if Lorene needed her company. There were often houseguests or callers who came out of obligation to the Earl of Tinmore. Most were polite to Lorene, but Genna knew everyone thought her a fortune hunter. Genna often sat through these tedious meetings so Lorene would not be alone, even though it was entirely Lorene's fault she was in this predicament.

A footman entered the breakfast room with a folded piece of paper on a silver tray. 'A message arrived for you, sir.'

Tinmore acknowledged the servant with a nod. The footman bowed and left the room again.

Tinmore opened the folded paper and read. 'An invitation,' he said, although neither Lorene nor Genna had asked. He tossed the paper to Lorene. 'From your cousin.'

'My cousin?' Lorene picked up the paper. 'It is from Lord Penford, inviting us to dinner tomorrow night at Summerfield House.'

Genna's heart beat faster. Was she included?

'We must attend, of course,' Tinmore said officiously. 'He peered over his spectacles at Genna. 'You, too, young lady.' He never called her by her name.

'I would love a chance to see Summerfield House again!' she cried.

Lorene did not look as eager. 'I suppose we must attend.'

The next day Genna was determined not to agonise over what to wear to this dinner. After all, it would be more in the nature of a family meal than a formal dinner party. There would not be other guests, apparently, save his houseguest, perhaps. A small dinner party, the invitation said, to extend his hospitality to his neighbour and his cousins.

Genna chose her pale blue dress because it had the fewest embellishments. She allowed her maid to add only a matching blue ribbon to her hair, pulled up into a simple chignon. She wore tiny pearl earrings in her ears and a simple pearl necklace around her neck. She draped her paisley shawl over her arm, the one with shades of blue in it.

She met Lorene coming out of her bedchamber.

Lorene stopped and gazed at her. 'You look lovely, Genna. That dress does wonders for your eyes.'

Genna blinked. Truly? She'd aimed to show little fuss.

'Do I look all right?' Lorene asked. 'I was uncertain how to dress.'

Lorene also chose a plain gown, but one in deep green. Her earrings were emeralds, though, and her necklace, an emerald pendant. The dark hue made Lorene's complexion glow.

Lorene looked like a creature of the forest. If Lorene were the forest, then Genna must be—what? The sky? Genna was taller. Lorene, small. Genna had blonde hair and blue eyes; Lorene, mahogany-brown hair with eyes to match. No wonder people whispered that they must have been born of different fathers. They were opposites. One earthbound. The other…flighty.

Genna put her arm around Lorene and squeezed her. 'You look beautiful as always. Together we shall present such a pretty picture for our cousin he will wish he had been nicer to us.'

Lorene smiled wanly. 'You are speaking nonsense.'

Genna grinned. 'Perhaps. Not about you looking beautiful, though.' They walked through the corridor and started down the long staircase. 'What is he, anyway? Our fourth cousin?'

Lorene sighed. 'I can never puzzle it out. He shares a great-great-grandfather or a great-great-great one with our father. I can never keep it straight.'

Genna laughed. 'He got the fortunate side of the family, obviously.'

They walked arm in arm to the drawing room next to

the hall where Lord Tinmore would, no doubt, be waiting for them. Before they crossed the threshold, though, they separated and Lorene walked into the room first, Genna a few steps behind her. Tinmore insisted on such formalities.

Lord Tinmore was seated in a chair, his neckcloth loosened. His valet, almost as ancient as the Earl himself, patted his forehead with a cloth. Tinmore motioned the ladies in, even though they were already approaching him.

Lorene frowned. 'What is amiss, sir? Are you unwell?'

He gestured to his throat. 'Damned throat is sore and I am feverish. Came upon me an hour ago.'

Lorene put her cloak and reticule on the sofa and pulled off a glove. She bent down and felt her husband's wrinkled, brown-spotted forehead. 'You are feverish. Has the doctor been summoned?'

'He has indeed, ma'am,' the valet said.

She straightened. 'We must send Lord Penford a message. We cannot attend this dinner.'

Not attend the dinner? Genna's spirits sank. She yearned to see her home again.

'I cannot,' Tinmore stated. 'But you and your sister must.'

Genna brightened.

'No,' Lorene protested. 'I will stay with you. I'll see you get proper care.'

He waved her away. 'Wicky will tend me. I dare say he knows better than you how to give me care.'

So typical of Tinmore. True, his valet had decades more experience in caring for his lordship than Lorene, but it was unkind to say so to her face.

'I think I should stay,' Lorene tried again in a more forceful tone.

Tinmore raised his voice. 'You and your sister *will* attend this dinner and make my excuses. I do not wish to insult this man. I may need his good opinion some day.' He ended with a fit of coughing.

A footman came to the door. 'The carriage is ready, my lord.'

'Go.' Tinmore flicked his fingers, brushing them away like gnats buzzing around his rheumy head. 'You mustn't keep the horses waiting. It is not good for them to stand still so long.'

Typical of Tinmore. Caring more for his horses' comfort than his wife's feelings.

Genna picked up Lorene's cloak and reticule and started for the door. Lorene caught up with her and draped the cloak around herself.

At least Lord Tinmore was too sick to admonish Lorene for not waiting for the footman to help her with her cloak.

'I really do not want to go,' Lorene whispered to Genna.

'Lord Tinmore will be well cared for. Do not fret.' Genna was more than glad Tinmore would not accompany them.

'It is not that,' Lorene said. 'I do not wish to go.'

'Why not?' Genna was eager to see their home again, no matter the elevated company they would be in.

Lorene murmured, 'It will make me feel sad.'

Goodness. Was not Lorene already sad? Could she not simply look forward to a visit home, free of Tinmore's talons? Sometimes Genna had no patience for her.

But she took her sister's hand and squeezed it in sympathy.

They spoke little on the carriage ride to Summerfield House. Who knew what Lorene's thoughts must be, but Genna was surprised to feel her own bout of nerves at the thought of seeing Rossdale again.

The Marquess of Rossdale.

If he expected her to be impressed by his title, he'd be well mistaken. *She* would not be one of those encroaching young ladies she'd seen during her Season in London, so eager to be pleasing to the highest-ranking bachelor in the room.

Heedless of the cold, she and Lorene nearly leaned out the windows as they entered the gate to Summerfield House, its honey-coloured stone so familiar, so beautiful. She'd seen the house only from afar. Up close it looked unchanged, except that the grounds seemed well tended. At least what she could see of them. A thin dusting of snow still blanketed the land.

When the carriage pulled up to the house, Genna saw a familiar face waiting to assist them from the carriage.

'Becker!' she cried, waving from the window.

Their old footman opened the door and put down the stairs.

'My lady,' he said to Lorene, somewhat reservedly. He helped her out.

'So good to see you, Becker,' Lorene said. 'How are you? In good health?'

'Good health, ma'am,' he replied.

He reached for Genna's hand next and grinned. 'Miss Genna.'

She jumped out and gave him a quick hug. Who cared if it was improper to hug a servant? She'd known him all her life.

'I have missed you!' she cried.

His eyes glistened with tears. 'The house is not the same without you.'

He collected himself and led Lorene and Genna through one of the archways and up the stairs to the main entrance. A guidebook had once described the house:

Summerfield House was built by John Carr, a contemporary of Robert Adam, in the Italianate style, with the entrance to the house on the first floor.

Genna loved that word. *Italianate*.

The door opened as they reached it.

'Jeffers!' Genna ran into the hall and hugged their old

butler, a man who had been more present in her life than her own father.

'Miss Genna, a treat to see you.' He hugged her back, but quickly released her and bowed to Lorene. 'My lady, how good to have you back.'

Lorene extended her hand and clasped Mr Jeffers's hand in a warm gesture. 'I am happy to see you, Jeffers. How are matters here? Is all well? Are you well?'

He nodded. 'The new master has had much needed work done, but it is quiet here without you girls.'

Genna supposed Jeffers still saw them in their pinafores. She touched his arm. 'We were never going to be able to stay, you know.'

Jeffers smiled sadly. 'That is true, but, still...' He blinked and turned towards the door. 'Are we not expecting Lord Tinmore?'

'He sends his regrets,' Lorene explained. 'He is ill.'

'I am sorry to hear it. Nothing serious, I hope?' he asked.

'Not serious.' Lorene glanced away. 'You should announce us to Lord Penford, I think.'

How very sad. Lorene acted as if Lord Tinmore was looking over her shoulder, ready to chastise her for performing below her station with servants. These were servants they'd known their whole lives, the people who had truly looked out for their welfare, and, even though Tinmore was nowhere near, Lorene could not feel free to converse with them.

Jeffers looked abashed. 'Certainly. They are in the octagon drawing room.'

He and Lorene started to cross the hall.

'Wait!' Genna cried.

She stood in the centre of the hall and gazed up at the plasterwork ceiling. There was the familiar pattern, the rosettes, the gold gilt, the griffins that hearkened back to her grandfather's days in India. Why had she never drawn the ceiling's design? Why had she not copied its pale cream, green and white?

'Come,' Lorene said impatiently. 'They are waiting for us.'

Genna took one more look, then joined her sister. As they walked to the drawing room, though, she fell back, memorising each detail. The matching marble stairs with their bright blue balustrades, the small tables and chairs still in the same places, the familiar paintings on the walls.

They reached the door to the drawing room. Would it be changed? she wondered.

Jeffers opened the door and announced. 'Lady Tinmore and Miss Summerfield.'

Two young gentlemen stood. One, of course, was Lord Rossdale, dressed in formal dinner attire, which made him look even more like a duke's heir. The other man was an inch or two shorter than Rossdale and fairer, with brown hair and blue eyes.

Jeffers continued the introductions. 'My lady, Miss Summerfield, allow me to present Lord Rossdale——'

The Marquess bowed.

'And Lord Penford.'

But Penford was so young!

He approached them. 'My cousins. How delightful to meet you at last.' His voice lacked any enthusiasm, however. He blinked at Lorene as if in surprise and stiffly offered his hand. 'Where is Lord Tinmore, ma'am?'

Lorene blushed, which was not like her. She might be reserved, but never sheepish. Unless Tinmore had cowed her into feeling insecure in company. Or perhaps she was as surprised as Genna that Penford was not their father's age.

'Lord Tinmore is ill.' Lorene put her hand in Penford's. 'A trifling illness, but he thought it best to remain at home.'

Penford quickly drew his hand away. 'I am delighted you accepted my invitation.' He glanced past Lorene and looked at Genna with a distinct lack of interest. 'And your sister.' He perfunctorily shook Genna's. 'Miss Summerfield.'

The stiff boor. Genna made certain to smile at him. 'Call me Genna. It seems silly to stand on ceremony when we are family.'

'Genna,' he repeated automatically. He glanced back to Lorene.

'You may address me as Lorene, if you wish,' she murmured.

'Lorene,' he murmured. 'My friends call me Dell.'

Which was not quite permission for Lorene and Genna to do so.

Rossdale stepped forward.

'Oh.' Penford seemed to have forgotten him. 'My friend Ross here is visiting with me over Christmas.'

'Ma'am.' Ross bowed to Lorene. When he turned to Genna, he winked. 'Miss Summerfield.'

She felt like giggling.

'Come sit.' Penford offered Lorene his arm and led her to a sitting area, with its pale pink brocade sofa and matching chairs that their mother had selected for this room. He placed her in one of the chairs and he sat in the other.

The Marquess gestured to Genna to sit, as well.

She hesitated. 'May I look at the room first?'

'By all means,' Penford responded.

'You lived here, I believe,' Rossdale said, remaining at her side.

'I did, sir,' she said too brightly.

So far he was not divulging the fact they'd met before. He stood politely while she gazed at another familiar plasterwork ceiling, its design mimicked in the octagon carpet below. Again, nothing was changed, not one stick of furniture out of place, not one vase moved to a different table, nor any porcelain figurines rearranged. She gazed at her grandmother's portrait above the fireplace, powdered hair and silk gown, seated in an idyllic garden.

Rossdale said, 'A magnificent painting.'

'Our grandmother.' Although neither she nor Lorene bore any resemblance to the lady. 'By Gainsborough.'

'Indeed?' He sounded impressed.

Genna had always loved the painting, but it was Gainsborough's depiction of the sky and greenery that fascinated her the most, so wild and windy.

'I am pouring claret. Would you like some, Genna?' Penford called over to her.

She felt summoned. 'Yes, thank you.'

She walked over and lowered herself on to the sofa. Rossdale sat next to her.

'Does the room pass your inspection?' Penford asked, a hint of sarcasm in his voice.

He handed her the glass of wine.

Was he censuring her for paying more attention to the room than the people in it? Well, how ill mannered of him! It was the most natural thing in the world to want to see the house where one grew up.

'It is as I remember it,' she responded as if it had been a genuine question. 'I confess to a great desire to see all the rooms again. We were in much turmoil when we left.' When he'd sent them packing, she meant.

Penford's face stiffened. He turned to Lorene, shutting Genna out. 'Do you also have a desire to see the house?'

Lorene stared into space. 'I have put it behind me.'

'I imagine Tinmore Hall is much grander than Summerfield,' he remarked.

Grander and colder, Genna thought.

'It is very grand, indeed,' Lorene responded.

Genna turned to Rossdale. 'I expect the house where you grew up would make both Summerfield House and Tinmore Hall look like tenants' cottages.'

His brows rose. Now *he* knew *she* knew his rank.

'Not so much different.' His eyes twinkled. 'Definitely grander, though.'

'Ross grew up at Kessington,' Penford explained to Lorene. 'You have heard of it?'

Her eyes grew wide. Now Lorene knew Rossdale's rank, as well. Wait until Lorene told Tinmore whom he'd missed meeting.

'Yes, of course.' Lorene turned to Rossdale. 'It is in Suffolk, is it not?'

'It is,' he replied. 'And it is a grand house.' He grinned. 'My father should commission someone to paint it some day.'

He leaned forward to pour himself more wine and brushed against Genna's leg.

Secretly joking with her, obviously. What fun to flaunt a secret and not reveal it.

'I paint, you know,' she piped up, feigning all innocence. 'I even paint houses sometimes.'

'Do you?' Penford said politely. 'How nice to be so accomplished.'

Genna waited for him to ask Lorene her accomplishments, which were primarily in taking excellent care of her younger siblings for most of their lives. He did not ask, though, and Lorene would never say.

Genna could boast on her sister's behalf, though. 'Lorene plays the pianoforte beautifully. And she sings very well, too.'

Lorene gazed at her hands clasped in her lap. 'I am not as skilled as Genna would have you believe.'

'Perhaps you will play for us tonight,' Penford said, still all politeness.

'After dinner, perhaps?' Genna suggested.

'Perhaps after dinner you would show me the house, Miss Summerfield,' Rossdale asked. 'It would kill two birds with one stone, so to speak. Ease my curiosity about the building and give you your nostalgic tour.'

How perfect, Genna thought. Lorene would simply spoil her enjoyment if she came along and Lord Penford's presence only reminded Genna that all her beloved rooms now belonged to him. With Rossdale, she could enjoy herself. She smiled. 'An excellent plan.'

Chapter Three

Ross enjoyed the dinner more than any he could recall in recent memory. Genna regaled them with stories about the house and their childhood years. She made those days sound idyllic, although if one listened carefully, one could hear the loneliness of neglected children in the tales.

Still, she made him laugh and her sister, too, which was a surprise. Heretofore Lady Tinmore had lacked any animation whatsoever. Dell was worse, though. He'd turned sullen and quiet throughout the meal.

It had never been Dell's habit to be silent. He'd once been game for anything and as voluble as they come. He'd turned sombre, though. Ross could not blame him. He simply wished Dell happy again.

In any event, Ross was eager to take a tour of the house with the very entertaining Genna.

After the dessert, he spoke up. 'I propose we forgo our brandy and allow Miss Summerfield her house tour. Then we can gather for tea afterwards and listen to Lady Tinmore play the pianoforte.'

Dell would not object.

'Very well,' Dell responded. He turned to Lady Tinmore as if an afterthought. 'If you approve, ma'am?'

'Certainly.' Lady Tinmore lowered her lashes.

She'd never let on if she did object, Ross was sure.

'What a fine idea! Let us go now.' Genna sprang to her feet and started for the door.

Ross reached her just as the footman opened it for her. She flashed the man a grateful smile and fondly touched his arm. These servants were the people she grew up with. Ross liked that she showed her affection for them.

They walked out the dining room and into the centre of the house, a room off the hall where the great staircase led to the upper floors.

'Where shall we start?' Ross asked.

Genna's expression turned uncertain. 'Would you mind terribly if we started in the kitchen? I would so much like to see all the servants. They will most likely be there or in the servants' hall. You may wait here, if you do not wish to come with me.'

'Why would I object?'

She smiled. 'Follow me.'

She led him down a set of stairs to a corridor on the ground floor of the left wing of the house. They soon heard voices and the clatter of dishes.

She hurried ahead and entered the kitchen. 'Hello, everyone!'

He remained in the doorway and watched.

The cook and kitchen maids dropped what they were doing and flocked around her. Other maids and footmen came from the servants' hall and other rooms. She hugged or clasped hands with many of them, asking them all questions about their welfare and listening intently to their answers. She shared information about her sisters and her half-brother, but, unlike her cynical conversation with Ross about her siblings, all was sunny and bright when she talked to the servants. So they would have no cause to worry, perhaps?

'Lorene—' she went on '*Lady Tinmore*, I mean—asked me to convey her greetings and well wishes to all of you. She is stuck with our host, I'm afraid, but I am certain she will ply me with questions about all of you as soon as we are alone.'

Ross remembered no such exchange between the sisters,

but it was kind of Genna to make the servants believe Lady Tinmore thought about them.

Finally Genna seemed to remember him. She gestured towards him and laughed. 'Lord Rossdale! I do not need to present you, do I? I am certain everyone knows who you are.' She turned back to the servants. 'Lord Rossdale begged for a tour of the house, but really only so I could see all its beloved rooms again and make this quick visit to you. I am told little has changed.'

'Only the rooms that were your parents,' the house-keeper told her. 'Lord Penford asked for a few minor changes in your father's room, which he is using for his own. He asked for your mother's room to be made over for Lord Rossdale.'

Ross turned to the housekeeper. 'He needn't have put you to the trouble, but the room is quite comfortable. For that I thank you.'

Genna looked pleased at his words. 'We should be on our way, though. I am sure Lady Tinmore will wish to return to Tinmore Hall as soon as possible, so we do not overstay our welcome.' She grinned. 'I am less worried about that. I'm happy for our cousin to put up with us for as long as possible. I am so glad to be home for a little while.'

But, of course, it would never be her home again.

There were more hugs and promises that Genna would visit whenever she could.

Ross interrupted the farewells. 'Might we have a lamp? I suspect some of the rooms will be dark.'

A footman dashed off and soon returned with a lamp. Genna extricated herself and, with eyes sparkling with tears, let Ross lead her away.

When they were out of earshot, she murmured, 'I miss them all.' She shot him a defiant look. 'No doubt you disapprove.'

'Of missing them?'

'Of such an attachment to servants,' she replied.

He lifted his hands in protest. 'That is unfair, Miss Summerfield. What have I said or done to deserve such an accusation?'

She sighed. 'You've done nothing, have you? Forgive me. I tend to jump to conclusions. It is a dreadful fault. After this past year mixing in society, I learned to expect such sentiments. Certainly Tinmore would have apoplexy if he knew I'd entered the servants' wing. No doubt that is why Lorene stayed away.'

'Does your sister disapprove of fraternising with servants as well?' He would not be surprised. She seemed the opposite of Genna in every way.

'Lorene?' Her voice cracked. 'Goodness, no. But she tries not to displease Tinmore.' She shrugged. 'Not even when he could not possibly know.'

'What shall we see next?' he asked, eager to change the subject and restore her good cheer.

'I should like to see my old room,' she responded. 'And the schoolroom.'

They climbed the two flights of stairs to the second floor and walked down a corridor to the children's wing.

She opened one of the doors. 'This was my room.'

It was a pleasant room with a large window, although the curtains were closed. She walked through the space, subdued and silent.

'Is it as you remember?' he asked.

She nodded. 'Everything is in the right place.'

'You are not happy to see it, though.'

She shook her head. 'There is nothing of me left here. It could be anyone's room now.' She continued to walk around it. 'Perhaps Lorene knew it would feel like this. Perhaps that is why she did not wish to come.'

He frowned. 'I am sorry it disappoints you.'

She turned to him with a sad smile. 'It is odd. I do feel disappointed, but I also like that I am seeing it again. It helps me remember what it once was, even if the remembering makes me sad.'

Ross had rooms in his father's various residences, rooms he would never have to vacate, except by choice. For him the rooms were more of a cage than a haven.

'Let us continue,' she said resolutely.

They entered every bedroom and Genna commented on whose room it had been and related some memory attached to it.

They came to the schoolroom. She ran her fingers over the surface of the table. 'We left everything here.' She opened a wooden chest. 'Here are our slates and some of the toys.' She pointed to a cabinet. 'Our books will be in there.' She sighed. 'It is as if we walked out of here as children, probably to run out of doors to play.'

'To become Boadicea?' Ross remembered.

She smiled. 'Yes! Out of doors the fun began.' She clasped her hands together and perused the room one more time. 'Let us proceed.'

They peeked in other guest bedchambers, but she hesitated when they neared the rooms that had been her parents'. 'I certainly will not explore Penford's room.' She said the name with some disdain.

'You seem inclined to dislike my friend,' he remarked.

'Well, he might have let us stay here a while longer.' She frowned.

'Dell only inherited the title last summer. I believe your resentment belongs to his father.'

Her eyes widened. 'Oh. I did not know.'

Dell might not desire him to say more. Ross changed the subject. 'I have no objection to your seeing your mother's bedchamber.'

She recovered from her embarrassment and blinked up at him with feigned innocence. 'Me? Enter a gentleman's bedchamber accompanied by the gentleman himself? What would Lord Tinmore say?'

'This will be one of those instances where Lord Tinmore will never know.' He grinned. 'Besides, for propriety's sake we will leave the door open and I dare say my valet will be inside—'

Her eyes widened in mock horror. 'A witness? He might tell Lord Tinmore! We would be married post-haste, I assure you.'

She mocked the idea of being married, so unlike the other young women thrown at him.

Her expression turned conspiratorial. 'Although I am pining to show you something about the house, so we might step inside the room just for a moment.'

With no one else would Ross risk such a thing, for the very reason of which she'd joked.

He opened the door and, as he expected, his valet was in the room, tending to his clothes.

'Do not be alarmed, Coogan,' he said to his man. 'We will be only a moment.'

'Yes, Coogan.' Genna giggled. 'Only a moment.'

'Do you require something, m'lord?' Coogan asked. 'I was about to join the servants for dinner, but I can delay—'

'We are touring the house and Miss Summerfield wishes to show me something about the room,' Ross replied. 'Stay until we leave.'

Ross was glad to have a witness, just in case.

She stepped just inside the doorway and faced a wall papered in pale blue. She pressed on a spot and a door opened, a door that heretofore had been unnoticed by Ross.

'We'll be leaving now,' she said to his valet and gestured for Ross to follow her.

They could not have been more than a fraction of a minute.

As soon as he stepped over this secret threshold, she pushed the door closed. Their lamp illuminated a secret hallway that disappeared into the darkness.

'My grandfather built this house so that he would never

have to encounter his servants in the house unless they were performing some service for him. He had secret doors put in all the rooms and connected them all with hidden passages. The servants had to scurry through these narrow spaces. We can get to any part of the house from here.' She headed towards the darkness. 'Come. I'll show you.'

Dell remained in the dining room with Lorene until they'd both finished the cakes that Cook had made for dessert. Their conversation was sparse and awkward.

He'd never met his Lincolnshire cousins, knew them only by the scandal and gossip that followed the family and had no reason to give them a further thought. He'd not been prepared for the likes of Lorene.

Lovely, demure, sad.

When he and Lorene retired to the drawing room, he was even more aware of the intimacy of their situation. What had he been thinking to allow Ross and the all-too-lively Genna to go off into the recesses of the house? Why the devil had Tinmore not simply refused the invitation? Why send his wife and her sister alone?

He realised they were standing in the drawing room.

She gestured to the pianoforte. 'Shall I play for you?'

'If you wish.' It would save him from attempting conversation with her, something that seemed to fail him of late.

She sat at the pianoforte and started to play. After the first few hesitant notes, she seemed to lose her self-consciousness and her playing became more assured and fluid. He recognised the piece she chose. It was one his sister used to play—Mozart's *Andante Grazioso*. The memory stabbed at his heart.

Lorene played the piece with skill and feeling. When she came to the end and looked up at him, he immediately said, 'Play another.'

This time she began confidently—*Pathétique* by

Beethoven—and he fancied she showed in the music that sadness he sensed in her. It touched his own.

And drew him to her in a manner that was not to be advised.

She was married to a man who wielded much influence in the House of Lords. Dell would be new to the body. Ross was right. He needed to tread carefully if he wished to do any good.

When Lorene finished this piece, she automatically went on to another, then another, each one filled with melancholy. With yearning.

The music moved him.

She moved him.

When she finally placed her hands in her lap, they were trembling. 'That is all I know by heart.'

'Surely there is sheet music here.' He looked around the pianoforte.

She rose and opened a nearby cabinet. 'It is in here.' She removed the top sheet and looked at it. 'Oh. It is a song I used to play.'

'Play it if you like.' After all, what could he say to her if she stopped playing? His insides were already shredded.

She placed the sheet on the music rack, played the first notes and, to his surprise, began to sing.

> *I have a silent sorrow here,*
> *A grief I'll ne'er impart;*
> *It breathes no sigh, it sheds no tear,*
> *But it consumes my heart.*
> *This cherished woe, this loved despair,*
> *My lot for ever be,*
> *So my soul's lord, the pangs to bear*
> *Be never known by thee.*

Her voice was clear and pure and the feeling behind the lyrics suggested this was a song that had meaning for her.

What was her *'cherished woe'*, her *'loved despair'*? He knew what his grief was.

She finished the song and lifted her eyes to his.

'Lorene,' he murmured.

There was a knock on the door, breaking his reverie.

The butler appeared. 'Beg pardon, sir, my lady.'

'What is it, Jeffers?' Dell asked, his voice unsteady.

'The weather, sir,' Jeffers said. 'A storm. It has begun to snow and sleet.'

Lorene paled and stood. Dell stepped towards the window. She brushed against him as he opened the curtains with his hand. They both looked out on to ground already tinged with white. The hiss of sleet, now so clear, must have been obscured by the music.

She spun around. 'We must leave! Where is Genna?'

'I sent Becker to find her,' Jeffers said.

'Well done, Jeffers. Alert the stables to ready the carriage.' Dell turned towards Lorene. 'You might still make it home if you can leave immediately.'

Lorene placed her hands on her cheeks. 'We did not expect bad weather.'

Dell touched her arm, concerned by her distress. 'Try not to worry.'

'Where is Genna?' she cried, rushing from the room. 'Why did she have to tour the house?'

Genna led Ross through dark narrow corridors, stopping at doors that opened into the other bedchambers. On the other side, the doors to the secret passageways were nearly invisible to the eye. While they navigated this labyrinth, sometimes they heard music.

'Lorene must be playing the pianoforte,' Genna said.

The music wafting through the air merely made their excursion seem more fanciful.

It was like a game. Ross tried to guess what room they'd come upon next with the floor plan of the house fixed in his mind, but he was often wrong. Genna navigated the spaces with ease, though, and he could imagine her as a little girl running through these same spaces.

She opened a door on to the schoolroom. 'Is it not bizarre? The passageways even lead here. Why would my great-grandfather care if servants were seen in the nursery?'

'I wonder why he built the whole thing,' Ross said.

She grinned. 'It made for wonderful games of hide and seek.'

He could picture it in his mind's eye. The neglected children running through the secret parts of the house as if the passages had been created for their amusement.

'It even leads to the attic!' They came upon some stairs and she climbed to the top, opening a door into a huge room filled with boxes, chests and old furniture. Their little lamp illuminated only a small part of it.

Ross's shoe kicked something. He leaned down and picked up what looked like a large bound book.

'What is that?' she asked, turning to see.

He handed it to her and she opened it.

'Oh! It is my sketchbook.' Heedless of the dust, she sat cross-legged on the floor and placed the lamp nearby. She leafed through the pages. 'Oh, my goodness. I thought this was gone for ever!'

'What is it doing up here?' he asked.

'I hid it for safekeeping and then I could not remember where it was.' She closed it and hugged it to her. 'I cannot believe you found it!'

'Tripped over it, you mean.' He made light of it, but her voice had cracked with emotion.

When had he ever met a woman who wore her emotions so plainly on her sleeve? And yet…there was more she kept hidden. From everyone, he suspected. With luck the Christmas season would afford him the opportunity to see more of her.

She opened the book again and turned the pages. Illuminated by the lamp, her face glowed, looking even lovelier than she'd appeared before. Her hair glittered like threads of gold and her blue eyes were like sapphires, shadowed by long lashes. What might it be like to comb his fingers through those golden locks and to have her eyes darken with desire?

He stepped back.

For all the scandal in her family she was still a respectable young woman. A dalliance with her would only dishonour her and neither she nor he wished for something more honourable—like marriage.

The time was nearing when he would be forced to pick among the daughters of the *ton* for a wife worthy of becoming a duchess. Not yet, though. Not yet.

She looked up at him. 'What should I do with it?'

'Take it, if you wish. It is yours.'

Her brow creased. 'Would Lord Penford mind, do you think? He might not like knowing I was poking through the attic.'

He shrugged. 'I cannot think he would care.'

She stood and, clutching her sketchbook in one hand, brushed off her skirt with the other. 'We were not supposed to take anything but personal items.'

He pointed to the book. 'This is a personal item.'

She stroked it. 'I suppose.'

He crouched down to pick up the lamp. 'In any event, we should probably make our way back to the drawing room.'

She nodded.

He helped her through the door and down the stairs. She led him through the secret corridor down more stairs to the main floor where they heard their names called.

'Genna! Where are you?' her sister cried.

'Ross! We need you!' Dell's voice followed.

Genna giggled. 'They must think we have disappeared into thin air.'

'Does your sister not know of the secret passageway?'

'She knows of it, but we really stopped using it years ago.' She paused. 'At least Lorene and Tess did.' She seized his hand. 'Come. We'll walk out somewhere where we will not be seen emerging from the secret passageway.'

They entered another hallway, and Ross had no idea where they were.

'This is the laundry wing.' She led him to a door that opened on to the stairway hall, but before stepping into the hall, she placed her sketchbook just inside the secret passage.

'Genna!' her sister called again, her voice coming from the floor above.

'We are here!' Genna replied, closing the door which looked nearly invisible from this side. 'At the bottom of the stairs.'

Her sister hurried down the stairs, Dell at her heels. 'Where have you been? We have been searching for you this half-hour!'

Genna sounded all innocence. 'I was showing Lord Rossdale the house. We just finished touring the laundry wing.'

'The laundry wing!' Lady Tinmore cried. 'What nostalgia did you have for the laundry wing?'

'None at all,' Genna retorted. 'I merely thought it would interest Lord Rossdale.'

'I assure you, it did interest me,' Ross replied as smoothly as his companion. 'I am always interested in how other houses are run.'

Dell tossed him a puzzled look and Ross shook his head to warn his friend not to ask what the devil he was about.

'Never mind.' Genna's sister swiped the air impatiently. 'The weather has turned dreadful. Jeffers has called for the carriage. We must leave immediately.'

Genna sobered and nodded her head. 'Of course.'

Jeffers appeared with their cloaks and Ross hurriedly

helped Genna into hers. As they rushed to the front door and opened it, a footman, his shoulders and hat covered with snow, was climbing the stairs.

'The coachman says he cannot risk the trip,' the footman said, his breath making clouds at his mouth. 'The weather prevents it.'

They looked out, but there was nothing to see but white.

'Oh, no!' Lady Tinmore cried.

Genna put her hands on her sister's shoulders and steered her back inside. 'Do not worry, Lorene. This could not have been helped.'

'We should have left earlier,' she cried.

'And you would have been caught on the road in this,' Dell said. 'And perhaps stranded all night. We will make you comfortable here. I will send a messenger to Lord Tinmore as soon as it is safe to do so.'

'We will have to spend the night?' Lorene asked.

'It cannot be helped,' Genna said to her. 'We will have to spend the night.'

Chapter Four

The lovely evening was over.

Although Lord Penford had tea brought into the drawing room, Lorene's nerves and Penford's coolness spoiled
Genna's mood. Lorene was worried, obviously, about what
Lord Tinmore would say when they finally returned and
who knew why Penford acted so distantly to them? Why
had he invited them if he did not want their company? Had
he done so out of some sense of obligation? Even so, it was
Lord Tinmore who'd compelled them to accept the invitation and she and Lorene certainly had not caused it to snow.

Not that it mattered. If Tinmore wished to ring a peal
over their heads, reason would not stop him.

All the enjoyment had gone out of the evening, though.

Lord Penford poured brandy for himself and Rossdale
and sat sullenly sipping from his glass while Rossdale and
Genna made an effort to keep up conversation. With no
warning Penford stood and announced he was retiring for
the night. Rossdale was kind enough to keep Genna and
Lorene company until the housekeeper announced that
their bedchambers were ready. At that point they also felt
they must say goodnight.

The housekeeper led them upstairs. 'We thought you
might like to spend the night in your old rooms, so those
are what we prepared for you.'

'Thank you,' Lorene said.

Genna gave the woman whom she'd known her whole
life a hug. 'Yes, thank you. You are too good to us.'

The older woman hugged her back. 'We've found clean

nightclothes for you, as well. Nellie and Anna will help you.' Nellie and Anna had served as their ladies' maids before they'd moved.

They bade the housekeeper goodnight and Genna entered her bedchamber for the second time that night. At least now there was a fire in the grill and a smiling old friend waiting for her.

'How nice it is that you can stay the night,' Anna said. 'In your old room. Like old times.'

'It is grand!' Genna responded.

Anna helped her out of her dress and into a nightgown. 'Come sit and I'll comb out your hair,' Anna said.

Genna sat at her old familiar dressing table and gazed in her old familiar mirror. 'Tell me,' she said after a time. 'What are the servants saying about Lord Penford?'

Anna untied the ribbon in her hair. 'We are grateful to him. He kept most of us on and we did not expect that. He does seem angry when he learns of some new repair to the house, but his anger is never directed at the servants.'

'He must be angry at my father, then,' Genna said. Did his anger extend to the daughters, too? That might explain why he was so unfriendly.

'I suppose you are right.' She pulled out Genna's hairpins and started combing out the tangles. 'He paid us our back wages, you know.'

Genna glanced at her in the mirror. 'Did he? How good of him.'

Paying their back wages was certainly something Lord Penford could have avoided if he'd chosen to. What could the servants do if he'd refused to pay them?

Anna gave her a sly grin. 'Why are you not asking about Lord Rossdale?'

Genna felt her cheeks grow hot. Why would that happen? 'Lord Rossdale? Whatever for?'

She stopped combing. 'Is he sweet on you? We were wondering.'

'He's not sweet on me!' Genna protested. 'Goodness. He's far beyond my touch. Besides, you know that I'm not full of romantic notions like Lorene and Tess. He knew I wanted to see the house so he asked for a tour.'

'So he said in the kitchen.' Anna resumed combing. 'I am still saying he's sweet on you.'

Genna stilled her hand and met Anna's gaze in the mirror. 'Please do not say so. At least not to anyone else. I admit Lord Rossdale and I do seem to enjoy each other's company, but it is nothing more than that and I do not want any rumours to start. It would not be fair when he has merely been kind to me.'

Anna shrugged. 'If you say so.'

As soon as Anna left, Genna started missing her. She missed all these dear people. Now she would have to get used to not seeing them all over again. It was so very depressing.

She stared at the bed, not sleepy one bit. All she'd do was toss and turn and remember when her room looked like *her* room. She spun around and strode to the door.

Like she'd done so many times when she was younger, she crossed the hallway to Lorene's room and knocked on her door.

'Come in,' Lorene said.

Genna opened the door. 'I came to see how you are faring. You were so upset about the weather and our having to spend the night.' How the tables had turned. Genna used to run to Lorene for comfort, now it was the other way around.

Lorene lowered herself into a chair. 'I confess I am distressed. What will he think?' She did not need to explain who *he* was. 'Knowing we are spending the night with two unmarried gentlemen without any sort of chaperon.'

Genna sat on the floor at her feet and took Lorene's wringing hands in hers. 'We are home. Among our own servants. And Lord Penford and Lord Rossdale are gentlemen. There is nothing to worry over.'

Lorene gave her a pained look.

Genna felt a knot of anger inside. 'Will Tinmore...give you a tongue lashing over this?' Or worse, he might couch his cruelty in oh-so-reasonable words.

Lorene leaned forward and squeezed Genna's fingers. 'Do not worry over that! Good heavens, he is so good to us.'

Only when it suited him, though. He liked to be in charge of them.

Well, he might be in charge of Lorene, but Genna refused to give him power over her—even if she reaped the advantages of his money. She could not escape admitting that.

She smiled at Lorene. 'Let us enjoy our time back in our old rooms, then. Back *home*. Does it not feel lovely to be here?'

Lorene pulled her hands away and swept a lock of hair away from her face. 'I cannot enjoy it as you do, now that it is no longer our home.'

Genna secretly agreed. She did not enjoy seeing the rooms empty of any signs of her sisters or brother or herself, but she'd never admit it to Lorene. The best part of the house tour had been showing Rossdale the secret passages; the rest merely made her sad, just as Lorene had anticipated.

Genna stood. 'I love being back. I'm glad we can stay. I'll sleep in my old bed. I'll wake to sun shining in *my* windows. Cook will make us our breakfast again. It will be delightful.'

Lorene rose, too, and walked to the window. 'We had better hope the sun shines tomorrow.' She peeked out. 'It is still snowing.'

Genna gazed out on to the familiar grounds, all white now. 'We must not worry about tomorrow until it comes.' She turned to Lorene. 'How did you and Lord Penford fare while we toured the house?'

Lorene averted her face. 'I played the pianoforte.'

'We heard,' Genna said. 'You learned to play on that piano. How nice you were able to play on it again.'

'Yes,' Lorene replied unconvincingly. 'Nice.'

Cheering up Lorene was not working at all. It was merely making Genna feel wretched. 'Well, I believe I will go back to my room and snuggle up in my old bed. You've no idea how I've yearned to do so.'

Even if she feared she'd merely toss and turn.

She bussed her sister on the cheek and walked back to the room where she'd slept for years, ever since she'd left the nursery.

But once in the room, she found it intolerable. She paced for a few minutes, trying to decide what to do. Finally she made up her mind. She picked up a candle from the table next to her bed and carried it to the hidden door. She opened the door and entered the passageway.

She made her way downstairs and to the space where she'd left her sketchbook. As she picked it up and turned to go back to her room, the light from another candle approached. Her heart pounded.

'Miss Summerfield.' It was Lord Rossdale.

He came closer and smiled. 'I came to pick up your sketchbook. I see you had the same notion. I am glad you decided to keep it.'

She clutched it to her chest. 'I have not decided to keep it. I just wished to look at it in my room. I cannot take it back with me. It is too big to conceal and I do not wish to cause any problems.'

'I am certain Dell would wish you to have it,' he said.

She could not believe that. Even so, Lorene would probably worry about her taking it out of the house. 'I do not wish to ask him or to have my sister know. She would not like him bothered.' Genna was certain Lorene would not wish her to ask anything of Lord Penford.

Rossdale did not move, though, and the corridor was too narrow for Genna to get past him.

'Enjoy the book tonight, then,' he said finally. 'Come, I'll walk you back to your room.'

She laughed softly. 'More like you want me to show you the way so you do not become lost.'

He grinned. 'I am found out.'

He flattened himself against the wall so she could get by, but she still brushed against him and her senses heightened when they touched.

How strange it was to react so to such a touch. She did not understand it at all.

And she dared not think about it too much.

The next morning did indeed begin with the sun pouring in Genna's bedroom window. For a moment it seemed as if the last year had never happened. That was, until her gaze scanned the room.

Still, she refused to succumb to the blue devils. Instead she bounded from the bed and went to the window. Her beloved garden was still covered in snow, not only sparkling white, but also showing shades of blue and lavender in the shadows. The sky was an intense cerulean, as if it had been scrubbed clean of clouds during the night, leaving only an intense blue.

Genna opened the window and leaned out, gulping in the fresh, chilled air, relishing the breeze through her hair, billowing under her nightdress to tingle her skin.

'It is a lovely day!' she cried.

On a rise behind the house, a man riding a horse appeared. A grey horse and a grey-coated man.

Lord Rossdale.

He took off his hat and waved to her.

Imagine that he should see her doing such a silly thing. In her nightdress, no less! Perhaps he had heard her nonsense, as well.

She laughed and waved back before drawing back inside and shutting the window. She sat at her small table and turned the pages of her old sketchbook, remembering when life was more pleasant here.

Unfortunately, some of her drawings also reminded her of unhappy times. Hearing her father bellow about how much his daughters cost him, or rail against her mother who'd deserted them when Genna was small. Then there were the times when he'd consumed too many bottles from the wine cellar and she'd hidden from him. Her drawings during those times were sombre, rendered in charcoal and pencil, all shadowy and fearful.

Most of the pages, though, were filled with watercolours. Playful scenes that included her sisters and brother. Sunny skies, green grasses, flowers in all colours of the rainbow.

Her technique had been hopelessly childish, but, even so, her emotions had found their way on to the paper. The charcoal ones, obviously sad. The watercolours, happy and carefree.

A soft knock sounded at the door. Before Genna could respond, Anna opened the door and poked her head in.

She paused in surprise. 'Good morning, miss. I thought you would still be sleeping.'

Genna smiled. 'The sun woke me.' She closed the sketchbook and gestured to the window. 'Is it not a beautiful day?'

'It is, indeed, miss.' Anna entered the room and placed a fresh towel by the pitcher and basin Genna had used since a child. 'Mr Jeffers sent one of the stable boys with a message to Tinmore Hall.'

'That should relieve Lorene's mind.' Genna swung back to the window. 'How I would like it if I had my half-boots with me. I would love to be outside.' Even if she had her watercolours and brushes with her, she could paint the scene below and include all the colours she found in the white snow. That would bring equal pleasure.

She gazed out of the window again, wishing she were

galloping across the snow-filled fields. On a grey horse, perhaps. Held by a grey-coated gentleman.

She turned away with a sigh. 'I suppose I might as well wash up. Then you can help me dress.'

Anna also arranged her hair in a simple knot atop her head.

When she was done, Genna stood. 'I might see if Lorene is awake yet.' She turned to Anna and filled with emotion again. 'I do not know when I will see you again.' She hugged Anna. 'I shall miss you!'

Anna had tears in her eyes when Genna released her. 'I shall miss you, too, miss. We all miss you.'

Genna swallowed tears of her own. 'I will contrive to visit if I can.'

She left the room, knowing she was unlikely to see it again, ever, and knocked on Lorene's door.

Lorene was alone in the room seated in one of the chairs. Doing nothing but thinking, Genna supposed.

'How did you sleep?' Genna asked.

'Quite well,' Lorene responded. Of course, Lorene would respond that way no matter what.

'Anna told me a messenger was sent to Tinmore Hall,' Genna assured her.

Lorene merely nodded.

Genna wanted to shake her, shake some reaction, some emotion from her, something besides worry over what Lord Tinmore would think, say, or do. She wanted her sister the way she used to be.

'Shall we go down to breakfast?' Genna asked.

Lorene rose from her chair. 'If you like.'

They made their way to the green drawing room where breakfast was to be served. Lord Penford sat at the table, reading a newspaper. He looked startled at their entrance and hastily stood.

'Good morning,' he said stiffly. 'I did not expect you awake so early.'

'We are anxious to return to Tinmore Hall,' Lorene said.

'Yes,' Penford said. 'I imagine you are.'

'*I* am not so eager to return,' Genna corrected. 'I have enjoyed my visit to our old home immensely.' She looked over the sideboard where the food was displayed. 'Oh, look, Lorene. Cook has made porridge! It has been ages and ages since I've tasted Cook's porridge!

Becker, one of the footmen, attended the sideboard. Lorene made her selections, including porridge, and was seated next to Lord Penford at the small round breakfast table.

Becker waited upon Genna next, placing a ladle of oatmeal into a bowl for her. She added some cheeses, bread and jam.

'Thank you, Becker.' She smiled at him as he carried her plate to the table and seated her opposite her sister.

Penford sat as well although he did not look at either of them. 'I trust you slept well.'

Lorene hesitated for a moment before answering, 'Very well, sir.'

'Fabulously well!' added Genna. 'Like being at home.'

Lorene shot her a disapproving look, before turning to Penford. 'It was a kindness to put us in our old rooms.'

He glanced down at his newspaper. 'The housekeeper's decision, I am sure.'

Goodness! Could he be more sullen? 'I hope you did not disapprove.'

He shot her a surprised look. 'Why would I disapprove?'

She merely answered with a smile.

Why had he invited them if he seemed to take no pleasure in the visit? Unless his main purpose was to curry favour with Tinmore. If so, Genna was glad Tinmore had not accompanied them. Well, she was glad Tinmore had not accompanied them, no matter what Penford thought. Perhaps if Penford had been a more generous man, he might have left his cousins in the house to manage it in his absence.

He might have come to their rescue instead of tossing them out of the only home they'd ever known and forcing Lorene to make that horrible marriage.

Lorene broke in. 'The porridge is lovely. Just as I remembered it.'

Penford's voice deepened. 'I am glad it pleases you.' He put down his paper and darted Lorene a glance. 'I sent a man to Tinmore Hall early this morning. The roads are passable. You may order your coach at any time.'

He was in a hurry to be rid of them, no doubt.

'Might we have the carriage in an hour?' Lorene asked this so tentatively one would think she was asking for the moon instead of what Penford was eager to provide.

'Certainly.' Penford nodded towards Becker, who bowed in reply and left the room to accomplish the task.

Genna sighed and dipped her spoon into the porridge. She'd hoped to see Lord Rossdale one more time, but likely he was still galloping over the fields.

The rest of the breakfast transpired in near silence, except for the rattle of Lord Penford's newspaper and the bits of conversation exchanged between Genna and Lorene. Genna used the time to think about the house. Her time away had seemed to erase it as her home. Leave the place to the dour Lord Penford. Her life here was gone for ever. More of its memories had been captured in her sketchbook, but she had no confidence that it would ever return to her possession. Likely she would not even see Rossdale again.

When it came time for them to leave, the servants gathered in the hall to bid them goodbye, just as they had done when Genna and her sisters first removed to Tinmore Hall. This time the tears did not fall freely, although many bid them farewell with a damp eye. Lorene shook their hands. Genna hugged each of them. Lord Penford stood to the side and Genna wondered if he felt impatient for them to depart.

When the coach pulled up to the front, Penford walked

outside with them, without greatcoat, hat, or gloves. One of the coachmen helped Genna climb into the coach.

Lord Penford took Lorene's hand to assist her.

Lorene turned to him, but lowered her lashes. 'Thank you, sir, for inviting us and for putting us up for the night.' She lifted her eyes to him.

For a moment Penford seemed to hold her in place. He finally spoke. 'My pleasure.' He'd never seemed to experience pleasure from their visit. 'I shall remember your music.'

Lorene pulled away and climbed into the coach.

'Safe journey,' Penford said through the window.

As the coachman was mounting his seat, a horse's hooves sounded near. A beautiful silver-grey steed appeared beside the coach.

Rossdale leaned down from his saddle to look inside the coach. 'You are leaving already!'

Genna leaned out the window. 'We must get back.'

'Forgive me for not being here to say a proper goodbye.' His horse danced restlessly beside them.

Genna spoke in a false tone. 'I do not believe I shall forgive you.' She smiled. 'But thank you for allowing me to give you a tour of the house. It was most kind.'

He grinned. 'It certainly was more than I ever thought it would be.'

The coach started to move.

'Goodbye!' Genna sat back, but turned to look out the back window as the coach pulled away.

Rossdale dismounted from his horse and stood with Penford watching the coach leave.

They watched until the coach travelled out of their sight.

Chapter Five

Lorene fretted on the road back to Tinmore Hall. 'I wish we had not gone. He will have been frantic with worry when we did not return last night.'

Did she fear the effect of Tinmore's worry on his health or that he would blame her for their absence?

'He wanted us to go,' Genna reminded her. 'He ordered us to go.'

Lorene curled up in the corner of the carriage, making herself even smaller. 'Still, we should not have gone.'

Genna tried to change the subject. 'What did you think of our cousin, then? *Lord Penford.* Did you know he just inherited the title this summer?'

Lorene did not answer right away. 'I did not know that,' she finally said. 'Perhaps that was why he was so sad.'

'Sad?' Genna had not considered that. Perhaps he had not been disagreeable and rude. Perhaps he'd still been grieving. His father would have died only a few months before. She felt a pang of guilt.

'He's taking care of the house,' Genna said, trying to make amends, at least in her own mind. 'Anna said he paid the servants their back wages.'

'Did he?' Lorene glanced back at her. 'How very kind of him.'

Genna might have continued the conversation by asking what Lorene thought of Rossdale, but she didn't. She felt Lorene really wished to be quiet. Instead Genna recounted their tour of the house, intending to fix in her memory the details of each room they'd visited. More vivid, though, were Rossdale's reactions to those details. She'd enjoyed showing him the rooms more than she'd enjoyed visiting them.

Their carriage crossed over the bridge and the cupolas of Tinmore Hall came into view. The snow-covered lawn only set off the house more, its yellow stone gleaming gold in the morning sun. Genna's spirits sank.

She hated the huge mausoleum. The house hadn't seen a change in over fifty years. At least her mother had kept Summerfield House filled with the latest fashion in furnishings—at least until she ran off with her lover.

The carriage passed through the wrought-iron gate and drove up to the main entrance. Two footmen emerged from the house, ready to attend them. Moments later they were in the great hall, its mahogany wainscoting such a contrast to the light, airy plasterwork of Summerfield House.

Dixon, the butler, greeted Lorene. 'It is good you are back, m'lady.'

'How is Lord Tinmore?' she asked.

'His fever is worse, I fear, m'lady,' he responded. 'He spent a fitful night.'

Oh, dear. This would only increase Lorene's guilt.

'Did the doctor see him yesterday?' Lorene handed one of the footmen her cloak and gloves.

Dixon nodded. 'The doctor spent the night, caught in the storm as you were. He is here now.'

The doctor's presence should give Lorene some comfort.

'I must go to him.' Lorene started for the stairway. 'I ought to have been at his side last night.'

'He would not have known it if you were,' Dixon said.

Lorene halted and turned her head. 'He was that ill?'

'Insensible with fever, Wicky told us.'

'That is good, Lorene,' Genna broke in. 'He cannot be angry at you if he does not know you were gone.'

Lorene swung around. 'It is not good!' she snapped. 'He is ill.'

Genna felt her face grow hot. 'I am so sorry. It was a thoughtless thing to say.'

'And very unkind,' Lorene added.

'Yes,' Genna admitted, filled with shame. 'Very unkind. I am so sorry.'

Lorene turned her back on Genna and ran up the stairs.

Why could she not still her tongue at moments like these? She must admit she cared more about Lorene's welfare than Tinmore's health, but she did not precisely wish him to be seriously ill, did she?

She took a breath and glanced at Dixon. 'Is Lord Tinmore so very ill?'

His expression was disapproving. 'I gather so from Wicky's report.'

Genna deserved his disdain. By day's end the other servants would hear of her uncharitable comment and would call her an ungrateful wretch.

Which she was.

Over the next three days Genna hardly saw Lorene, who devoted all of her time to her husband's care. Genna would have happily assisted in some way—for Lorene's sake, not Tinmore's—but no one required anything of her and anything she offered was refused. She kept to her room, mostly, and amused herself by drawing galloping horses with tall, long-coated riders. She could never quite capture that sense of fluid movement she'd seen that day when she'd gone to make a painting of Summerfield House.

She had just finished another attempt and was contemplating ripping it up when there was a knock at her door. Her maid, probably. 'Come in,' she called, placing the drawing face down on her table.

'Genna—' It was Lorene.

Genna turned and rose from her chair. 'How is—?' she began.

Lorene did not let her finish. 'He is better. The fever

broke during the night and now he is resting more comfortably.'

'I am glad for you,' Genna said.

Lorene waved her words away.

Genna walked over to her. 'You look as if you need rest, too. Might you not lie down now?'

Lorene nodded. 'I believe I will. I just wanted you to know.'

'Thank you.' Genna felt careful, as if talking to a stranger. 'I am glad to know it.'

Lorene turned to leave, but a footman appeared in the corridor.

'My lady, two gentlemen have called to enquire after his lordship's health,' he said. 'Lord Rossdale and Lord Penford.'

Genna's heart fluttered. She would be excited for any company, would she not? Of course, they had not come to call upon her.

Lorene put a hand to her hair. 'Oh, dear. I am not presentable.' She turned to Genna. 'Would you entertain them until I can make myself fit for company?'

'Certainly. Anything to help.' Genna turned to the footman. 'Where are they?' There were so very many rooms in this house where visitors might be received.

'I put them in the Mount Olympus room,' he replied.

The room with the ceiling and walls covered with scenes from mythology, cavorting, nearly naked gods, all painted over a century before.

'Very good,' Lorene told him. 'Have Cook prepare some tea and biscuits.'

'Tea?' Genna said. 'Offer them wine. Claret or sherry or something.'

Lorene pursed her lips. 'Very well. Some wine, then, as well as tea and biscuits.'

The footman bowed and rushed off.

Lorene glanced at Genna.

'I can go down directly.' Genna took off the apron she wore to cover her dress and hurried to wash the charcoal off her fingers. She dried her hands. 'I'm off!'

Ross craned his neck and stared in wonder at the ceiling. It looked as if the mighty Zeus and all the lesser gods surrounding him might tumble down on to his head.

'This is quite a room,' he remarked. 'I am reminded of our Grand Tour—the palaces of Rome and Venice. Remember the murals? On every ceiling it seemed.'

'A man cannot think. The room fills the mind too much,' Dell responded.

Ross grinned. 'We did not do much thinking in those days, did we?'

Dell nodded, his face still grim. 'None at all, I recall.'

Ross perused the ceiling and walls again. 'In those days we would have been riveted by the naked ladies.' He stopped in front of one such figure, a goddess who appeared as if she would step out from the wall and join them.

Dell paced. 'Remind me again why we were compelled to come here?'

Ross had already explained. 'You wanted to become acquainted with Lord Tinmore, so calling to enquire after his health is only polite, especially after his illness kept him away from your dinner.'

The door opened and both men turned. Ross smiled. It was Genna, the one person he'd hoped to see when he concocted this scheme to call at Tinmore Hall.

Genna strode over to them. 'Rossdale. Penford. How good of you to call. My sister will be here in a few minutes. She has ordered refreshment for you, as well.'

Dell frowned. 'Lord Tinmore is still ill, then?'

'Lorene can better answer your questions.' She gave Dell a cordial smile. 'But, yes, Tinmore remains unwell.'

She gestured to the gilt stools cushioned in green damask that lined the walls of the room. 'Do sit.'

The room was in sore need of a rearrangement of furniture more conducive to conversation, Ross thought. A style more in tune with the present.

'Tell me, how is the weather?' Genna asked politely. 'I see our snow still covers the fields. Was it not terribly cold to ride this distance?'

'Not so terribly cold.' Ross kept his expression bland. 'I suspect some people would consider walking this far even when it is cold outside.' He darted a glance her way and saw she understood his joke.

'We felt it our duty to enquire into Lord Tinmore's health,' Dell said solemnly.

'How very good of you,' she responded, her voice kind.

Ross gave her an approving look.

'How were the roads?' she asked.

Dell shrugged. 'Slippery in places, but the horses kept their footing.'

'I think they relished the exercise,' Rossdale added. He'd relished it, as well.

She looked at a loss for what else to say. He fished around to find a topic and rescue her from having to make conversation.

She beat him to it. 'Tell me, do you plan to stay at Summerfield House for Christmastide?'

'At present that is our plan,' Dell responded.

Genna looked surprised. 'Do you not travel to visit your families?'

Dell averted his gaze and Rossdale answered. 'We decided to avoid all that.'

He hoped his tone warned her not to ask more about that. Dell's grief at the loss of his entire family was still raw. It was why Ross had elected to pass up a Christmas visit to his father at Kessington Hall. So he could be with his friend at such a time.

That and because he preferred his friend's company

to the politically advantageous guests his father always invited.

'What are your plans?' Ross asked her.

She sighed. 'Lord Tinmore plans a house party. Several of his friends will come to stay.' She did not seem to look forward to this. 'Guests should arrive next week.'

'No, they will not.' Her sister entered the room. Genna and the gentlemen stood. 'How do you do, sirs? It is kind of you to call.'

Dell's voice turned raspy. 'How—how fares Lord Tinmore?'

Lady Tinmore glanced up at him, then gazed away. 'He is better. The fever broke, but he remains too weak to receive callers.'

'We do understand,' Dell said stiffly. 'Please send our best wishes for his recovery.'

Lady Tinmore darted another glance at him. 'I will. Thank you, sir.'

Dell seemed uncomfortable around these sisters. Not ready for even this relatively benign social call?

Genna turned to her sister. 'What did you mean the guests will not arrive next week?'

Her sister replied, 'Tinmore has asked that the house party be cancelled. His secretary is to write to the guests today.'

The refreshments arrived. Ross and Dell accepted glasses of wine and offers of biscuits.

Ross stepped away while Lady Tinmore poured for Dell. To his delight, Genna joined him.

He wanted a chance to speak to her. 'Are you disappointed about the house party?' he asked.

She laughed. 'Not at all. I do not rub well with Lord Tinmore's friends.'

Her sister heard her and snapped, 'It is cancelled because Lord Tinmore needs the time to recover. He has been very sick, Genna.'

'I know that, Lorene,' Genna said softly.

Ross felt for her. No one liked being reprimanded in front of others.

He took a sip of his wine. 'Tell me about this room, Lady Tinmore. It is quite unusual.'

'It is called the Mount Olympus room,' Lady Tinmore responded, sounding glad to change the subject. 'Depicting the Greek gods. My husband said it was painted over one hundred years ago by the Italian muralist, Verrio. He painted a similar scene even more elaborate at Burghley House. And one at Chatsworth, as well. My husband prefers this one, though.'

Ross noticed Genna gazing at the walls and ceiling as if seeing them for the first time.

'It is hard to imagine one even more elaborate,' he said diplomatically. 'Although it does remind me of rooms we saw in Rome and Florence and Venice.'

'You've visited Rome and Florence and Venice?' Genna's eyes grew wide.

'We did indeed,' Ross replied. 'On our Grand Tour. You would have appreciated the fine art there.'

'Lord Tinmore's grandfather and great-grandfather collected many fine pieces of Italian art. They are hung in almost every room of this house,' Lady Tinmore said almost dutifully.

'They are?' Genna looked surprised.

Dell drained the contents of his wineglass and placed it on the table. 'We must take our leave.' He spoke to Lady Tinmore, but did not quite meet her eye. 'I do hope Lord Tinmore continues to improve.'

'Thank you,' she murmured.

Ross bowed to her. 'It was a pleasure seeing you again, ma'am.' He turned to Genna. 'And you, Miss Summerfield. I hope we meet again.'

'Yes.' Genna smiled. 'I would enjoy that.'

Perhaps he could convince Dell to call upon Lord Tinmore again. Or he could call upon the gentleman himself, although he had less reason to do so and no interest in meeting the man. He merely wanted to see Genna again.

And he still must devise a way to deliver her sketchbook to her as he had promised.

Before Ross could say another word, Dell strode out of the room as if in a hurry. Ross was compelled to follow, although he did so at a more appropriate pace.

He also turned back to the ladies when he reached the door. 'Good day, ma'am. Miss Summerfield.'

When he caught up to Dell in the hall, Dell had already sent the footman for their greatcoats, hats and gloves.

'What the devil was the rush?' Ross asked him.

'We were intruding.' Dell did not meet his eye. 'Tinmore is still ill. Sick enough for him to cancel his house party. The last thing Lady Tinmore needs are callers.'

'She did not seem to mind,' Ross insisted.

The footman brought their coats and assisted in putting them on. 'Your horses are being brought from the stable.'

They waited in uncomfortable silence until the horses were outside the door.

They were on the main road from the estate before Ross spoke. 'What is amiss, Dell?'

'Amiss?' he shot back. 'I told you. We were intruding. I should not have allowed you to talk me into this visit.'

Ross spoke in a milder tone. 'I did not see any indication that we were not welcome. Lady Tinmore seemed very gracious. I think she appreciated our concern for her husband.'

'She was gracious,' Dell admitted, sounding calmer. 'She was—' He cleared his throat. 'Perhaps we might call again. In a week or so, when we are certain of Tinmore's recovery.'

Genna and Lorene waited at the window until they saw Rossdale and Penford ride away.

Lorene then turned to tidy up the wineglasses and plate of biscuits, putting them back on the tray, something for which her husband would chastise her if he knew of it.

Acting like a servant, he would say.

Genna liked those old habits of Lorene's—her tendency to take care of things and save others the trouble.

Genna put her hands on her hips and stared at the Mount Olympus mural. 'I had not noticed before, but this really is a remarkable painting.' Verrio had painted the perspective so skilfully the figures in the painting appeared to be stepping into the room. Remarkable.

A footman had stepped into the room, ready to take the tea tray away.

Genna walked out of the room with Lorene. 'How serious is Lord Tinmore's illness?' she asked. 'I confess, I was surprised he cancelled the house party.'

'He is very weak, but his breathing is less laboured.'

The footman opened the door for them and Genna wondered what he thought about her ladyship tidying the room.

Lorene continued talking. 'If he had not cancelled it today, there would not have been enough time for letters to reach everyone. He did not want guests arriving with him lying abed. He said I should have known to cancel the house party two days ago.'

'Did he?'

And if Lorene had cancelled it, he would have been angry at her for interfering with his plans. But Genna would not say so to Lorene, who was still too sensitive on the subject of her husband. Genna missed being able to speak her mind to Lorene, but even more she wished she could ease Lorene's hurt feelings. Lorene would never complain to her, though.

They entered the hall and started up the stairway.

'How did you find Lord Penford?' Genna asked instead. That seemed like a safe subject.

Lorene avoided looking at her. 'What do you mean?' Her voice was sharp.

That took Genna by surprise. 'No special reason. You thought him sad before. I wondered if that was why he seemed so uncomfortable.'

'I think he realised it was not a good day to call,' Lorene said, as if defending him.

Genna had not intended any criticism of the man. 'Perhaps.' Better to agree than risk an argument. 'I suspect you are right.'

They reached the first floor where Lorene's set of rooms were located. And Lord Tinmore's.

'Is there anything I can do for you, Lorene?' Genna asked.

'Nothing,' her sister said.

'You will rest this afternoon, then?' Lorene still looked very fatigued.

'I will.' Lorene smiled wanly. 'I believe I will have dinner sent up to my room. May I tell Cook you will not expect to be served at the table?'

'Of course you may!' Genna assured her. 'A simple plate will do very nicely for me. Whatever is on hand.'

She was not the servants' favourite at any time, even though she tried never to put them to too much trouble for her. Like expecting a full meal prepared and served to her alone.

She reached over to buss Lorene's cheek. 'Promise you will rest.'

Lorene nodded.

Genna walked up another flight of stairs to her bedchamber. As she entered the room, a wave of loneliness washed over her. She had never felt lonely at Summerfield House—well, almost never. But here she felt so very alone.

She hadn't felt lonely with Rossdale. In fact, she'd felt happy, as if she'd found a real friend.

Right now, he felt like her only friend.

Chapter Six

Having dinner in the dining room was no pleasure. Lord Tinmore recovered well over the next few days, well enough to dress for dinner and to expect his wife and her sister to do the same. Genna complied, of course, and placed herself on her best behaviour. She was well capable of being agreeable at mealtime, especially when Lord Tinmore expected an audience rather than conversation.

They dined in the formal dining room, but at one end of the table. Lord Tinmore sat at the table's head. Lorene sat to her husband's right and Genna to his left. He was a little deaf in his left ear so there was little need for Genna to speak. Mr Filkins, his secretary, who was nearly as old as he, also dined with them. Filkins was seated next to Lorene, the side of the table upon which Tinmore focused most of his attention.

By the time the main course was served Tinmore had exhausted a recitation of the frequency of his cough, the colour of his phlegm and the irregularities of his bowels, to which Mr Filkins made appropriately sympathetic comments.

He went on to lament his decision to cancel the house party.

'I now see I will be quite well enough,' he said. 'I should have known I would recover swiftly. I have a strong constitution.'

'That you do, sir,' agreed Mr Filkins. 'But you had to decide quickly and I believe you made the most prudent of choices.'

'Yes,' Tinmore readily agreed with him. 'Besides, what is done cannot be undone.' He pointed his fork at Genna. 'Although I had high hopes for you, young lady. There was many a good catch invited to that party.'

Yes. Eligible men of Tinmore's age looking for a young wife to take care of them and their sons and grandsons looking for a dowry big enough to tempt them.

'A lost opportunity,' Genna said.

'What?' Tinmore cupped his ear.

'A lost opportunity,' she said louder.

Tinmore stabbed a piece of meat with his fork and lifted it to his mouth. After he chewed and swallowed it, he glanced at Lorene. 'You never told me about the dinner with Lord Penford.'

How like Tinmore to accuse rather than merely ask.

'You were so ill, I put it entirely out of my mind,' Lorene said.

'Put it out of your mind? Something as important as all that? Where is your head, my dear?' He took another bite of meat and waved his fork at her. 'Well, how was it? Were you treated well?'

Lorene responded as if she'd been asked with some kindness. 'We were treated very well, I assure you. Were we not, Genna?'

Genna nodded. 'Very well.'

Lorene went on, 'Although Lord Penford was disappointed you were unable to attend.'

Tinmore looked pleased at that. 'What did he serve?'

Goodness. Genna hardly remembered. Lorene, though, provided a rather thorough list of the courses. Genna wondered if she made up some of them.

'Was he a reasonable fellow, this Penford?' he went on to ask. 'I knew his father.' He would have seen the late Lord Penford in the House of Lords last Season. 'I have great hopes of turning the son to my views. Get them while they are new, you know.'

Mr Filkins laughed appreciatively.

'He was very amiable,' Lorene said. 'Although he and his friend did not talk politics with us at all, did they, Genna?'

'Not at all,' Genna agreed.

Tinmore straightened. 'His friend? Who was this friend?'

'Lord Rossdale,' Lorene responded.

Tinmore half-rose from his seat. 'Rossdale? Rossdale? The Duke of Kessington's son?'

'Yes, that is who he was,' Lorene responded. 'He was very nice, as well.'

'The Duke's son?' He pounded his knife down on the table. 'You should have told me you dined with the Duke's son.'

'Well, you were ill,' Genna said.

Tinmore turned to her. 'What, girl? Speak up. Do not mumble.'

She raised her voice. 'You were ill!'

He ignored her response. 'Kessington is the last man I would wish to offend. We must do something about this immediately!'

'I do not believe Lord Rossdale was offended,' Lorene assured him. 'He offered kind condolences over your illness when they called here the other day.'

'The Duke's son called here the other day?' Tinmore's face was turning red.

Lorene reached over and patted his arm. 'Do not make yourself ill over this. I am sure they understood completely that you were too ill to receive them. Perhaps we can invite them for dinner one night when you are a little stronger.'

'Dinner. Excellent idea,' Tinmore said.

'Excellent idea,' Mr Filkins agreed.

Tinmore pointed the knife towards him. 'But we must not wait. Must do something immediately.'

'Might I suggest a letter?' Mr Filkins offered. 'I will

pen something this very night and if it meets with your approval it can be delivered to Lord Rossdale in the morning.'

'A letter. Yes. A letter is the thing.' Tinmore popped a piece of potato into his mouth. 'But address it to Penford. He was the host. Make certain you mention Rossdale in it.'

'I quite comprehend, sir,' the secretary said. 'An excellent point.'

Genna smiled to herself. At least she would see Rossdale again.

'In fact,' Tinmore went on, 'invite them for Christmas Day.' He turned to his wife. 'Do you know if they are staying through Christmastide?'

Lorene nodded. 'That is what they told us. Through to Twelfth Night, at least.'

'Ha!' Tinmore laughed. 'We shall have a house party after all. At least Christmas dinner with elevated company.' He tossed a scathing look at Genna. 'Rossdale is not married. But you come with too much baggage to tempt him.'

Baggage?

The sins of her mother and father, she supposed. As well as her sisters and brother. She'd not done anything to deserve society's censure.

At least not yet.

On Christmas Day Ross and Dell made an appearance at the parish church for morning services and later in the day rode over to Tinmore Hall in Dell's carriage. The invitation to Christmas dinner had been somewhat of a surprise, albeit a welcome one for Ross. He was eager to call upon Genna again and curious to meet the formidable Lord Tinmore. Dell seemed less enthusiastic. Less enthusiastic than he'd been when first he'd invited Tinmore to dinner. Then he'd thought it prudent to ingratiate himself to the old lord, but now he seemed to relish meeting the man as much as one might look forward to having a tooth pulled.

The nearer the carriage brought them to Tinmore Hall, the bigger Dell's frown seemed to grow.

'Are you certain it will not be thought presumptuous to bring presents?' Dell asked.

Gifts had been Ross's idea. 'Presumptuous? Guests always brought my father gifts for his Christmas parties.'

Dell shot him a glance. 'Then if Tinmore seems offended, you must tell him that it was your father's custom.'

'I will.' Ross grinned. 'I dare say that will make the practice quite appreciated.'

The roof line of Tinmore Hall came into view in all its Elizabethan glory. As they passed through the gate, a herd of deer bounded across the park, their hooves kicking up clods of snow from the patches that still dotted the grass.

'At least it is merely a dinner and not a house party,' Dell said. 'I would detest having to spend the night.'

That would not have brought pleasure, would it? Ross agreed silently. No secret passages to explore. No surprise meetings when others were abed. Still, a conversation with Genna would prove stimulating. The closer Christmas Day came, the more withdrawn Dell had become. Ross supposed his friend remembered what his Christmases used to be like.

The carriage drew up to the entrance and four footmen emerged, forming a line to the carriage door. They were ushered into the hall, their cloaks taken and packages carried behind them as the butler led them to the Mount Olympus room and announced them.

The room was fragrant with greenery and spice. Garlands of evergreen were draped around the windows, holly, red with berries, lined the mantelpiece. Bowls of apples sat on the tables. Ross glanced up. Mistletoe hung in the doorway.

Seated in the huge room were Lord Tinmore and his wife, an incongruous pair. Tinmore, who must have been in his seventies at least, had the pallor and loose skin typical of an aged man who'd lost whatever looks he might have once possessed. He was thin, with rounded posture, but still his presence seemed to dominate the room. His wife, on the other hand, was a beauty in her prime. Flawless skin, rich dark hair, clear eyes and pink lips. A figure any man would admire, but she seemed a mere shadow in the wake of her husband's commanding presence.

Ross preferred her sister, who sparkled with life.

Tinmore, using a cane, rose from his chair. 'Good to see you. Good to see you. Happy Christmas to you.'

Ross and Dell crossed the room to him.

Lady Tinmore stood at her husband's side and made a more personal introduction. 'May I present my cousin, Lord Penford, and his friend, Lord Rossdale?'

Dell bowed. 'A pleasure, sir, to meet you.'

'And you, sir,' Tinmore said to Dell. He turned to Ross. 'Knew your grandfather. A decent man.'

'I have always heard so.' Ross hardly remembered his grandfather. The only image he could conjure up was of a remote figure, always busy, too busy to bother with an inquisitive, energetic boy. Rather like his father became after Grandfather died.

'Please, do sit,' Lady Tinmore said. 'We have refreshments.' She turned towards the fireplace where a bowl sat on the grate. 'Wassail, for you.'

A footman in attendance ladled wassail into a glass, which Ross took gratefully. The carriage ride had given him a thirst.

Tinmore asked about the carriage ride. The conditions of the road were discussed and the weather, of course, and the fine quality of the drink. The church services and sermons were compared, a devious way for Tinmore to discover whether they had attended the services at their parish.

Tinmore had not attended church, but his wife and her sister had.

And where was her sister?

He took the first opportunity to ask. 'Will we have the pleasure of Miss Summerfield's company today?'

Lady Tinmore frowned slightly. 'She should be here. I dare say something has detained her.'

'I am here!' Genna burst into the room, her arms laden with packages wrapped in brown paper and string. 'I was wrapping gifts.'

'Gifts?' Tinmore said disparagingly.

Ross rose from his chair. 'We also brought gifts. My father always insisted on gifts on Christmas Day.' He looked around. 'Although I am not quite sure what has become of them.'

Tinmore gestured to a footman, who bowed and left the room.

Genna placed her packages on a table and walked up to Dell and Ross. 'How delightful you could be with us today.' She smiled. 'Happy Christmas!'

Ross shook her hand. 'Happy Christmas, Miss Summerfield.'

Tinmore had not stood at her entrance. 'You are late, girl.'

Her smile stiffened. 'I do apologise, sir. I fear the wrapping took longer than I had anticipated.'

She sat on the sofa next to her sister, which placed her next to Ross's chair. She glanced at him as she sat and her smile softened again.

'I hope you have not been extravagant, girl,' Tinmore said. 'I do not provide you an allowance for frivolities.'

How ungentlemanly of Tinmore to make it a point that her allowance came from him.

She lowered her voice. 'I assure you. I was not extravagant.'

The footman handed her a glass of wassail and she took a sip.

Dell asked a question about the next session of Parliament and Ross was grateful to him for deflecting Tinmore's attention from Genna.

Not wanting to spend the holiday discussing politics, Ross turned to the ladies. 'The room smells and looks like Christmas.'

'It was Lorene's doing,' Genna said. 'I think it turned out lovely.'

'Lovely, indeed.'

Lady Tinmore's cheeks turned pink at the compliment. 'Genna helped.'

Genna grimaced. 'She means I supervised the gathering of the greens. The decoration was completely up to Lorene.'

'You did well, ma'am,' he said.

Genna gazed around the room and looked as if she was trying to stifle a laugh. 'It is a bit incongruous, though, do you not think? All these Roman gods amidst greenery meant to celebrate the Christian holiday.'

'The gods appear to be joining in the revelry,' he responded.

It was amusing that this room in particular was used to entertain guests on this special day, especially because this house must have several other drawing rooms that would be suitable. Was this chosen as the most impressive?

Lady Tinmore's brows knitted and Ross suspected she did not see the humour so evident to her sister.

Lady Tinmore changed the subject. 'We will eat dinner early. In a few minutes, perhaps. I hope that will be to your liking?'

Ross took a sip of his wassail. 'I am usually ready to eat at any moment of the day, so whatever you have planned will suit me very well.' He glanced at Genna. 'Perhaps after dinner there will be time for you to give me a tour of this house.'

She smiled. 'I would be pleased to do so.'

* * *

They'd had time enough to finish the wassail when Dixon announced dinner.

Mr Filkins, Tinmore's secretary, had not been included in the meal. Genna supposed the poor man was eating in his room alone on this day, which did not seem at all right to her.

The conversation was not as lively or amusing as it had been when she and Lorene had shared a meal with Rossdale and Penford at Summerfield House. It was dominated by Lord Tinmore and, as such, did not include Genna. She was seated across from Rossdale, but unable to speak with him. If only he'd been seated at her side they might have been able to have a little private conversation.

'Your father is Whig, is he not, Rossdale?' Tinmore asked.

'Very,' Rossdale responded.

'And yourself?' Tinmore went on.

'Me?' Rossdale responded. 'I am not in politics.'

'But you must have a party, a set of beliefs?' Tinmore took a bite of roast goose.

'Must I?' he answered. 'I can see no reason at the moment. When my father dies, I will choose, but I am in no hurry to do so.'

'Odd thing, not declaring your party.' Tinmore turned to Penford. 'And you, sir? Do not say you are Whig.'

The Whigs advocated reform, to give more power to the people and Parliament and less to the monarchy.

Penford nodded. 'I must say so, at least in desiring to ease the suffering of our people. There is more suffering to come, I fear, now that the war is over.'

'Now that the war is over, we must protect our property and the prices of our crops. That is what the Corn Laws are all about.' Tinmore landed a fist on the table for emphasis.

The Corn Laws fixed the prices of grain and imposed

tariffs to prevent imported grain from undercutting those prices.

'I do understand, sir,' Penford replied. 'But I fear the high prices will cause many to go hungry.'

Tinmore turned to Rossdale. 'I suppose you were against the Corn Laws. Your father certainly held out until the last, but we won him to our side.'

'I did not have to make the choice,' Rossdale said. 'But it would be hard to vote for a hardship for so many.'

Tinmore jabbed a finger in Rossdale's direction. 'If our farms fail, we all go hungry.'

Had Rossdale's father voted against his beliefs? 'It must be very difficult to choose,' Genna said. 'Especially when one does not know what the future will bring.'

'Humph!' Tinmore said. 'What do you know of such things?'

She had forgotten for a moment. Tinmore did not expect her to have opinions.

Rossdale spoke up. 'I quite agree with Miss Summerfield. Those in Parliament must live with many difficult decisions. It can be a great burden.'

Rossdale stood up for her? When was the last time anyone had done that for her?

Tinmore straightened in his chair. 'It is a great privilege! And one's duty!'

'I agree it is both of those things, as well,' Rossdale responded.

Tinmore seemed unexpectedly at a loss for words.

Ross rescued him, as well. 'Sir, I must tell you I am intrigued by this house. I have heard there is much to admire here.'

Tinmore swelled with pride. 'The first Earl of Tinmore was in the service of Queen Elizabeth. In her honour, the house was designed like the letter E, which might not be apparent to you. One can see it is shaped like an E if one climbs to the roof, though.'

'I should like to see that,' Rossdale said.

'I'll have Dixon take you around after dinner.'

'We do not need to trouble your butler. Miss Summerfield gave me a tour of Summerfield House. I am certain she will do a fine job of showing me Tinmore Hall.'

Genna felt herself go all warm. First he stood up for her; now he complimented her.

Tinmore waved his fork. 'Dixon will do it. The girl knows nothing of this house.'

Genna tensed, but tried to keep her voice composed. 'Then I should like to go along, if I may. To learn what Dixon can teach me.'

'Suit yourself,' Tinmore said, swallowing another bite of goose and smiling ingratiatingly towards Rossdale. 'I'll have Dixon take you around after tea.' He signalled to the butler who then had the footmen remove the main course. 'Time for the pudding,' Tinmore said.

Chapter Seven

After the pudding, Genna and Lorene left the gentlemen to their brandy and retired to the drawing room again.

'Do be careful, Genna,' Lorene warned as they walked to the Mount Olympus room. 'You know how he is. And I do not believe he is as recovered as he makes us believe. His temper is easily piqued, I fear.'

How did Lorene know? Had he lost his temper with her? 'I am being careful. I forgot myself for one moment, that is all.'

'Being late did not help matters either,' Lorene added.

'Yes, I realise it.' Genna doubted Tinmore cared whether she'd been present or not. 'I do wonder, though, why he is not throwing me at these two *eligible* gentlemen. He is so eager for me to make a match and here they both are.'

She meant it as a joke, but Lorene answered her in all seriousness. 'He thinks they are too high for you, Genna. Marrying you would not give either of them any advantage.'

Lorene's words stung. 'I was not being serious. Do you not think I know they are too high for me?'

They entered the room and sat on the sofa where they had been before dinner. Genna's back was stiff and with effort she kept her hands still in her lap. She could not think of a word she wished to say to her sister, at the moment.

Or rather, she could not think of a civil word she wished to say.

Once upon a time she would have shared with her sister that she had no plans to marry, that she intended to make her own way in the world unshackled by any man.

But Lorene's decision to marry Tinmore had altered matters. Lorene and she did not look upon the world with the same eyes.

'What are these gifts you are giving?' Lorene asked, breaking the silence.

'They are gifts,' Genna said. 'You discover the gift when you open it, not before.'

Lorene's brow furrowed. 'You have gifts for Lord Rossdale and Lord Penford?'

'For our guests, you mean? Yes, that was rather the point of it all.' Although she would have given Lorene her gift before the day was over, even if there had been no guests.

Lorene bit her lip. 'I do hope Lord Tinmore finds them appropriate.'

What were the chances of that? 'Do not worry, Lorene. They are mere trifles.'

The footman brought in tea and they lapsed into silence again. Genna occupied herself by staring at the paintings that covered the walls of the room, studying Verrio's use of colour, of movement and illusion. Whatever room she had found herself in these last few days she'd examined the paintings. How had she not allowed herself to see them before?

Ross felt as if he was sitting at his father's table with all Tinmore's talk of the politics of the day. Ross was not oblivious to the issues facing the country now that the war was over and he was not indifferent, but while his father was still alive he had no role to play in deciding such matters as what should be taxed, what prices should be fixed and what tariffs imposed. He also did not have to consider the consequences of whether he voted aye or nay. His day would come for all this, but now it was in the hands of others.

Tinmore slapped the table with the palm of his hand. 'The power must remain with the King and the aristocracy! We shall never go the way of France!'

His words became lost in a paroxysm of coughing. His butler quickly poured more brandy for him.

He downed the drink in one gulp. 'Shall we join the ladies?' His voice still choked.

'Excellent idea.' Ross tried not to sound too eager—or sarcastic.

Tinmore leaned heavily on his cane as he led them back to the drawing room. His butler followed rather solicitously.

The ladies looked up at their entrance.

'Would you like tea, gentlemen?' Lady Tinmore asked as they approached.

Lawd, no, thought Ross. More tea, more conversation.

'They don't want tea,' Lord Tinmore snapped. He signalled to the butler. 'Bring more brandy.'

The butler bowed and left the room.

In Ross's mind, the Earl had imbibed quite enough brandy already. He glanced at Lady Tinmore, who looked both chastened and concerned. Genna merely looked furious. Even Dell looked displeased.

Such a disagreeable man, especially to his wife and her sister.

The brandy was brought quickly and poured by the butler.

Ross detested the pall brought on by Tinmore's ill humour. He'd be damned if he let the evening go on like this. 'Shall we open the presents?' Tinmore would not dare contradict him.

Few men contradicted the son of a duke.

'If you desire it,' Tinmore agreed, sipping his brandy.

Genna turned to Ross. 'Do you mind if we open my gifts first? They really are mere trinkets.'

Ross smiled at her. 'If it pleases you, Miss Summerfield.'

She jumped out of her seat. 'It does, indeed!' She rushed over to the table where she'd placed her packages and brought them over. Handing them out, one to her sister, one to Dell, one to Ross. Even one to Tinmore, who, after all, provided her with lovely clothes, a roof over her head and an allowance.

'Please, do open them.' Her eyes sparkled in anticipation.

Dell was the first to open his. 'It is Summerfield House!'

The gift was a small framed watercolour of Summerfield House, obviously painted by Genna. It was not the one with the wild colours that she'd made the day he'd met her, though. This one showed snow on the ground and candlelight shining from the windows.

'It shows the night of your dinner party,' Genna said.

'So it does.' Dell looked up at her.

'I painted it for you,' she said.

He gazed at it appreciatively. 'It is a fine remembrance of that evening.'

Genna beamed with pleasure.

Ross opened his next. Another watercolour of a similar size, this one of a man on a galloping horse, his greatcoat billowing behind him. It was meant to be him, he realised, riding Spirit. He caught her eye to show he knew.

'I surmised that any gentleman would like a picture of a horse,' Genna explained.

So it was to be just between them that she'd drawn him?

He grinned. 'I like it very much.'

She smiled back, her face radiant.

Lord Tinmore tore open his gift next. His was smaller. He looked at it without comment.

'It is a miniature of Lorene,' Genna said.

She'd made a very small ink-and-watercolour painting of her sister and placed it in a frame small enough to be carried in the pocket of a coat.

Tinmore turned to his wife. 'It does you no justice, my dear. Amateur work.' He tossed it aside and it fell on the carpet by Dell's feet. 'When we go to London I will commission a proper portrait of you from the finest miniature artist in town. Perhaps Cosway or Engleheart are still painting. If not, someone quite as renowned.'

Genna's cheeks turned red, as if she'd been slapped in the face. She might as well have been.

Ross was too outraged to speak. How unspeakably rude and cruel to both women.

Dell picked up the small painting and looked at it. 'I disagree, Tinmore.' He turned to Genna. 'Well done, Miss Summerfield. This is a charming likeness of your sister.' He placed it carefully on the table, catching Lady Tinmore's eye as he did so.

She immediately glanced away. 'Let—let me open mine,' she said, her voice shaking and her fingers tremulous. 'Oh, Genna!' Lady Tinmore turned her small painting around for the others to see.

It showed four children, a boy and three little girls, playing at a folly, the folly where Ross and Genna had taken refuge from the weather.

'It is us,' whispered Genna.

Her sister looked up at her with glistening eyes. 'Look how happy we were.'

Tinmore tapped his cane on the carpet. 'We should allow our guests to present their gifts, since they have gone to the trouble.' He glanced at the butler who gestured to a footman to bring the gifts to them.

'I fear our gifts will pale in comparison to such thoughtfulness on Miss Summerfield's part,' Ross said. 'As you shall see.'

Ross took the gifts from the footman and handed one to each of them. Even in the wrapping, it was pretty obvious what he and Dell had brought for Lord Tinmore.

The man opened it eagerly. 'Cognac. Remy Martin 1780!'

'From my father's cellar,' Ross said.

Tinmore gushed. 'This is a fine gift indeed. A very fine gift. Even finer that it came from the Duke's cellar.'

'Open yours, Lady Tinmore,' Dell said.

It was a large and heavy box that she balanced on her knees. When she opened the box, she gasped, 'The music!'

Dell spoke, 'I am merely returning what is yours.'

She lifted each sheet of music as if it were as precious as jewels. 'I did not think to bring the music with me when we left Summerfield House. You have restored it to me.'

'Look,' Genna said, 'some are the pieces from which we first learned to play.'

'Lovely memories,' Lorene murmured.

Genna looked up. 'It is my turn, I suppose.' She untied the string and opened her box. 'My sketchbook!'

'Again, we merely return what is yours,' Dell said.

Ross had talked Dell into bringing Genna's sketchbook and presenting it as a gift. He had, after all, promised to return it to her. It was Dell who thought of the piano music, though.

Genna opened the book and glanced at some of the pages before closing it again and clasping it to her breast. 'I am so happy to have it. I thought it lost for ever.' She faced Ross and her smile widened. *Thank you*, she mouthed.

Ross turned to Lord Tinmore. 'See, sir, nothing precious.'

Tinmore looked affronted. 'I assure you, the cognac is quite precious!'

Ross had brought it for Dell and rather wished the two of them had made short work of it instead of leaving it with this disagreeable man who did not even have the courtesy to offer to share it with them.

Ross suddenly could not stand to be in this man's presence another second.

He stood. 'I desire to prevail upon your butler for the house tour now. I have a great need to stretch my legs.'

Tinmore was still examining his bottle of cognac, turning it around in his hands. He looked up and smirked at Ross. 'I am certain Dixon would be delighted to start the tour.' He snapped his hand to his butler. 'Dixon, show Lord Rossdale the important rooms of the house, the state rooms.'

Dixon bowed. 'Very good, sir.'

Ross glanced at Dell. 'Do you come, too, Dell?' Perhaps Dell needed a break from this disagreeable man, as well.

Dell darted a glance at Lady Tinmore and shook his head. 'I am content to stay.'

Genna rose from her chair. 'I will go.' She faltered and turned to Tinmore. 'You gave your permission, sir.'

Tinmore waved her away. 'Go, then.'

'This way, m'lord,' Dixon said, leading the way.

When they crossed the threshold, Ross glanced up at the mistletoe, but this would certainly not be an opportune time to take advantage.

Besides, it would send the wrong message to her.

Instead he whispered to her, 'Tinmore is unpleasant and cruel. I am sorry for you and your sister.'

'I am able to bear it,' she whispered back, 'but I worry about Lorene.'

'We will begin at the hall,' the butler said, cutting off more conversation.

Genna inclined her head towards the butler. 'Dixon will repeat anything we say to each other.'

Ross took the warning and stepped away from her.

The hall, the first room seen when one entered the house from the main entrance, was wainscoted in dark mahogany and its walls were adorned in armament of early times, when it was important that a lord show his military strength. Though the swords, battleaxes, lances, rapiers and pikes were arranged in decorative patterns, the sheer numbers were a warning.

'You can see,' the butler intoned, 'the power that has always been a part of the Earls of Tinmore.'

Rossdale Hall had an armament room with twice as

many weapons on display and countless more stored away in an attic somewhere, but Ross did not mention that fact.

'Depressing, is it not?' murmured Genna just loud enough for Ross to hear.

Dixon gestured to a huge portrait of a gentleman on the left wall. 'This is the first Earl of Tinmore, a favourite of Queen Elizabeth and one of her trusted advisors. He was given this land and title as a reward for his faithful service to the Queen.'

The first Earl had the pointed beard, ruff and rich velvets of his era.

'And on the right is his Countess.'

The portrait matched the size of the first Earl of Tinmore's. His Countess wore a black gown with an even wider white ruff and huge puffed sleeves.

'The house has over one hundred rooms...' Dixon said.

He led them from salon to dining room to gallery and Ross made no more attempt to talk with Genna. This house tour had none of the delight of her tour of Summerfield House. His only consolation was that they were free of Tinmore's company.

And he could watch Genna.

In each room, Genna paid close attention to the paintings. The house contained an impressive array of them. Most were Italian, as Tinmore had suggested. Ross recognised the style from the Grand Tour he and Dell had taken in their youth, but there was also an impressive number of Dutch paintings, classical sculpture, and later portraits by Lawrence and Reynolds.

What was she thinking as she examined the artwork? Ross wondered. Her mind was alive, he could tell, but he did not have an inkling what was passing through it.

He rather liked that.

Tinmore waved a hand towards the pianoforte. 'Play for our guest,' he demanded of his wife.

Dell steeled himself. He'd managed to act as if he was not affected by Lorene, but he did not know how long he could tolerate Tinmore's company. He would have fled the room with Ross and Genna, but he could not bear to leave Lorene alone with him.

Foolish. She was his wife. She would be alone with him the moment they left for Summerfield House.

She rose from her sofa and gracefully moved to the pianoforte in one corner of the room. The pianoforte was a work of art unto itself, like the walls of the room with their Roman gods spilling over each other. Trimmed in ebony and gold, the pianoforte sparkled in the candlelight, as dreamlike as the Mount Olympus scene.

Dell held his breath as her hands touched the keys. Since the night she had played for him at Summerfield House, he could not get her music out of his head—or the vision of her playing it. It came back to him during moments of solitude when he could not keep himself busy enough to stop thinking.

She began with the Beethoven piece she had played for him before, the one that revealed to him all her sadness and loneliness and so reminded him of his sister. It took a few bars of the music to transport her and then her lovely face glowed as if the music had lit her from within. He had to close his eyes from the sheer beauty of her.

'No. No,' her husband interrupted. 'Do not play your gloomy nonsense!'

She stopped with a discordant note and her back stiffened.

Tinmore had downed another glass of brandy. How many had he consumed? Dell and Ross prided themselves on being able to empty a few bottles at night, but where they'd restrained themselves, Tinmore had indulged.

'Our guest does not want to hear this.' He pounded on the carpet with his cane.

'I assure you I do wish to hear whatever your wife chooses,' Dell said through clenched teeth.

Tinmore smirked at him. 'You need not be polite, Penford. She can play something cheerful. Something fitting for Christmas Day.'

She paused for a moment, as if collecting herself, before she played the first notes of *Here We Come A-wassailing.*

Lord Tinmore started to sing, *"'Here we come a-wassailing among the leaves so green—"'*

Another fit of coughing overtook him.

Lorene rose and hurried over to him. 'My lord, you are ill again.'

Dell poured him a cup of tea, tepid now. Better tea than more brandy. He handed it to Tinmore without milk or sugar. Tinmore gulped it down and the coughing eased, but his breathing was laboured.

'You are wheezing.' Lorene placed a hand on Tinmore's forehead. 'Let me help you to your room.'

Tinmore pushed her hand away. 'Stop fussing. Think of your duty, woman. We have a guest. You stay and entertain our guest. Wicky will take care of me.' He motioned for the footman attending the room to approach. 'Help me to my room and get Wicky for me.'

'His valet,' Lady Tinmore explained.

Dell did not care who tended to Tinmore.

The old Earl hobbled out of the room with the footman bearing his weight. His coughing came back, echoing behind him.

This damned man. How could he be so churlish towards his wife, even while she showed him great solicitude? How did she bear moments like this, being callously dismissed and rebuffed?

She still faced the door from which her husband exited. Dell indulged in his desire to gaze at her, so graceful, so perfect.

Lawd! Why should this woman be married to such a man?

He raised his arm, wanting to comfort her, but he had no right. He had no right to even speak to her about her husband.

But he could not help it. 'Does he always speak to you so?'

She turned and lifted her eyes to his. 'Quite often.'

'He should not,' he answered in a low voice. 'You do not deserve it.'

She lowered her lashes. 'It is kind of you to say so.'

There was so much more he wished to say. He wanted Tinmore to go to the devil and never do her feelings an injury again.

Instead the two of them stood there, less than an arm's length apart. Too close. Much too close.

He could not help but reach out and touch her arm. 'Would you play the Beethoven piece for me?' he murmured. 'I would very much like to hear it again.'

She nodded. 'Of course.'

She returned to the pianoforte and began *Pathétique* and the notes of the music transformed into sheer emotion. He could not quiet the storm inside him. As she played he walked back to the chair where he had been sitting, spying on the table the miniature Genna had painted of her. Lorene's back was to him and, for the moment, there was no one else in the room. He picked up the miniature and placed it in his coat pocket.

When she finished *Pathétique*, she turned to him. 'Do you mind if I play some of the music you brought to me?'

'Not at all,' he responded. He picked up the box and brought the sheet music to her. She set it on the piano bench and started to look through it.

'Some of this is so frivolous,' she said. 'Some too simple.'

'Like what?' he asked.

'King William's March,' she responded. 'This is one of the first pieces I learned to play.'

She put the sheet of music on the stand and played the crisp lively notes. He stood behind her and watched the confident movement of her fingers on the keys and was glad that the music had led her to something more cheerful. When the piece was done her mood seemed to have lifted.

She looked through her box again. 'Let us look for a nice song!'

'The wassail song?' he asked.

She laughed. 'No, not that one.' She continued to riffle through the pages. 'This one.' She handed him a sheet.

'Barbara Allen?' He placed it on the stand. 'Even I know that one.'

She placed the box on the floor and moved over on her bench. 'Then sit and sing it with me.'

They sang the old song together, her voice high and crystalline; his deeper.

> *In Scarlet town where I was born*
> *There was a fair maid dwelling...*

The song was a tragedy, two lovers dying.

She played other pieces of music from her box, all songs of thwarted love, it seemed. He remained at her side, watching her, joining in on the songs when he knew them. Time seemed suspended as her music went on.

'You select one,' she said, handing him the box.

He picked out *The Turtle Dove.* She played and he sang.

> *Fare you well, my dear, I must be gone,*
> *And leave you for a while,*
> *If I roam away I'll come back again,*
> *Though I roam ten thousand miles...*

He sang to the end of the song:

O yonder doth sit that little turtle dove,
He doth sit on yonder high tree,
A-making a moan for the loss of his love,
As I will do for thee, my dear.

When he finished, she placed her hands on the bench at her sides, but continued to stare at the piano keys. The room turned very quiet.

He touched her hand, a bare touch with only two fingers entwined with hers. He was merely feeling sympathy for her, was he not? She was a relation of sorts so it stood to reason he would care about her.

Very slowly she faced him and met his gaze.

Dell stopped thinking.

She leaned towards him, still holding his eyes.

The door opened and Genna's laughter reached their ears.

Genna and Ross entered the room.

'We are finished with the tour!' Genna said.

Dell stood up and moved away from the pianoforte. 'And we must take our leave,' he said.

'Now?' Ross looked surprised.

'Yes—now—' Dell sputtered. 'Lord Tinmore took ill again. We should leave. Now.'

Chapter Eight

London—February 1816

Six weeks later Genna sat behind her sister in the recesses of Lord Tinmore's box at the Royal Opera House. On-stage was *Don Giovanni* and all the *ton* were keen to see it—and to be seen seeing it. Thus, the boxes were packed with ladies in silks and gentlemen in impeccably tailored formal dress. Those in the orchestra were not so fashion-ably dressed, but those people mattered very little to the fashionable world.

Genna loved to see the fashionable clothes the London ladies wore. Genna, though, considered it important to set herself off from the latest fashion, with a twist on whatever was the rage. She and Lorene used a modiste who used to be their sister Tess's maid. Nancy was a par-ticularly creative collaborator in Genna's quest to express herself in her dress.

Her wardrobe, of course, was possible only through the benevolence of Lord Tinmore, a fact which niggled at Gen-na's conscience a little, even though he considered her dress mere pretty packaging to attract suitors. Tinmore's inten-tion was to marry her off this Season. Genna was just as determined to resist.

If she could only hold out this Season. In the autumn she would turn twenty-one and then she intended to do as she pleased.

In the meantime she would enjoy the Season's entertain-ments, like this lovely opera, so filled with humour and drama. The Season was hardly at its height, but more of the fashionable elite arrived every day and more and more were hosting balls, breakfasts, or musical soirées.

Not that Genna expected to be invited to many of them. Tinmore was a generation or two too old to be on everyone's guest list and Genna was certain many hostesses seized on any excuse to keep from inviting the scandalous Summerfield sisters.

'Look! Look there!' Tinmore cried above Leporello's solo. 'I do believe that is the Duke of Kessington.' He lifted his mother-of-pearl opera glasses to his eyes. 'Yes. Yes. It is. Rossdale and Penford are in his company.'

Rossdale. Her heart skittered.

She knew there was a chance she would see Rossdale during the Season. It was unlikely they would attend the same entertainments, but it was possible that their paths would cross somewhere like this. She hardly knew what greeting to expect from him, if he deigned to greet her at all. He and Penford had left so abruptly on Christmas Day. They quit Lincolnshire entirely within that same week, she'd heard, even though they'd said they would stay past Twelfth Night.

Something must have offended them. What other explanation could there be? Something must have happened while she and Rossdale were touring the house. Lorene professed to know nothing, but Genna did not know whether to believe her or not.

She'd missed Rossdale. She fancied him her friend and Genna had enjoyed his company more than anyone she could remember.

Although perhaps he'd merely been kind to a silly chit with scandalous parents and siblings.

'Who is Tinmore talking about?' her sister Tess leaned over to ask.

Another of the delights of London was the opportunity to see Tess, who now stayed in town most of the time with her husband and his parents, Viscount and Viscountess Northdon.

Genna answered her. 'He is talking about our cousin, Lord Penford, and his friend. They sit in the Duke of Kessington's box.'

'Our cousin attends the opera with a duke?' Tess's brows rose. 'Impressive.'

'His friend is the Duke's son,' Genna explained.

The Duke's box was positioned almost as advantageously as the King's box, which seemed a great distance from Genna at the moment.

Once she would have told Tess about every moment with a man like Rossdale, but since Lorene married and turned their world on its ears, Genna had become too used to keeping secrets.

Tess glanced at the Duke's box again. 'Lorene told me you had dined with our cousin, but I did not know about his friend.'

Genna joked, 'I suppose Lorene and I are so accustomed to lofty acquaintances that it quite slipped our minds to tell you.'

Tess laughed. 'Who would ever have thought any Summerfield sister would be acquainted with a person of such high rank?'

'Indeed.' Though he might pretend not to know her now.

Ross saw Tinmore gazing at his father's box through opera glasses. Whether Dell saw Tinmore, too, Ross could not tell. He didn't dare ask either. Ever since Christmas night Dell had acted very strange. First he'd insisted they leave Tinmore Hall abruptly, then he'd decided to quit Lincolnshire entirely. Ross thought he would have left on Boxing Day if he could have, but it took a little longer than that to complete his business there.

Ross asked once what had happened to make Dell so adamant about leaving. Dell told him he did not want to risk having to be in Tinmore's company again. Neither he nor Ross could abide the man, but Ross had been disappointed that their visit was cut so short. He'd have risked a few moments in Tinmore's company if it meant spending more time with Genna. He'd at least hoped they would have had a chance to discuss the house tour or the artwork she'd examined that night.

Now every time he saw a painting, even the familiar ones in his father's town house, he thought of her. Would she see the painting as he did? Would she learn something from the artist's technique?

He must confess, he'd never given artistic technique a thought until meeting her, until seeing her wild use of colour in that watercolour of Summerfield House.

Was she in Tinmore's box? he wondered. He could not see her and he certainly did not wish to call upon Tinmore during the intermission if she were not present.

Could he renew his friendship with Genna here in London? He did not see how. Eligible men and marriageable women could not simply enjoy one another's company without wagging tongues putting them both in parson's mousetrap.

On stage Don Giovanni attempted to seduce Zerlina. *'This life is nought but pleasure,'* he sang in Italian.

But life was not all pleasure, Ross thought. For many there was nothing but suffering. He and Dell had visited some of the Waterloo wounded who'd been in Dell's regiment, men merely hanging on to life by a thread. He'd brought them bottles of brandy, but what they'd really wanted was food for their families. He'd seen to that later. Those families would never go hungry again.

If his father the Duke knew of his charity, he'd scoff and insist that the real solutions lay in Parliament. To his father, Parliament and its politics were everything. Even the guests the Duke had selected to share his box were chosen to bring some political advantage. Ross was not even sure his father and his wife paid any attention to the marvel of this opera.

What about merely inviting friends because you enjoyed their company? And why not help suffering individuals now? What was wrong with doing things his own way, not like his father?

Ross and Genna were alike in that way. They both wanted to choose their own way.

Ross stared at Giovanni, so determined to do as he wished, as reprehensible as his wishes were. Ross's desires were not reprehensible. He wished to do good for people. But the important thing to him was to assist by his own choice, not someone else's, not what the politics of the situation would require of him.

He shifted his gaze to Tinmore's box. Somehow he'd cross paths with Miss Genna Summerfield again. Why not?

When the opera was over the crowds spilled on to the street where the carriages were lined up to gather them. A fine mist of rain dampened the air and kept most of the crowd waiting in the shelter behind the Opera House's columns.

Genna stood with Tess and her husband, Marc Glenville, a few feet from Tinmore and Lorene, who remained under the portico. The rain was too thin to be of much concern and, after the close air and crowds inside the theatre, Genna relished the night air. The lamplight shone on the wet pavement and cobbles, making a play of light and dark that captivated her. How did artists paint such reflections?

Something else to try. There was always something about art that she discovered she did not know. Thanks to Rossdale, she'd begun to look at the paintings around her more carefully to try to answer some of these questions.

She took a breath.

Rossdale. Where was he? Somewhere in the crowd?

Odd to know he was so close. It made her skin tingle with excitement.

'What is the delay?' she heard Tinmore complain. 'I distinctly told the coachman to be at the head of the line. I detest waiting.'

Next to her, Tess gave an exasperated sigh. 'At least it is not pouring rain.' She clasped her husband's arm. 'It feels rather refreshing out here.'

Marc smiled and held her even closer. 'It does look as if we are in for a bit of a wait.'

'We could walk back faster,' Genna said.

'I would not mind,' Tess said.

Most of those from the orchestra seats seemed to be doing just that, filling the streets and blocking the carriages.

Tess hummed. 'Do you not have the music still in your head? I do.'

'It was good music,' her husband agreed.

Genna held on to the costumes, the stage designs and the colours and patterns of the theatre itself.

'Miss Summerfield?' A low masculine voice sounded behind her.

She turned. 'Lord Rossdale!' Her insides skittered with something like joy.

He tipped his hat and bowed. 'I thought that was you.'

'Rossdale! Rossdale!' Tinmore called out. 'Saw you in the theatre. You and your father. Give him my regards.'

Rossdale turned slowly and merely nodded to Tinmore before turning back to Genna. 'I hope you are well, Miss Summerfield.'

She smiled. 'I am always well, sir!' Her voice dropped. 'It is good to see you.'

She caught his gaze for a moment, when Tess, standing right beside her, said, 'Genna?'

'Oh.' She gestured from Tess to Rossdale. 'Tess, may I

present Lord Rossdale, with whom we became acquainted when he visited Lincolnshire. My sister, Mrs Glenville.'

Tess smiled at him. 'Lord Rossdale.'

Tess's husband spoke up. 'Rossdale. Good to see you again.'

'And you, Glenville.' He shook Marc's hand. 'Under better circumstances, yes?'

Marc glanced at his wife. 'Much better circumstances.'

'There it is!' Tinmore shouted. 'There is our carriage. Do not tarry!' He walked quickly, his cane tapping loudly on the pavement.

Genna exchanged a glance with Rossdale.

He stepped back. 'Goodnight, Miss Summerfield.' He nodded to Tess and Marc. 'Goodnight.'

'Make haste!' Tinmore called from the carriage door. 'I do not wish to remain here all night.'

They had no choice but to rush to the carriage.

Genna took a glance back as she was assisted into the carriage, but Rossdale seemed to have melted into the crowd.

Shortly after Lord Tinmore's carriage pulled away, Ross climbed into his father's carriage.

'Is Dell with you?' his father asked. They had all been invited to a supper after the opera.

'He is making his own way,' Ross replied.

Dell had left him right after the performance. Rather abruptly, Ross thought.

'I wanted to talk to him about this income-tax business,' the Duke said. 'We must settle this question. It is vital.'

Income taxes had been high during the war with Napoleon and now, with the peace, the citizens were eager for some relief.

'I heard much discussion among the others who called upon our box during the intermission,' the Duchess said.

Ross's father's second wife was perhaps even more serious about politics than was his father.

The carriage started to move.

Ross, though, had heard his father's discussion of the income tax—and the Duchess's—many times since joining them in London. He'd contributed all his thoughts on the subject already. Not that his father credited his opinion.

He turned his thoughts instead to Genna. To devising some way to see her again soon.

It was possible that eventually they would be invited to the same social affair, but that was leaving too much to chance. He needed to figure out a way to see her soon and he knew just how to arrange that.

'I heard something as well,' he began. 'Well, not so much heard, but noticed.'

'Something of importance?' his father asked sceptically.

His father believed Ross was merely pleasure-seeking, but, then, his father never knew Ross to do anything of importance. He never knew of Ross's voyages across the channel during the war, transporting spies like Glenville, Genna's brother-in-law, and of bringing exiles to safety. He certainly did not know of his assistance to Waterloo veterans and their families.

'Do you recall that Dell and I had some acquaintance with Lord Tinmore when we were in Lincolnshire?' Ross asked.

'That unpalatable fossil?' his father spat.

Ross suppressed a smile. His father did have a way with words. 'The very one. I ran into him tonight right before the carriage came. He asked me to give you his regards.'

His father peered at him. 'Ross, Tinmore's regards are of no importance to me.'

'I think they are,' Ross countered. 'The thing is, Tinmore is dazzled by you. He acted the complete toad-eater when Dell and I saw him in Lincolnshire. I believe he fancies being one of your set. I think he'd be easily swayed to

vote with you if he had the impression you favoured him.'
This was half-true at least. Tinmore was enamoured of
being in the company of a duke—or even his son. Whether
he'd change his vote was total speculation.

Ross's father nodded thoughtfully. 'You might be correct. And if I secure his vote, those old cronies of his might
follow suit.' He shook his head. 'No. If I befriend him now
he'll think I am merely seeking votes.'

Which was precisely what his father wished to do.

'Be subtle,' Ross urged. 'Do not approach him directly.
Invite him to some of your entertainments.'

The Duchess, who had been listening with keen interest,
spoke up. 'Invite him…I believe it could work, although I
hesitate to include that fortune-hunter wife of his.'

'I can ease your concern on that score,' Ross said
quickly. 'Lady Tinmore is actually a mild-mannered, well-
meaning woman. I think you might actually take a liking
to her.'

'Is she?' The Duchess's brows rose. 'Difficult to believe. Everyone knows her mother was as wanton as they
come even before she ran away with a foreign count.' She
leaned forward. 'You know people say each of the Summerfield daughters were fathered by different lovers. And
there is that bastard son. And Summerfield lost his fortune, of course.'

Leave it to the Duchess to know all the gossip there
was to know.

'I also heard the bastard son married Lord Northdon's
daughter,' she went on. 'A patched-up affair that was, I
am certain. Northdon packed them off to some farm in
the Lake District.'

How did she retain all this information?

'I do not dispute the sins of the parents,' Ross said.
'And I have never met the son. But the daughters are not
cut from the same cloth.' Genna was an original, that was

certain, but he saw nothing wanton in her. 'They would not embarrass you.'

She leaned back on the seat. 'I confess I am curious about them.'

'Invite them to your musicale next week,' he suggested.

Her mouth turned up in a calculating grin. She turned to the Duke. 'Shall we?'

He returned her expression. 'By all means.'

Chapter Nine

The invitation to the Duchess of Kessington's musicale was quite unexpected, but it put Lord Tinmore in raptures. He became nearly intolerable. From the moment he'd opened the gold-edged invitation bearing the Kessington crest his warnings and instructions had been incessant. He was convinced that Lorene or Genna would behave improperly and would prove to be an embarrassment to him.

Genna had no fears that she and Lorene would offend anyone. Tinmore's capacity to be objectionable, though, was another story altogether.

Along with a litany of dos and don'ts in the society of dukes and duchesses, Tinmore desired to select what gowns they were to wear and how they ought to style their hair. Goodness! He would probably have put them in stomachers and powdered wigs.

Somehow Lorene had been able to prevent that ghastly idea. It was a good thing, because Genna would have refused to wear whatever Tinmore selected, even if it had been her finest dress.

On the night of the musicale, with the assistance of Nancy, their modiste, they managed to look presentable, but that hardly eased Tinmore's nerves. When their carriage pulled through the wrought-iron gates of Kessington House on Piccadilly, he was nearly beside himself.

'Now remember to curtsy to the Duchess and, whatever you do, do not open your mouths. The less you say the less chance you will utter some drivel.'

They entered the hall, a semicircular room all white and

gold with marble floors and cream walls with gilded plasterwork. The curve of the room was repeated in the double-marble staircase, as was the gold. Its wrought-iron banister was gilded, the curves appearing again in its design.

A footman in fine livery took their cloaks and another led them toward the sounds of people talking and soft violin music playing.

The butler announced them, 'Lord and Lady Tinmore. Miss Summerfield.'

Genna noticed heads turn towards them. Because of Tinmore or because two of the scandalous Summerfield sisters had arrived? She lifted her chin and allowed her gaze to sweep the room. Its walls were covered with huge paintings and mirrors, its ceiling a marvel of plasterwork design. Hanging from the ceiling was the largest crystal chandelier she had ever seen. The room was all pattern and opulence.

Tinmore impatiently tugged at her arm to follow him to where His and Her Graces greeted other guests who had arrived just before them. Rossdale stood next to them and caught Genna's eye as they approached.

He smiled and she knew the smile was just for her.

Tinmore effusively greeted the Duke and thanked the Duchess for including them. He made a big show of presenting Lorene to them before mumbling, 'My wife's sister, Miss Summerfield.'

'Very good of you to come,' the Duke said. 'I trust we will have some time to talk before the night is through.'

'It would be my honour.' Tinmore bowed.

The Duchess smiled graciously at Lorene and Genna. 'I must learn who your modiste is. Your appearance is charming. Charming.'

Rossdale stepped forward, extending his hand to Tinmore. 'Good of you to come, sir.'

'Rossdale.' Tinmore shook his hand eagerly. 'Good to see you again. Looking forward to this evening.'

Rossdale also took Lorene's hand. 'Welcome, ma'am. I dare say there should be some people you know here. Your cousin is here somewhere.'

'Lord Penford?' she said. 'Yes, I already glimpsed him.'

Finally he clasped Genna's hand and even through her glove she could feel his warmth and strength. 'Miss Summerfield. I hope you will allow me to show you the art work in this house. We have a considerable collection.'

She was so happy to see him, but feared it would show. She glanced at the paintings gracing the walls instead. 'I can see that already! There are so many wonderful paintings here.'

He released her. 'I took time to learn of them so you will be impressed with me.'

She laughed.

Tinmore took her arm and pulled her away. 'Do not waste the gentleman's time.'

'She is not—' Rossdale started, but other guests arrived and he had to turn away.

Tinmore led Genna and Lorene through the throngs of people and deposited them in a corner before insinuating himself into a group of other lords probably discussing their political matters.

'Do you suppose anyone will speak to us?' Lorene asked. 'I cannot help but feel this company is too high for us. Why were we invited, I wonder?'

'I wonder, too.' Did Rossdale have anything to do with it?

Two of the ladies seated nearby gave them curious looks. Did they disapprove of their being invited?

Lorene nodded to them and smiled sweetly. How could anyone not adore her sister?

Genna turned her attention to the painting on the wall behind them, a portrait of an old man in a turban. This was not an Italian artist, she would guess by the clothing and the style of painting. The colours were dark and the figure seemed to blend into the background, although his face seemed bathed in light.

'Lady Tinmore.' A male voice came from behind.

Genna turned. It was Lord Penford.

'How do you do, sir,' Lorene said, her voice barely audible.

'Penford!' Genna said lightly. 'Are you going to speak to us? No one else has dared!'

'I thought I might take you around and introduce you,' he said.

It was what Tinmore ought to have done.

'How very nice of you, Cousin.' Out of the corner of her eye Genna saw Rossdale working his way through the crowd. 'Take Lorene around. I wish to study these paintings a little longer.'

Neither he nor Lorene acted as if she'd said something odd. They left her. A footman brought her a glass of champagne which delighted Genna, who had only tasted the bubbly light wine two or three times during the last Season.

The two ladies seated nearby glanced at her again. They were of an age with her parents, Genna guessed. Perhaps they knew Genna's mother and father. If so, no wonder they stared.

Genna used Lorene's response and smiled at them. They smiled back. Did they wish her to speak with them? Genna could not tell.

No matter. Rossdale was coming closer.

'You are here alone,' he said when he reached her.

She turned to the wall. 'I was studying this painting. It is not Italian, is it?'

He grinned. 'Good girl. It is Dutch. Rembrandt.'

She looked at it again, more closely. 'I have never seen a Rembrandt. Look how he paints the black cloak of the man. It blends into the background, but it is still clear it is a coat if you look closely.'

He nodded. 'Do you wish a tour of the other paintings in the room?' he asked.

She glanced at the ladies nearby who looked her way again. 'I am afraid it would look odd with all your guests here.' She leaned closer to him. 'Tinmore might have apoplexy if I do anything to draw attention to myself. He has a great fear that Lorene and I will do something to mortify him.' She huffed. 'Of course, as soon as he could, he left us in this corner. I suppose he thought we would stand here like statues.'

He inclined his head. 'I saw Dell introducing your sister to other guests. Would you like me to introduce you?'

She giggled. 'Let Tinmore worry that I'll do something objectionable in your company.'

He started with the two ladies who had made her and Lorene an object of interest. 'May I present Miss Summerfield, sister-in-law to Lord Tinmore? Miss Summerfield, the Duchess of Archester and the Duchess of Mannerton.'

Genna executed a perfect curtsy. 'Your Graces. I am honoured to meet you.'

The Duchess of Archester peered at her. 'I knew your mother, Miss Summerfield.'

And she probably knew about all her mother's lovers and how her mother had left her children with a father who cared nothing for them and ran off with a foreign count.

'Did you, ma'am?' Genna smiled and held her gaze steady.

'I knew her quite well,' the Duchess said. 'How is she faring? I hope she is in good health.'

Genna managed to keep her composure. 'I have not seen her for many years.' Since she was three years old. 'But my sister, Mrs Glenville, met her in Brussels last summer. By her report my mother is in good health and prospering.'

'Is she still with Count von Osten?' asked the Duchess of Mannerton.

Was this any of their concern?

'Yes, she is.' Genna still smiled. 'My sister reports they are quite happy together.'

She was not about to give them the satisfaction of imagining her mother going to rack and ruin by leaving a loveless, desolate marriage for a man who loved her and could give her everything she desired.

Except her children.

To her surprise, though, the Duchesses looked pleased. 'I am delighted to hear it,' the Duchess of Mannerton said. 'A bad business it was, but she found her way in the end.'

Rossdale asked if the Duchesses needed anything and if they were enjoying themselves while Genna still reeled from this reaction to her mother.

'I cannot believe it,' she said as Rossdale escorted her away. 'I think they actually liked my mother. I thought they were looking at Lorene and me because they disapproved of us.'

'Perhaps they knew your mother well enough to realise she did the right thing,' he said.

She stiffened. 'Right for her, perhaps.'

He walked her around the room and introduced her to guests who were not deep in conversation. It seemed as if most of the guests were high in rank or important in government and all were quite uninterested in her.

'Ah, Vespery is here,' Rossdale said. 'Now, he is someone you must meet.'

He brought her over to a rather eccentrically attired gentleman, his neckcloth loosely tied, his waistcoat a bright blue. His black hair was longer than fashionable, very thick and unruly. As were his eyebrows.

The gentleman's eyes lit up upon seeing Rossdale.

'Rossdale, my lad,' he said. 'Are you in good health?'

'Very good, Vespery.' Rossdale turned to Genna. 'Miss Summerfield, allow me to present Mr Vespery to you.'

'How do you do?' Genna extended her hand, over which Vespery blew a kiss.

'Charmed,' the man said.

'Vespery is a friend of the Duchess's,' Rossdale explained. 'He is painting portraits of her and my father.'

'You are an artist!' The first true artist she'd ever met.

His eyes assessed her. 'Are you in need of an artist? Please tell me you wish to have your portrait painted. I would be more than delighted to immortalise you on canvas.'

She laughed. 'I am not important enough to be immortalised.'

'Miss Summerfield is an artist herself,' Rossdale told him.

'Are you?' Vespery's rather remarkable brows rose.

Genna rolled her eyes. 'An *aspiring* artist is more precise. But I am very serious about it.'

Vespery leaned forward. 'Do tell me. What is your medium?'

'Watercolours,' she replied. 'But only because I've never been taught how to use anything else.'

At that moment the Duchess of Kessington came up to Rossdale. 'I need you Rossdale. I must take you away.'

The Duchess took him out of earshot. 'What are you about, Ross? Spending all your time with the Summerfield girl? We have other guests.'

'Is that why you took me away?' Ross frowned.

'You know how it will look if you favour one young lady.' She kept her smile on her face. 'Especially a Summerfield.'

'Both Lord Tinmore and her sister left her standing alone,' he said. 'There is no one of her acquaintance here. Would it not be rude to leave any guest in that circumstance?'

'Well, be careful,' the Duchess said. 'You would do well to join some of the conversations among the peers tonight.

These are very important times, you know. You will learn much from the experience of these gentlemen.'

'Constance.' He looked her directly in the eye. 'Do not tell me what I must do.'

She released his arm. 'I speak for your father.'

Ross doubted that. Although her father and she were perfect partners, both working hard to further his political power and influence, Ross was reasonably certain his father was motivated by duty to the country and its people. Ross feared the Duchess merely liked power and influence for its own sake.

Ross's father married Constance when Ross was in school. Her connection was to his father and his role in society, not to Ross. It was fortunate that she had no interest in mothering Ross, because no one could replace the mother he had adored. The duty in which Constance revelled was what had killed his mother.

Ross scanned the room and found his father deep in conversation with his cronies. Tinmore, who looked very gratified, was included.

'I dare say the Duke has not given me a thought since the party began,' Ross told her. 'So do not tell me he has spoken of me to you.'

'You are impossible.' She swept away.

Ross glanced towards Genna, who seemed to be delighted to be in conversation with Vespery. As much as he hated to admit it, the Duchess was correct that people would notice if he spent the whole of the evening in Genna's company. He must make the rounds of the room and speak with other guests before returning to her. That should keep his father's wife satisfied.

He approached Dell, who still remained at Lady Tinmore's side, obviously not feeling the same obligation to limit his time with any one person.

'Is Dell taking good care of you?' he asked Lady Tinmore.

She blushed, although why she should blush at such a statement he could not guess.

'He has been very kind,' she said.

Ross glanced over at her husband, who was listening intently to something Ross's father was saying. 'Lord Tinmore seems quite preoccupied.'

'Indeed,' she said. 'I fear Lord Penford took pity on me. I am grateful to him.'

Dell looked like a storm ready to spew lightning and thunder.

'I know some ladies who might be very interested to speak with you.' Ross meant the Duchesses Archester and Mannerton.

'Would you like that?' Dell asked her.

'Of course.' She lowered her lashes. 'And it would free you from having to act my escort.'

Dell nodded, but Ross could not tell if he wanted to be rid of Lady Tinmore or not. Nor could he tell what Lady Tinmore really wished.

Lady Tinmore took Ross's arm and Dell followed.

Ross presented Lady Tinmore to the Duchess of Archester and the Duchess of Mannerton. 'The Duchesses told your sister that they knew your mother,' he told Lady Tinmore.

'Come sit with us, dear.' The Duchess of Archester patted the space next to her on a sofa.

Ross bowed and he and Dell walked away.

'Tinmore appears to have forgotten his wife,' Ross remarked.

'Yes.' Dell's voice was low. 'I thought it my duty to step in.' He took two glasses of champagne off a tray offered by a passing footman and handed one to Ross. 'Cousin and all. Why ever did your stepmother invite them?'

'Do not call her my stepmother.' Ross had told him this many times. She was his father's wife, but not any sort of mother to him. 'She invited them at my suggestion.'

'Your suggestion?' Dell gaped at him.

Ross shrugged. 'I had a desire to see Miss Summerfield again.'

'Miss Summerfield?' Dell took a sip of champagne. 'I am surprised.'

'Are you?' Ross responded. 'She is refreshing.'

Dell's brows knit. 'Your father will not approve, you know.'

'There really is nothing for him to approve or disapprove,' Ross said. 'I merely enjoy her company.'

'Will you court her?' Dell asked.

'I do not intend to court anyone,' Ross replied. 'You know that. I am in no hurry to be leg-shackled or to be shackled to a title. Time for that later.' His father was in good health. The need to produce an heir and be about the business of a duke was some years away yet.

Dell put a stilling hand on Ross's arm. 'Take care not to trifle with that young woman. She's got enough of a trial merely living with Tinmore. Besides, she's barely out of the schoolroom.'

'She's not as young as all that. She'll reach her majority within a year.' A friendship with Genna was sounding more and more impossible.

But it should not be. They should be free to be friends if they wished to.

'Take care, Ross,' Dell said. 'Tinmore means for her to be married. And he is just the sort to force the deed, if you give him any reason.'

Genna could not help but keep one eye on Rossdale. She fancied she could tell precisely where he stood in the room at any time. It made her heart glad merely to be in the same room with him, knowing he would eventually speak to her again. In the meantime what could be more delightful than to be in the company of a true artist, a man who made his living by painting! There was so much she wanted to ask Vespery, so much of his knowledge and skill she wished to absorb.

She asked him about the paintings.

'What of this one?' She pointed to a nearby landscape, a pastoral scene with a cottage, a stream, horses and a wagon, cattle, men working.

He pulled out spectacles and perched them on his nose. 'This painting? This painting is Flemish, of course.'

She wondered how one could tell a Flemish painting from a Dutch one. Although even she had been able to tell the Dutch painting was not Italian.

'It is a Brueghel, I believe,' he went on. 'Jan the Younger, if I am not mistaken. There were several generations of Brueghels. Some of them painted fruit.'

'How old is it?' she asked.

'Oh, possibly two hundred years old. Seventeenth century.'

She looked at it again.

Vespery moved closer to the painting. 'Notice the composition. All the triangles.'

She stared at it. 'Yes! The roof of the cottage. The shape of the stream. Even the tree trunks.' Patterns. Like the pattern of curves in the hall of this house. 'It makes it pleasing to look at.'

She wished she could find Rossdale and tell him what Vespery had taught her.

She glanced around the room and saw Rossdale speaking to an older woman and a younger one, possibly the older woman's daughter. The excitement in her breast turned into a sharp pain.

Why should she ache? Rossdale was merely speaking to a young woman who was his social equal. Genna could not aspire to be anything but a friend to him, not that they could manage a friendship in London during the Season when everyone and everything centred on marriageable young ladies finding eligible gentlemen to marry.

Chapter Ten

The musicale was announced and the guests filed out of the drawing room.

Genna excused herself from Vespery. 'I should find my sister.' No doubt Tinmore would leave her to walk into the music room alone.

She found Lorene near where Tinmore had first deposited them.

'I have had the most remarkable conversation with two duchesses,' Lorene said when Genna reached her. 'You spoke with them, too, Rossdale said. They knew our mother.'

The Duchesses of Archester and Mannerton. 'Yes. I did.'

'They knew her when she eloped with Count von Osten. I must tell you all about it later.' Lorene glanced around the room.

Tinmore had attached himself to another grey-haired gentleman and was leaving the room, but Lorene did not remark on it. Genna walked with Lorene as if it was the most natural thing in the world to be left without an escort.

Except Lord Penford appeared. 'I will escort you ladies to the music room.'

They followed the other guests to another huge room, this one painted green with cream accents and more gold gilt at the border of the ceiling and along the chair railing on the walls. Chairs upholstered in a brocade the same shade as the walls were lined up facing an alcove whose entrance was flanked by two Corinthian columns, their elaborate ornamentation painted gold.

'This is a lovely room,' Lorene exclaimed.

'Let me find you seats,' Penford said.

Tinmore hobbled up to them. 'There you are!' he said peevishly. 'Come. Come. Let us sit.'

Penford stepped back and when Genna next glanced his way, he'd disappeared.

'Here. Sit here.' Tinmore gestured with his cane.

They were near the centre of the room, several gentlemen having chosen seats in the back and Tinmore knew better than to take the front seats that more properly went to those of higher rank. On each chair was a printed card edged in gold like the invitation had been. It listed the program.

When everyone was seated, the butler stood at the front of the alcove and announced the program. 'Mozart's Quintets in D Major and G Minor.'

He backed away and five musicians entered the alcove through a door hidden in the wall, two violins, two violas and a cello. They sat and spent a few minutes tuning their instruments before beginning the first piece.

Lorene gasped and leaned forward, her colour high and the hint of a smile on her face. Genna silently celebrated. Her dear sister was awash in pleasure from the beautiful music. It was a joy to see her so happy. Genna glanced around the room, looking for Rossdale.

He stood in the back of the room, his arms folded across his chest, looking perfectly comfortable—and slightly bored. And very handsome. How lovely to have a handsome friend.

But she must not be caught staring at him.

She turned her attention instead to the lovely array of colours of the ladies' gowns, like so many flowers scattered about. She looked for patterns and shapes, but, unlike the symmetry of the room's decor, the guests were a mishmash. How would one put a pleasing order on a painting of this event?

Feeling like a hopeless amateur, she gave up and closed her eyes.

To her surprise she heard a pattern of sounds in the music, a repeated melody, but as soon as she identified it, the music changed and the pattern was lost. Sometimes it came back; sometimes a new pattern of notes emerged. Frustrating.

After talking with Vespery she'd entertained the idea that all art used pattern. Hearing it in the music expanded the idea. But then Mozart broke the pattern and her idea seemed suddenly foolish.

She opened her eyes again and looked around her.

Lord Tinmore leaned on his cane, his eyes closed and his breathing even. The music had put him to sleep. Goodness! She hoped he would not snore.

Rustling in the back suggested that other guests were restless. Lorene, though, was rapt and that was enough for Genna.

She wanted to glance behind her to see Rossdale's reaction to the music, but she feared it would be noticed.

When the first piece finished there was a short intermission during which the musicians left the room and the footmen served more champagne.

Some guests rose from their seats, but Lorene and Genna remained seated. Tinmore woke, but his eyes remained heavy.

'What did you think of the music?' Genna asked her sister.

'I thought it marvellous.' Lorene said. 'I wonder if there is sheet music for piano. I should love to learn it.'

'Perhaps we can visit the music shops and find out.' The shopping was another of the delights of London. There was a shop selling anything one could imagine.

After a few minutes the glasses were collected and the musicians returned to the alcove.

They began to play.

This piece was not as light-hearted as the first. It was melancholic. Sorrowful.

It reminded Genna of all she had lost. The home in which she'd grown up. Her mother.

And now her sisters and brother whose lives really did not involve her any more.

She blinked rapidly. She would not give in to the blue devils. She would not. No matter how dismal her life became. She was in London, a city of many enjoyments. She would enjoy as many as she could and would take it as a challenge to thwart any of Tinmore's plans for her to marry.

She would do just as she pleased.

The last movement began, a slow cavatina. It was a veritable dirge, pulling Genna's spirits low again. Then the music paused and Genna braced herself against a further onslaught of depression.

Instead, the music turned ebullient. Genna almost laughed aloud in relief as the notes danced cheerfully along, brushing away all that darkness.

That was what she would do. She'd brush away the darkness, make her own happy life and leave the rest behind.

She smiled and dared to glance back at Rossdale.

Ross scanned the supper room, although he knew precisely where Genna sat. Lord Tinmore had brought his wife and her sister into the supper room, but Ross's father had called him over to his table and Tinmore never looked back. The ladies were again left alone. Ross had been ready to cross the room to them, but both Dell and Vespery approached their table and sat with them. So he made the rounds again, but kept his eye on her, determined to spend a little more time with her before the night was over.

He moved through the room and finally stopped at their table.

Genna smiled up at him. 'Might you sit with us a little while?'

'I would be pleased to,' Ross answered truthfully. 'I do not believe I have sat down since the evening began.'

'Not even during the Quintet,' she stated.

'I stood in the back.' He turned to Lady Tinmore. 'Did you enjoy the performance?'

Lady Tinmore certainly had appeared as if she had. Of all the guests, she was the one whose attention to the music did not waver.

Her face lit up. 'Oh, yes! I do not know when I have so enjoyed music.'

He was baffled. The music had been competently played by the musicians and the pieces were pleasant enough. 'Why do you say so?'

'The first piece. In D major. It lightened my heart. There were so many musical ideas in it that I could not see how Mozart would be able to make it into a coherent whole.' She smiled. 'But, of course, he did.' She looked at the others. 'Did you not think so?'

'I listened for patterns of melody,' Genna said. 'But as soon as I heard one, the music changed to something else.'

'That is what I mean! So many ideas,' her sister cried. 'Please someone say they heard what I heard.'

Vespery threw up his hands. 'I do not analyse. I merely listen.'

Dell's chair had been pulled back as if he were not quite a part of this table. He stared into his glass of wine. 'I thought it complex. And beautiful.'

Lady Tinmore nodded. 'Yes,' she whispered. She looked shyly at Ross. 'What did you think?'

'I agree it was pleasant to listen to.' Music had never captured his interest. Neither had art of any sort, really. He liked what he saw or not, liked what he heard. Or not.

'What of the second piece?' Genna asked. 'That was not pleasant.'

'Beautiful.' Vespery raised a finger. 'But not pleasant.'

'But there were so many surprises in it!' Lady Tinmore cried. 'Like those harsh chords in the minuet.'

One thing Ross could say. Lady Tinmore had suddenly come to life. She had a personality after all. And emotion. Hidden, he supposed, because of her overbearing yet neglectful husband.

Genna spoke up. 'I thought I should be driven to a fit of weeping by those movements. Right when I was beginning to completely despair, that happy ending came.'

'Yes!' her sister cried. 'Was that not marvellous?'

Ross liked both the Summerfield sisters, he decided.

Lord Tinmore appeared at the table, but he spoke only to Ross. 'Rossdale, I was just telling your father, the Duke, that this was a most competently played musical evening. I am honoured to have been in the audience.'

Ross saw Genna cover her mouth, but her eyes danced. Tinmore did not notice. His attention was only on Ross. He also did not see Dell pull his chair further back and slip away.

'Kindly said, Tinmore,' Ross responded.

'I fear, sir, that I must bid you goodnight,' Tinmore went on. 'I already bade goodnight to your father and the Duchess. I hope that my years will excuse me to you and your family. Fatigue plagues me.'

They were leaving? He'd hardly had time to speak to Genna.

'Come!' Tinmore snapped to his wife and Genna. 'We must leave now.'

Lady Tinmore rose. 'I must thank the Duke and Duchess first.'

'They do not want to be bothered, I assure you,' Tinmore said. 'I said all that was required.'

All the life glimpsed a moment ago seemed drained from Lady Tinmore now. Genna looked red-faced with anger.

This boor.

Ross put on a smile he did not feel. 'I must agree with your wife, sir. My father and the Duchess take great offence when guests do not bother to thank them. I will accompany your wife and her sister to bid their farewells. You rest here.'

As Ross offered his arms to each of the ladies, Tinmore looked at Vespery and demanded, 'Who are you?'

Ross did not wait to hear Vespery's reply.

When they stepped away from the table, Genna murmured, 'It was nonsense.'

'What was?' Ross asked.

'He fell asleep during the whole concert,' she said. 'He did not hear it competently played at all.'

Ross inclined his head to her. 'I noticed. I could see from the back.'

She giggled.

'Want to hear more nonsense, ladies?' Ross asked.

'Indeed!' Genna said.

Her sister remained subdued.

He stopped and looked from one to the other. 'My father and the Duchess do not care a fig if you bid them goodnight.'

Genna's eyes sparkled. 'Oh, you are trying to make me laugh out loud!'

Yes. He definitely wanted to see more of Genna Summerfield.

Because she made him want to laugh out loud, too.

The next morning Ross strode down Bond Street and entered a shop he had never set foot in before. Mori and Leverne's Music Shop. He'd passed it countless times on his way to Gentleman Jackson's Boxing Salon, but he'd never had a reason to enter it before.

He had a whim to purchase sheet music to the Mozart pieces performed at the Duchess's musicale to give to Lady

Tinmore. It seemed the one thing that made her happy. He'd present it to Lord Tinmore for his wife and no one would think anything of that, not that any member of the *ton* would know of it. Tinmore would take it as a compliment to him, Lady Tinmore would receive some pleasure from it and perhaps Genna would also be pleased with him.

He stood inside the door without a clue how to find the piece he desired. The music seemed to be arranged in aisles, filed in some order that escaped him.

The clerk stood behind a counter at the far end of the shop, speaking to two ladies.

As Ross approached one of the ladies turned and broke into a smile. 'Rossdale!'

Genna. And her sister.

'What a surprise to see you!' Genna said. 'We came looking for the music from last night's musicale, but the last copy was sold just this morning.'

'I am terribly sorry,' the clerk said. 'The gentleman came early when the shop opened. You might try Birchall's down the street.'

'We did try there,' Lady Tinmore said.

So much for his idea of giving the music to her.

'What are you here for, Rossdale?' Genna asked. 'Do not tell me you were searching for the same music.'

Very well. He would not tell her. 'I was considering a gift,' he said.

Her smile faltered. 'Oh.' She seemed to recover, though. 'Perhaps we can help you. What sort of music did you have in mind?'

He shrugged. 'Perhaps something by Mozart. For the piano.'

'Ah!' said the clerk. 'I have some over here.'

'Help him, Lorene,' Genna said. 'You will be able to tell him what music is best.'

Lady Tinmore acted as reserved as usual. 'If you like.' She lowered her lashes.

'I would be grateful,' Ross said.

She riffled through the sheets of music the clerk indicated. 'Here is one.' She pulled out the sheet and studied it. 'A piano sonata. Number eleven.'

She handed it to him and he glanced at the page. He could follow almost none of it. 'Do you have this music?' he asked her.

'No,' she replied. 'I merely think it would be a pretty one to play.'

He handed the sheets to the clerk. 'I will purchase this one.' He gave his information to the clerk.

Upon learning where the bill was to be directed, the clerk became even more solicitous. 'Allow me to place this in an envelope for you, my lord.'

'Did you want to look for something else?' Genna asked her sister.

Lady Tinmore shook her head.

Ross, music in hand, walked with the ladies to the door. At the door, though, he stopped and handed the envelope to Lady Tinmore. 'This is for you, ma'am,' he said.

'For me?' Some expression entered her face.

'Lorene!' Genna broke into a smile.

'But, why?' Lady Tinmore asked.

'For being the guest last night who most enjoyed the concert,' he replied.

And to give her some happiness since she certainly did not have that in her marriage.

Ross opened the door and held it. Lady Tinmore walked out first.

Genna paused and looked up at Ross. 'Take care, Lord Rossdale. You might make me like you very much.'

He grinned. 'There must be worse fates than that.'

Although what good would it do them to like each other? Unless they could spend time together.

He was determined to figure out a way, but unless he made a formal gesture, he could not even call upon her.

All he could do was wait until they saw each other by accident, like this, or were invited to the same parties. And who knew when that would be?

Chapter Eleven

What was he thinking? They were together now. Ross could contrive to spend more time with Genna, even if her sister was also present.

'Where are you ladies bound after this?' he asked when they were out on the pavement.

'I believe we will go home,' Lady Tinmore said.

Genna looked disappointed. Perhaps she wanted more time together, as well. He was not surprised they were of one mind.

'May I escort you?' he asked.

Genna's eyes pleaded with her sister. The walk back to Curzon Street and Tinmore's town house would be a short one, but to accompany them would be more enjoyable than if he simply left them here.

Lady Tinmore lowered her lashes. 'If you like.'

Genna smiled.

As did Ross.

He offered his arm to Lorene, who, as a countess, had precedence. Genna walked next to her.

They strolled past the shops on Bond Street and turned on Bruton Street.

'Are you enjoying your Season in London?' Ross asked in a polite tone.

'Yes, quite,' Lorene answered agreeably.

He leaned over and directed his gaze at Genna. 'And you, Miss Summerfield?'

Genna appeared for a moment to be doing battle with

herself. Trying not to say something she really wanted to say.

Her words burst forth. 'To own the truth, I am feeling a bit restrained.' Apparently what she wanted to say won out. 'There is so much to do and see here in town and, as I cannot go out alone, I am confined to the house.'

'Genna!' her sister chided.

'Well, it is true,' Genna protested hotly.

They had reached Berkeley Square.

Ross deflected the impending sisterly spat. 'Shall we do and see something right now?' he asked. 'Here is Gunter's. Shall we stop and have an ice?'

Lady Tinmore's brows knit. 'I do not know if we should.'

'It would be respectable,' Ross said. 'I would not have asked otherwise.'

'Oh, let's do, Lorene.' Genna pleaded. 'It will be fun.'

Lady Tinmore looked as if she were being dragged to a dungeon instead of the most fashionable tea shop and confectioner in Mayfair.

'Very well,' she finally said.

Genna skipped in apparent delight.

'The day is overcast, though, as well as being chilly,' Ross said. 'Let us not eat in the square under the trees. We should go inside.'

They entered the shop and sat at a table.

A waiter stepped up to serve them. 'Sir? Ladies?'

'What would you like?' Ross asked Genna and her sister.

'Not an ice,' Lorene said. 'Not on such a cold day. I shall have tea.'

Genna huffed. 'I do not care how cold it may be, I am having an ice!'

The waiter handed them cards that had the flavours printed on them. 'Your choice, miss.'

Genna read part of the list aloud. 'Barberry, elderflower, jasmine, muscadine, pistachio and rye bread…' She handed the card back to the waiter. 'I shall be adventuresome. I will try the rye-bread ice.'

'Rye-bread ice,' repeated the waiter in a voice that showed her exotic choice was commonplace for him. 'And you, sir?'

'Pineapple,' Ross said.

The waiter bowed and left.

'Pineapple?' Genna looked at him in mock disapproval. 'That is not very daring.'

'It is what I like,' he explained.

'But how do you know that you will not like another flavour better unless you try it?' she asked.

'Genna fancies whatever is new and different,' her sister said.

'You make me sound frivolous,' Genna complained, but she turned to Ross and laughed. 'What am I saying? Lorene is correct! That is me! Liking whatever is new and different.'

Therein was her charm. 'And you are eager to see new and different sights while you are here?' he asked.

'I am eager. Not very hopeful, though.' She frowned and her face tightened in frustration. 'I think I might be content to do anything but stay in the house.'

'Genna!' her sister again chided. 'You must not say such things. They can be misinterpreted. You'll sound fast.'

'Oh, I think Lord Rossdale knows what I mean,' she said with confidence. 'I just want to *do* things. The places I see do not even have to be new. Something I've liked before and wish to do or see again would be fine.'

'Like what?' he asked.

'Well.' Her mouth widened into an impish smile. 'Like having an ice at Gunter's.'

He liked her humour. 'What else?'

Lady Tinmore answered for her. 'Genna wishes to see Napoleon's carriage at the Egyptian Hall.'

Ross laughed inwardly. He wanted to see Napoleon's carriage, as well.

'I do wish to see it!' she protested. 'Who would not?'

'It has created quite a stir,' he admitted.

Genna gave Lorene a smug look. 'See, Lorene, I am not the only one.' Lorene folded her arms across her chest and glanced away.

He had no idea what to do with sisterly disputes. He had no brothers or sisters. It was one of the reasons his father was so eager for him to marry and produce an heir.

Perhaps if his mother had lived it would have been different. Perhaps there would have been little sisters or brothers for him to spat with.

Genna went on. 'I would love to see everything in the Egyptian Museum. I also want to see Astley's Amphitheatre, the menagerie at the Tower, and—' She paused and looked away. 'I want to see the Elgin Marbles.'

She was game for everything.

Like his mother had been.

Until his father inherited the title and the burden of that responsibility fell upon him. And her.

'You cannot see the Elgin Marbles,' Lady Tinmore said. 'No one can. They are stored away until Parliament decides whether or not to purchase them for the British Museum.'

They were stored at Montagu House.

Their ices and Lady Tinmore's cup of tea were brought to them.

Genna dipped into hers eagerly. And made a face, but she took another spoonful and another.

Ross's spoon was poised to taste his. 'How is it?'

She put on a brave smile. 'It is—it is—it is...' She faltered. She finally laughed. 'It is quite dreadful, actually.'

Her sister murmured, 'Of course it is.'

Ross pushed his untouched pineapple ice towards her. 'Here. Have mine. I only ordered it so you would not have to eat alone.'

She looked at it longingly, then pulled it the rest of the way towards her. 'Oh, thank you! I love pineapple ices.'

Her sister stood and Ross quickly stood, as well.

'I believe I will choose some confections to bring to Lord Tinmore,' she said.

'Shall I assist you?' he asked.

'Not at all. The clerk will help me.'

There was a clerk behind a counter who had just assisted someone else.

Ross sat again as Lady Tinmore walked away.

'She is purchasing confections for Lord Tinmore,' he repeated, finding it difficult to believe.

Genna's countenance turned serious. 'She tries very hard to please him. An impossible goal, I believe.'

He thought he ought to be careful what he said. 'Tinmore is very…critical…of her.'

She swallowed a spoonful. 'He is an awful man, but do not say so in front of her. She will defend him.'

He was puzzled. 'She has a regard for him?'

She shook her head. 'Not in the way you mean. She is grateful to him for marrying her. She married him so that my sister Tess, my brother and I would have a chance to make good matches and not be required to be governesses or ladies' companions, or, in my brother's case, to stay in the army and be sent some place terrible like the West Indies.'

'She married him for you and your sister and brother?' Marrying for money took on a different meaning in that case.

She nodded and glanced over at her sister. 'Although I never wanted any of it. I won't use his dowry, no matter what Tinmore thinks.'

'Surely you wish to marry, though,' he said.

She scoffed. 'With no dowry, I cannot expect to marry, but that does not trouble me. I do not wish to marry.'

'How would you live, then?' he asked.

Young ladies of good birth had few choices in life except to marry. The few they had were dismal. Ladies' companions or governesses, as she'd said.

'Well, if you must know, I wish to make my living as an artist. Like your Mr Vespery.' She took another spoonful.

'You wish to paint portraits?' That was how Vespery made his living.

'I would prefer to paint landscapes, but I doubt that will bring me enough money.' She shrugged.

He smiled. 'Ones with purple skies and blue grass?'

She laughed. 'I doubt that sort of landscape would bring me any income at all!' She glanced down at her almost finished ice. 'I have so much more to learn, though. I do not even know how to paint in oils.'

Maybe Vespery could be persuaded to give her lessons, Ross thought. But would Tinmore allow such a thing?

She smiled and took the last bite. 'I can always become a lady's companion. I would make a good one, do you not think?'

He grinned. 'You would keep some lady on her toes, that is true.'

Lady Tinmore walked back to the table, a small package in hand. Ross stood.

'I believe we should go, Genna,' she said.

Genna rose. 'Thank you, Lord Rossdale. That was a lovely interlude.'

'My pleasure.'

It was his pleasure, a pleasure to have a candid conversation with an intelligent young woman who enjoyed new experiences as much as he did. He was not going to leave their next meeting to chance. After he delivered Genna and her sister to the town house on Curzon Street, he would make another call nearby. The Duchess of Archester was planning a ball in two weeks' time. He would wager she could be persuaded to invite the daughters of her old friend, Lady Summerfield.

* * *

After Rossdale left Genna and Lorene at their door and the footman carried away their cloaks, Lorene turned to Genna. 'Do you not think you are acting a bit too free with Lord Rossdale?'

She should have known Lorene would have something to say about her behaviour. Too often her husband's words seemed to be coming out of Lorene's mouth.

'Too free? I do not take your meaning.'

They started up the stairs.

'You say too much. About wanting to go to the Egyptian Museum, and Astley's and all. Might he not take it you want an invitation from him?'

She made herself laugh. 'Perhaps I did! How else am I going to do things unless someone invites me?'

'Not the son of a duke!' Lorene cried. 'You must not mistake his father's interest in Lord Tinmore for the son's intention to court you.'

Sometimes Lorene could sound every bit as dispiriting as her husband.

She continued up the stairs, a few steps ahead of her sister. 'I like Lord Rossdale. And I think he likes me. But he is not going to court me. It is not like that.'

No one would court her if she had anything to do with it. Tinmore could not force her to marry. She just needed a little more time to be ready to forge her own way.

Lorene went on. 'You must not speak so familiarly to gentlemen. It is not the thing to do. You must be careful. The last thing we want is to be the objects of gossip.'

Of scandal.

Genna did not have the horror of gossip and scandal that her two sisters did. She did not care what others thought of her.

Had her mother been like her?

If she should ever again be in the company of the Duchesses of Archester and of Mannerton, she would ask them.

They were met on the first floor by the butler. 'A package arrived for you, my lady.'

'For me?' Lorene sounded surprised.

'It is in your sitting room.' He bowed.

Lorene had a parlour near to her bedchamber where she could receive callers—if anyone called on her, that was.

'Let us go see what it is!' Genna cried, the sharp words between them forgotten.

They rushed to the sitting room. On the tea table was an envelope very similar to the one Lorene held in her hand, the music Rossdale had purchased for her. She placed that envelope on the table and picked up the other. It was tied with a ribbon like a gift. A card was stuck underneath the ribbon.

Lorene pulled the card out and read it. She handed it to Genna.

'"*For your enjoyment*",' Genna read. She looked up at Lorene. 'It is not signed.'

Lorene opened the envelope and pulled out sheets of music. She gasped. 'The Mozart pieces from the musicale last night!'

'Oh, my goodness,' Genna exclaimed. 'It must have been purchased by that gentleman the clerk mentioned. Who could it be?'

Lorene traced her fingers along the lines of music, a strange, soft expression on her face. 'I do not know.'

Not Tinmore, that was for certain.

Two weeks later Lord Tinmore, Lorene and Genna were invited to the Duchess of Archester's ball, the first important ball of the Season. It was a coup Tinmore credited to his new alliance with the Duke of Kessington, Rossdale's father. He was more certain than ever that Lorene or Genna would embarrass him completely, so every dinner for over a week had been consumed with his incessant instructions.

He insisted both Genna and Lorene have new ball

gowns, as if they would not want a new gown themselves. Their modiste made certain their dresses were beautifully fashionable. Genna's was a pale blue silk with an over-dress and long sleeves of white net. The hem of the skirt was trimmed in white lace as were the neckline and cuffs.

Tinmore insisted that a hairdresser be hired as well, but Genna disliked what the man did. She had her own maid take down her hair and rearrange it to a style less fussy and more comfortable for her. She wound up with curls around her face and the rest pulled high on her head. A long string of tiny pearls was wrapped around her head and up through the crown of curls.

Lorene's gown was white muslin embellished with gold embroidery that shimmered in the candlelight. She wore a gold-and-diamond band in her hair and diamonds around her neck. Her usually straight hair had been transformed into a mass of curls. How anyone could look at another lady there, Genna did not know. Her sister took her breath away.

When they were announced at the ball, Genna felt se-cure in their appearance—and totally mismatched with the grey-haired, wrinkled man who escorted them. They first waited in a line to greet the Duke and Duchess of Archester. When it was finally Genna's turn, the Duchess greeted her warmly.

The Duke held on to Genna's hand for a moment. 'You are the image of your mother, young lady,' he said with feeling.

Genna felt a stab of pain. She could not remember what her mother looked like.

She curtsied. 'Thank you, your Grace.' What else could she say?

Tinmore quickly whisked them away from the Duke and Duchess.

As they crossed the ballroom floor, Tinmore whispered, 'There will be some eligible men here, girl. I expect you to be on good behaviour. Make a good impression. I have already spoken to some gentlemen on your behalf, so you will have some dance partners.'

Genna forced a smile. 'I never want for dance partners, sir.'

She had no intention of encouraging his matchmaking. She was perfectly capable of having a good time all on her own.

'Now, do not come bothering me if I am in conversation,' he whispered to Lorene. 'It will likely be about a matter of importance. There will be other ladies for you to speak to. Make certain you are agreeable.'

Lorene was always agreeable, Genna wanted to say, but Tinmore left them before she could open her mouth.

'There are so many people here!' Lorene looked around nervously.

Genna scoured the room. 'Good! Perhaps Tinmore's gentlemen will not be able to find me. If I spy them coming, I'll hide behind a jardinière of flowers.'

'He merely wants to see you settled,' Lorene said defensively.

'He wants me out of his house so he can have you all to himself,' Genna retorted in good humour, although she really meant it.

She caught sight of two men walking towards them. 'Here are two gentlemen we know.'

Rossdale and Penford.

Rossdale smiled. 'Good evening, ladies.'

Lord Penford merely nodded and asked, 'May I get you some refreshment?'

Genna saw liveried servants carrying glasses with what she hoped was champagne. 'Yes, Penford. Thank you.'

Was he Lorene's secret admirer?

Impossible. Genna could not tell whether or not Penford even liked Lorene. He was all obligation, Genna feared.

'Are you available for the first set?' Rossdale asked Genna.

Her heart danced in her chest. 'I am.' There was no one she would rather dance with.

He turned to Lorene. 'Will you be dancing, ma'am? Perhaps you will favour me with a set?'

Now Genna's heart melted. He'd included her sister who desperately deserved to enjoy herself.

Lorene's eyes darted towards where her husband was conversing with other men. 'I am not certain if I should.'

'Of course you should,' cried Genna. 'It is a ball and you look so lovely many gentlemen will want to dance with you.'

Penford came up and handed her and Genna a glass of champagne.

'Dance the second set with me,' Rossdale said. 'Then you may retire if you wish.'

'Oh, say yes, Lorene!' Genna said impatiently.

She lowered her eyes. 'Very well.'

By the time they finished the champagne, couples were lining up for the first dance. Rossdale took Genna's hand to lead her on to the dance floor. Genna turned back to smile at her sister. She felt a little guilty for leaving Lorene, but Penford, taciturn as he was wont to be, stood by her side and was some company, at least.

Genna filled with excitement. To see Rossdale again. To be dancing with him. To have a friend.

Ross smiled as they faced each other in the line, waiting for others to join.

The music started and the couples at the head of the line began dancing their steps and figures. Each couple would repeat the figures, couple by couple, down the line.

'Do you enjoy dancing?' Ross asked Genna, although it was clear she did.

Her colour was high and her eyes sparkled.

'I do indeed.' she responded. 'It is so lively. And I love

how pretty it is when all the couples perform the figures together.'

Ross mostly considered dancing a social obligation, but it was impossible not to catch Genna's excitement and enjoy himself along with her. There was a rhythm to it, a pattern, he found pleasant, especially if he forgot anything but the dance.

And Genna.

He noticed that Dell and Lady Tinmore had joined the line. When he and Genna came together in the figures, he said to her, 'Your sister dances.'

'I noticed,' she replied as the dance separated them.

It brought them together again.

'Do you suppose Penford felt an obligation?' she asked.

His answer had to wait until they came together again. 'That is what he says.'

'I am delighted she is allowing herself some fun,' Genna said. 'I wonder if Tinmore even notices.' They parted and came together once more, turning in a circle. 'I hope she thinks of nothing but the dancing.'

He decided to offer Genna what she wanted for her sister—a chance to think of nothing but the dancing. He did not attempt more than a comment or two after that.

The sets often lasted a half-hour or more and this one was no exception. Ross usually succumbed to boredom after the first ten minutes, but this time he was not even aware of how much time had passed.

When the music stopped, he stood facing Genna again. They both stared at each other as if shocked the dance had ended. Finally she curtsied, he bowed, and he took her hand to return her to where she had stood with her sister.

Her step quickened when they neared her. 'Was that not lovely?' she asked.

Lady Tinmore darted a glance at Dell, who quickly looked away. 'Lovely. Yes.'

A footman bore a tray with champagne and they each took a glass.

It made perfect sense for Ross to remain with Genna and her sister. He would be dancing with her sister the next set, but after that he must leave them and dance with others. He could swing back for a second dance. Two dances were the limit unless he wished for there to be speculation about a betrothal between them.

He glanced around the room and saw his father's wife standing with the Duchess of Mannerton. His father was deep in conversation with the Duke of Mannerton and Lord Tinmore was hovering around the edges of these higher-ranking men. His father's wife, on the other hand, kept tossing disapproving looks Ross's way.

Another reason why he must leave Genna and seek out other partners. The Duchess could be a formidable enemy if she so chose and he certainly did not wish her to choose Genna as an enemy.

A young gentleman with whom Ross had a passing acquaintance, approached them.

He bowed to Genna. 'Miss Summerfield, how good to see you.'

She smiled at him. 'Why, good evening, Mr Holdsworth.'

Holdsworth was the younger son of Baron Holdsworth. He could not be more than twenty-one, more of an age with Genna than Ross, who was nearing thirty.

Holdsworth nodded nervously to Ross and Dell, who easily outranked him.

His attention returned to Genna. 'Are you engaged for the next set? If not, would you do me the honour of dancing with me?'

'Yes, of course, Mr Holdsworth,' she responded right away. 'I remember dancing with you last Season. I enjoyed it very much.'

The young man beamed with pleasure. He bowed and withdrew.

Ross's mood turned sour.

'Do you know Mr Holdsworth?' she asked Ross. 'I should have introduced you, shouldn't I?'

'I am acquainted with him,' Ross answered.

'He is quite fun to dance with, as you will see.' She laughed. 'Very energetic.' She leaned closer to his ear. 'And he is not one of Lord Tinmore's choices.'

Ross frowned. 'Tinmore has chosen who will dance with you?'

'Widowers with a dozen children to manage or younger sons needing the dowry Tinmore offers.' She glanced around the room. 'I shall avoid them if I am able.'

Lorene glared at her. 'Genna, may I speak with you for a moment?'

Her sister drew Genna aside. 'What are you saying to Rossdale about Lord Tinmore—?'

Ross could not hear the rest.

He turned to Dell, who looked preoccupied. 'How are you faring, Dell?'

'Well enough, I suppose.' Dell composed his features, but only briefly. His eyes shone with pain. 'Actually, not well at all. I need some respite.'

'Is there anything I can do?' Ross asked. He'd been surprised that Dell had danced at all. In fact, he was surprised Dell had agreed to come. These social events were not easy for him.

'No. Nothing.' Dell glanced towards Genna and her sister. 'Please make my excuses to the ladies.' He turned and walked away without waiting for Ross's agreement.

Both sisters, looking somewhat heated, returned to where Ross stood. Neither looked very happy.

'Dell had to excuse himself,' he told them. 'He bids you goodnight.'

'Oh?' Genna glanced at her sister. 'I do hope he comes back.'

'Was there anything amiss?' Lady Tinmore asked. 'He appeared upset.'

'He is not yet completely recovered from the loss of his family,' Ross replied. 'It strikes him unawares at times.'

'What happened to them?' Genna's face looked pinched.

'They were killed in a fire. All of them,' he said in a low voice.

Lady Tinmore gasped.

'You and your sisters and brother, Lady Tinmore, are all the relations he has left,' he added.

The musicians signalled the next set and couples began to line up on the dance floor. Mr Holdsworth strode over eagerly and extended his hand to Genna, who seemed to have lost her sparkle.

He ought not to have spoken. Both ladies immediately grasped the enormity of Dell's loss and were affected by the news.

Ross turned to Lady Tinmore. 'This is our set, I believe.'

She glanced up at him and for a moment he thought she would start weeping. 'You do not have to dance with me, Lord Rossdale. I—I feel it is almost unseemly to dance after hearing...' Her voice trailed off.

'Forgive me,' he said. 'This was not the proper time to tell you of Dell's loss. He would be vexed with me if he found out I ruined this ball for you. Please dance with me.'

She nodded.

They took their place in the line not far from Genna and Mr Holdsworth.

Lady Tinmore noticed him looking Genna's way.

He changed the subject. 'I hope you and your sister settled your quarrel.'

'Quarrel?' She could not quite meet his eye. 'She has such lively spirits. Sometimes she is too forward and her tongue runs away with her.'

Ross responded, 'I admire your sister's forthrightness. It is a refreshing change from those who only say what is expected.'

'Then do understand. She is not trying to get you to court her.'

The music had begun and the first figures were starting down the line of dancers.

He knew that. Even from his first meeting with Genna, he knew she was not trying to trap him into marriage. But it depressed him to hear her sister say it aloud.

It was Genna's and Mr Holdsworth's turn to dance. They were quite well matched in lively steps and grace, which somehow did not please him. Genna seemed to regain some of her former enthusiasm, though.

At the end of the set, Lady Tinmore thanked him and added, 'I do hope Lord Penford returns to the ballroom.'

He bowed to her. 'I hope so, as well.'

He escorted her back to the place they'd been standing and she lowered herself into a nearby chair. 'I believe I will sit for a while.'

'Shall I bring you some refreshment?' he asked, although he also watched Genna and Mr Holdsworth still on the dance floor talking together.

'I would love something to drink.' Lady Tinmore fanned herself.

He brought her a glass of champagne and noticed Genna leaving the dance floor.

'I see your sister is returning to you,' he said to Lady Tinmore. 'I must take my leave.'

She thanked him again for the dance and said goodbye.

He made himself walk through the ballroom and converse with various people he knew. His father was doing the same, as was his father's wife, but they had an agenda—to turn as many members of Parliament as possible to their way of thinking. Important work, but when did his father ever simply enjoy himself? His father used to smile and laugh and be willing to do things just for the doing of them.

Ross spied Genna conversing with yet another young man. A man who looked to be in his forties—one of Lord Tinmore's choices, perhaps?—hung around her for a bit, but gave up trying to get her attention away from the young buck. A quadrille was called and the young man escorted her to the dance floor.

Ross asked the daughter of one of his father's closest allies to dance the quadrille with him, which certainly would meet with the Duchess's approval. The young lady was in want of a partner and Ross did not wish to leave her a wallflower.

But he intended to get a second dance with Genna before the night was through.

Unless another gentleman claimed her first, that was.

Chapter Twelve

After the quadrille, Ross noticed Genna leave the ballroom. She disappeared into the ladies' retiring room and he waited in the corridor to catch her when she came out.

The door opened and Genna peeked carefully around before stepping into the corridor. She seemed in no hurry to return to the dancing.

He approached her from behind. 'Genna?'

She jumped and put her hand on her chest when she saw it was him. 'Oh, Rossdale! You startled me. I thought you were someone else.'

'Who?' One of the young men who occupied her time?

She waved a hand. 'Oh, one of Tinmore's widowers. I am eager to avoid him.'

He took her arm. 'Then let's not return to the ballroom.'

He led her outside on to a veranda. The Duke of Archester's town house was one of the few in Mayfair to have a garden of any size behind it. They were not the only ones to seek a quieter, more secluded place. Other couples stood close together on the veranda or on benches in the garden. After the close, warm air of the ballroom, the chilly March air felt welcome, although Ross doubted that all the couples outside were merely seeking fresh air.

Genna inhaled deeply. 'Oh, how nice. I can breathe out here.'

It occurred to him that she smiled at him the way she smiled at her other dance partners. He didn't like that thought, though. 'You appeared to be having a good time dancing.'

She sobered. 'I am having a good time, although I cannot help thinking about Lord Penford. Has he returned to the ballroom?'

'Not that I've seen.' It pleased him that she felt concern for his friend.

Her lovely forehead knitted.

'Do not let it spoil your enjoyment, though. He would not wish that and I should feel quite regretful that I spoke of his family.'

She nodded. 'I have enjoyed the dancing.' She slid him a sly smile. 'So far I have not had to dance with any of the men Tinmore picked to court me.'

'Is he so determined to get you married?' he asked.

She nodded. 'But I only have to get through this Season. I will be twenty-one soon and I can go my own way.'

He thought about her desire to become an artist. It was a daring choice. Women artists were rare, but some had made a good living with their art.

She shivered and he led them to a corner more protected from the cool air.

She gazed at him with curiosity. 'But what of you? There seem to be several young ladies with whom to dance. Are you not looking to make a match?'

He stiffened. 'I am in no hurry to take on that responsibility.'

She peered at him. 'You do not seem the sort to wish to shirk responsibility.'

'Perhaps responsibility is not the proper word.' How could he explain? 'My station dictates that a match should be a carefully considered one. Advantageous to both parties.'

Her expression turned sympathetic. 'How dreadful.'

He was not ready to explain it all, though. 'I know I must marry and produce an heir. It is my duty. I know I will have to bear the mantle of the title eventually, but my father is in excellent health. There is no reason for me to rush. There is so much more I wish to do.'

Her face relaxed. 'Like what?'

What did he wish to do? Since the war's end, he hadn't been sure, although there certainly was plenty to do for the returning soldiers. With the war's end, several regiments would disband and the soldiers would return home without a pension and many without a trade to support them.

He'd already cast Genna and her sister into the dismals by talking of Dell's loss; he certainly did not wish to depress her further with the plight of the soldiers.

'I'd like to travel, perhaps,' he said instead. Who would not wish to travel? 'Visit Paris, for one thing. The rest of the Continent. Maybe return to Rome and Venice.'

Her eyes lit up. 'And see the works of art there! Would that not be wonderful?'

Lately, because of Genna, he'd been noticing the artwork wherever he went. He'd like to learn more, appreciate it more.

She laughed. 'Here I am, pining merely to see the sights of London. You are thinking of the world!'

He smiled. 'Not the world, perhaps.' Although he was intensely curious about the Colonies. 'But certainly the Continent. Do a Grand Tour all over again, but widen my horizons.'

She sighed. 'You did a Grand Tour?'

'With Dell,' he said. 'We have been friends since we were boys.'

'How lovely!'

A footman came to the veranda door. 'Supper is being served.'

'We missed the supper dance,' she said, sounding relieved.

'You wanted to miss it?' he asked.

She grinned. 'One of Tinmore's widowers was searching for me. That is why I left the ballroom. Imagine being trapped with him through supper.'

'You know this gentleman?'

She nodded. 'Tinmore introduced us last Season, but he was not out of mourning yet, so he's been encouraged to court me now.' She glanced away and back again. 'He is a perfectly nice man. I do not mean to make a jest of him. I merely do not want him to court me. There are so many ladies who would love to marry him, but I would feel imprisoned.'

Other couples crossed the veranda and re-entered the house.

'Would you consider it undesirable to be trapped with me through supper?' he asked.

Her gaze rose to meet his. 'I can think of no one else I would rather be trapped with.'

Sitting with Rossdale for supper was a delight. With anyone else she would have restrained herself and taken care what she said, but with Rossdale she felt free to say anything. Even better, she was not beneath the watchful eye of her sister, who she finally spied in a group of other ladies and gentlemen. And Lord Penford.

She was relieved to see Lord Penford back.

After supper some of the young gentlemen with whom she became acquainted the previous Season engaged her to dance. Lord Rossdale asked her for the last dance.

A waltz.

It was exciting that the Duchess of Archester allowed the waltz, still considered scandalous by some. Genna usually did not relish the less lively dances, but she did love to dance the waltz. She liked being free of the lines of the country dances or the squares of the quadrilles. You stayed with your partner throughout the whole dance. With the right partner, the waltz was heaven.

And Rossdale was the right partner.

When the music began, they walked on to the dance floor with hands entwined and, finding a place, faced each other. She curtsied. He bowed. She put her hands on his shoulders. He placed his hands at her waist. Her heart fluttered.

Why did her body react so when he touched her? She could only think that it was because they liked each other so well and were as alike as two peas in a pod.

He led her in the dance, moving in a circle together.

Usually in the waltz, Genna relished the sight of the couples all turning on the dance floor, the ladies' dresses like spinning flowers. This time, though, she could not take her eyes off Rossdale. She was taller than fashionable, but it hardly mattered when dancing with him. She had to tilt her head to see his face and she much preferred that to staring at the top of some gentleman's head.

Especially because Rossdale's lovely eyes and smiling mouth made her feel happy inside.

Staring only at him made the rest of the room a blur. Genna felt as if they were alone in the room, moving to the music, like one unit. She was tired from the dancing and giddy from a bit too much champagne and it all felt like a lovely dream, one she did not want to end.

But end it did. The music stopped and it took a moment longer for Genna to tear her eyes from his.

'What a lovely way to end a ball,' she murmured.

He nodded.

He took her hand and they walked through the guests, looking for her sister. Or Tinmore. How lucky Genna had not seen Tinmore during the whole ball. That in itself had contributed to the night's enjoyment.

Lorene had returned to where Tinmore had originally left them and she stood with poor Lord Penford, although they were not speaking to each other. Lorene had danced many of the dances, Genna had been glad to see.

'There you are,' Genna cried. 'Did you dance the waltz?'

Lorene glanced at Penford. 'Yes. We did.'

Goodness. Penford even asked her to dance the waltz.

'I would have been without a partner otherwise,' Lorene added.

'We have had such a nice time,' Genna said, squeezing Rossdale's hand before he released hers. 'I must find the Duchess and thank her for including us.'

'I had an opportunity to speak with her,' Lorene said. 'I did convey our thanks.'

Genna laughed. 'I was too busy dancing.'

Penford inclined his head towards the door of the ballroom. 'Lord Tinmore is bidding you to come.'

Tinmore was leaning on his cane with one hand and waving the other. He looked very impatient.

'I wonder where he was all this night,' Genna said.

Lorene pulled her arm. 'Come, Genna.'

She turned and smiled at Rossdale and Penford. 'Goodnight!'

Ross and Dell watched the Summerfield sisters rush to where Lord Tinmore was beckoning.

'You spent a great deal of time with Miss Summerfield,' Dell said.

'As much as possible.' Ross slid him a sideways glance. 'And you with Lady Tinmore, I might add.'

Dell frowned. 'By happenstance.'

Ross clapped his friend on the shoulder. 'I am glad you came back.'

Dell nodded.

Dell was living with him in Ross's father's house while the shell of his burned London town house was restored.

'The thing is, I like them. I like both of them,' Ross said.

'They are not what I expected,' Dell said. 'I will agree to that.'

The two men followed the crowd out of the ballroom, taking their time, having no reason to hurry. They caught up with his father and the Duchess. His father's wife had remained in the ballroom the whole time, making her rounds and keeping an eye on Ross's activities. His father spent most of the time in the card room, where Ross imagined Tinmore stayed, as well.

His father and the Duchess joined them and they all stood waiting for the carriage.

Ross's father pointed to him. 'Brackton's daughter.' His father spoke as if their conversation had begun earlier than this moment. 'She'd be a good match for you. Marquess's daughter. A step up for her. Good family, too.'

Obviously the Duchess had reported to his father that he'd danced with Lady Alice.

'I danced with her, sir,' Ross said. 'I did not make an offer.'

'You should,' his father responded. 'You are not getting any younger and neither am I.'

Ross glanced towards Dell, who averted his gaze. Both had heard this conversation before. 'I am not ready to consider marriage,' Ross said. 'Not yet.'

'What are you waiting for?' his father snapped.

'There are things yet I wish to do.' He never discussed his activities with his father and certainly not with the Duchess. They both assumed he merely caroused.

His father sliced the air with his hand. 'Marry. Beget an heir. Then do as you wish until the title is yours.'

Ross gave him a scathing look. 'Do you hear yourself? What sort of marriage would that be for the woman?'

'If the woman is a proper partner, she will understand,' the Duchess said. 'She will have her duty, as well.'

'Do not spout any romantic nonsense,' his father said.

'I was not planning to.' Ross's anger rose.

Once his father had engaged in romantic nonsense. When Ross's mother had been alive. When it had been just the three of them. His father had loosened his reserve and expressed the love and affection he had for both his wife and son. When Ross's grandfather died and his father inherited the title, everything had changed. His father grew distant, always busy, too busy. Too busy to notice when Ross's mother became ill.

'No romantic nonsense,' his father repeated more softly. To Ross's surprise what looked like pain etched the corners of his father's eyes. His father gave him a fleeting bleak look that told him his father, indeed, remembered those halcyon days when he and Ross's mother engaged in romantic nonsense.

The Duchess did not see. She was too busy looking smugly at Ross. 'You need a wife who will understand that being a duchess is not play. It is serious business.'

Ross understood, though. A duchess needed to be more like her, more in love with the title than the man, because she had to run her own enterprise, something for which his gentle mother with her freedom of spirit had not been suited.

His father's countenance hardened again. 'You have waited long enough, Ross. This is the Season. No more tarrying.'

The carriage arrived and they all climbed in.

The next day Lorene and Genna called upon the Duchess of Archester to thank her for the ball. They stayed only fifteen minutes. Tinmore had made such a fuss about how they should behave with decorum that Genna said very little during the visit. Several other ladies and gentlemen had also called, including Mr Holdsworth, who left at the same time as Genna and Lorene.

'May I walk with you?' the young man asked.

Lorene nodded and walked a little ahead of them.

'It is a lovely day, is it not?' Mr Holdsworth said.

He continued to utter the sort of polite conversation that contained very little of interest to Genna. He was also visibly nervous, which puzzled her. They were acquainted. What was there to be nervous about?

She found herself comparing him to Rossdale, which was rather unfair. Rossdale had years on him and the experience with it. Rossdale made her laugh. Rossdale listened. He talked to her about art. Did Mr Holdsworth even know she painted watercolours?

They reached the corner of Curzon Street.

'May—may I call upon you, Miss Summerfield?' His voice shook.

Ah! She understood now. He wanted to court her.

Why on earth would he want to court her? There was so much more he could see and do before settling down to marry. So many more young ladies to meet who would suit him better.

She slowed her pace. 'Oh, Mr Holdsworth!' She spoke in exaggerated tones. 'If it were up to me, I would say yes, because we have such fun dancing together. But Lord Tinmore would never allow it. He is looking for someone much grander for me.'

Holdsworth looked wounded, as well he should. She'd just told him he was not good enough because of something he could do nothing about—the status of his birth. Better that, though, than telling him he simply did not interest her.

'Do tell me you understand, Mr Holdsworth,' she said pleadingly. 'I should not like Tinmore to ruin our friendship.'

He brightened a little. 'I do understand.'

They reached the door of the town house.

His brow furrowed. 'You do not think Lord Tinmore will change his mind? I will have money.'

She shook her head. 'It is status with him, you see.'

'I value your candour.' He bowed. 'And I must bid you good day.'

'Good day, Mr Holdsworth.'

He walked away with shoulders stooped.

Lorene glared at her. 'What are you about, Genna? Lord Tinmore would find Mr Holdsworth perfectly acceptable, I am certain.'

'But I do not find him acceptable, Lorene,' she said.

'Why not? He's the son of a baron. And he's a very nice young man.'

Maybe that was it. Genna felt years older than Mr Holdsworth. 'You know I would run rings around him. Why make him miserable being stuck with the likes of me? And what happened to all your romantic notions? Were you not the one who wanted Tess and Edmund and me to marry for love?'

'Of course I did,' Lorene shot back. 'I still do, but—'

Tess and Edmund did not marry for love. They married to escape scandal. It was just by sheer luck they found happiness and who knew how long it would last?

'Then do me the honour of allowing me my own choice of a husband.' Or no husband at all.

'Well.' Lorene huffed. 'Do not say it is Lord Tinmore who must approve your choice.'

'I had to say something,' she said. 'Would you have me wound the poor fellow? Say I simply do not fancy him?'

'It would be more honest,' Lorene countered. 'But let us not debate this at the door to the town house. We can continue inside.'

Where the servants would hear and report whatever they said to Lord Tinmore.

A footman attended the door and took their things. 'A gentleman to see you, Miss Summerfield. He is waiting in the drawing room.'

'To see me?' Her spirits plummeted. One of Tinmore's widowers, no doubt. 'Who is it?'

'Lord Rossdale,' the footman said.

She smiled. 'How delightful!' She started to climb the stairs to the drawing room.

Lorene hurried to catch up with her. 'I should come with you.'

To chaperon? She'd been alone with Rossdale more than once.

But she would not argue. 'Of course.'

When they entered the room, he was standing and gazing at one of the paintings on the wall. He turned at their entrance.

'Why, hello, Rossdale,' Genna said. 'How nice of you to call.'

He bowed. 'Lady Tinmore. Miss Summerfield.'

'Would you care to sit, sir?' Lorene said. 'Shall I send for tea?'

He held up a hand. 'No, please do not go to that trouble. I will only stay a minute.' He turned to Genna. 'I merely stopped by to ask if you would care to take a turn in the park with me this afternoon.'

She grinned at him, but looked askance. 'I do not know, sir. It depends upon your vehicle…'

He smiled in return. 'A curricle. Nothing too fancy, though. It will have a matched pair, however.'

She pretended to think. 'A matched pair, you say?'

'Matched chestnuts.'

She sighed. 'Oh, very well.' Then her grin broke out again. 'I would be honoured to. Really.'

He nodded. 'Three o'clock?'

Four was the fashionable hour.

'Yes.' Her voice turned a bit breathless. 'I will be ready.'

'Then I must take my leave.' He bowed again.

When he left, Lorene shook her head. 'I do not understand you. The way you talk.'

'Oh, Lorene.' Genna groaned. 'It is all in fun. Rossdale knows that.'

Her sister gave her an exasperated look. 'If you wish to gain his interest, it is no way to talk to him, though.'

'I am not trying to gain his interest,' Genna retorted. 'As you have said many times, he is too far above me.'

Besides, she knew Rossdale's desire was to avoid marriage.

Lorene's brows rose. 'Then why would he ask you to take a ride in the park?'

'I think he is taking pity on me.' Why else? 'I did moan to him about wanting to go places and see things.'

'Well…' Lorene turned to leave the room '…do heed your behaviour on this outing. Lord Tinmore's new connection to the Duke of Kessington is important to him.'

After Lorene left the room, Genna said, 'Oh, yes. Lord Tinmore's well-being is of the utmost importance to us all.'

Chapter Thirteen

Ross pulled up to the Tinmores' town house in his curricle with its matched chestnuts. Gone were his days of driving high flyers and racing down country roads. Those had been exhilarating times, but, once experienced, he'd no need to repeat them. His curricle was the latest in comfort and speed, though he'd not tested how fast he could push it.

He suspected Genna would not care if he pulled up in a mere gig.

His tiger jumped off and held the horses while he knocked on the door.

As the footman let him inside, Genna was coming down the stairs, putting on her gloves. 'I saw you drive up.'

She wore a pelisse of dark blue and a bonnet that matched, nothing too fussy.

'Shall we go, then?' he asked.

'Absolutely!' she cried. 'I am ready.'

He helped her into the carriage. She pretended to examine it. 'I suppose this will have to do.' She sighed.

He took the ribbons from his tiger and climbed in next to her. 'It must do, because it is the only one I possess.'

She blinked at him. 'Truly? A duke's son with only one carriage?'

He smiled. 'All the others belong to my father.'

She laughed. 'All the others! At Summerfield House we had one pony cart and one coach.' Her smile fled. 'My father had a curricle.'

He'd prefer her laughing. 'Shall we take a turn in Hyde Park?'

She smiled again. 'By all means.'

The park was mere steps away from Curzon Street. They entered through the Stanhope Gate. Right inside the gate, he stopped the curricle and the tiger jumped off. He'd pick him up again on their way out. He drove the curricle towards the Serpentine. The weather was overcast and a bit chilly, not the best, but at least it was not raining.

'There is a rug beneath the seat,' he told her. 'Let me know if you feel cold.'

'I like it,' she said. 'It feels so good to be out of doors.'

He turned to her. 'And you are one to set up your paints while the snow is falling.'

She protested, 'Not fair! I packed up when it began to snow.'

'That you did.'

He'd guessed correctly that the Park would be thin of other vehicles at this hour. He'd wanted to be as private with her as possible. He waited until they'd passed the Serpentine, where some children were playing under the watchful eyes of their nannies and others were feeding the ducks.

'You probably wondered why I asked you for this ride—' he began.

'No.' She looked surprised. 'I didn't wonder.'

'I have a proposition for you.'

'A proposition?' She pretended to look shocked.

'It will indeed be shocking,' he said. 'But hear me out.'

The carriage path was edged with shrubbery and there were no other vehicles in sight. He slowed their pace.

Her expression conveyed curiosity, nothing more. This was why he could ask what he planned to ask. She would not take advantage, nor would she assume more than he intended.

He continued. 'I have a plan that will get us both through the Season without feeling like commodities in the marriage mart.'

Her interest kindled. 'Indeed?'

'It will also give you the freedom you desire, freedom to explore London, and it will satisfy my father who has begun to pressure me into marriage.' He glanced to the horses who were plodding along.

'What is this plan?' she asked.

'We become betrothed.'

She stared at him, but did not speak.

He quickly added. 'Betrothed. Think of it. If we are betrothed, I could escort you all around London. We could see the sights you wish to see. Do the things you wish to do. The cost of doing so would be no object.'

Her brows knitted. 'But a betrothal means becoming married. You just implied you do not wish to marry.'

'Not any more than you,' he responded. 'I said *betrothed*, not married. We would not have to marry. You could cry off, but not until you turn twenty-one and are free to do as you wish.'

And he had the funds to be certain she could do as she wished, but now was not the time to offer her money, not when she might misconstrue his intent. He meant merely to help her become the artist she wished to be. At least one of them would be free to do as they wished.

'No one would know it was not a real betrothal,' he added. 'It would be our secret.'

She stared at him again.

He actually began to feel nervous inside. 'Tinmore would see it as a feather in his cap if you were betrothed to a duke's son. He would stop sending you suitors.' Had he misread how daring she might be? 'There might be a little scandal. I fear you might receive some criticism for ultimately refusing me, but it is also likely that it will be assumed I was at fault.'

'What would your father say?' Her voice lacked enthusiasm.

He shrugged. 'What could my father say? He has been

pressuring me to marry and it would seem as though I was doing what he asked of me.'

'But surely he has someone else in mind besides me. My father was a mere baronet.'

'That is the beauty of it,' he explained. 'He cannot complain that I've become betrothed, but he is likely not to complain when you cry off.'

'Because I am not suitable for you.' She turned away and he feared he might have offended her.

'Betrothed,' she murmured.

He gazed at the horses and gripped the ribbons. 'I will understand if you do not wish this.'

She swivelled back to him, seizing his arm as she did so. 'Betrothed?'

He dared look at her again.

Her eyes were sparkling. 'A pretend betrothal.'

'Yes. To free us both.'

A smile lit up her face. 'It is a capital idea! We can go anywhere, do anything and no one will wonder over it.'

'That is the idea. We can enjoy this Season in a way that would have been impossible before.'

At their social engagements they would be free to be together the whole time. They could dance more than two dances. No greedy suitors would bother her; no matchmaking mamas would throw their frightened or eager daughters at him.

She frowned. 'I do not like the idea of keeping secrets from my sisters.' She paused and broke into a smile again. 'Why do I worry? They both kept secrets from me.'

He tilted his head. 'Then you say yes?'

She took a breath and he thought she would say yes. Instead she said, 'Let me think about it a little.'

'Take all the time you need,' he responded, disappointed. A delay usually meant no.

He flicked the ribbons and the horses moved faster. They

continued to circle the park, turning at the Cumberland Gate and proceeding along the perimeter of the park.

She finally spoke again. 'Would—would you take me to see places like the Egyptian Museum and Astley's Amphitheatre?'

He glanced at her. 'It would be my pleasure to do so.'

She fell silent again for so long Ross felt like fidgeting.

'You do realise, I could make you honour your promise to marry me,' she said in a serious tone. 'You would be taking a great risk.'

He turned to her again. 'But you won't. You are not the sort to break your word.'

Her eyes glowed as if satisfied by his response.

'You realise *I* might make you honour your promise,' he countered.

Her eyes danced in amusement. 'But you won't. You are not the sort to break your word. Besides, I have the right to cry off.'

They rode on, nearing the Serpentine again.

She bit her lip. 'Do you think that we can stretch it out until I am twenty-one?'

'When is your birthday?'

'October.'

He nodded. 'We can stretch it out that long.'

She shifted in her seat, as if setting her resolve. 'Then let us do it, Rossdale! Let us have this false betrothal. We'll fool everyone and have a lovely time of it!'

He turned to her and grinned and, to his surprise, had an impulse to embrace her. He resisted it.

'Then you had better call me Ross, if we are to be betrothed,' he said instead.

She laughed. 'Ross. And you'll call me Genna.'

He wouldn't tell her he'd been thinking of her as Genna since that first meeting.

Genna threaded her arm through Ross's and squeezed her cheek against his shoulder. 'I already feel as if I am set free. No longer can Tinmore dictate to me. I can simply direct him to you.'

'I should speak to him first,' Ross said. 'Ask his permission.'

She bristled. 'He is not my guardian. He has no say in who I marry, no matter what he thinks.'

'No,' he agreed. 'But let us use his arrogance. Appeal to his vanity. Let him think he has some say. If he believes he has given his permission, he is less apt to question the validity of the betrothal. He'll be less apt to exert control over your activities.'

She nodded. 'I see your point, though it rankles with me.' It was really no different than the way she'd always handled Tinmore, though. Make him think she would do as he desired, but really do what she pleased. 'Promise me one thing, though.'

He turned his head to glance at her. 'What?'

'Promise me you will refuse the dowry he has offered me.' She did not want Tinmore to think his money had any influence, even on this pretend-betrothal.

'Genna.' He looked her straight in the eye. 'We are not really to be married. The dowry makes no difference, because I will never receive it.'

'It makes a difference to me.' Her voice rose. 'I want Tinmore to know that I do not need his dowry money, that it had nothing to do with you proposing to me. It is bad enough I must accept his money for my dresses and such.'

She had to admit that Tinmore's money had given her a rather comfortable life these last two years. She had as many dresses as she could want, food aplenty and enough spending money to keep her in paints and paper. It was the cost to Lorene that ate at Genna's insides.

Ross nodded. 'I promise you that if the subject of the dowry comes up, I will refuse it.'

'The subject will come up. Tinmore will want you to know what a huge sacrifice he has made for me.'

He glanced at her and back at the road. 'Then I will make a very convincing refusal.'

While he was attending to the road and the horses, Genna had a chance to study him in detail. His was a strong profile, high forehead, gracefully sloping masculine nose, strong jaw and lovely thick brows and lashes. She loved that his face was expressive when he wished it to be and devoid of all expression when he did not.

She was so lucky, so fortunate that he would do her this great favour. Certainly she would receive more benefit from it than he. Tinmore's dictates that she marry would be silenced now, because Tinmore would think she was marrying Rossdale.

Ross.

The mere thought of his name brought flutters inside her. These sensations, all so new to her, were a puzzle and one she did not wish to examine too closely. She just wanted to enjoy his friendship.

This plan of his made it so they could be friends.

'So you will call upon Lord Tinmore tomorrow.' She had to keep talking or the flutters would take over.

'Correct.'

She did not mind keeping this secret from Tinmore and the rest of the world, but this was another huge secret to keep from Lorene and Tess. She'd told them nothing of her intent to be an artist or her determination to refuse marriage to anyone. This would distance them from her even further.

'Will you tell Lord Penford the truth?' she asked.

He thinned his lips and took his time to answer her. 'I would like to tell Dell,' he said finally.

She frowned. Since learning he'd lost his family in a fire, Genna's heart went out to him, but she still was not certain how he felt about her and Lorene. Sometimes Penford looked at them as if he wished they were in Calcutta, but at other times he behaved in a most thoughtful and attentive manner.

'Surely he will not approve of our scheme,' she said. 'Who would?'

'Even if he does not approve, we can trust him to keep the secret.' Ross met her eye. 'I would trust him with my life. In any event,' he added, 'we may need an ally.'

But if Penford disapproved, would he be an ally?

She examined Ross's face.

If she embarked on this plan of theirs, she must trust Ross. 'Very well. You may tell Lord Penford.'

'Do you wish to confide in your sisters?' he asked.

She shook her head. 'I shall wait to announce this betrothal to Lorene, though,' she said. 'And to Tess and Marc.'

They fell into silence again until they neared the Stanhope Gate. Ross signalled to his tiger to get on the back and in what seemed like the blink of the eye, they pulled up to the town house.

The tiger jumped down again and held the horses while Ross helped Genna out of the curricle and walked her up to the door. When the footman opened the door, Ross bid her good day and she skipped inside, wanting to dance through the hall and up the stairs. How could she be expected to contain her exuberance?

Once in her room, she gave in to her impulse and spun around in joy.

Until there was a knock at her door. 'Come in,' she said tentatively.

Lorene entered. 'I saw Lord Rossdale pull up. How was your outing?' Her voice was filled with expectation.

Genna felt a great pang of guilt. She was about to lie about the lie they were going to tell everyone. 'It was lovely. We do get along famously, so there was a great deal to talk about.'

'Did you get any notion of why he asked you?' Lorene persisted.

'None except companionship.' This was not precisely
a lie. Companionship was what they'd agreed upon, was
it not?

The next day Ross called upon Lord Tinmore. When
the butler announced him to Lord Tinmore in his study,
Tinmore's head was bowed. It snapped up at the footman's
voice. The old man had fallen asleep.

When Ross approached the desk, Tinmore fussed with
the papers there as if he had been busy with them. He tried
to stand.

Ross gestured with his hand. 'Do not stand, sir. No need
of ceremony with me.'

'Kind of you, Rossdale. Kind of you,' Tinmore muttered. 'And how is your father? And the Duchess? In good
health, I hope?'

'In excellent health,' Ross replied. 'And you, sir?'

'Excellent!' he repeated. 'Could not be better.' Tinmore
sat back in his chair.

Ross wasted no time. 'I know you are a busy man, sir,
so I will not waste your time with prattle. I have come to
talk with you about Miss Summerfield.'

'What?' Tinmore straightened. 'What has the girl done
now?'

Tinmore's automatic disapproval chafed. 'You assume
she has done something of which you would disapprove?'

Tinmore's expression turned smug. 'Why else would
you come here?'

'To ask your permission to marry her.'

Tinmore recoiled as if Ross had struck him in the chest.
'Marry her!'

Genna would like that reaction. Sheer surprise.

'Yes,' Ross stated. 'Marry her. Assuming she will accept me, that is.'

'Accept you?' Tinmore continued to look dumbfounded.
'She's naught but the daughter of a baronet. She's not fit—'

Ross's anger flared. 'I assure you, she is my choice.' He glared at the man. 'I might remind you that you married the daughter of a mere baronet.'

'An entirely different matter, sir!' Tinmore said indignantly. 'An entirely different situation.'

Ross inclined his head. 'In any event, I wish to become betrothed to Miss Summerfield and I would like your permission to ask her to marry me.'

'I would not refuse you.' Tinmore shook his head. 'But I feel an obligation to your father to advise you against this idea.'

This man was intolerable. He ought to be looking after Genna's best interests, not the best interests of a duke's son.

'Then I will be obliged to explain your reticence to my father, sir. I thought you would be pleased to unite our families.' Let him ponder that. 'What will he conclude but that you do not desire to be so closely connected?'

Tinmore's eyes bulged. 'No. No. No. I do not mean that. I would not offend— Mustn't think so. Mustn't think so.'

'Then I have your permission?'

The Earl still looked reluctant, but he finally nodded his head. 'Yes. Yes, my boy. If that is what you want.'

'I want her,' Ross said. Hearing his words, he could almost believe it himself, that he wanted Genna, to marry her.

'She comes with a handsome dowry, my boy. Very respectable amount. I made certain of that.'

Ross rubbed his chin. 'About the dowry, sir.'

'Is it not enough?' Tinmore looked anxious. 'We can negotiate the amount. Might be fitting for me to increase it for marrying the heir to a dukedom.'

'I do not wish an increase,' Ross said. 'I do not want it at all.'

'Do not want it?' Tinmore's voice rose.

'I have no need for it,' Ross responded. 'I am wealthy in my own right and my wealth will increase when I inherit the title. Make some other use of the dowry. Gift it to the poor. God knows there are plenty of hungry people in England with these Corn Laws.' Very likely Tinmore voted for the Corn Laws that made bread so expensive that many people could no longer afford it. 'I can advise you on where the money might do the most good.'

'If you insist,' Tinmore said, like air leaking from a bellows. 'Give it to the poor.'

Ross raised his eyebrows. 'May I see Miss Summerfield now?'

'You want to speak with her?' Tinmore seemed completely rattled.

Ross straightened and looked down his nose as his father did when his father wanted to intimidate someone. 'It is my wish to speak with her now.' He made it sound like a command.

'Yes. Yes.' Tinmore's head bobbed up and down. 'I will make certain she sees you.'

Ross felt quite certain Genna would need no pressure from Tinmore to receive him.

'Now, if you please,' Ross mimicked his father.

Tinmore popped up from his chair so fast he needed to hop to get his balance. 'Dixon!' he cried. 'Dixon!'

The butler opened the door. 'My lord?'

Tinmore waved one hand. 'Escort Lord Rossdale to the drawing room, then find my wife's sister and send her to him.'

The butler bowed.

'Now, Dixon! Now,' Tinmore cried.

Ross followed the butler to the drawing room, but he wound up cooling his heels for several minutes before Genna entered the room.

She grinned at him. 'I waited ten minutes so I would not look too eager.' She took his hands and led him to the sofa. 'How was it? Did he faint away in shock?'

'He was gratifyingly surprised.' Ross would not tell her how Tinmore tried to talk him out of proposing to her.

'Did he bring up the dowry?' she asked eagerly.

He nodded. 'As you predicted.'

'And did you refuse it?' she pressed.

'I refused it and told him to give the money to the poor.'

Her eyes sparkled. 'Oh, that is famous! He won't do it, of course. It is not in his nature. Why waste good money on poor people?'

'Are you ready for me to propose to you now?' he asked.

Her fingers fluttered. 'You already did so yesterday.'

'I think I must repeat the event.' Ross glanced towards the door. 'Is there a crack between the door and the door-jamb?'

She looked startled. 'I have no idea. What does it matter?'

'Just in case there are curious eyes watching, I will do this right.' He slid to the floor on one knee. 'Will you become betrothed to me, Miss Summerfield?' He lowered his voice. 'Now you must act surprised. Slap your hands on your face. Cry out. Act as if you are being proposed to by a duke's son.'

She giggled. 'I *am* being proposed to by a duke's son.' But she slapped her cheeks and squealed with pleasure. 'Oh, Lord Rossdale,' she said louder. 'This is so sudden.'

'Do not keep me in suspense.' He put his fist to his heart. 'Let me know if I will be the happiest man in all of Mayfair, or cast me down into the depths of despair.'

'What should I do?' she cried, playing along with his joke. 'I cannot decide.'

'Why, say yes, of course.'

Her smile softened. 'I will accept your proposal, Lord Rossdale. I will become betrothed to you.'

Chapter Fourteen

After Ross left, Genna danced around the drawing room, the way she'd danced in her bedchamber the day before. No one would guess that her happiness was not in anticipation of marriage to a duke's heir. It was because he'd set her free to be herself for the whole Season and more.

It would be impossible to keep her happiness a secret. It burst from her every pore. The source of it might need to be kept secret, but the emotion could not be held in. Still, it felt so precious to her she wanted to keep it to herself a little while longer, savour it alone in all its aspects. Unfortunately Tinmore would tell Lorene soon enough. Genna would rather her sister hear the news from her.

She smoothed her skirt and tidied her hair and took a deep breath. She could pretend to be composed, at least for a little while. She left the room with her head held high and her step unhurried, when she really felt like skipping and taking the stairs two at a time.

Lorene would probably be in her sitting room where she spent a great deal of her time practising on the pianoforte there. It was not as grand as the pianoforte in the drawing room, but it was the one she preferred.

As she neared the room's door, though, she did not hear music—except the joyous refrain inside her.

Genna knocked anyway and heard Lorene say, 'Come in.'

Genna opened the door.

Lorene stood. 'Genna, I was just about to send for you. Look who is here.'

Her sister Tess came up to her and bussed her cheek. 'I thought I would call upon my sisters. I have not seen you since the opera. Lorene has been telling me all about the musicale you attended and the Duchess of Archester's ball. Did you enjoy yourself?'

Ross had engineered those invitations, Genna was sure. 'I did.'

She could hardly keep from hopping from one foot to the other. How fortunate that both of her sisters were here. She could tell them both at once.

'I am glad you are here, Tess,' she said, 'because I have some news.'

'That Lord Rossdale called upon Tinmore?' Lorene broke in. 'I told her of it.'

Genna hesitated. Had Lorene been told why he called? Did they already know?

Lorene turned to Tess. 'Tinmore has lately become better acquainted with Rossdale's father, the Duke of Kessington.'

'Did you tell Tess that Rossdale took me for a ride in Hyde Park yesterday?' she asked instead.

Tess looked surprised. 'He did?'

'That is not all,' Genna said. 'He called upon me today after seeing Tinmore.'

'He has been attentive to Genna, that is true.' Lorene made it sound as if she'd forgotten such an unimportant event.

'He had a reason for calling upon me,' she said.

Genna looked from one sister to the other. 'I am betrothed to him.' The words sounded awkward to her ears, but she could not make herself say he'd asked her to marry him. He had not done that. The proposal was for a betrothal, not marriage.

'What?' Lorene cried.

Tess gave a surprised laugh, but immediately seized

Genna's hands. 'Do not say so! He asked you to marry him? Just now?'

Genna nodded. 'First he spoke to Lord Tinmore and then to me.' She glanced at Lorene. 'Yesterday he spoke to me about it a little. To see if I might be willing.'

Lorene looked dazed. 'I did not expect this—I—I feared his intentions were dishonourable.'

'Dishonourable?' Genna retorted. 'Rossdale is an honourable man.'

If you did not count his willingness to engage in a scandalous secret, that was.

Tess pulled back and peered at Genna. 'One moment—was this another of Tinmore's machinations? Did he put pressure on Rossdale?'

Tinmore had forced Tess and Marc to marry. Marc rescued Tess from a storm and the two were forced to take refuge overnight in a deserted cabin. Tinmore insisted Marc had compromised Tess.

'No,' Genna told her. 'Rossdale really asked me. There was no pressure or any such thing. I believe he merely sought Tinmore's approval before asking me.'

'Not that you would want Tinmore's approval,' Lorene said sarcastically.

Genna met her gaze. 'You have the right of it, Lorene. I do not care a fig whether your husband approves or not, but it was a respectful thing for Rossdale to do.'

Tess sat down on a sofa near Lorene. Genna was too excited to sit.

'A duke's son,' Tess said breathlessly. Her voice changed to shock. 'Oh, my stars. He is the heir, is he not? You will be a duchess some day!'

No, I will not, Genna said to herself. But her sisters could not know that. Genna felt her insides squirm with guilt.

'It makes no sense, does it?' Lorene said. 'A duke's son and a penniless baronet's daughter.'

'We get on well together,' Genna said defensively.

'Of course you do,' Tess said soothingly.

'We must do something for a formal announcement.' Lorene frowned. 'A ball or something.'

'I do not know—' Genna plopped down next to Tess. This was becoming too big. A formal announcement seemed wrong when the betrothal was not real.

'Of course you must do something,' Tess agreed. 'If not a ball, *something.* You will be marrying a man who will be a duke. You cannot go higher than that unless you married one of the royal princes.'

Genna was as likely to marry one of them as to marry Ross.

A small pang of disappointment struck her at that thought, but she pushed it away immediately. She did not wish to marry a duke. She did not wish to marry anyone and be trapped the way Lorene was trapped.

'A ball.' Lorene sounded stressed. 'I do not know how to host a ball.'

Genna had not thought that she would distress her sister. She felt as small as a bug. 'A ball is too much fuss! I do not see why you should even think of it.'

'Oh, it must be done,' Tess said with decision. 'It would cause more talk not to have some sort of event to announce your engagement.' She laughed. 'Do you realise this will be the only wedding in the family that adheres to propriety?'

'The wedding,' Lorene groaned. 'What is proper for a future duke's wedding?'

This was all going too far. Genna felt miserable. 'Do not talk of wedding plans. It will not be before next autumn at the earliest.'

'So long a wait?' Tess looked surprised. 'Whatever for?'

How could she explain? 'Because that is what we've decided.'

'Oh, but never mind that.' Tess took Genna's hands in hers again. 'Tell us about Rossdale! He is very handsome, is he not?'

Genna had to agree. 'He is handsome.' But that was not the half of it. They could laugh together. But he did not laugh at her plans or her ambitions.

Lorene and Tess would never understand how important both those things were to her.

Lorene leaned towards her. 'Genna, do you have a genuine regard for him? Or do you feel obligated to marry him? Because you do not have to accept the first offer you receive. I will support you in waiting for a love match. It is all I've ever wanted for you.'

Now Genna felt even worse. Lorene wanted her to be happy so much she'd defy her husband for it. And all Genna was doing was deceiving her.

Genna softened her tone. 'I do have a great regard for Rossdale. What is more, I believe he feels the same towards me.'

They *liked* each other and that was the truth.

'Oh!' Tess had tears streaming down her cheeks. She hugged Genna. 'You have found the dream! A husband you love who loves you!'

Genna stiffened. 'You found it as well, Tess.'

'Yes, but mine was hard won. Luck was a big factor in it, too.' She shuddered. 'If I had been rescued by some wretched man my life would be a misery.'

Like Lorene's, Genna thought.

'I care only that my sisters are happy,' Lorene said, her voice catching.

Tess gestured for her to join them on the sofa and the three sisters wrapped their arms around each other. Genna was filled with love for them.

And consumed with guilt for deceiving them.

Dell sat at a desk in the bedchamber he used in the Kessington town house. He tried to make sense of a line of figures representing crop yields and estimates of the effect of allowing foreign grain and produce to undercut prices.

He tried to make his own calculations based on the figures provided, but his results did not match the author of the material he'd been studying.

He sat back and pinched his nose.

A knock sounded at the door and a familiar face peeked in. 'Do you need an interruption?'

Dell glanced up and smiled. 'Ross! An interruption would be most welcome.'

Ross approached the desk and sat in a nearby chair. 'What are you reading?'

'Writings about grain prices. This author seems to have fabricated his results, however. I don't know how one ever knows who to believe.' Dell set the papers aside. 'What do you wish to see me about?'

Ross looked defensive. 'What? I cannot simply knock on your door?'

'I think you have a reason,' Dell said. It was written all over Ross's face.

Ross stood again and paced. 'I do have a reason. Something I want to talk over with you. Something I want to tell you.'

Dell watched him and waited.

Ross finally faced him. 'I've become betrothed to Genna Summerfield.'

Dell could not believe his ears. 'What? You don't want to marry. You've always said.'

'I don't want to marry,' Ross agreed. 'At least, not yet.'

Dell felt alarmed. 'Do not tell me you are being forced into this.'

Ross held up his hand. 'No. Not at all. Hear me out. I'll explain the whole thing.'

Dell crossed his arms over his chest.

'It is not a real betrothal—' Ross looked uncomfortable. 'Genna does not wish to be married any more than I do. We are merely pretending to be betrothed so that my father will take the pressure off me and Tinmore will no longer plague her. I'll take her all the places she wishes to go, to see what she wishes to see. We will have an enjoyable Season instead of one spent dodging suitors or matchmaking mamas.'

Dell looked sceptical. 'You never had difficulty resisting your father's pressure before or dodging matchmaking mamas. Why take such an extreme step? It makes no sense.'

Ross sat again. 'You are correct. It is not for me, but for her. I want to help her.'

'Help her resist pressure from Tinmore?' Dell scoffed. 'Genna seems strong-willed and self-assured. I'd wager she knows just how to resist whatever Tinmore wants her to do.'

'That may be so, Dell.' Ross rose again. 'But why should we have to fight everyone when there is enjoyment to be had instead?'

Dell frowned. 'Enjoyment?' Surely Ross did not intend to trifle with the young woman?

'Nothing untoward, I assure you,' Ross said.

'You've told me over and over that you find no pleasure in a frivolous life any more. So do not tell me you do this for enjoyment.'

'I like her company, Dell.' He paced. 'There are places to show her here in London that I could not show her unless we are betrothed.'

Dell peered at him. 'You will pretend to be betrothed so she can see the sights of London?'

'It is more than that,' Ross insisted. 'I cannot explain. I cannot see the harm.'

Dell raised his brows. 'Can you not? I can think of all kinds of harm. People will be hurt over this; you mark my words.'

'It is only for a few months,' Ross added. 'Next autumn she'll cry off and that will be the end of it.'

'Oh, yes.' Dell spoke with sarcasm. 'That will not cause harm. Nor gossip. Nor scandal.'

Ross leaned across Dell's desk. 'It will not be that bad.'

'I disagree,' Dell said. 'This is a mistake.'

'I'll prove you wrong,' Ross challenged.

'We'll see,' Dell said.

They glared at each other, as they had done when they were boys and argued about something or another.

Ross backed away. 'No matter. It is done. I simply wanted you to know the truth of it all.'

So he was burdened with the secret as well? He wouldn't mention that bit to Ross, though.

'Just take care,' Dell said. 'I'd not like to see either of you hurt.'

Ross met Dell's eyes again. 'May I have your word you will keep this in confidence?'

Dell nodded. 'You have my word. I will keep your secret.'

'Even if you believe it is a mistake?' Ross pressed.

'Even so,' Dell said.

Ross left Dell's bedchamber with some of his high spirits dampened. He supposed he harboured the hope that Dell would understand his reasons for this betrothal, not that he could tell him the whole of it.

He had an idea of how to make certain Genna's plans worked out just as she wished, even though he had more to work on how to make that happen. To help her live the life of her own choosing was all he desired. He might be destined for duty, but he'd make certain Genna could be free, like he, his mother and father had been free in the days before duty took over.

Ross's next task was to inform his father and the Duchess. He dreaded it.

It was nearing time to dress for dinner. With luck he'd catch his father and the Duchess alone for a few minutes before guests arrived. There were always guests for dinner, it seemed. Dinner was one of the venues where his father could influence others to agree with his views.

He had his valet dress him hurriedly and he was the first to enter the drawing room where they would wait for dinner to be announced. A decanter of claret was on the table. Ross poured himself a glass and sipped it while he waited for his father and the Duchess.

They walked in the room, discussing the impending marriage of the Princess Charlotte to Prince Leopold of Saxe-Coburg-Saalfeld and the various monies and property Parliament would vote to bestow upon the young woman who might some day become Queen.

'Ross!' his father exclaimed upon seeing him there.

Ross was rarely early.

'Do you stay for dinner, Ross?' the Duchess asked. 'I do hope so. It will even out our numbers. I already told the butler you would dine with us.'

'I will stay, then,' he said. 'When do the guests arrive?'

'Not for a half-hour,' she said. 'Unless they are late, which they usually are.'

He poured them each a glass of claret. His father took a long sip of his.

No reason to delay, Ross thought. 'There is something I wish to tell you.'

Interest was lacking in both their eyes. His father considered most of what Ross talked about to be of no consequence, usually about some poverty or injustice he'd discovered. His father thought only in terms of the fate of the country, not individuals. The Duchess merely regarded Ross as the heir and not as a person who could further the Duke's influence and power.

'I have done something you have begged me to do—' he began.

They both glanced at him then.

'I have become betrothed.'

'What?' cried the Duchess.

'This is excellent!' His father's face lit with excitement. 'Who is the lady?'

'As long as she is suitable,' the Duchess said warily.

Ross met her eyes. 'She suits me very well.'

The Duchess blanched. 'Please do not say it is that woman—'

Ross knew that his father and the Duchess would not approve. That was part of what would make the scheme work, but it angered him, nonetheless.

'Miss Summerfield, do you mean?' He did not want the Duchess to say her name first. 'Yes. I have made Miss Summerfield an offer and she has accepted.' Which was the truth.

'Summerfield?' His father raised his voice. 'That chit connected to Tinmore?'

'Ross, she is a nobody,' the Duchess said quickly. 'Worse than that, look at her family. There is not a one of them who has not been the subject of gossip. Her mother and father—bad blood, indeed.'

'Has Miss Summerfield done anything objectionable?' Ross challenged.

The Duchess's lips thinned. 'Not as yet.'

In that she was correct. In a few months, Genna would cry off and that would certainly cause gossip. Not to mention what people would say when she became an artist and lived as an independent woman.

'Will you not reconsider?' his father pleaded. 'I'll never get Tinmore off my neck if you are married to his wife's sister.'

Of course, his father would think of himself. 'Miss Summerfield will have no difficulty distancing herself from Lord Tinmore, if that is your only objection.'

'Not my only objection,' his father snapped. 'She's not spent any time in town. She knows nobody of importance. What does she know of entertaining? Of managing houses as grand as our family's?'

'She has a quick intelligence,' Ross said. 'These matters can be learned.'

His father's eyes turned pained. 'Some women cannot learn.'

Like Ross's mother. She'd never adapted to the strains of being a duchess.

Ross's anger at his father melted a little.

'You are in your prime, Father,' he said softly. 'There will be time for Genna to learn how to be a duchess.'

But it would never get that far. He'd forgotten that for a moment.

His father's wife broke in. 'Why could you not court Lady Alice? She is a sweet girl. And her father is a marquess. It would be much wiser for you to court the daughter of a marquess and bring some advantage to the union.'

'It is done, Constance.' There was no use arguing over what would never come to pass. 'I am betrothed to Miss Summerfield.'

'But we could induce her to cry off even before word gets out,' she persisted. 'It is not too late.'

'I do not want to break this engagement. I have a high regard for Miss Summerfield.' Which was very true. 'And I intend to honour my promise to her.'

Both the Duchess and his father's faces were pinched in disappointment.

For no reason. The marriage would never take place.

'Regard this,' he told them. 'I have done as you wished, as you have begged me to do for years now. I have become betrothed. We will marry in the autumn, probably.'

The Duchess lifted a shoulder as if to say that was not concession enough.

'Well, if you say it is done, it is done and we will have to devise the best way to approach this.' His father poured himself another glass of claret. 'I beg you not to speak of it at dinner. Let us think upon how to have this announcement made.'

'As you wish.' Ross finished his claret.

Chapter Fifteen

For the next week Ross called upon Genna every day, taking her to all the places she'd desired. They'd battled the crowds to see Napoleon's carriage at the Egyptian Museum, gaped at the beasts kept at the Tower, and sat in choice seats at Astley's Amphitheatre. Every day brought new delights and new ideas and Genna could not have been happier.

She had almost been able to forget that Lord Tinmore had invited the Duke and Duchess of Kessington and Ross to dinner to discuss the announcement of the betrothal.

She wished the announcement could be made in the newspapers, rather than for her to face the stares and whispers of those who wouldn't think a duke's son would actually wish to marry her. It made it worse knowing she and Ross were deceiving everyone about their true intent.

The dinner with the Duke and Duchess was the only entertainment for Tinmore and Lorene this week. It had taken that many days to find an evening the Duke and Duchess could attend. Ross requested that Lord Penford be invited, to which Tinmore readily agreed, but about whom Genna and Lorene heard Tinmore's endless complaints that the table would be uneven.

Lorene had little to do with the planning of the dinner. Nothing would do but for Tinmore to see to every detail, in consultation with Mr Filkins, his secretary, and Dixon, the butler. She knew nothing of planning important dinners, Tinmore had said, so Lorene spent long hours practising her new music instead. Genna regretted leaving her for the pleasures Ross's outings provided, but she shoved her feelings aside. She must learn to see to her own well-being and leave Lorene to cope with the life she'd chosen.

Even though Lorene had chosen this dismal life for Genna's sake.

When the evening of the dinner came, Genna's mood darkened. She did not need Ross to tell her that the Duke and Duchess would disapprove of the betrothal. No one would approve such an unbalanced pairing. Besides facing them, she would also be seeing Lord Penford for the first time since he'd learned the truth of the betrothal. And she would have to endure Lord Tinmore, who took credit for the match.

In a way, Tinmore deserved credit. If he were the least bit tolerable, she might never have decided to pursue a career as an artist. Truth be told, she was nowhere near being able to do that. She'd solved one problem by agreeing to this pretend betrothal, but she still needed to learn so much more before she could begin to support herself with painting and she'd not painted for days.

Before her maid came in to help her dress, she sat down with her crayon and sketched some of the images she'd seen over the week. A lion from the African continent. Dancing horses from Astley's. The crowd gaping at Napoleon's carriage. She forgot everything else and lost herself in her drawings.

When the maid entered the room carrying her dress, Genna jumped in surprise.

'Is it time already?' She closed her sketchbook and walked over to her pitcher and basin and washed the chalk from her fingers.

'I'll dress your hair first,' the maid said.

Genna missed the camaraderie she'd had with Anna, her maid at Summerfield House. She did not dare confide in this woman even in simple ways. Tinmore's servants had a habit of reporting back to Tinmore everything Genna or

Lorene said or did. So she merely told her how she wished to wear her hair and what dress she desired.

This night she was donning a pale rose dinner dress, a nice complement to the deeper red Lorene had chosen. She wanted to take some care with her appearance for Ross's sake, so the Duke and Duchess would not find fault with her looks.

The maid seemed to be moving particularly slowly this evening. Genna feared she would be late in presenting herself in the drawing room where they would all have a drink of wine before dinner.

Before the line of buttons down the back of her dress were fastened, Genna heard a carriage arrive. 'Please hurry, Hallie. I believe they have arrived.'

'Yes, miss,' the maid said, but she went no faster.

When the maid finally finished, Genna dashed down the stairs to the drawing room. She forced herself to stop at the door and compose herself. Why did she worry? The more the Duke and Duchess disliked her, the less dust they would kick up when she broke the sham betrothal.

She lifted her chin, put a smile on her face and walked in.

'About time, girl,' Tinmore snapped.

He stood near the fireplace with the Duke and Ross. The Duchess sat on the sofa with Lorene and Penford stood apart from them all.

Ross was the only one to smile at her entrance. 'Genna!' He walked up to her and took her hand.

She curtsied to the Duke. 'Good evening, Your Grace.' And to the Duchess. 'Your Grace. Forgive my tardiness.' She decided to give no excuse.

'We have been discussing how to make an announcement of this betrothal,' the Duchess said, making it sound like it was something loathsome. 'We have decided that it should be done at the ball we are already scheduled to give in two weeks' time.'

Tinmore spoke up. 'I would be honoured to host the entertainment where the announcement is made. I think it only appropriate—'

The Duchess held up a hand. 'No. We've settled it. It will be at our ball.'

Genna glanced at Lorene, but her face was blank and she could not tell how Lorene felt about this.

'I should most like to do what my sister wishes to do,' Genna said. 'If you have her approval, then I am happy to have the announcement at your ball. I do wish for my whole family to be included. Our brother will not come, of course. He and his wife are too far away, but I insist my sister Tess and her husband be included. And his parents, of course.'

'Lord and Lady Northdon?' the Duchess said through a sneer.

Lord and Lady Northdon were practically shunned by the *ton*, because Lady Northdon was a French commoner by birth and the daughter of French Jacobins.

'Yes.' Genna kept her gaze steady. 'I consider them part of my family.'

The Duchess glanced away. 'If we must.'

'Certainly we must,' added Ross. He turned to Genna. 'Would you like some Madeira?'

'I would.' Lots of it, in fact.

It was Penford who poured her the wine and handed it to her.

'How are you, sir?' she asked him.

He met her eyes. 'Very well.'

His expression was as blank as Lorene's, but not hostile. Genna supposed she must be content with that.

He turned to Lorene. 'More wine?'

'Thank you,' she murmured, handing him her glass.

The dinner was a stilted affair. What troubled Genna the most was her sister, who seemed even more unassuming than usual. It was as if all the life had been sucked out of her. Genna had caused it, she knew, and it ate at her. But

what could she do about it now? She could not blurt out to
them all that the betrothal was a sham and they should not
take it all so seriously.

Her saving grace was having Ross seated across from
her. When Lord Tinmore and the Duke's conversation became particularly tedious, Ross needed only to look at her
and she could smile inside.

After dinner when the ladies left the gentlemen to their
brandy, the Duchess spent the time lecturing Genna and
Lorene in proper behaviour at this upcoming ball, as if
they did not know how to behave. She also discussed the
politics of the day, to which Lorene and Genna agreed to
her every word merely to be polite.

When the men returned to the drawing room, Ross
rolled his eyes at Genna, making her smile again. Dell
looked bleak. Lord Tinmore and the Duke continued to
discuss Princess Charlotte's impending wedding and the
Duchess joined in.

Dell looked down on Lorene. 'Do you play for us this
evening, ma'am?'

Her gaze rose to his. 'If you wish it.'

Dell extended his hand to Lorene to help her rise. She sat
at the pianoforte in the corner of the room and played softly
the Mozart piece that had been performed at the musicale.

While Tinmore, the Duke and Duchess discussed politics and Lorene played Mozart, Ross gestured for Genna
to come with him. They sneaked out of the room and into
the hallway. Genna pulled him into the library, which was
dark. She could hardly see his face.

'Has it been too ghastly for you?' he asked.

She smiled. 'Perhaps a bit more than dinners here usually are.'

He stood close. 'The Duchess is intent on having her
own way. I apologise for that.'

She felt the warmth of his body even though they were

not touching, such an odd but pleasant sensation. 'I wish we did not have to make a formal announcement.'

'Do not put too much on it,' he responded. 'No one else will. We will be stared at for a while, whispered about and then they will forget us. They will be talking of Princess Charlotte and no one else.'

The wedding of the Princess was a welcome distraction. As the only child of the Prince Regent, she would be Queen one day.

'I hope you are right,' she said.

He held her hands. 'I will call upon you early tomorrow. Are you able to spend the day with me?'

She smiled. 'I would be delighted.'

He gave her a kiss on the cheek, then stepped away. 'We should go back.'

She put her fingers where his lips had touched and where she still felt the sensation of the kiss. 'Yes. Let us go back.'

The next day Genna stopped by Lorene's sitting room before leaving for her outing with Ross.

Lorene was playing the pianoforte when Genna knocked and entered the room. 'I'm off with Ross in a few minutes. I just wanted to let you know.'

Lorene made an attempt at a smile. 'Where do you go this time?'

Genna sat in a chair near the pianoforte. 'I do not know. It is to be a surprise.'

'A surprise? How nice.'

Genna had not had a chance to speak with Lorene after the Duke and Duchess left after dinner. 'I wanted to see if you are all right.'

'All right?' Lorene blinked. 'Of course I am. Why ever would I not be all right?'

'You—you seemed different last night,' Genna said. 'So very subdued. I worried about you.'

Lorene turned back to the keyboard. 'Oh, there is nothing to worry about. I—I merely had little to say. The Duke and Duchess and Tinmore had so many strong opinions on what should be done, I merely let them sort it out.'

Genna rose and leaned over to give her sister a hug from behind. 'I am certain I would have been happier with whatever plan you could come up with.'

Lorene covered Genna's hand with her own and squeezed it. 'A very small dinner party with family and close friends?'

'Perfect!' Genna said. Especially if the betrothal were real.

Lorene turned to her again. 'I cannot tell you how delighted I am that you are going to marry Rossdale. The two of you are so fond of each other. Your happiness shows.' She still held Genna's hand and squeezed it again. 'It is what I dreamed of for you.'

Genna felt her guilt like a dagger twisting in her chest. How shameful to deceive such a loving sister! Still, she had to steel herself. She needed to find her own way.

'I am happy,' she said and realised there was truth in those words. When she was with Ross, she could push aside all the other feelings that swirled around inside her.

A footman came to the door. 'Lord Rossdale has arrived, miss.'

She hugged Lorene again. 'I'll stop in when I return and let you know where it is he has taken me.'

'Yes,' Lorene gave her that forced smile again. 'Do enjoy yourself.'

Genna always enjoyed herself when in Ross's company.

She raced to her room and had the maid help her into her pale pink pelisse and bright blue bonnet. She hung her reticule over her arm and pulled on her gloves as she hurried down the stairs.

When she entered the drawing room, Ross stood with another man.

'Look who will accompany us today,' Ross said, gesturing to the man standing next to him.

'Mr Vespery!' She smiled at the artist who'd been so kind to her at the Duchess of Archester's ball. 'How lovely to see you.'

The artist blew a kiss over her hand. 'Miss Summerfield, it is my pleasure to be in your company.'

She turned to Ross, even more excited than before. 'Where are we going?'

Instead of answering her directly, he said, 'Somewhere you will like. But first I have a gift.'

He handed her a package wrapped in brown paper. She looked at him, puzzled.

'Open it,' he said.

She removed the paper. It was a beautifully bound book. She opened it and found the title page. '*A Treatise on Painting* by Leonardo da Vinci,' she read aloud, then words failed her.

'It is the only book on art I could find,' he said apologetically.

'It is wonderful,' she finally managed, leafing through the book and glancing at da Vinci's words.

'A classic work,' Vespery added.

'And a hint about where we are bound today,' Ross said. 'We are going to look at art.'

Genna looked up and grinned. To be with Ross gazing at art and learning from Vespery. This day was going to be wonderful.

Ross had come with one of the Duke's carriages so they all sat comfortably for the short ride to their destination. When the carriage stopped and Ross helped her out, she was even more puzzled. They were in front of Carlton House, the residence of the Prince Regent.

'Here we are,' Ross said.

'But this is—'

He threaded her arm through his. 'This is our destination.'

The palace of the Prince Regent.

As they walked through the portico and up to the door, he explained, 'With His Royal Highness's permission, we will meet one of his art advisors, Sir Charles Long, who will take us on a tour of His Royal Highness's collection.'

Before Genna could form a coherent thought, the door opened and they were greeted by a line of four footmen and a nattily dressed gentleman.

'Ah, you must be Lord Rossdale. Welcome.' He bowed to Ross and turned to Vespery. 'Good to see you again, sir.'

Vespery bowed.

The gentleman then regarded Genna. 'And you must be the young lady who Rossdale insisted be shown the collection.'

Ross stepped forward. 'Miss Summerfield, may I present Sir Charles Long, one of His Royal Highness's art advisors.'

Genna curtsied. 'Sir Charles, I am in awe already!'

They stood in the entrance hall, which was as bright as daylight with its white marble floors, white walls and domed ceiling accented with yellow-gold columns and statues in alcoves.

The footmen took their coats.

'His Royal Highness is quite a collector of fine art. There are one hundred thirty-six paintings in the principal rooms and another sixty-seven in the attics and bedrooms. We will not see those, of course. We will not intrude on His Royal Highness's private rooms,' Sir Charles said. He gestured for them to follow him. 'Come.'

Genna lost track of time as they walked from one spectacular room to another. The architecture and decor rivalled the paintings on the walls. So opulent. So beautiful. So much like pieces of art in themselves. The grand staircase deserved its name as it rose in graceful, symmetrical curves. Gilt was prominent in almost every room. Light from the candles and the fireplaces reflected in the gold, making them seem to glow from within. There were rooms of all colours and styles. Round rooms. Blue rooms. French rooms. Gothic rooms. She wished she had a sketchbook with her to record the unique beauty of each.

Then there was the art. Almost every wall displayed a painting or several. Vespery and Sir Charles pointed out the different styles and time periods and artists. There were old paintings, many of them by the Dutch masters—Rembrandt, Rubens, Van Dyck, Jan Steen. And newer ones like Reynolds, Gainsborough and Stubbs. And countless others. Genna tried to keep everything they said in memory, but she knew she would forget half of it. She listened as intently as her excitement allowed her.

When it was possible, Vespery had Genna look closely at the brushwork of the paintings. He explained how the artists created the effects, some of which were so real looking that Genna thought the people would come alive and join them on the tour. Sir Charles spoke of how the Prince Regent was able to purchase so many paintings so quickly. In the aftermath of the French Revolution, a glut of paintings came on the market, paintings once owned by aristocrats.

Genna gasped. 'The owners must have died on the guillotine!'

'Indeed,' agreed Sir Charles, his expression sombre. 'Or drowned at Nantes.'

'At least the Prince Regent rescued the art,' Vespery said.

'Because one could not save the people,' added Ross.

Snatches of memory came back to Ross, memories of the Terror—or what he'd heard of it from his parents or other adults who seemed to have spoken of little else during that time. What he remembered was mostly feeling their fear and anguish. His mother had known some of the aristocrats who'd been executed. A cousin had been killed.

That whole time was fraught with upheaval and tension. His grandfather had just died and his father disappeared into his new role as Duke. His mother, so carefree and gay, turned fearful of an uprising in England such as had happened in France. She feared she, his father and even Ross would be targets if the people rose against aristocrats, high aristocrats especially, like dukes and duchesses.

His mother never recovered from that time, Ross realised later. She tried to fulfil her duties as duchess, but without any pleasure whatever. His father did not help, always too busy with Parliament and running the estates. Ross had been sent to school by that time. On holidays, his mother seemed even more anxious and withdrawn.

When she became ill, she simply gave up.

He was at school, his father in town and she in the country at Kessington Hall when the last fever took her away for ever.

He'd vowed then to live as his mother had once lived, for adventure and enjoyment, like his family used to do. He'd succeeded, too, until he realised men like Dell and other friends were putting their lives at risk fighting in Spain. Then he tried to do his part, meagre as it was, transporting men across the Channel.

He'd been thinking more about his mother lately. Since meeting Genna, actually. Like his mother, Genna embraced new experiences and was not afraid to let her enjoyment of them show. He liked that about her.

Genna, though, was brave. She was unafraid of a very uncertain future.

He was perhaps a bit more realistic about what she would face trying to support herself as an artist, but he was determined to help her succeed.

Vespery, Genna and Sir Charles continued to discuss the paintings in these rooms while Ross stood nearby. Afterward Sir Charles returned them to the entrance hall where the footmen were waiting with their things.

'I do not know how to thank you, Sir Charles,' Genna said, her voice still ebullient. 'And please convey my thanks to His Royal Highness. Tell him you have made a lady artist very happy.'

'I will do so at my first opportunity,' Sir Charles said.

Vespery also bade him goodbye.

Ross extended his hand to Sir Charles. 'Thank you, sir, and convey my regards to His Royal Highness.'

When they went out the door, their carriage was waiting for them.

Genna clasped Ross's arm as they walked to the carriage through the portico with its Corinthian columns. 'I do not know how to thank you, Ross. Nothing could duplicate that experience!' She reached one arm out to touch Mr Vespery's hand. 'And to you, sir. I learned so much by listening to you.'

When they were seated in the carriage, Ross said, 'There is more planned, Genna. Not for today, though.'

'Good.' She sighed. 'I do not think I could endure any more today. I am already bursting with new knowledge.'

The carriage first took Mr Vespery to his rooms in Covent Garden.

When he left the carriage, Genna said, 'Thank you again, Mr Vespery.'

His eyes twinkled. 'I will see you again soon, my dear.'

'I hope so, sir.'

When the carriage pulled away she turned to Ross. 'What did he mean by "I will see you soon"? Do you have another outing planned?'

He grinned. 'Perhaps.'

She leaned against his shoulder. 'You could not possibly please me more than you have done today.'

He could try, though. He could try.

Chapter Sixteen

The next day, Genna eagerly watched out the window for Ross's arrival. This time he drove up in his curricle with his tiger seated on the back. She rushed down the stairs and was in hat and gloves by the time he was admitted to the hall.

'I am ready!' she cried.

His ready smile cheered her. 'Then we shall be off.'

The footman held open the door as Ross escorted her out of the house. He helped her on to the curricle and climbed up beside her. The tiger jumped into his seat.

When they pulled away, Genna could not resist asking, 'Where are we bound?'

Ross grinned at her. 'Do you actually think I would tell you?'

She pretended to be petulant. 'I had hoped you would not be so cruel as to leave me in suspense.'

'But that is my delight,' he countered.

She spent the rest of the time guessing where they might be bound.

He turned down Park Lane to Piccadilly. 'Are we to visit the shops?'

'No.' He looked smug.

'Westminster Abbey!' she cried. 'Are we headed there? I've always wanted to see Westminster Abbey.'

'Another time, perhaps,' he said.

He turned on Haymarket.

She had a sudden thought, one that made her heart beat faster. 'Somerset House?'

Somerset House was the home of the Royal Academy of Art.

'Not today,' he said.

She gave up and felt guilty for being disappointed, but her hopes grew again when they turned down Vespery's street. 'Will Vespery accompany us again?' If so, where would he sit? This curricle sat two comfortably; three would be a crush.

'No,' he said.

He pulled up in front of the building where Vespery had his rooms. The tiger jumped down and held the horses. Ross climbed down and reached up to help Genna. He held her by her waist and she put her hands on his shoulders. She felt the strength of his arms as he lifted her from the curricle. When her feet hit the ground she lurched forward, winding up into his arms. Her senses flared at being embraced by him and she did not wish to move away. Ever.

It was he who released her. 'We are calling upon Mr Vespery.'

That was the surprise? She'd enjoy spending time with Vespery, especially because he was so filled with helpful information, but her mind had created something grander. How nonsensical was that? To be disappointed in whatever nice thing Ross created for her. What an ungrateful wretch she was.

'Calling upon Vespery will top Carlton House?' she said in good humour.

'Oh, indeed it will,' he assured her in a serious tone.

He must be making a jest. What could top Carlton House?

The housekeeper answered the door. 'He is in his studio.' She turned and started walking. 'This way.'

Genna's interest was piqued. 'I've never been in an artist's studio before.'

His studio was in the back of the building with a wall of large windows facing a small garden patch. As they entered, he turned from his canvas to greet them. 'Ah, Miss Summerfield. Lord Rossdale. Welcome to my studio.'

The housekeeper left.

In the corner of the room was a chair behind which was draped red velvet fabric. Obviously this was where his clients sat for him. Facing that area was a large wooden easel with a canvas on it large enough for a life-sized figure to be painted upon it. The painting in progress, Genna noticed right away, was of the Duchess of Kessington.

She approached the painting. 'Oh! Am I to have the honour of watching you work?'

Next to the easel was a table stained with paint of all colours. Vespery's palette was equally as colourful. Several brushes of all sizes stood in a large jug.

'You will watch me work, my dear,' Vespery said. 'And you will paint, as well. Lord Rossdale has asked me to give you lessons in oil painting.'

She swivelled around to Ross. 'Painting lessons?'

'As many as you need,' Ross said. 'You said you had much to learn.'

She ran to him and clasped his hand, lifting it to her lips. 'Ross! How can I thank you?'

He covered her hand with his. 'When you are ready, paint my portrait.'

She stood on tiptoe and kissed his cheek. 'It will be my honour.'

'Come,' Vespery said. 'I have a smock to cover your dress. Let us begin.'

Ross found a wooden chair in the studio and sat in it, stretching out his legs in front of him. He watched as Vespery showed Genna the easel, palette, brushes, paints, canvas, and other necessities Ross had purchased for her at Vespery's direction.

Vespery started by teaching Genna about the paint. How the colours were made. How they could be mixed to create any colour she wished. She seemed to pick up the concepts quickly from her knowledge of watercolours and Ross learned more than he'd ever known before about this basic element of oil painting. She practised mixing the colours and then she practised putting them on a canvas stretched on a wooden frame. Vespery showed her how to draw on the canvas, either with paint or with a pencil. It seemed that artists did not make detailed drawings on the canvas, but rather bare outlines.

Next Vespery taught her about the different brushes and the effects produced by each and she practised with each one.

'You are quick enough to begin a painting,' Vespery told her. He wiped the paint off her canvas, though an imprint of the colours remained. 'With the oil paints, you are able to paint over them. You can scrape off your mistakes and start again. You can change what you don't like in the painting.' He set a plain bowl on a table covered with a dark cloth. 'Try painting this.'

Ross watched her with pride. She painted a credible likeness of the bowl, although she was not satisfied with it. She scraped it off with a palette knife and started over.

The time passed with impressive speed. From a distant room, Ross heard a clock chime. 'By God, we've been at this for three hours. I believe I must return you to your home and leave Vespery to finish the Duchess's portrait.'

'Oh!' She dipped her brush in the turpentine and cleaned it off with a nearby rag. 'I had no idea we were here that long! I hope I did not take you too long from your work, Mr Vespery.'

'The light is always better in the morning,' the artist said. 'That makes the afternoon perfect for your lessons.' He took her palette and covered it with a cloth. 'That should keep your paint moist until tomorrow. Let me show you how to clean your brushes.'

When Vespery finished instructing her how to clean up at the end of a session, they retrieved their hats and gloves and overcoats. Vespery walked them to the door.

'Thank you, Mr Vespery,' Genna said, shaking the man's hand.

'My pleasure, Miss Summerfield,' he responded.

Ross said his goodbyes, as well.

When he and Genna stepped outside, the curricle was not there.

'We are at least a half-hour later than when Jem was told to bring the carriage here,' Ross explained. 'He will be walking the horses around the streets, I expect.'

'I do not mind waiting,' She met his gaze. 'That was—' She paused as if searching for words. 'That was—marvellous.'

'I am glad you thought so,' he responded. 'You will have as many lessons as you need.'

She blinked. 'I should not accept this. I am certain it is costing you dear.'

'I have wealth enough to afford it.' He wanted to spend it on her. 'Think of it as a betrothal gift.'

She gave a nervous laugh. 'But we are not really betrothed.'

'Then think of me as being a patron of the arts. That is a long tradition, is it not?'

She smiled up at him. 'Then I accept.'

His tiger appeared at the end of the street. 'Ah, here is Jem now.'

During the drive back to Mayfair, Genna kept hold of his arm and sat close to him. He found it a very comfortable way to ride.

'Where do you go after you drop me off?' she asked.

He paused, uncertain of what to say. 'Somewhere I cannot take a lady.'

'Oh.' She let go of his arm.

He glanced at her, but she turned her head away.

'I am sorry.' Her voice was strained. 'I did not mean to pry into your—your affairs.'

Did she think he was going carousing? He certainly did not wish to give her that impression. 'I—I do not make a habit of speaking of this,' he began. 'I am driving to a workhouse. There are some soldiers there. I am paying their debts so they can be released.'

She turned back to him. 'You are paying their debts?'

He glanced away. 'It is a trifle to me, but will mean a great deal to them and to their families.'

She took his arm again. 'How did you find out they were in the workhouse? Did they tell you? Or did someone else tell you.'

He turned the curricle on to the next street. 'Someone told me. One of the other soldiers I help.'

'Other soldiers? What other soldiers?'

The soldiers should thank Dell for this. If Dell had not taken Ross to the hospital to see those wounded men from his regiment, he never would have sent baskets of food to their families. He never would have created a system where several needy families received food from him on a regular basis. Enough to keep them, their wives and children in good health.

'There are several soldiers and their families who I help.'

He lifted a shoulder. 'I simply went to the workhouse and asked if there were any soldiers there. I gathered their names and the amounts of their debts and today I return to pay them and secure their release.'

She lay her head against his shoulder. 'How good of you, Ross. How very good of you.'

After Ross brought her home, Genna could not get out of her mind how wonderful this man was. To her and to others. He was giving her the best chance for her to achieve her desire to support herself with her art. How could she ever repay him?

'Lady Tinmore wishes to see you,' the footman attending the hall told her.

How could she repay her sister? Look what Lorene had done for her, misguided as it was. She must become a success. What other choice did she have than to give them what they desired for her?

'Will I find her in her sitting room?' she asked him.

'I believe so, miss.'

Genna hurried up to her bedchamber where she removed her hat, gloves and redingote. She looked at her fingers. All the paint had not washed off them. She scrubbed them some more at her basin without complete success, gave up and hurried to Lorene's sitting room.

She knocked and entered without waiting for an invitation. 'I am back. You wanted to see me?'

Lorene sat at her pianoforte, but Genna had not heard her playing. She looked up at Genna with an expression of disapproval. 'We had a fitting scheduled this afternoon. Did you not remember?'

Genna placed her hand over her mouth. 'I completely forgot.' She had been so enthralled with painting that everything else dropped out of her mind. 'Lorene, I am so sorry.'

The fitting was for their new ball gowns, the ones they were to wear to the Duke and Duchess of Kessington's ball.

'I sent word that we would come tomorrow.'

'What time?' Genna asked.

'Morning.'

Excellent! She would not have to miss her art lesson.

She did not want to tell Lorene about her lessons, afraid Lorene would somehow stop them.

'I promise I will be ready tomorrow,' she said. 'Will Tess come?'

'Tess and Lady Northdon,' Lorene responded.

Nancy, Tess's former maid turned modiste, had come up with an idea for their gowns to complement one another, so when they stood together, they would make one pretty picture.

'I will not fail you tomorrow,' Genna vowed.

She turned to go, but Lorene stopped her.

'Will you attend the rout with me tonight?' There was an edge to Lorene's voice that made Genna pause.

'Is Tess not going?' Genna asked over her shoulder.

'No,' Lorene said. 'They did not receive an invitation.'

It was shameful how often Tess's husband's family was shunned by the *ton*. If Tess was not attending this rout, then who would Lorene talk to? Tinmore would leave her for the card room.

Genna turned back to her sister and gave her a reassuring smile. 'Of course I will attend with you. It should be very enjoyable.'

Dell walked through the crush of guests at the rout and kicked himself for attending. Why had he come?

He knew why. He suspected Lord Tinmore would receive an invitation and Dell wanted a moment with Lorene to see how she was faring.

The last time he'd seen her—at that ghastly dinner party with the Duke and Duchess—she'd looked even more beaten down than usual. Not that he'd believed Tinmore beat her—God knew what he would do if he discovered her husband was beating her. It was bad enough to witness Tinmore slashing at her spirit.

He was concerned because they were cousins—was that not so? Distant cousins, though. They shared a great-great-grandfather. That made them family and he had no one else but the Summerfield sisters.

If only he'd known their plight perhaps he could have convinced his father to allow them to stay at Summerfield House. Then Lorene would not have needed to marry Tinmore for his money. His father might have helped them instead.

Foolish notion. His father would never have listened to his younger son. Had his brother Reginald spoken it would have been a different matter, but Dell could not see either his father or his brother taking pity on the scandalous Summerfield sisters.

He heard a grating voice. 'Duke! How good to see you!' It was Tinmore greeting Ross's father. 'Do you play cards tonight?'

Tinmore was abandoning her again. Did the man not realise he left her adrift like a ship without a rudder? Someone must guide her, protect her from those pirates who delighted in attacking the vulnerable.

He found her in the crowd. Standing with her was her sister, a young woman made of sterner stuff than Lorene.

'Good evening, ladies.' Dell bowed.

Lorene lowered her gaze. 'Good evening, sir.'

'Lord Penford!' Genna responded. 'At last we see a friendly face. I was beginning to think that no one would know us here.'

Though he suspected several of the guests had been introduced to these two ladies before. 'I am happy to be of service. Would you like some refreshment?'

'Would you get us whatever is in those wine glasses we keep seeing the servants carry?' she asked.

'My pleasure.' He bowed and went in search of a footman carrying a tray.

When he returned, Lorene was conversing with the Duchess of Archester, but she accepted the wine with a fleeting smile. He bowed to her again.

Genna stood close to him. 'I hope you are speaking to me, Lord Penford.'

'Why should I not?' he asked.

She gave him a knowing look. 'Because of the betrothal.'

He met her gaze. 'I am not fond of keeping secrets. No good comes of it.'

She lowered her gaze for a moment, then raised her chin. 'Have you no secrets?' she asked.

He resisted the impulse to glance at her sister. 'I have your secret,' he said. 'I gave my word to keep it.'

She placed her hand on his wrist. 'I thank you for it, I really do. I know you do not approve.'

He lifted one shoulder. 'It is between you and Ross, ultimately.'

She glanced over to her sister. 'I know it will affect others, but Ross will make certain everything concludes well.'

'I hope so.' But he could not keep the scepticism from his voice.

She glanced around the room. 'I never know what to do in these entertainments. Everyone seems to stand around and talk and take some refreshment.'

'One is supposed to mingle,' he said.

She laughed. 'You make it sound very easy, but there are few people who wish to mingle with Lorene and me. That is why I am here. To be certain she is not alone.'

Lorene was one of the most alone people Dell had ever known. 'That is kind of you.'

She sighed and tapped her foot. 'She will never know what a sacrifice it is! I have yet to devise a way to make a rout enjoyable.' She watched a young man approach. 'But I shall try.'

It was Baron Holdsworth's younger son. 'Good evening, Lord Penford.' He tossed a shy glance to Genna. 'Miss Summerfield.'

She gave the young man a big smile. 'Hello, Mr Holdsworth! How good to see you. I was just trying to make Lord Penford explain to me how one should act at a rout. Do you know?'

He looked stricken. 'Why—why—you merely talk to people.'

'Ah.' She shot a mischievous glance to Dell. 'How lucky I am, then. I will talk to you.'

Dell took a step back, intending to leave Genna with Holdsworth, an obvious admirer. He slid a glance to Lorene, who was still conversing with the Duchess of Archester. He slipped away.

Better not to be seen paying too much attention to the Summerfield sisters. All he needed—all *Lorene* needed—was to be talked about because he paid too much attention to her.

He had just found another footman with a tray of wine, when the Duchess of Kessington, Ross's stepmother, sidled up to him.

'I see *she* is here with her sister,' the Duchess said in scathing tones.

Dell knew precisely whom she was talking about. 'Who with what sister?'

'You know who I mean. Those odious Summerfields.' She glanced towards Genna.

Dell took a sip of his wine. 'You forget, Duchess, that I am a Summerfield.'

'But you are not one of *those* Summerfields,' she protested. 'You have a title and property.'

He'd trade it all to have his family back.

She leaned towards his ear. 'What are we to do about this betrothal?'

'What can be done of it?' he countered. 'Ross made his decision.'

'He cannot marry her!' she said in an agitated whisper. 'She is entirely unsuitable. Why, her mother is still living in Brussels with the man she ran away with years ago. And her father—'

He held up a hand. 'I have heard the gossip.'

'Even Lord Tinmore cannot put enough shine on her,' the Duchess went on. 'Why, the girl received no offers last Season. She was not even admitted to Almack's, you know.'

'Many young ladies have Seasons without offers. Many do not attend Almack's.'

She sniffed. 'Obviously she was waiting for a duke's son.' She placed a hand on his arm. 'I hope I can rely on you to do what you can.'

He faced her. 'Duchess, recall the lady you are discussing is my relation.'

She lifted her nose. 'A distant relation. You cannot credit it.'

But he did credit it. He held on to that distant family connection much more firmly than he would have imagined he could. 'In any event, the matter is between Ross and Miss Summerfield. I will not interfere.'

Her eyes flashed. 'I see I cannot rely on you. I must act alone to prevent this ghastly mistake.'

She turned with a swish of her skirts and strode away, joining another group with a cordial smile and ingratiating manners.

Chapter Seventeen

During the next week, Genna had lessons with Vespery almost every day and when she was not at the easel in Vespery's studio, she snatched time to read the da Vinci book Ross gave her. Vespery said she was progressing very quickly, but not quickly enough for her. She had only half a year to prepare to be a working artist. Painting still life—vases of flowers, food, cloth of various textures—like Vespery had her doing was not going to earn her money. She needed to paint portraits and she needed to be good at it.

She sighed. Patience was not one of her virtues!

Genna paced the floor of her bedchamber. There would be no lesson today, no outing with Ross. She sat at the desk in her room and pulled out her latest sketchbook from the drawer.

If she could not paint, she could at least draw.

The pencil in her hand made some sweeping curves on the page, but, before she knew it, she was making a sketch of Ross, how he appeared when his face was in repose. For practice, she told herself. For when she would paint his portrait.

She had to admit, she missed Ross as much as the painting lessons. He stayed during most of her lessons, always ready to assist, to bring them food, to shop for supplies. He professed to find the process interesting, but he must become bored some of the time. When Vespery left her to paint, Ross talked with her. Or rather she talked with him, telling him all the inconsequential details of her unvaried life at Summerfield House. She told him about the governess who'd taught her to draw and paint in watercolours. What a talented woman that governess was, nurturing Lorene's love of piano, as well.

Until their father, who'd stopped paying the woman, forced her to find employment elsewhere. She was their last governess. After that, Tess and Lorene took over teaching Genna mathematics, and French and history and such. Genna and Lorene tended to their talents on their own.

Ross listened to her tell all this nonsense. She wished he would tell more about himself, but he did not. There was so much she wished to know about him.

Tonight was the night of the Kessington ball, the night their betrothal would be announced and more people deceived by the secret they kept. The announcement would not be applauded, she suspected. Who would think it a good idea for a duke's heir to marry one of the scandalous Summerfields?

Tinmore had insisted she stay home this day, to be rested and ready for the ball. Her maid would be coming in at any time to help her dress. She'd refused a hairdresser this time, setting off a tirade from Tinmore, but his tirades had become a mere annoyance now that he had no power over her.

Her maid Hallie entered the room, carrying her ball gown. 'Are you ready to dress, miss?'

'I am indeed.' She closed her sketchbook and put it away.

She promised herself she would not worry about her appearance. She would wear her hair in her favourite way, high on her head with curls cascading. Her dress was lovely, a blush so pale it was almost white. It matched Lorene's and Tess's and even Lady Northdon's, Tess's mother-in-law. Genna's was designed to shine the brightest. She was eager for the scandalous Summerfield sisters and the notorious Lady Northdon to be seen together as the very height of fashion.

While Hattie was putting the last pins in her hair, there was a knock at the door.

A footman handed Hattie a package. She brought it to Genna. 'This came for you.'

First she read the card. 'It is from Lord Rossdale.'

Genna unwrapped the paper to discover a velvet-covered box. She opened it.

'Oh, my!' she exclaimed.

It was a pendant and earrings. The pendant was a lovely opal surrounded by diamonds set in gold and on a gold chain. The earrings were matching opals.

It would go perfectly with her gown.

'But how did he know?' she said aloud.

'Do you wear them tonight?' Hattie asked without enthusiasm.

'Of course I will!' Genna cried.

With a gift such as this, who could ever guess their betrothal was a sham? She must remember, though, that such a gift must be returned when their charade was over.

When Lord Tinmore's carriage pulled up to the Kessington town house, Tess, her husband and his parents were waiting for them on the pavement.

Tess hurried up to Genna and Lorene as they were assisted from the carriage. 'We saw you coming and Lady Northdon said we should wait. We can be announced at the same time and walk in together!'

Genna gave her sister a buss on the cheek. She said hello to Lady Northdon. 'It is a wonderful idea.'

'Let us give them a spectacle, no?' Lady Northdon said in her French accent.

Lord Tinmore grimaced when he greeted Lord Northdon, who looked no happier, but Lord Northdon's expression changed to completely besotted when his wife took his arm. Lord and Lady Northdon might defy Genna's disbelief in happy marriages, except for the fact that the Northdons had been miserable together until very recently. Who knew how long this period of marital bliss would last?

They all walked into the house and were attended by footmen in the magnificent marbled hall whose vaulted ceiling rose over two floors high. Other guests were queued on the double stairway of white marble with its gilt-and-crystal bannisters. It struck Genna that the design of this stairway mimicked the one at Carlton House. Or was it the other way around? Surely this house had been built first. It was a majestic sight, one Genna tried to commit to memory. What a lovely painting it would make with all the ladies in their colourful finery gracing the stairs like scattered jewels.

'Come. Hurry,' Tinmore snapped. 'There are enough people ahead of us as it is.'

They hurried to their place on the stairs. Genna looked down and noticed that each step was made of one complete piece of marble.

Her sister Tess stood beside her. 'Do you realise that all this will be yours some day?'

'I cannot think that,' Genna said honestly.

A quarter of an hour later they reached the ballroom door.

The butler announced, 'Lord and Lady Tinmore and Miss Summerfield.'

Tinmore marched ahead, but Genna and Lorene held back until Lord and Lady Northdon and Mr and Mrs Glenville were announced. The four ladies crossed over the wide threshold together as heads turned towards them and a murmur went through the crowd already assembled in the ball room, a room even bigger than the ones they had been before.

A *frisson* of excitement rushed up Genna's spine. They presented a lovely picture, each dressed in a shade of pink, Genna's the palest, Lady Northdon's the richest. Their gowns were not identically styled, but the fabric was the same, net over fine muslin so that their skirts floated around them.

Genna leaned to Tess. 'Tell Nancy her styles have triumphed.'

'How gratifying it is,' Tess responded. 'Because you know half these guests were certain we would not come off so well.'

Genna glanced at the receiving line, where Lorene had hurried to catch up with Lord Tinmore. Ross shook the hand of the gentleman who'd been announced before them, but when the man moved on, Ross glanced up and smiled at Genna.

Suddenly all that mattered was that he like her gown.

She touched the opal pendant and stepped forward to greet the Duke and Duchess.

The Duchess greeted her with a fixed smile. 'Don't you look sweet, my dear.'

She curtsied to the Duke.

'Good. Good. You are here.' He made it sound as if he wished she wasn't.

'I am honoured to be here, Your Grace,' she responded.

Then she came to Ross who clasped her hand and leaned close to her ear. 'You look beautiful.'

Her spirits soared.

She touched her opal. 'Thank you, Ross. It is lovely.'

'Save me the first dance,' he added.

She smiled at him. 'With pleasure.'

Lady Northdon waited behind her. 'There are guests behind us,' she reminded Genna.

Genna stepped away from Ross, but waited for Lady Northdon and Tess to be finished. Together they walked across the ball room to where Lorene stood with Tinmore.

As soon as they reached her, Tinmore glanced from Lorene to Tess. 'I am off to the game room, but I will return for the announcement. In the meantime, behave with decorum. I'll not have the Tinmore title besmirched by hoydenish antics.'

As if Lorene could ever be hoydenish. Genna felt like creating a fuss just to upset him.

'Look at this room!' Tess said in awed tones.

The walls were papered in red damask, but were covered with huge paintings depicting scenes from Greek mythology. Genna wished she could get up close to examine the brushwork, the use of colour. She knew so much more now than when she first met Vespery.

'Look at the ceiling!' Tess said.

The ceiling had intricate plasterwork dividing the ceiling into octagons and squares, each of which were painted. It made the ceiling of the drawing room where they had been the night of the musicale look plain in comparison.

Her husband came to her side. 'This is a magnificent room, is it not?'

Lorene said, 'There is Lord Penford standing alone. I believe I will walk over to him and say hello.'

Ross joined Genna as soon as he could leave the receiving line. He danced with her, with each of her sisters and even with Lady Northdon, whom he'd never met before but liked immediately. He noticed plenty of disapproving stares, which angered him. Why should the Summerfields and Lord and Lady Northdon be judged so negatively? Nothing they had done deserved this denigration. Except maybe for Lady Tinmore, who did marry for money, but after five minutes seeing her with Lord Tinmore, one could feel nothing but pity for her.

One of the footmen approached him. 'Her Grace says you should come now.'

Time for the announcement. 'Thank you, Stocker.' Ross turned to Genna, who was laughing at something Lady Northdon said. 'It is time,' he told her.

Her face fell, but she nodded and said to her sisters, 'I think they are ready for the announcement.'

'Oh,' cried Tess. 'Let us all go up front where we can see you better.'

Ross and Genna led the way and the rest of their party followed. In their wake were audible murmurs from the other guests.

Ross's father and the Duchess stood at the far end of the ballroom where, on an elevated platform, the orchestra still played quietly. The Duchess looked crestfallen; his father, grim.

'Are you ready?' his father asked.

Ross smiled down on Genna. 'Indeed we are.'

She straightened her back, lifted her chin and smiled back at him. Brave girl.

His father and the Duchess, all smiles now, climbed on to the orchestra's platform. The musicians sounded a loud chord and went silent.

Ross's father raised his hands. 'May I have your attention? Attention!'

The guests turned towards him and fell silent.

'We have an announcement to make,' his father said. 'A happy announcement.' He gestured to Ross. 'As you know, the Duchess and I have long desired to see my son Rossdale settled and tonight I am delighted to report that he has done as we wished.'

The crowd murmured.

Ross's father went on. 'My son, the Marquess of Rossdale, has proposed marriage to Miss Summerfield, daughter of the late Sir Hollis Summerfield of Yardney and ward of Lord Tinmore—'

Tinmore waved and bobbed from nearby.

The Duke continued, 'And I am happy to report that Miss Summerfield has accepted him.'

'No!' a lone female voice cried from the back of the

room amidst other shocked sounds from other guests. The Duchess's smile faltered.

Ross stepped on to the platform and helped Genna up to stand beside the Duke and Duchess. 'Thank you, Father.' He turned to the crowd. 'Miss Summerfield is not well known to many of you, but I am confident you will soon see all the fine qualities she possesses. I could not be a happier man.'

He put his arm around Genna, who smiled at him with much admiration in her face. Her family beamed from below them, but only a few others in the crowd looked pleased.

Ross knew this world, where birth and titles and wealth mattered more than character. He and Genna knew the disapproval they would face. So why should he feel so angry at these people and so protective of Genna?

He lifted her off the platform. 'There. It is done.'

She grinned at him. 'And I am still standing!'

Her sisters, Glenville and his parents clustered around her with hugs and happy tears of congratulations. Lord Tinmore disappeared into the card room again. Several others offered congratulations, a few genuinely meant, others so as not to offend the Duke of Kessington.

Dell approached them just as the music for the supper dance began. 'I thought I should congratulate you as well, or it might look odd.'

'I appreciate it.' Ross kept a smile on his face as he shook Dell's hand. 'I'm glad this part is over. Now we can simply enjoy the rest of the Season.'

Dell turned to Genna. 'How are you faring?'

She smiled, too, as if accepting good wishes. 'I am actually surprised that some people with whom I have no connection seemed happy for me.'

It had surprised Ross, too. He planned to make a note of those people.

'Are you dancing the supper dance?' Genna asked Dell.

'With your sister,' he responded. 'As it is likely Lord Tinmore will not escort her in to supper.'

'So good of you,' Genna said.

His face turned stony. 'My duty to my cousin.' Dell bowed and presumably went in search of Lady Tinmore.

Ross took Genna's hand. 'Let us skip the supper dance. There is someone here I should like you to meet.'

'As you wish,' Genna said in exaggerated tones. 'I am a biddable fiancée.'

He laughed. 'Biddable?'

He brought her to a pleasant-looking woman in her forties who sat among other ladies not dancing.

'Lady Long.' He bowed. 'Allow me to present to you my fiancée—'

'Your very biddable fiancée,' Genna broke in.

'My *biddable* fiancée,' he corrected. 'Miss Summerfield.'

'How do you do, ma'am.' Genna curtsied.

'Not as well as you, young lady,' the woman said in good humour. 'Landing yourself a future duke.'

Genna made a nervous laugh.

Ross quickly spoke. 'Your husband was gracious enough to give Miss Summerfield and me a tour of the artwork at Carlton House.'

'You are Sir Charles's wife?' Genna exclaimed. 'I am so delighted to meet you. Your husband was too generous to take the time for that wonderful tour. I learned so much!'

Ross continued. 'Lady Long is an accomplished artist, Genna. She has exhibited at the Royal Academy.'

Genna's eyes grew wide. 'You have?'

Ross turned to Lady Long. 'Miss Summerfield is also an artist.'

'It is my abiding passion,' Genna said. 'What do you paint? Portraits?'

'Landscapes,' Lady Long responded. 'I suppose you could say that gardens and landscapes are my abiding passion.'

'Landscapes,' Genna repeated in awed tones.

'And what do you paint, my dear?' Mrs Long asked.

'I am hoping to learn to paint portraits, but most of what I've done before are landscapes.'

Like the one she'd painted of Summerfield House with the purple and pink sky and blue grass.

'What medium do you use?' Genna asked.

'Watercolours,' the lady said.

'I love to paint landscapes in watercolours.' Genna sighed. 'Tell me, Lady Long, do your watercolours sell for a good price?'

'Sell?' Mrs Long scoffed. 'Goodness me, no. I do not *sell* my paintings, my dear. I enjoy painting and am lucky enough to have my skill recognised, but I enjoy many pastimes. I adore designing my garden, but I would never hire myself out to design anyone else's.'

Ross saw disappointment in Genna's eyes, but she kept a pleasant expression on her face for the older woman. 'Do you design your own garden, then?'

Ross suspected Genna was not very interested in moving trees and shrubbery about.

'Sir Charles and I are creating our garden. We've been inspired by Repton and Capability Brown, but the ideas are our very own,' she answered proudly.

'That is an art as well, is it not?' Genna added diplomatically.

The lady smiled. 'It is, indeed, my dear. You must call upon me some time and I will show you my garden—in my sketchbook, that is. Our house is some distance away. We are staying in town while Parliament sits.'

'That would be lovely,' Genna said. 'I would love to see your sketchbook.'

Genna curtsied and Ross bowed and they walked away.

'I am ever so much more interested in the sketchbook than actually seeing the gardens,' she told him in a conspiratorial tone.

'I would have surmised that,' he responded.

She drew closer to him. 'Thank you for introducing me to her. Imagine. She has exhibited at the Royal Academy!'

'I thought you would like to meet a fellow lady artist,' he said.

'I should like to meet one who earns enough to live on from her art. Someone like Vigée-LeBrun.'

'Who?'

'Madame Vigée-LeBrun. She was Marie Antoinette's portraitist.' She peered at him. 'You really know very little about art, do you not?'

'Only what I have learned from you, Sir Charles and Vespery,' he told her. 'Before that I either liked a work of art, disliked it, or noticed it not at all.'

Her eyes looked puzzled. 'Then why become an artist's patron?'

He raised his brows. 'Because of you, of course.'

She gave him a puzzled look. 'I do not understand.'

The music was loud and the guests who were not dancing tried to talk above it. He did not fancy shouting at her to be heard.

'Let us go somewhere quiet.' He escorted her out the ballroom door and down a hallway to a small parlour.

The room was lit by a crystal chandelier. Most of the rooms were lit in case the guests should wander in. The Duke refused to appear as if he needed to economise about such things as the cost of candles.

As soon as they entered, though, Genna was distracted by the decor. 'Oh, more plasterwork and gilt. Is every room in the house so beautiful?'

Her attention was caught by a painting in the room, a long painting depicting some Classical battle scene, with overturned chariots, rearing horses and fighting soldiers in gleaming helmets, swords and shields.

'Who painted this?' she asked.

'I have no idea,' he responded. 'I grew up with these

paintings, but I knew nothing of them. I liked this one when I was a boy, because it was a battle scene—not that I saw it often when my grandfather was alive. He would not allow children in the public rooms, in most of the rooms, actually, but sometimes my mother would sneak me out of the nursery and take me on a tour of the house.'

She turned from the painting to him. 'I think I would have liked your mother.'

He gestured to a sofa in a part of the room set up as a seating area.

She sat on the sofa and he sat next to her.

'I think I understand why you are helping me,' she said. 'It is like your soldiers, is it not? When you discover someone in need, you help them.'

His reasons for helping her were a great deal more personal than that. 'Genna—' he began.

From the hallway they heard a loud voice making an announcement.

She grimaced. 'It must be time for supper.'

He extended his hand to help her up, but pulled too hard. She wound up in his arms, her body flush against his.

She laughed and looked up into his eyes. 'If anyone saw us now, they would think we truly were betrothed.'

The blood surged through his veins, as powerful an arousal of his senses as he could remember experiencing.

'Let us convince them even more.' He lowered his head and took possession of her lips, suddenly ravenous for her.

An eager sound escaped her lips. She put her arms around his neck and pressed her mouth against his. Her lips parted, giving his tongue access. He backed her up until she was against the wall and he could hold her tighter against him. His lips left hers and tasted the tender skin of her neck. She writhed beneath him, her hands holding his head as if she feared he would stop kissing her.

From the hallway, the butler's voice rose again.

Ross froze. Good God. 'We must stop,' he managed, releasing her and stepping away.

Her chest rose and fell, her breath rapid. 'Oh, my!'

He filled with shame. 'Genna, I—'

She expelled one more deep breath before smiling up at him. 'That was quite wonderful, Ross! Last Season a fellow or two pecked at my cheek, but now I feel I have been truly kissed!'

He'd resisted such impulses so many times when they'd been together. Why had he weakened now? 'It was poorly done of me.'

She laughed and threw her arms around his neck again, giving his mouth a quick kiss. 'I would say your kiss was rather skilfully done.'

He held her cheeks in his palms. 'You are outrageous, Genna Summerfield.' He released her again. With difficulty.

She straightened the bodice of her dress and smoothed her skirt. 'Me? You are the one who kissed me.'

He checked his own clothing and made certain he was together. With any luck the visible evidence of his arousal would disappear by the time they reached the dining room.

Chapter Eighteen

Genna hardly knew what to think as Ross escorted her to the dining room. Such a kiss! She'd never imagined a kiss could be so sublime. Could leave one so…wanting.

She should have been furious at Ross. She should have slapped his face.

Instead, when he'd pulled away from her, she'd wanted to pull him back and start the kiss all over again. Was this the sort of physical thing that made men and women desire to marry? Or, like her unhappily married mother and father, was this what made them seek other lovers?

If a mere kiss could be so powerful, what, then, would marital coupling be like? For the first time, she wanted to know. If Ross's kiss could bring such breathless pleasure, what could his lovemaking bring?

The supper was set out in three separate rooms, the dining room and two others set up with tables and chairs. Unlike the musicale, the food would be served at the table. She and Ross were expected in the dining room where the guests of highest rank were to be seated. When they entered the dining room, most of the guests had already taken their seats. The Duke at the head of the table, the Duchess at the other end, but, beyond that, precedence was abandoned. One supped with one's recent dance partner.

From across the room, the Duke stood and called, 'Ross!' He gestured for them to come to him. Two empty chairs next to the Duke had obviously been intended for them.

A footman held Genna's chair for her. To her dismay,

Lord Tinmore procured a place almost directly across from her. She glanced down the table and spied Lorene seated with Lord Penford.

The room was another grand exhibition of opulence. Walls of green damask, two marble pillars at each end of the room, another intricate plasterwork ceiling, its designs outlined in gilt. The paintings on the walls were huge and awe-inspiring, depicting scenes from ancient history.

'You are late,' the Duke chastised.

'A bit late,' Ross responded without a hint of apology.

'You disappeared from the ballroom.' The Duke's tone did not change.

'Only briefly,' Ross said.

A gentleman on the Duke's other side asked him a question and he turned away.

The white soup was served, but the guests selected other fare from the dishes set before them on the table. Because a hot meal would never have stayed hot for so many guests, the dinner consisted of cold meats and fish, jellies, pastries, sweetmeats and ices, among a myriad of other dishes. The room was soon filled with the noise of conversation, and silver knives and forks clanking against dinner plates of fine porcelain china.

The Duke and the other gentleman began a heated exchange about the rash of violence occurring lately, of several break-ins, thefts and murders by gangs of men.

The Duke half-stood, his face red. 'We cannot ignore that people are hungry, sir!'

Genna wanted to tell him that Ross fed hungry people. Perhaps the others should do the same. But she did not dare.

The Duke sat down again, drained the contents of his wineglass and suddenly clasped his hand to his chest, with a cry of pain. He collapsed on to the table, scattering dishes and food and spilling wine.

One of the guests screamed in alarm.

'Father!' Ross was first to his feet and first to reach his

father. He sat his father back in the chair. 'Wake up, wake up,' he cried.

His father moaned.

Ross turned to the butler. 'Fetch the doctor immediately.'

The butler rushed from the room.

Penford ran up from where he had been sitting. 'Shall we carry him to his bedchamber?'

'Yes,' Ross immediately agreed.

The two men picked up the Duke and carried him out of the room.

The Duchess stood and tried to make herself heard above the rumblings of the guests. 'He's merely had a spell. He will recover soon. Please let us continue with supper.'

Finish supper? Genna could not finish supper. She left the room to see if she could help in some way. Out in the hallway, she looked for Ross and Dell, but they were out of sight.

She found a footman. 'Show me where Rossdale took his father.'

There was no reason the footman should do what she demanded, but he did. She caught up with them right as they reached the Duke's bedchamber door.

'May I help?' she asked.

Both men looked surprised to see her.

At that moment, though, the Duke made a sound and struggled to get out of Ross's and Penford's arms. 'What? What happened?'

'You lost consciousness, Papa,' Ross told him. 'We're bringing you to your room.'

'Nonsense. Must be—we are giving a ball. Perfectly fine.' He stumbled and Ross caught him before he lost his balance.

Genna spoke up. 'Your butler has sent for your physician. You should lie down until he comes.'

The Duke peered at her as if never having seen her before, then the puzzlement on his face cleared. 'Oh, I remember you.'

'See?' She smiled at the Duke. 'That is a good sign. You remember me. But you continue to be unsteady on your feet. Best to wait for your physician.'

'Come on.' She stepped forward and took his arm. 'If you feel dizzy you may simply hang on to me.'

'I do feel dizzy,' he murmured.

He was inside the door of his room when his valet appeared. 'They said below stairs that His Grace took ill.'

'A little spell, that is all,' His Grace said.

The valet lost no time in getting him in the room and over to his bed. Ross remained with him.

Genna walked back to the hall.

'I was amazed he would follow your orders,' Penford said.

She slid him a smile. 'So was I. Sometimes people do, though.' She peeked in the room where the valet and Ross were convincing his father to lie down. 'I hope he is not seriously ill.'

'Indeed.' Penford closed the door all but a crack. His voice turned low. 'We should not like to lose him.'

Another death for Penford to endure? How hard for him. 'You must know the Duke well.'

He shrugged. 'I know Ross well. The Duke is too busy and too steeped in politics to be known well. I do not believe he ever spoke to me until I inherited my title.'

'Ross is so unlike that,' she said.

He nodded in agreement. 'According to Ross, his father was never like that.'

'What do you mean?' she asked.

He peeked through the crack in the door. 'They are dressing him for bed,' he said before answering her question. 'According to Ross, his father was light-hearted before he inherited the title. He and Ross's mother were always taking Ross to some new place for some new adventure. His father was game for anything, apparently. His mother, too.'

'Did you know Ross's mother?' she asked.

Penford shook his head. 'I met her once, but by then she was ill and much altered, Ross said.'

She glanced away. She had no memory of her own mother and her father had never bothered with her at all.

'Let us hope he does not lose his father as well,' she murmured.

Penford's face was grim.

Ross came out the door. 'He is in bed resting. His valet will stay until the physician arrives. I should return to the guests. Apprise them of his condition.'

'And the Duchess. She will be worried,' Genna said.

Ross frowned.

'What does that frown mean?' she asked.

'She should be here,' he said bitterly. 'Not trying to salvage her social event.'

Another less-than-ideal marriage? Genna was not surprised.

'Everyone will still be at supper,' she said. 'While you go to the Duchess, shall I tell the guests in the other rooms what occurred and of your father's present status?'

Ross did not answer right away.

'I'll do it,' Penford said.

Ross threaded her arm though his. 'Come with me. Stay by my side.'

At this moment, if they were truly betrothed, she would be expected to stay by his side. Oddly enough, at this moment, it was also where she most wanted to be.

Although the Duchess had wanted the ball to go on in spite of her husband's sudden malaise, no one wished to dance and pretend to enjoy themselves while the host of the party had taken to his bed.

So Ross stood where his father would have stood, at the

Duchess's side, while one after the other, the guests approached to say goodbye and to extend their good wishes to the Duke.

In the midst of all this, the doctor arrived and, since the Duchess showed no inclination to accompany the physician to her husband's room, Ross accepted that duty, as well. He managed only the briefest goodnight to Genna, a mere glance as he hurried behind the doctor.

After examining him, the doctor told his father, 'It is your heart. We have talked of this before. You must curtail your activity. Now it is imperative that you rest. For at least a month.'

'A month!' the Duke cried. 'I cannot rest. There is much to do in Parliament. And my duties to the wedding of Princess Charlotte— I will be expected to participate.'

The doctor was unfazed by these excuses. 'If you fail to rest, another episode like this one could put a period to your existence.'

Ross's father crossed his arms over his chest and pursed his lips like a sulking child.

The doctor stepped away from the bed. 'I will stop in to see how you are faring tomorrow, but now I am very desirous of returning to my bed.'

'We are grateful you came,' Ross said, extending his hand.

The doctor shook it. 'I'll see myself out.'

Ross walked him to the door. Ross was also eager to get some sleep.

His father called to him. 'Ross?'

He turned. 'Yes, Father?'

'You must take over for me.'

Ross knew this even before the doctor gave his diagnosis. 'Yes, whatever you require, but sleep now. I'll come in the morning. Tell me then what you need me to do.'

The next day instead of Ross coming to pick up Genna for her painting lesson, he sent a message and a carriage, explaining why he could not go with her. She understood. Goodness! His father was ill; what else could he do? He promised to call upon her in the afternoon.

When she arrived at the studio, Vespery was disappointed that Ross was not there. 'I was going to have him pose for you. You are ready to try a portrait.'

The portrait seemed suddenly much less important to her than before.

'I could paint you,' she said.

'No, *you*. Paint you.' He brought over a mirror and set it up where she could look at herself and her canvas.

Genna began as he'd taught her to begin on other paintings. Make a few lines as a guide, a rough idea of the shape of her head, where to place her eyes, nose and mouth. At each step, he stopped his own work and taught her what she needed to know next. What colours to mix for skin pigment, what colours for shadow and highlights. How to block in the colours, then how to refine them. By the end of the day she had a portrait of herself in a rough, unpolished form.

'This is a very good effort,' Vespery said. 'A very good effort, indeed.'

She wondered if Ross would be pleased.

'I am becoming used to the paints,' she said to Vespery.

When the carriage came to take her home that day, all she could think of was seeing Ross that afternoon.

She entered Tinmore's town house more subdued than at any other time when returning from her art lessons. She'd barely stepped into the hall when Lorene came down the stairs.

'Where were you?' Lorene's voice was angry. 'You were not with Rossdale. I saw you leave. You were alone.'

'He sent a carriage for me,' she stalled.

'You did not meet him, though, did you?' Lorene accused. 'Lord Tinmore said it was Rossdale, not the Duke, who met with some of the other lords to discuss the changes in coinage.'

Parliament would vote on changing the currency to a fixed gold standard. She'd heard gentlemen talking about it at the ball last night.

Lorene glared at her. 'If Rossdale was there, he was not with you.'

'No, he was not with me,' Genna admitted. Her art lessons were another secret she kept from her sister.

'Then where did you go alone in Rossdale's carriage?' Lorene demanded.

Genna glanced around her. The footman who had opened the door for her was standing stony-faced, but in hearing distance. 'May we go up to your sitting room? I will explain everything there.'

Lorene answered her by simply turning and climbing the stairs again. When they reached the sitting room, Lorene remained standing.

'Explain, then,' Lorene said.

'I have been taking lessons in oil painting,' Genna said.

Lorene's brows rose. 'Oil painting?'

'From Mr Vespery. Do you remember him? He was at Her Grace's musicale. He is painting portraits of the Duke and Duchess.'

Lorene shook her head in disbelief. 'Lessons? With a man? Unchaperoned?'

'Well, Ross was with me until today, but, I assure you, Mr Vespery is merely my art teacher, not my paramour.'

Lorene's eyes scolded. 'Genna! Honestly! You are much too free-speaking.'

Genna lowered her gaze. 'I am sorry, Lorene. I should not have been so sharp.'

Lorene waved a hand. 'Never mind that. Whatever possessed you?'

'To get art lessons?' How much could she explain without telling all of it? 'We've been surrounded by astounding paintings in this house, at Tinmore Hall, in every house we've visited. I want to paint like that.'

'Genna, those paintings were done by masters. You cannot expect to paint like them.'

Lorene's words stung, but Genna wanted her to understand. She took her sister's hand and pulled her over to the chairs. 'I love it, Lorene. And I am progressing very quickly at it. Please do not make it so I cannot continue.' In other words, tell Lord Tinmore.

'But why? How did you even start it?' Lorene asked.

'One day I mentioned to Ross that I would like to learn to paint in oils and the next day he took me to Mr Vespery's studio. Ross bought me all the supplies and paid for the lessons.'

Lorene looked shocked. 'You cannot accept that!'

'Why not?' Genna countered. 'He is my fiancé. If he gave me a diamond bracelet, you would think that a fine thing.' If he were really her fiancé, she should say.

Lorene's eyebrows knitted. 'I do not know. In some ways Lord Rossdale seems the perfect husband for you, but it is difficult to see you as a duchess.'

On that Genna could agree. She would make a horrible duchess.

Genna leaned forward. 'Please do not spoil this for me, Lorene. I am doing no harm and I do love it so.'

Lorene glanced away. 'I suppose…'

Genna sprang from her chair and kissed her sister on the cheek. 'You do understand! It is like your music.'

'Like my music,' Lorene said wistfully. 'Like if I could take lessons…'

'You could!' Genna seized her sister's hands. 'London is the perfect place to find a wonderful piano master. We can ask if anyone knows of one. I'll ask Ross. Or Lord Penford.'

'No!' Lorene said sharply. 'It is a lovely idea, but I cannot do it.'

'You could.' Genna sat again, but kept hold of Lorene's

hands. 'Ask Lord Tinmore. He likes to do things for you.' But not for anyone else. She shook her sister's hands. 'Think of it! You already play beautifully, but you were mostly self-taught. There might be all sorts of things you could learn.'

'Perhaps...' Lorene glanced away.

When Ross called that afternoon Genna met him in the drawing room. Seeing him standing, waiting for her, she had an impulse to rush into his arms. It stunned her. The events of the previous night, seeing Ross so distressed, it had changed something in her.

'Ross,' she managed.

He walked towards her and took her hand. 'Forgive the message this morning. I hope you got to your lesson with no difficulties.'

'None at all.' She led him to the sofa and they sat. 'But, tell me, how is your father?'

His brow furrowed. 'Weaker than he will admit. The doctor said he must rest for at least a month. The only way I could get him to agree to do that was to take over whatever of his duties I am able to perform.'

'Of course you must.' But she felt sad for him. It must be a great deal of responsibility thrust upon him so suddenly.

'I must renege on my promise to take you wherever you wished to go,' he said.

She put her hand on his. 'Do not fret over that.'

'Tell me.' He gave a wan smile. 'What did you paint today?'

The stress on his face put all thoughts of painting out of her mind. She did not wish to cause him worry so she exclaimed, 'It was the very best day! Vespery started teaching me to paint portraits. At last!'

'Who did you paint?' he asked.

She'd not mention that he was supposed to have been her first model. 'I painted myself. Vespery gave me a mirror.'

'I would like to see that,' he said.

She laughed. 'No, you would not. It is rather awful at the moment, but I will improve it.' She took a breath. 'I can master this, Ross. I can paint portraits. Thanks to you, I will be able to earn money.'

'And that is what you desire more than anything,' he stated as if finishing her sentence.

She sobered. 'But how are you faring?'

He smiled sadly. 'I can manage. I suppose I absorbed more of my father's thinking than I guessed. I still hope to break away one of these days and come and visit Vespery's studio.'

'Whenever you are able,' she said. 'I would welcome you.'

Chapter Nineteen

Ross returned to the Kessington town house after calling upon Genna. The footman attending the hall told him his father wished him to come to his bedchamber.

Ross knocked and was admitted.

He walked to his father's bedside. 'How do you fare today, Father?'

His father, always so strong and commanding by nature, looked shrunken and pale against the bed linens. 'I'm tired, is all. Merely need a little rest.'

'The doctor listened to your heart. You need to heed him,' Ross countered.

His father made a dismissive gesture. 'I know. I know. I am doing as he says.'

His father's valet, who was in the room folding clothes, spoke up. 'Your Grace, I dare say the physician would not have approved of your getting up and working at your desk for over an hour.' His father's desk was in his study attached to the library on the floor below.

'You may leave us, Stone,' his father snapped.

The valet bowed and left the room.

'Gossips worse than an old woman,' Ross's father muttered.

'He is concerned about you.' Ross's brows knitted. 'You must rest, Father. It has only been a day since your spell.'

'Sitting at my desk did not seem such an exertion,' his father said.

'But walking there. Climbing stairs. Stay in this room.

Please. I can take care of what you cannot.' What other choice did Ross have?

'Very well. Very well,' His father gestured to a chair by his bedside. 'Sit, my son.'

Ross sat.

His father glanced away as if uncertain what he wished to say. Finally he spoke. 'This spell has alarmed me, if you must know. Your grandfather died of such a spell. He was about my age.'

Yes. Everything changed when his grandfather died.

'It is time for you to settle down, my son,' he said.

Ross's brows rose. 'I am. I am betrothed—'

His father interrupted. 'But you plan to marry in autumn! I may not be here in autumn. I do not know how long I will be here. I would like to know if there will be an heir to the title before I die.' He leaned forward in the bed. 'Get on with it! Get a special licence and marry right away. What is this waiting?'

This deception of his and Genna's suddenly felt like a foolish mistake.

His father's voice rose. 'It is nonsensical to wait. Are you wishing to get out of it? Believe me, Constance and I would be delighted to see you look elsewhere. But if it must be this Summerfield chit, marry her now, even though I doubt she is up to the rigours of becoming a duchess!'

Ross disagreed. Genna would make a duchess unlike any other. The problem was, if he truly wished to make her his wife, he would kill her dreams. His mother's dreams had been dashed; Ross would not see the same for Genna.

She'd become that important to him.

Ross answered the Duke defensively. 'Stop trying to control when I marry and what I do.' He rose from the chair. 'I will take over whatever duties you need me for. I will do that for your sake and for the sake of the title and all the people dependent upon us, but allow me my own choice of who to marry and when.'

'You are a disappointment to me!' his father shouted. He pressed a hand to his chest and sank back against the pillows.

'Calm yourself, Papa!' Ross cried in alarm. He softened his tone. 'Just rest. Trust me. You will get well. All will work out as it should.'

His father turned his face away.

Ross stepped back. Curse his idea of this false betrothal!

'Rest, Papa,' he said again. 'I'll come see you later.'

His father continued to ignore him. Ross turned and strode out of the bedchamber.

The Duchess stood right outside the door. She joined him as he walked away.

'I am not in favour of your marrying right away,' she said.

He did not look at her. 'Eavesdropping, Constance?'

She huffed. 'I was walking by. Your voices were raised. I could not help but hear.'

Ross did not believe her.

'You can change your mind about marrying Miss Summerfield,' the Duchess went on. 'I am certain she can be persuaded to cry off. She has not the vaguest notion of what it will take to be a duchess. She is entirely unsuitable.'

'It is none of your affair, ma'am,' he warned.

She continued anyway. 'Now that your father is ill, you can see how important it is to marry well, to have a dignified, capable woman for a wife, not a frivolous girl with a scandalous upbringing.'

What had his father ever seen in this woman? Ross wondered. She was all calculation and no heart.

He stopped and faced her. 'Take care, Constance. If my father's health fails completely—if he dies—you will want to be in my good graces. I will be Duke then.'

He left her and did not look behind.

For the next three weeks, Ross barely had time to think about his father's wishes and the Duchess's mean-spiritedness. He was too busy going from one task to another. There always seemed to be problems on the estates, decisions to make about finances, Parliamentary bills to advocate for, or Court functions to attend.

There were more Court functions than a typical Season. All to celebrate the upcoming wedding of Princess Charlotte. To these functions he was required to escort the Duchess. They were dreary affairs.

When he could Ross included Genna in his attendance to other parties, but those were infrequent. There were one or two functions which she attended with Lord Tinmore and her sister.

All in all, though, he saw very little of her.

He missed her.

He stopped in at Vespery's studio a few times. It was clear she was thriving there. Her portraiture was remarkably skilled, he thought. He coveted the self-portrait she painted. Perhaps he could own it, to remember her by.

He found himself dreading the day they must part. Too often he wished their betrothal to be real.

But it was time for him to face truth. She did not want to marry. Even if she did want it, marrying him would rob her of everything she desired—to be an artist. To answer to no one but herself. To live free of constraints.

Life with him would be nothing but constraints.

His father gained strength, enough that the doctor allowed him to participate in Princess Charlotte's wedding, but afterwards Ross must continue to assume the lion's share of his father's burdens.

On the day of the wedding, his father seemed his old robust self. Perhaps the excitement over this event would carry him through.

Ross had not been included in the wedding invitation, but ladies and gentlemen were allowed to stand in the entrance hall of Buckingham House to greet the Princess and other royal personages as they came out to their carriages.

Ross took the opportunity to escort Genna and Lady Tinmore to the event. Also in their party were their other sister, her husband and his parents. And Dell. To everyone's delight, Tinmore begged off, unable to bear the exertion of the event.

When the royals emerged, Genna's excitement burst from her and spilled over all of them.

'Look! There is the Queen! I never thought to see the Queen!' She jumped up and down.

Princess Charlotte appeared.

'Tess! Look!' Genna cried. 'Look at the Princess's gown. It shimmers!'

She commented on all of the Royal Princesses, as well. Ross was surprised she recognised them.

'I've seen engravings of their portraits in magazines,' she explained.

Afterwards they all walked to the Northdons' town house for a breakfast.

'It is said that Charlotte's choice of a husband is a love match,' Tess remarked over the meal.

'Yes, but what about Prince Leopold?' Genna retorted. 'Surely the prospect of becoming the Queen's consort had much to do with his agreeing to the marriage. Much higher status than the prospect of ruling a duchy.' Leopold was one of the German princes of a duchy that had been taken over by Napoleon. 'Did he fall in love with the Princess or with the idea of being the husband of an extremely wealthy queen?'

'One can fall in love even if a marriage has political advantages, can one not?' Tess asked. 'Look at you and Rossdale. People will say you marry him because of his rank.'

Genna reddened. 'I assure you, Ross's rank is of no consequence to me.'

Again, their deception reared its ugly head. These good people thought them to be in love, thought they would marry. Ross could now admit to himself that he loved Genna, but he would never marry her.

After leaving the Northdons' breakfast, Genna walked with Ross through the streets of Mayfair to Tinmore's town house on Curzon Street. Lorene had left earlier, escorted home by Lord Penford. It was already dusk and the streets were a lovely shade of lavender against a pink sky.

The exhilaration of the day had settled into melancholy and Genna fought an urge to simply burst into tears. To see the royal family had been thrilling, but now sadness swept over her. How could she explain it to Ross when she did not understand it herself?

She forced herself not to dwell on it. 'I rather hope they will be happy.'

'Who?' Ross asked.

She held his arm. 'Princess Charlotte and Prince Leopold. They have little chance, of course, but it would be nice if they could be happy. Goodness knows, Princess Charlotte's parents were not happy with each other.'

It was well known that the Prince Regent and his wife, Caroline of Brunswick, detested each other from first sight.

'You cannot judge every marriage after that of the Prince Regent. Think of the King and Queen. Theirs has been a long and, by all reports, a happy marriage.'

He was right, of course, but she resisted any evidence contrary to what she believed. 'Well, he turned insane. That can't be happy.'

'You won't hear of a happy marriage, will you?' His voice turned low.

'There are far more unhappy ones, you must agree,' she said. 'Better to be like my mother and take a lover.'

He said nothing for several steps. 'Is that what you plan to do? Take a lover?'

'I suppose,' she said without enthusiasm, although what

other man could she possibly want for a lover besides Ross?
'It seemed to be what made my mother happy.' Even at the
expense of her children's happiness, but Genna would turn
into a watering pot if she thought about that too much.
'What about your parents? Were they happy?'

He frowned. 'For a long time, very happy. Until my
father inherited the title.' He paused. 'The revolution in
France, becoming a duchess, it was all too much for my
mother, not to mention my father's complete preoccupation with the role. It killed her.'

'Oh, Ross!' She leaned against him in sympathy. 'Could
unhappiness truly kill her?'

He shrugged. 'She contracted a fever, but I believe she
could have fought harder to live if she'd wanted to.'

'Both our mothers left us,' she murmured, blinking away
tears, but it was not losing her mother that most pained her
now. It was knowing she and Ross would have to part. In
many ways, she'd already lost him.

Like his mother, she realised. She'd lost Ross to his new
duties just as his mother had lost the Duke.

She continued to hold on to him tightly, as if that would
keep him with her for ever.

They walked for half a street before he spoke again. 'We
should talk—' he began.

That sounded ominous.

'My father's illness has changed things. He is pressing
for us to marry right away. He wants to know the succes-
sion is secured in case his heart gives way completely. You
might say he wants us to get on with it.'

With creating an heir, he meant.

He went on. 'Father doesn't know, of course, that we
will not marry—'

'Do you want me to cry off sooner?' She tried to keep
her voice from cracking.

He'd be free to marry someone else, then.

'No,' he said quickly. 'I tell you this only so you will be prepared if he speaks to you. I want us to continue as we planned. To make certain you are ready to become the artist you wish to be.'

To ultimately part in the autumn, when everyone expected they would marry. Would he marry someone else then? He must, she thought. What other choice did he have?

She made herself speak brightly. 'Yes! Let us enjoy the rest of the Season. You will have more time, will you not, now that your father is more recovered? You must let me paint you.'

'I would be honoured,' he said, but his eyes looked as sad as she felt inside.

The next morning Ross called upon Vespery before Genna was expected. His housekeeper sent him to Vespery's studio where the artist was at work on a portrait.

'Ross, my boy, how good to see you.' Vespery put down his brushes and palette and greeted him. 'To what do I owe the pleasure of this visit? Without Miss Summerfield?' He gestured to the seating area where Ross used to sit to watch Genna paint.

'I am here about Miss Summerfield,' Ross said, taking a chair. 'How is she faring?'

'She progresses very rapidly, Ross.' He motioned for Ross to rise again. 'Come. I'll show you.' He walked over to several canvases leaning against the wall. He turned one of them, Genna's self-portrait. 'Here is her first effort at portraiture. It is competent, is it not?'

Ross thought it looked very much like Genna. It even captured some of her irrepressible personality.

'I am no judge of competence,' Ross admitted. 'It is very like her, though.'

'Yes. And that was her first effort.' He walked over to another canvas still on an easel and removed the cloth covering it. 'Here is another.'

It was the housekeeper and even Ross could tell Genna had improved her technique.

'The woman's personality shows, does it not?' said Vespery.

'Indeed.'

'I believe there is nothing she could not paint if she wished to.' Vespery covered the painting again and walked back to the chairs.

Ross sat with him. 'Painting is what Miss Summerfield wishes to do and I want to make certain she can do it. So I have a proposition.'

Vespery's brows rose. 'Yes?'

'I will continue to pay you to take her on, but as an assistant, not a student.' He paused to gauge the artist's reaction. The man still looked interested. 'I will pay her salary, too, but she mustn't know it comes from me. It must seem as if you are paying her. I want this plan to continue until she has enough commissions to set up her own studio.'

Vespery looked puzzled. 'But you are to marry her, are you not?'

Ross stopped to think. Could he trust Vespery with the whole truth?

The artist's expression turned to alarm. 'Do not tell me you are planning to renege on your promise!'

'No,' Ross said. 'Not me. But lately I have thought perhaps—perhaps Miss Summerfield would like to cry off. The painting makes her much happier than being a duchess would do. I think that is beginning to dawn on her. When—if—she decides to end our engagement, I want her to have what she most desires—to support herself as an artist.'

'An artist's assistant makes a pittance,' Vespery cried. 'She cannot support herself on it!'

Ross lifted a stilling hand. 'You and I might know what an artist's assistant would make in salary, but she does not. I will pay enough for her to live comfortably.'

Vespery stared at him for a long time before answering.

'I will do it, of course. I would be a fool not to. I can double my output, be paid and have a skilled paid assistant at no cost to myself.' He leaned towards Ross. 'Are you certain, my lord, that Miss Summerfield would prefer art over marriage to you? I am not convinced.'

'I am certain,' Ross answered.

And he was also certain he wanted it for her.

Chapter Twenty

Three days later Genna put on her gloves, ready to be transported to Vespery's studio. It was time for the carriage to come and pick her up and she waited in the anteroom.

A knock sounded at the door. The footman announced, 'Your carriage, miss.'

She hurried out to the hall and was happily surprised. Ross stood there, hat in hand, looking magnificent in his perfectly tailored black coat, white neckcloth and buff-coloured pantaloons.

'Ross!' she cried, stilling an impulse to rush into his arms. Instead she approached him with her hands extended.

He clasped them and gave her a peck on the cheek. No doubt she would feel the sensation of his lips against her skin for the rest of the day.

'I was able to take the time.' There was only the hint of a smile on his face. 'Much has slowed down now that the Princess's wedding is over and my father is feeling better.'

'I'm glad.' She filled with hope. 'Will I see more of you, then?'

'As often as I can manage,' he responded, as she took his arm and they walked to the door.

The footman opened it and they stepped outside.

'You have your curricle!' she cried. 'It has been weeks since we were out in your curricle.'

He helped her up into the seat. 'I warn you, it is chilly today. I am regretting leaving my topcoat at home.'

'I do not care.' She cared about nothing else except that he was with her.

He took the ribbons and his tiger jumped on the back.

As soon as they started, Genna turned to him. 'Oh, Ross! I have some wonderful news!'

He glanced from the road to her. 'What is it?'

She could hardly get the words out. 'Vespery wishes to hire me to be his assistant. He will pay me a handsome amount, enough for me to live on.'

'That is wonderful news.' His voice did not sound as enthusiastic as she'd anticipated.

But, then, she did not feel as excited as she'd sounded.

She went on. 'I must tell him when I am ready, he said, but I am able to take as little or as much time as I wish.'

'That is good, is it not?' he responded.

'Yes. Very good.' She swallowed. 'It—it means we can break the betrothal whenever we wish.'

'I suppose it does.' His voice turned low. 'When do you wish it?'

'Never!' she cried, threading her arm through his and leaning her head against his shoulder. 'I wish everything could remain exactly as it is this minute.'

'Riding in a chilly curricle, you mean?' he quipped, but his throat was thick.

She tried to smile. 'You know what I mean.'

He turned on to Piccadilly. 'I was hoping you would want a break from the studio. A little outing. Two outings, actually.'

'Will you have that much time?' She hoped.

'I will.'

'I still want you to sit for a portrait for me,' she said.

He turned to gaze at her. 'I will make the time.'

When they reached Vespery's studio, Ross handed the ribbons to his tiger who would take the curricle back to the stable until it came time to pick them up again. Ross knocked at the door and the housekeeper admitted them.

The housekeeper broke into a smile when she saw

Genna. 'Good afternoon, miss,' the woman said brightly. 'And to you, sir.'

'Good afternoon, Mrs Shaw!' Genna turned to him. 'I painted a portrait of Mrs Shaw. She was my second one.'

'Did you?' He knew it, of course, having called upon Vespery the day he made his bargain with him. Ross glanced at Mrs Shaw. 'And have you seen it?'

'Oh, yes, my lord.' The housekeeper beamed. 'Miss Summerfield made me look so very nice.'

'I merely paint what I see,' Genna said. 'Lord Rossdale has agreed to sit for me next. Is that not brave of him?'

Brave because it would put them in each other's company for an extended period. They'd not been together so much since he'd kissed her, since he'd realised how much he wanted her.

The housekeeper patted Genna's arm. 'You will do a fine job of it, miss.'

They left Mrs Shaw to her duties and walked to the back of the house to the studio.

Genna burst into the light-filled room. 'Look who I have brought with me!'

Vespery put down his brush. 'Lord Rossdale. Good to see you,' he said, a bit stilted.

'Ross will be able to stay the afternoon, too,' Genna added. 'Is that not grand?'

Ross nodded to the artist and placed his hat and gloves on a table by the door. 'It seems I am to be Miss Summerfield's next model.'

He helped her off with her redingote.

'I can hardly wait to get started.' She glanced around the room. 'Do we have a canvas already stretched that I can use?'

Vespery pointed to several stacked against the wall. 'Pick whatever size you wish.'

He gave Ross a conspiratorial look while she selected her canvas and carried it to her easel.

'Ross knows of your kind offer, Mr Vespery,' she said.

Vespery jumped and his voice turned high. 'He does?'

She gestured for Ross to sit in the chair in the corner. 'I told Ross today.'

Genna looked at home in the studio, comfortable around the canvases and paints. More so, she looked relaxed and happy. He had no doubt she would ultimately be as big a success as Vespery himself, but, in the meantime, he would watch and make certain she wanted for nothing.

She positioned him, stepped back and surveyed him, then positioned him again. 'You must remember to sit this way tomorrow, too,' she said. 'You can come tomorrow, can you not?'

'I had planned one of those outings for tomorrow,' he said, trying to remain still.

'The next day, then.'

Vespery spoke up from his side of the room. 'As of tomorrow I will not be here. I will be away for a week on a commission out of town.'

'But we can come in, can we not?' she asked. 'Mrs Shaw can let us in.'

'Mrs Shaw will be away, too,' Vespery said. 'She will be visiting her sister.'

'Then might we have a key?' Genna pressed. 'If I am to be your assistant, surely you would trust me with a key.'

Vespery shrugged. 'I suppose.'

She ran over and gave him a hug. 'Thank you!'

The clock Vespery kept in the room chimed two o'clock.

'Two o'clock?' the artist said. 'I must be off. I am delivering the portraits to your father and the Duchess.'

'Would you prefer I take them?' Ross asked, though it would necessitate explaining to them why he'd been at Vespery's studio.

Vespery hurriedly cleaned his brushes. 'No. The Duchess will want me to bring them. I must ensure they are acceptable.' He wiped his hands and bid them good day.

Ross attempted to remain still.

'It has been a long time since you and I were alone together,' Genna remarked.

'Since the ball.' He remembered that moment. He'd kissed her.

And then everything changed.

She paused, brush in the air, and gazed at him. 'I liked being alone with you that night,' she murmured.

'As did I,' he responded.

She met his gaze.

It was a good thing he needed to remain in the chair, in that pose. Otherwise he might have crossed the room and kissed her again. God knew he wished to do so.

She turned back to her painting, making quick big strokes with the brush. Soon he could tell she was lost in the work, the concentration on her face enhancing her beauty. The pose he needed to keep gave him a great advantage. He needed to look in her direction. He could indulge in watching her all he liked.

The next day Ross picked up Genna earlier than the usual time. They would have nearly the whole day together, plenty of time for what he had planned for her.

When she sat next to him in his curricle, she smiled happily. 'It has been so long since we've had an outing. I cannot imagine where you are taking me.'

He felt happy, too, happier than he'd been since his father took ill. A whole day together, a day she was bound to enjoy. He turned on to Audley Street, heading north to turn right on Oxford Street.

As they left Mayfair, Genna looked around at everything. 'I have never been in this part of town,' she said, commenting on whatever caught her eye.

When they reached the end of Oxford Street, she asked, 'What part of town are we in now?'

'Bloomsbury.' He hated to give her too many hints.

'Oh.' She turned silent.

He pulled up to their destination, what once was the mansion of a wealthy duke who sold it to the British government when the Bloomsbury neighbourhood was no longer the fashionable place to live. The mansion had a large expanse of garden in the front so it took some time for the curricle to reach the doorway.

Genna finally spoke. 'I know where we are. I've seen this building in books. This is Montagu House, is it not?'

'That it is.'

Ross's tiger jumped off to hold the horses. Ross climbed down and turned to assist Genna.

'You've brought me to see the exhibits of the British Museum!' she cried in delight.

He held her by her waist as he helped her down. 'Even better,' he said.

She landed on her feet, but he did not immediately let go of her. She tipped her head up and looked directly in his eyes. Her eyes darkened and she leaned a little closer.

He released her then, before he forgot they were in a public place.

She took a breath and recovered her composure. 'What could be better than the British Museum?'

He knew this would please her. 'We will see the Elgin Marbles.'

Her eyes grew wide. 'Truly?'

He offered his arm. 'Truly.'

Genna's excitement grew as they approached the door of the museum. Ross knocked as if visiting someone's residence.

'The museum is closed?' Genna asked.

'Not to us,' he responded.

Obviously he had gone to some effort for this outing. For her.

The door was answered by a well-dressed gentleman. His brows rose. 'Lord Rossdale?'

Ross nodded. 'Mr Hutton, I presume.'

'Welcome to the British Museum.' Mr Hutton swept his arm in an arc and stepped aside for them to enter.

Ross turned to Genna. 'Miss Summerfield, may I present Mr Hutton, who has made this excursion possible.'

'My pleasure, Miss Summerfield.' Mr Hutton bowed.

'I am so grateful to you, sir.' And to Ross for making this possible.

Mr Hutton looked apologetic. 'You do understand you will not be able to tour the entire museum at this time. Let me escort you to the courtyard.'

They walked by a grand staircase and Genna spied huge giraffes at the top of the stairs, appearing as they might have been when alive. Other curiosities could be glimpsed as they made their way to the back of the mansion and out the door to the courtyard. Mr Hutton then led them to a huge wooden shed, which he unlocked, and opened the doors, filling the space inside with light.

'I will return in an hour,' Mr Hutton said. 'Obviously you may not move any of the sculptures, but I doubt you could. They are quite marvellous. I think you will agree.'

He left them in the doorway.

Huge slabs of marble lined the sides of the shed. Scattered around were ghostly figures. Headless. Armless. Standing. Reclining.

Genna stepped inside reverently. 'Oh, Ross!'

She walked along the perimeter gazing at the long slabs of marble that used to decorate the frieze of the Parthenon. The sculpted figures depicted all sorts of figures: men on horseback, on foot or racing chariots, women carrying items—for sacrifice to the gods, perhaps? Everything seemed in motion. Rearing horses, figures interacting, no two the same.

'It must tell a story,' Genna said. 'I wish I knew what it

was.' She dared to touch the sculpture, almost surprised the figures were not as warm as flesh they were so realistic.

'Here is a Centaur fighting a Lapith,' he said.

It was one segment, not a part of the long procession of figures that had been part of the frieze. Had there been more Centaurs? Did they tell a different story?

'Lord Tinmore criticises Elgin for removing these sculptures from the Parthenon,' Genna said. 'He likens it to theft.'

'I have heard that sentiment,' Ross responded. 'I have also heard Lord Elgin praised for saving the marbles. Apparently the Parthenon was a ruin and local builders thought nothing of using its sculptures as building blocks in their own buildings, some of which were ground down for cement.'

Genna shook her head. 'Can you imagine these magnificent carvings ground down into nothing? It would be an abomination!'

She walked the length of a section of the frieze. Many of the men were naked, some riding horses, some on foot. Genna was not such a green girl that she'd never seen a naked man before, although her knowledge of such was confined to seeing other statuary or spying her brother, a boy then, swimming naked. These figures, though, were all well-formed, muscular, powerful beings.

She glanced at Ross, who was examining one of the pieces. His shoulders were broad, like the Greek figures on the marbles, his legs well formed. She remembered the feel of his body pressing against hers when he'd kissed her the night of the ball. His muscles were as firm as marble.

Her skin flashed with heat.

She resisted the impulse to fan herself and turned away to examine the other marbles. One was a horse's head from what must have been a huge statue. She ran her hand down the horse's forehead to its muzzle, but it only made her wonder what it would be like to run her hand over Ross's skin.

She walked further away from him, over to three headless statues, all women attired in lavishly draped cloth. For all three, it was easy to see the bodies underneath, as evident as if they were real.

Then she came to a naked reclining male, exuding raw masculine strength.

Like Ross.

'Here is another Centaur,' called Ross from across the room.

She crossed the shed to him and her insides fluttered at being so near. She forced herself to gaze at the marble.

A mistake.

The Lapith in this fragment had the better of the Centaur, even though the Lapith's head and feet were missing. His body, though, splayed across the marble, displayed the muscles of his abdomen, his ribs, his masculine parts.

Her cheeks burned, not from embarrassment, but from a sudden desire to see Ross without his clothes, to again experience the warmth of his mouth against hers. She wanted to experience that kiss again. And more.

Sensible, independent Genna wanted a man's kiss—no, not a man's kiss—*Ross's kiss*. Ross's lovemaking.

She finally understood. The sensations she experienced in Ross's presence were carnal ones. She desired him, the way her mother had desired many men.

Was she like her mother? She must be. Like her mother, she felt willing to abandon all propriety to make carnal love with a man. *With Ross*. At this moment she desired Ross more than anything. More than respectability.

More than…art.

Why not? She had no intention of living a conventional life. Artists were allowed their passions, were they not?

Ross jarred her from her thoughts. 'I seem to remember a legend about Centaurs fighting Lapiths. Something we read in school.'

She turned to him, her whole body vibrating with wanting him. 'Did you read Greek?'

He groaned. 'Not well, but it was part of my studies.'

She crossed her arms around herself and forced herself to sound unaffected by desire. 'This is likely as close as I may get to studying a man's body. Vespery told me that the Royal Academy barred women from the classes with naked models.'

'You would want to take such a class?' He sounded surprised.

'Yes. I would.' She turned to him. 'I would like to study a man's naked body—' Ross's body. 'Does that shock you?'

His gaze seemed to smoulder. 'Nothing about you shocks me, Genna.'

Did she know she was arousing him? Ross wondered. Something was different.

A change had come over her, a change that made him think of how it would be to touch her naked skin, how it would feel to kiss her again. To make love to her.

He became more aware of her hint-of-jasmine scent, more aware of how she moved, of how her eyes slanted up when she smiled.

Good God. Was he going to be able to keep his hands off her?

She gazed up at him and he caught her chin between his finger and thumb. He tilted her face so he was looking straight down at her.

'Genna,' he murmured.

She rose on tiptoe, bringing her face just a little closer.

No. Not again. Not here. He released her and stepped away.

Mr Hutton appeared at the door of the shed. 'I fear it is time, my lord, miss.'

Genna turned towards him. 'I am ready.'

They walked through Montagu House again and out

the front door where Jem waited with the curricle, just as Ross had arranged.

'Where are we bound now?' Genna asked when they started off again.

'To Vespery's, if you like.'

'Yes,' she murmured. 'I would very much like that, if you are able to stay with me.' She paused. 'For the portrait, I mean.'

He also paused before responding. 'Yes. I am able to stay.'

Chapter Twenty-One

Ross and Genna entered Vespery's studio, which, Genna was acutely aware, they had all to themselves. She put on her smock and uncovered her palette. Ross sat in the chair and assumed the pose she'd placed him in before. They said little while she painted. She felt his eyes on her, though, and it made her hand tremble.

'I have another outing planned for you,' he told her after an hour had passed. 'Are you able to make a morning call with me tomorrow?'

'A morning call?' Her brows rose. 'To visit someone?'

'Precisely.'

'Am I to know to whom?' she asked, knowing he would not tell her, that he delighted in surprising her.

'No.' He smiled. She loved how his smile reached his eyes.

She turned back to her canvas. 'What time?'

'Eleven o'clock.'

She kept painting. 'Nothing grander than the Elgin Marbles, I am sure. Nothing could be.'

'Different' was all he said.

The marbles had been so magnificent, so detailed, so beautiful and real. If only she could bring those elements to her painting. Her portrait of Ross was flat. The statues gave the sensation of skin under drapes of clothing. Or muscles and veins under skin. Surely there was a way to convey the same impression in paint.

She closed her eyes and tried to imagine the naked statues.

It was not the same, though.

'Ross, unfold your arms' Maybe if he stood differently, she could see differently.

He unfolded his arm, stretching them as if to get the stiffness out.

Still they were covered with cloth—his coat, his waist-coat, his shirt.

She stepped away from the canvas and walked over to examine one of Vespery's nearly completed portraits set on his easel.

'What is amiss?' Ross asked her.

'Mine is too flat.' She pointed to Vespery's. 'See? His gentleman has shape to him. A sense of his physique.' She put her hands on her hips and stared at Vespery's painting. 'I begin to understand why artists take classes with naked models. For that sense of the body under the clothes.'

He gave a dry laugh. 'Do not tell me you wish me to take off my clothes.'

She turned to him. 'Would you? It would help so very much.'

'Genna, do not jest.'

She hurried over to him. 'I am not jesting. I need to know what you look like under your clothes. So—so the portrait is not flat.'

His return look was very sceptical.

'Please, Ross?'

'Do not be nonsensical,' he countered. 'You saw enough naked men in the Elgin Marbles. Think of those.'

'It is not the same. They were ideal images, not real men at all.' Although she suspected he might also be an ideal.

She faced him and stood so close she could touch him.

His eyes darkened as he held her gaze.

'It is for the art,' she protested. 'So I can paint a decent portrait of you.'

His gaze did not waver. 'You propose we act indecently so you might paint a decent portrait.'

Her face flushed. 'What harm would there be? No one would know.'

Still seated in the chair, he leaned forward. 'Do you know what I think?' His voice turned to silk.

It was difficult to take a breath. 'What?'

'I think this has nothing to do with art. You just wish to see me naked.'

Her heart pounded. How dare he say this wasn't for her art? 'What if I match you?'

His brows rose. 'Match me?'

She untied her smock. 'Tit for tat.'

She pulled it off and tossed it on to the floor.

It was a game. A dare.

Ross had no doubt at all that Genna wanted to see what a real man looked like beneath his clothes. No doubt she resented that women artists were barred from such experiences. But there was something more there as well, something she did not yet understand.

She did not know her powers of seduction, how easily she could draw men to her and how easily they could take advantage.

He ought to teach her. Arm her with that knowledge so she could protect herself when he could no longer be there keeping other gentlemen away.

'Tit for tat, then.' He unbuttoned his coat and removed it.

He thought he saw a flicker of anxiety in her eyes, but she quickly recovered and stared directly in his eyes.

She removed the fichu tucked into the neckline of her dress.

He untied his neckcloth and unwound it from his neck. 'Your turn.'

He had his waistcoat yet to take off and he'd still be covered by his shirt. For Genna, her dress would be next.

She flashed a grin and kicked off her shoes.

'Coward,' he said, unbuttoning his waistcoat and shrugging out of it. He lifted his chin in a silent challenge.

'I cannot do it myself.' She turned her back to him.

He had not accounted for touching her. He unbuttoned the buttons at the back of her dress, too aware of her slender neck and her smooth skin. She pulled off her sleeves and let the dress slip to the floor.

Only her chemise and corset remained. She spun around again. 'Now you.'

He could not help his eyes sweeping over her. Her corset showed her slender waist and pushed her breasts up to their voluptuous fullness.

She twirled a finger at him, indicating he should remove his shirt.

He undid the button at his neck and pulled his white linen shirt over his head.

Genna took in a sharp, audible breath.

She reached out and touched him, very softly, her fingers cool against his suddenly heated skin. She traced the contours of his bare chest, like he'd seen her touch the Elgin marbles.

'Oh, Ross,' she whispered.

He, unlike the statues, was not made of stone. Her touch, the awed look on her face, set his senses on fire. He forgot this was a game or a lesson he was going to teach her. He was alone with her, protected from everything outside, cocooned in a world existing only for the two of them.

'Genna,' he groaned, lifting her on to his lap so her legs straddled him.

She leaned into him, pressing against his arousal, and twined her arms around his neck. She dipped her head to him and he strained to meet her, capturing her mouth with his ravenous lips. The kiss was long and lingering. Like their one other kiss, she opened to him and his tongue touched hers, soft, warm and wet. She dug her fingers into his hair and matched his lips' demand.

When finally they broke apart long enough to take a breath, Genna murmured, 'Make love to me, Ross. Please. I want you to show me. No one else.'

He longed to show her. He wanted no other man to possess her like this.

He lifted her and rose from the chair. Her chemise was bunched about her waist and her stockinged legs wrapped around him. He carried her out of the studio into a small drawing room. He sat her on a couch and unlaced her corset, slipping it off entirely. He ran his hands over her body, still covered by her chemise. He freed her breasts from the thin fabric of the undergarment and relished their soft flesh and the nipples that hardened under his touch.

'Mmm...' she hummed. 'You were right. Not the art. This. I wanted this. From you, Ross. Only you.'

He lay next to her on the couch and kissed her again, still rubbing his palm against her nipples. It seemed so right for him to make love to Genna. He could not think of another time or another woman who felt this right. He wanted to show her pleasure, a fair exchange for the pleasure just being with her brought to him.

She placed her hands in his hair again and pulled him into another kiss. He felt her hunger, her yearning resonate within his whole body.

They were surely kindred spirits, two of a kind, and at this moment they were as free as ever they would be, without anyone nearby to see. Her kiss was eager and urgent and he knew he could satisfy her urges. Why not make love to her? Why not show her? Bring her pleasure?

His lips made a path down her neck to her breasts to her nipple. He relished the feel and taste of her against his tongue. She twisted and squirmed beneath him. He backed off for a moment and rubbed her in long, sweeping strokes. She calmed again.

His hand splayed over her abdomen. She seized his wrist and guided his hand downward over her bunched-up skirts.

Her arousal must tell her where the greatest pleasure lay. He obliged her by sliding his hand lower and gently touching the soft moist skin around her most womanly place.

'Ross!' she rasped. 'Yes. Yes.'

She moved beneath his fingers and he could feel her pleasure building, building. He wanted to give her the pleasure, to feel her pleasure beneath his hand.

He found her tender spot and her voice became more urgent. 'Yes. More. More,' she cried.

He gave her more, able to feel the passion rising in her, higher and higher until her back arched and she cried out, writhing with the explosion of pleasure he'd released in her.

'Ross,' she cried as her spasm eased. 'Ross.'

Genna basked in the sensations he had created in her. She'd never dreamed lovemaking could feel so—so pleasurable and unsettling. His touch was so acutely pleasurable it very nearly was pain. Not hurting, but agonising her with wanting what she had not known would come, that— that explosion of pleasure.

She pressed herself against him on the narrow couch. 'I—I never knew a touch could feel like that, but that was not all, was it, Ross? That was a mere taste of lovemaking, was it not?'

She was not so green a girl, even if she was a maiden. She knew the barest of elements of lovemaking. She simply had not guessed such pleasure and need could be built by a touch.

She loved it. And wanted to feel it again. She wanted to feel everything about lovemaking. She tried to remember every part of this. How his lips felt against hers. How warm his tongue was. How it tasted of tea. She wanted her body to remember the feel of his hands against her skin. And how different it felt for his hands to touch her breasts, how that sensation touched off a veritable riot in her feminine parts. If she could paint this, what colours would she use?

All of them, she thought.

The cool, smooth blues blended into purple and gradually built from red to orange to a bright yellow, as bright as the sun. How would she paint such a feeling?

Like a rainbow that burst and turned into sunshine.

This very sort of sensation must have been what tempted her mother away from her father, she realised, more powerful and compelling than the mothering of children. Genna understood it a little. Right before Ross created that explosion of pleasure, Genna would have given up everything else for it.

Was she like her mother?

It must be so.

'Show me the rest of it, Ross,' she murmured. 'I want to do this with you. Make love to me.'

He kissed her, a demanding kiss, one she was delighted to accept. Who knew a kiss could radiate throughout one's whole body? Or a touch could set off such pleasurable pain? Who knew a kiss and touch could lead to a rainbow bursting? She could hardly wait to experience what lay ahead.

She unbuttoned the fall of his pantaloons, her heart racing with excitement. She would join with Ross.

Only Ross.

She thought she'd never want this attachment to a man, like her mother's attachment to her lover, so imperative she'd leave her children for it.

She gazed down and saw his male member, swollen and long and so unlike the ones on the marble statues. She wavered. Would there be pain? How could he possibly fit inside her?

His hands, so gentle now, reassured her. Ross would never hurt her. Never.

His hand did not linger this time, but it tantalised, igniting her need for that bursting of colour.

'Now, Ross,' she begged. 'Now. Please.'

He groaned and positioned himself on top of her. She

felt his member touch the now-throbbing skin of her feminine parts. She parted her legs wider and he began to push in gently, gingerly.

She did not wish for him to be gentle. She wanted him to hurry. She wanted that pleasure to explode inside her again. Now.

'Please,' she begged, feeling that agonising need.

He pushed in a little more, and more, and pulled out again.

'Mmm…' she urged, ready for more, relishing the feel of him entering her. Joining with her.

He broke away and moved off her. Moved off the couch to stand a pace away.

'No, Genna,' he cried, raking a hand though his hair. He buttoned his pantaloons. 'I will not do this with you.' He sounded angry.

She felt bereft. Deserted. 'Why not, if I want it?' she asked.

'You did not think, did you? Of what could happen? We could make a child.' He strode out of the drawing room.

She sat up, stunned.

She'd not given one single thought to the idea that she might get with child from this. Even though she knew what had happened to her brother, why he had to hurry to get married. She'd acted as if this was only about feeling good.

She picked up her corset and put it on, tightening the laces as best she could. She returned to the studio.

He had already donned his shirt and waistcoat. He picked up his coat off the floor and glared at her.

She spoke. 'I thought only of you and me.'

'I could have ruined your life,' he said.

She lifted her chin. 'If I am to be an artist, it does not matter. I will not need to be proper.'

He wrapped his neckcloth around his neck and tied it in a terrible knot. 'And how many members of the *ton* will pay to have their portrait painted by a baronet's daughter who has a bastard child in tow? How many would let you paint their daughters?'

She turned away.

All the colour had been leached away. Only the black-and-white truth remained. She could not simply do as she wished. She could no longer act as if she and Ross were in their own fairy tale.

He moved closer to her, close enough to hand her her dress. 'Do not make me the one who will ruin you, Genna.'

He despised her now. Why not? She did not like herself very much.

She donned her dress.

'We should not be together,' he said as he buttoned it for her. 'Tidy your things. Jem will not be here with the curricle for another two hours. I'll get us a hackney cab now.' He walked out of the studio.

She did not want a hackney cab. She did not want to leave. She simply wanted to perish.

The brisk air did not do a great deal to cool Ross's senses. He was still burning with desire and blazing with anger at himself. He'd nearly ruined her! He'd taken far too many liberties with her even before this. What had he been thinking?

He wasn't thinking. Probably had not been thinking since he'd met her. He'd simply craved her—why pretend otherwise? He'd come up with the harebrained idea of a pretend betrothal so he could be with her. Had he thought of where that would lead? To seduction? Ruin? Risk?

He felt as if a fog had cleared and he suddenly could see around him.

He could have killed her dreams of being an artist. He could have got her with child. What then? He'd have to marry her. She did not want that. If he didn't marry her, he'd embroil her in a scandal that would affect the rest of her life.

Perhaps he already had ruined her life by encouraging her, by coming up with this misguided betrothal. What were the chances of her—a woman—becoming a successful artist? Successful women artists were rare.

He found the corner where the hackney cabs waited and hired one.

When it pulled up in front of Vespery's door, Genna emerged, locking the door behind her. Ross jumped out of the carriage to help her inside.

She did not look at him.

When the coach starting moving, she asked, 'What happens now?' Her voice was so tiny he hardly heard her.

'I take you home,' he said.

'And, then?'

He did not understand. 'And then—nothing.'

She averted her face, then suddenly squared her shoulders and lifted her chin. 'It was not such an abominable request, you know. To make love to me. Is it not how men and women are meant to be with each other?'

'If they are married,' he shot back. 'If they are safe from the kind of scandal that will wreck a lady's life. Widows can manage it. Married women sometimes manage it. But not you, Genna. Not you.'

She went on. 'I am not going to marry. I will not be in society. Are not the rules looser for women such as me?'

'If you came from Italy, perhaps. Or France. Or anywhere besides the home of one of their own. You cannot fall from grace in the eyes of the *ton* and be acceptable to them. You know this, Genna.'

'I thought you would understand,' she accused. 'You, of all people. No one would know except you and me.'

'You and I have to face reality, Genna. Enough of these illusions.' He lowered his voice. 'Some things cannot be hidden, Genna.'

'It might not have happened,' she protested. 'I might not have got with child.'

He turned her face to him, like he had in the studio. 'What if we lost that gamble?'

She wrenched away.

They spent the last of the trip in silence.

When the coach pulled up to Tinmore's town house, Ross paid the driver and walked her to the door.

'This is goodbye, then?' she asked uncertainly.

'Yes. Goodbye,' he responded, sounding the knocker.

The door opened and she stepped over the threshold.

He called before the door closed again. 'Be ready tomorrow at eleven o'clock.'

She swivelled around to face him again. 'Tomorrow? You do not wish to cancel?'

'It is all arranged.'

She stared at him without speaking for several seconds. Finally she said, 'I will be ready.'

Chapter Twenty-Two

The next day Genna was ready early for Ross's outing. A bad idea. She had nothing to do while waiting except to think.

She'd deliberately sought to seduce him. That was the truth. She'd merely been deluding herself by saying she did it for her art. It had all been her fault and now he despised her for it.

Why he still wished to take her on this outing was a mystery to her. Their friendship was ruined now.

She had ruined it.

Consequences. The cost of keeping her head in the clouds. She'd liked him. More than liked him. He'd become the most important person in her life. Now she'd come crashing back to earth.

We should not be together, he'd said.

He'd leave her, too. After this outing, she supposed.

Her mother had left her. Her father never cared for her. Lorene and Tess and Edmund had left her, too, in their way when they married. She'd always known Ross would leave her. That was part of their secret plan. She'd cry off and they would part.

So why did it hurt so much?

She groaned in pain and rested her head on the table in front of her. She was making herself sick with all this self-pity.

The only person she could depend upon was herself. She'd known that since a child. She still had her painting.

She still would become Vespery's assistant. She could take care of herself.

Thanks to Ross. He'd given her the lessons with Vespery. He'd showed her so much more, as well.

A footman knocked at the door.

'Is Lord Rossdale here already?' she asked him. 'I'll be right down.'

'Not Lord Rossdale, miss.' He handed her a card.

The Duchess of Kessington, the card said. She glanced up at the footman. 'I will be down directly. Is she in the drawing room?'

'Yes, miss.' He bowed and left the room.

What on earth did the Duchess want with her?

She glanced in the mirror and smoothed her hair. She deliberately walked from the room at a normal pace. No good appearing before the Duchess out of breath from rushing.

When she entered the drawing room, the Duchess was examining a blue-and-white porcelain bowl. 'Chinese,' she stated.

'If you say so.' Genna did not smile. 'Good morning, Your Grace. Do have a seat. Shall I send for tea?'

'Do not bother.' The Duchess lowered herself into a chair. 'This will not take long.'

Genna sat nearby and folded her hands in her lap, trying to look calm. She certainly did not wish the Duchess to know her emotions were in turmoil.

She waited.

An annoyed look came over the Duchess's face, but she finally spoke. 'I came here to discuss something with you.'

Genna raised her brows.

The Duchess pressed her lips together before continuing. 'You cannot possibly marry Rossdale.'

'I cannot? I am betrothed to him.' Genna *would* not marry him, of course, but the Duchess did not know that.

'You are entirely unsuitable.' The Duchess leaned forward. 'I have learned that you spend your days unchaper-oned, alone with a man. That is scandalous, young lady.'

Alone with Ross? No. That could not be what she meant.

'Alone with Mr Vespery? I am taking painting lessons from him, Your Grace.'

'I know that,' she snapped. 'But it is what else goes on when you are alone with him that concerns me.'

The inference was appalling. 'Ask his housekeeper. She is always nearby.'

'Hmmph!' The Duchess scowled. 'A servant doesn't matter. This has the appearance of scandal. That is all I need to know. It is not fitting for the wife of a future duke to be so shameless.'

Genna felt her cheeks heat. With anger. 'Rossdale knows of the painting lessons. He arranged them. He provides me transport to and from Vespery's studio. If he does not object to the lessons, why should I be concerned with what you or anyone else thinks of it?'

'Because of the title, Miss Summerfield! You must think of the title. Some day Rossdale will be the Duke of Kes-sington. For five generations that title has been unstained by scandal. I will not allow you to tarnish it.'

Genna straightened her spine. 'You insult me, Duchess.'

'I speak the truth!' the Duchess cried. 'I assure you, I am prepared to do anything possible to ensure that this marriage does not take place.'

'Does Ross know you have come to speak to me like this?' He would not have sent her. There would have been no need. He knew they would never marry.

'Ross is as foolish as you are,' the Duchess said. 'We thought he was coming to his senses and then he became betrothed to you. He needs a proper lady for a duchess, not the supposed daughter of an improvident baronet.'

Supposed daughter? How cruel to throw that particular rumour in her face.

'If the scandals in my family do not concern Rossdale, I see no reason they should concern you. You have no say in his affairs.'

She lifted her nose. 'I am the Duchess.'

'But no relation to Ross.' Genna stood. 'I will hear no more of your insults, though, Your Grace. Please leave.'

The Duchess rose. 'I have one more thing to say.'

Genna held the woman's gaze and waited.

'If you break your engagement to Ross, I will pay you handsomely for it.'

'Pay me?' Genna could not believe her ears.

'I am prepared to pay very well. *Very* well.'

Genna glanced away.

Money would provide her security. It was not as if she didn't intend to cry off anyway. The joke would be on the Duchess, then.

'Do you not wish to know how much money I offer?' the Duchess asked smugly.

Genna paused a moment before facing her. 'I assure you, Duchess, no amount of money would induce me to break my engagement to Lord Rossdale.'

Because it was already broken.

Genna walked briskly to the door. 'You must now have nothing more to say.'

The Duchess huffed and strode towards the door. 'You will change your mind. I am certain of it. You will change your mind or suffer the scandal I can spread.'

Genna held the latch of the door, blocking the woman's way. 'That is an empty bluff. Any scandal you cause me will bring shame on the precious title. That is precisely what you profess to avoid.'

She opened the door and the Duchess swept out.

Genna sank into the nearest chair and put her head in her hands. She'd defended herself as if the betrothal were real, but it had never been. She and Ross had fooled everyone, but, in so doing, they'd affected everyone. They'd certainly put the Duchess in a panic.

But it had all been lies.

Ross pulled up to Tinmore's town house and spied his father's carriage pulling away from its door. Through the carriage window he glimpsed the Duchess.

That did not bode well.

He jumped down from his curricle and handed the ribbons to Jem.

Ross was admitted by a footman at the same moment Genna appeared in the hall.

'You are here.' Her voice was stiff—and sad.

He nodded, wanting to ask her about the Duchess, but not in front of the footman.

'Are you ready?' he asked.

'I need to fetch my hat and shawl.' She climbed the stairs and disappeared from view.

The footman spoke. 'Would you care to wait in the drawing room, my lord?'

'No. I'll wait here,' he responded.

When she returned, they walked out the door to the curricle. He helped her into the seat and climbed up beside her. His tiger jumped on the back and they started off.

He could finally speak. 'I saw the Duchess driving away from the town house. What did she want?'

'She wanted me to cry off,' Genna said with little animation in her voice. 'I am too scandalous, apparently, because I take painting lessons from Mr Vespery and am, at times, alone with him. That and merely being a Summerfield with uncertain paternity.'

His anger flared. 'She said those things to you?'

'Think if she knew how scandalous I truly am,' she added sadly.

He did not know how to talk to her about that. 'I am sorry you had to endure her venom.'

She shrugged. 'Her threats were empty ones.'

He could not lay all blame for Genna's bleak mood on the Duchess. He was at fault.

He'd been foolish not to realise what could happen, what could ruin her friendship with him.

Their destination was not far. A mere street north of Cavendish Square, but she did not tease him to tell her where they were going. When he pulled up in front of the town house at 47 Queen Anne Street, she still asked nothing.

He needed to prepare her, though. 'This is the home of Mr Turner. He is an artist and also a lecturer at the Royal Academy. His work is quite renowned. It is said that Canova visited here last year and pronounced Turner a great genius.'

Canova was an Italian sculptor famous throughout Great Britain and the Continent.

'Canova,' she whispered, but without enthusiasm.

Ross knocked on the door. They were admitted by a housekeeper and joined Mr Turner in his sitting room.

'It is an honour to meet you, sir,' Ross said. 'And a very great privilege to be shown your gallery.' Ross introduced Genna. 'Miss Summerfield is an artist herself, sir,' he explained. 'A student of Mr Vespery, but I wanted her to see your paintings. She has been living in the country and has not had an opportunity to see the works of artists such as yourself.'

Genna managed, 'How do you do, sir.'

'A pleasure to meet a fellow artist,' Turner kindly said. 'Let us go straight to the gallery, shall we?' As he led the way, he asked, 'What is your medium, Miss Summerfield?'

'Watercolour, mostly, sir,' she replied. 'But I am lately a student of Mr Vespery, learning to paint in oils.'

'I have done both.' He chuckled. 'I often do both at the same time.'

He opened the door to a room built on to the back of his house. The room was bright from a skylight in the roof.

Genna stepped inside and gasped.

'Landscapes!' she exclaimed.

Hung on all four walls, or sitting on the floor, everywhere she looked, were landscapes. Large ones. Beautiful landscapes unlike anything she'd seen before.

Ross had known. He'd known she loved painting landscapes most of all.

'They are not all landscapes,' Mr Turner said. 'Some are history paintings.' He took her arm and walked her over to one painting on another wall. 'Like this one. This one is called *Hannibal and His Army Crossing the Alps.*'

History paintings depicted the people involved in some event in history, but in this painting, the landscape dominated and Genna had to strain to see the people. The painting depicted a huge black storm cloud, black paint that looked like it had been dabbed on by mistake, but, somehow, the canvas conveyed the feeling of the storm and of how inconsequential even a strong warrior like Hannibal was when faced with the forces of nature.

She walked over to a sea scene. There were several sea scenes. Ships or fishing boats or men fighting a stormy seas. Each conveyed the power of the ocean and its danger.

Turner painted how it felt, just as she had in that first fanciful painting Ross had seen that day overlooking Summerfield House. He'd remembered and brought her here.

Each of Turner's paintings were emotional, each done in ways she'd never seen a landscape painted.

One pulled at her artistic soul.

'This is *Dewy Morning*,' Turner said.

It was a lake scene, pretty ordinary in its composition, but, oh, the colour! The sky was orange and purple, its reflection in the water almost pink. It wasn't real. Ross had found a renowned artist who painted landscapes that were not real, just as she had done.

And he'd wanted her to see. It made her want to weep, especially because she'd ruined everything with him.

After they bid Mr Turner good day and returned to the waiting curricle, Genna spoke, even though she could not yet look directly at Ross, 'I know why you brought me here.'

Ross flicked the ribbons and the horses pulled away from the curb. 'To see the landscapes,' he said. 'It is what you first painted. I thought you would like to meet an artist who made his name painting landscapes not unlike the first painting I saw of yours, the one with the purple sky and blue grass.'

Her heart lurched.

He knew—no matter how much she went on about portrait painting—somehow he knew what she loved most to paint. Who else knew her that well? Who else would have cared?

'Shall I drive you to Vespery's studio?' he asked. 'I will not be able to stay with you, though. I'm required to do an errand for my father.'

She suspected he no longer wanted to stay with her. She felt a pang of pain, like a sabre slashing into her chest.

What she really wanted to do was return to her bedchamber and weep into her pillows.

'Take me to Vespery's,' she said instead. 'I want to paint.'

She wanted to finish his portrait even though it felt like she'd already run out of time to do so.

Ross drove her to Vespery's and escorted her inside, despite her protest that it was unnecessary. She did not wish to be in his presence at the place of her greatest pleasure and worst mistake, but he insisted and she endured it, watching his gaze wander to the couch in the drawing room and quickly look away.

'Will you be all right here alone?' he asked.

'I am used to being alone,' she replied, although, in truth, there were usually people around her.

He glanced around the room again. 'I'll pick you up at the usual time, then?'

'Yes. Thank you, Ross.' Her voice was tight.

He nodded. 'Goodbye, then, Genna.'

'Goodbye, Ross.'

He walked towards the door.

'Ross?'

He turned back to her.

'Thank you for taking me to call upon Mr Turner.'

He stared directly into her eyes. 'It was my pleasure, Genna.'

When he left, she dropped her shawl on a chair and removed her gloves and hat. She donned her smock and uncovered the painting and palette. When she stood in front of the painting, it was like standing in front of him. Only the eyes in the painting did not look upon her with strain, but with something warmer.

Something she'd lost.

Chapter Twenty-Three

Ross finished his father's errand and returned to pick up Genna at Vespery's studio.

He found her ready to go, but as distant as she'd been with him the whole day. This chasm between them seemed impassable.

She spoke to him only if he spoke to her first and he struggled to think of things to say. Their trip back to Tinmore's town house was a nearly silent one.

'How fares the portrait?' he asked her.

'I've done all I can do,' she answered. 'I need Vespery's opinion.' Several streets passed before she spoke again. 'So I do not need to go to the studio until he returns.'

Ross would have no reason to see her, then, unless he invited her to the opera or some other entertainment. If so, would she even attend with him?

He pulled up to the town house and helped her out of the curricle, holding her by the waist like he'd done before. He caught her gaze, fleetingly, and saw, not her usual sparkle, but pain and regret. It pierced him like a shaft to the heart.

He walked her to the door. 'I will not see you tomorrow, then?'

Those pained eyes looked up at him. 'There is no reason.'

Before Ross could knock at the door, it opened and the Tinmore butler stood in the doorway.

'Goodbye, Ross,' Genna said.

The butler stepped aside so she could enter. Ross turned

to go, but the butler called him back. 'Lord Tinmore wishes a moment with you, sir.'

Ross and Genna exchanged puzzled glances.

'Certainly,' Ross told the man. He called back to his tiger, 'I'll be a few minutes, Jem. Just walk the horses.'

Ross entered the house.

The butler said, 'Follow me, sir.' He led Ross to the library. 'I'll announce you.'

Tinmore dozed in a chair, but woke with a start when the butler spoke to him.

'Show him in, show him in,' Tinmore said.

Ross entered the room. The butler bowed and left.

'You wished to see me, Lord Tinmore?' Ross asked.

'Indeed. Indeed.' Tinmore gestured to a chair.

Ross sat.

'This betrothal,' Tinmore began. 'It won't do. Won't do at all.'

First the Duchess, now Tinmore?

'Sir?' Ross said in a gruff tone.

Tinmore leaned forward. 'The way the two of you are carrying on, you cannot afford a long engagement.'

Ross straightened. 'Carrying on?'

'Come now,' the old man said. 'The two of you meeting every day. At this rate the girl's belly will be swollen with child by the time you say the vows.'

'Lord Tinmore—' Ross's voice rose.

Tinmore went on as if Ross had not spoken. 'I'll not have it. I demand you marry the girl straight away. None of this waiting.'

'Tinmore!' he said more loudly. 'Enough! I'll not have you speak about Miss Summerfield in that manner.'

Tinmore pursed his lips.

'We are waiting until autumn.' But not to marry.

'Not good. Not good at all.' Tinmore coughed. 'I want the matter settled now before everyone knows you are carrying on. I won't have scandal. Won't have it.'

Ross spoke through gritted teeth. 'There is no carrying on. Miss Summerfield is taking painting lessons.'

Tinmore gave him a leering look. 'Is that what you call it?' He leaned towards Ross. 'I do not want anything to spoil this marriage. I want it settled now. The longer you wait, the more I think you are not going to come up to the mark. You asked for her hand in marriage and, by God, you need to take it.'

'Certainly not under pressure from you,' Ross said.

'I've already told your father that I will vote with him on every issue, every issue, if he makes you marry now. Get a special licence. You can be married within days.'

This man was mad. What a reason to make a vote.

Ross stood. 'We wait until autumn, Tinmore.'

Tinmore smirked. 'Then I will make the girl's life a misery. No more *painting* lessons. No more parties or balls. I'll banish her back to Lincolnshire. See how she likes that.'

Ross leaned close again. 'If you make her suffer, your life will be a misery.'

He turned and strode out.

Genna waited outside the door. 'What did he want?'

'For us to marry by special licence now.' He wouldn't tell her the rest of it, the part about *carrying on*. Why upset her even more?

She walked with him. 'What did you say?'

He wanted to say that he'd protected her dream, that she would be free to live the life she chose, that he wished more than life itself he could live it with her.

'I said no.'

Ross left her then. Again.

Genna hurried back to the library, but met Lorene along the way.

'Was that Rossdale?' her sister asked.

'Yes,' Genna replied. 'He has just talked to Tinmore.'

Lorene made a frustrated sound. 'I'd hoped to warn you. I could not convince Tinmore to leave you both alone.'

'You tried?' Genna was surprised.

'Yes, of course,' Lorene said. 'He would only make things worse for you and Rossdale to interfere like that.'

'I am going to speak with him,' Genna told her. 'You may come if you wish.'

She would stop this.

She entered the library without knocking. 'I would speak with you, sir!' she demanded.

'Not now, girl, I am busy.' He was seated in a chair, the same one, she suspected, where he'd sat with Ross. There were no papers or books around him.

'I'll not be put off,' Genna persisted. She stood in front of his chair. 'I want you to know where your attempts at manipulation and control have led me.'

'Now, see here—' he sputtered.

She did not stop. 'I am not going to marry Rossdale. Do you hear? I am going to cry off. Rossdale and I will not suit.'

'Cry off?' His brows shot up. 'Oh, no, you are not. He will be a duke. You will marry him now, without delay.'

'I tell you we will not suit.' The previous day had showed her how unsuitable she was. 'And I will not marry a man if we do not suit.'

'Genna! Do not be hasty,' her sister cried. 'Anyone can tell he loves you and you love him.'

He'd done so many loving things for her, but she'd ruined it. Now, at least, she could do something for him— get him out of this foolish plan they'd made.

She turned to Lorene. 'We will not suit, Ross and me,' she said. 'I am everything the Duchess and your husband think of me. Too inconsequential to be the wife of a duke's heir. Too scandalous.'

Tinmore rose from his chair and waved his cane at her.

'Now you listen to me, girl. You will marry that man. I do not give a fig whether he loves you or you love him. It is a better match than you deserve. If you cry off there will be no dowry. You will not get another chance.'

She stood her ground. 'I will not marry him.'

He hobbled closer to her. 'Then pack your things! I'll not see your face in this house, not with the fuss you are making. Crying off. A duke's heir, no less. I can hear the gossip now.'

'You cannot send her away!' Lorene cried. 'She has a right to cry off.'

'She's a fool. I do not suffer fools.' He shook his cane at Lorene. 'And I'll not have you contradicting me, Wife. Enough of that talk from you.'

Genna turned to leave, but Lorene stopped her. 'You could go to Tess. You should stay in town. Work things through with Rossdale. I am certain he will want to. You are not inconsequential to him, I am sure of it.'

She gave her sister a quick hug. 'You are a romantic, are you not? Do not fret, though, Lorene. I want to go.'

Lorene faced her husband again. 'You cannot simply toss her out. It—it will reflect poorly on you.'

He waved a hand and his cane pounded his way to the door. 'She can go to Tinmore Hall, but she needs to be out by the time we return there. I'm done with her.'

When he left the room, Lorene spoke again. 'Genna, do not do this. Give love a chance. It is all I've ever wanted for you.'

She touched her sister's arm. 'A person can have love and ruin it, Lorene. I must pen a letter and pack. It is better this way.'

The next morning at breakfast, a footman handed Ross a letter. 'This just came for you, sir,'

He opened it and read:

Dear Ross,
Recent events have convinced me it is better if we
break the engagement now and that I leave town for a
while. You deserve, at the very least, a peaceful Sea-
son without interference in your affairs. Who knows?
Without me around, you might even meet a young
lady worthy of you.

Please know that you have my sincerest gratitude.
To you I owe my life and future livelihood, as well
as treasured memories of all the wonderful places
you took me. Carlton House. The Elgin Marbles. Mr
Turner's gallery. Words cannot express what it meant
to me to see those places. And to see them with you.

I realise we can never now be the friends we have
been over these last several weeks. I am to blame, but
please know you will always be my very best friend
in my heart.
With fondest regards,
G.

He felt punched in the chest.

'What is it, Ross?' his father asked. 'Bad news? Nothing to interfere with our meeting today, I hope.'

The estate manager of their Kessington estate was in
town expressly to meet with Ross, his father and his father's
man of business. Overseeing the Kessington estate was one
of the responsibilities Ross was assuming for his father.

'I'll be there,' he said.

With Genna gone, where else did he have to be?

Why did he feel as if a rug had been pulled out from
under him? This was what he had planned, after all. He'd
arranged it so she could become the artist she wished to be.
He'd pay Vespery to make certain of it. He'd had a fine Season full of new experiences, shared with her. And finally
she would cry off. He could search for what the Duchess
would call a more suitable match.

Although that idea made him faintly ill.

Very ill, actually.

He'd made a terrible mistake with this scheme he'd talked her into. He'd been attracted to Genna right from the first meeting. It was not enough that he liked her; he'd also desired her. He thought he could keep that side of him in check. He had no illusions any more. She would have defied Tinmore's pressures, as she'd defied the Duchess's. She did not break the engagement because of Tinmore, she did it because he'd allowed his desire for her to go unchecked. He'd known the power of lovemaking; she had no way of knowing it. It was because of him she'd cried off.

Now he would likely never see her again.

That thought made it hard to breathe.

He fought to get it out of his head.

He glanced over at his father. 'Did you know the Duchess called upon Miss Summerfield yesterday?'

His father lowered the *Morning Post*. 'Did she? Glad she is coming around. We all have reservations about your choice of Miss Summerfield...'

By 'all' Ross assumed his father meant the Duchess and his cronies.

'But she is your choice, so we might as well become accustomed to her.'

Well, if that was not damning with faint praise, Ross did not know what was. 'Is that how Grandfather perceived my mother when you became betrothed to her?'

His father placed the newspaper on the table, a faraway look in his eyes. 'No, but, in those days, I would not have cared what he or anyone thought.' He picked up the newspaper again. 'I was a great deal younger than you, though. I must suppose yours is a more mature choice, even if I cannot see it.'

Ross had been living a fantasy, the fantasy that he and Genna could be together without consequences. To others. To Genna. To him. He'd made everything worse.

'Do you regret marrying my mother?' Ross asked.

'No,' his father said wistfully, but his expression hardened suddenly. 'Yes. Yes, I regret it. If I had not married her, she might still be alive.'

Ross stared at him.

His father lifted his newspaper again and spoke from behind it. 'Your Miss Summerfield is made of sterner stuff, I hope.'

Genna had been honed by living under an umbrella of scandal. She'd forgone all expected roles for herself to embrace one that fed her soul. Yes, that pointed to sterner stuff.

His father put down the *Morning Post* and stood. 'Well, I have much to do today before our meeting—'

His father listed several things he had to do, but, as Ross listened, he realised most were not important. What, really, would be different if his father chose to use that time, say, to visit the Elgin Marbles? Ross suspected the Duchess's duties were like that, as well. Optional.

His father left the room. Ross opened Genna's letter again and reread it.

Chapter Twenty-Four

A week later, Genna sat on the hill overlooking Summerfield House, her wide-brimmed straw hat shading her face from the warm sun. What a contrast to the chill and snow of the last time she'd been in this same place.

She glanced down at her sketchbook. Painting Summerfield House in a snow storm was a challenge in itself, especially on this fine May day with the hills dotted with white cow parsley, blue forget-me-nots, and, like an exotic accent, purple snakes' heads.

Perhaps she should give up painting memories and commit to what was presently before her eyes. Paint what you have, not what is gone.

She turned the page of her sketchbook and started again.

It was time to stop dreaming and to face life as it was. Not as vibrant and exciting as her fanciful drawing of Summerfield House with its impossible sky and grass, but lovely enough nonetheless.

She added the colour she saw before her and a peace descended upon her for the first time in days. There was beauty enough in the world as it was. Why had she not seen that?

She stepped back from the watercolour she'd produced and decided to add one more thing to finish it, something not really in the picture in front of her.

One tiny memory could not hurt, could it?

She added a grey horse and rider, galloping across the field. The horse's mane and tail were raised in the wind and the man's grey topcoat billowed out behind him, just like it had last December.

She'd been at this vantage point for over two hours and the sun was getting lower on the horizon. It was time to pack up, although returning to Tinmore Hall held no real appeal. She was barely tolerated by the servants there, who seemed to go out of their way to let her know they resented serving her. Perhaps she would write to Lord Penford and ask if she might stay the rest of the time at Summerfield Hall. She'd be content to use a room in the servants' quarters and she'd be happy to perform whatever useful service he might require.

As she rinsed her brushes in her jug of water, something caught her eye. A horse and rider galloping over the same space in the field where she'd painted them. A grey horse. Its rider wore no topcoat, though, and he was too far away to identify.

Could it be? It made no sense that it would be.

Hope could turn fanciful, apparently.

She dried her brushes with a clean cloth and poured the water on to the ground. Packing up her paints and her rags and placing them in her large satchel, she remembered the last time she'd done this very thing. It had started to snow and he had been watching her.

She heard a rustle behind her and the sound of a horse blowing air from its snout. She spun around.

'I did not nearly run you over this time,' he said.

The breath left her body. 'Ross.'

He smiled at her. 'I came to see if you needed assistance. A creature of habit, I suppose.' He dismounted and his horse, Spirit, contently found some grass to nibble. 'I see you are a creature of habit, as well, drawing the same scene.' He walked over to her easel and examined it. 'You've captured it,' he said. 'With the real colours this time.' He did not mention the horse and rider, though, but he touched them lightly with his gloved finger.

'I still do not understand why you are here,' she said.

A gust of wind blew over the easel. Ross caught the sketchbook before it tumbled to the ground.

He did not answer her. 'Are you returning to Tinmore Hall?' he asked. 'If so, may I convey you there? There is a place I would like to see on the way back. We could talk there.'

She nodded and he helped her pack the rest of her things into her satchel. He helped her on to Spirit and climbed on behind her. She knew where he was heading.

To the folly.

This part of the estate was as overgrown as ever. Apparently Lord Penford's improvements had not yet reached here. The white wood anemone covering the barely visible path reminded her of the snow that dotted this same area last time they rode here. They came to the folly, now canopied with trees bright green with new leaves. It looked even more fanciful than it had in the snow.

Ross slid off Spirit and reached up to help her down, their eyes catching as he held her waist. She climbed the three steps of the folly and sat on the bench, dangling her feet as she had done before.

She looked up at him. 'So?'

He leaned against one of the columns. 'I missed you.'

The words were like needles. She'd missed him, too. 'That cannot be why you are here.'

He paced. 'Not entirely.' He stopped and looked down at her. 'You once were willing to take a very big chance and I would not let you. Are you willing to take another?'

'Am I willing to seduce you again?' She shook her head. 'No.'

'Not that—although I might not object this time, provided you are willing to take this other gamble.' His eyes were warm on her face and filled her with so many memories.

'Just tell me what it is, Ross.'

He sat next to her and took her hands in his. 'Marry me.'

'Marry you?'

'Take a chance on me.' His voice was low and earnest. 'I know you do not believe in love, but I do. I have felt it since I met you and it did not leave even when you did.'

She pulled her hands away. 'No, Ross. I am unsuited. The Duchess was right in that regard. I would make a terrible duchess.'

'You would make an unconventional one,' he corrected. 'And I've no objection to that. I've watched my father plan his day and discuss his activities afterwards. It struck me that most of what he does is unnecessary. I do not have to play politics all the time. I can be a duke differently than the one he is, than who my grandfather was. You can be who you wish to be, as well. God knows I do not wish you to be like the Duchess. You can paint portraits or landscapes or whatever you wish. I have no desire to limit you—'

Think of the good she and Ross could do! Perhaps they could help all the hungry people, all the out-of-work soldiers

No. Ross, perhaps, but not her. The *ton* would never accept one of the scandalous Summerfields as the Duchess of Kessington.

'I'm happy to use my rank to open doors for you,' he went on. 'And I will not require anything of you that you do not wish to do. All I ask of you is to take the chance to believe me. Believe that I love you and want you with me.'

He loved her now. Would he love her later? Or would he leave her like everyone else she loved?

'Would you answer me, Genna? Say something.' His voice sounded anxious.

She should stay safe and refuse him, but if she refused him now, it would guarantee losing him, would it not?

'I am too scandalous,' she said. Would he resent that some day? 'I have already caused scandal by breaking our engagement. I cried off. Surely the *ton* is abuzz with that news. Think what they will say if we wind up betrothed again.'

He stood and paced again. 'Do I care about that? Not a whit.' He turned and stood before her again. 'Besides, no one knows you cried off besides you and me. In the eyes of the *ton*, we are still betrothed.'

She looked up at him. 'Truly?'

He smiled. 'Truly.'

She glanced away again. 'I'm afraid, Ross. I'm afraid you will stop loving me, that I will do something odd or something scandalous, or something wrong and you will despise me for it.'

'I cannot promise to never be angry,' he said. 'Only to love you and be faithful to you.'

She thought of all the things he'd done for her. He'd known her better than anyone, even her sisters.

'Take a chance on me, Genna,' he murmured.

She rose and faced him. 'There is no one more important to me than you, Ross. No one. You have never failed me. Not once.' She took a deep breath. 'Very well, Ross. I will take a chance on you.'

He opened his arms and she bounded into them, holding him tight.

'I shall try to never fail you.' His lips caressed her ear.

'I love you, Ross.' Now she knew. Her feelings of friendship. The carnal desires. The wish for his well-being and happiness even over hers. What she felt was love.

'And I love you, Genna.' His head dipped down to hers. Before his lips touched hers, he added. 'For always.'

Epilogue

Lincolnshire—Christmas Day 1816

Summerfield House was fragrant with evergreen, with the turkey roasting in the kitchen and the flames licking around the yule log. The host and his guests burst into the hall, back from Christmas church services. Their cheeks were pink, and white flakes of snow on their hats, lashes and shoulders rapidly melted. They'd walked back from the village church, the one Genna and her sisters had attended all through their childhood. It was glorious to sit next to Tess again in the pew reserved for the Summerfields.

Almost all the Summerfields would be together to celebrate Christmas Day. Tess and Marc were staying at Summerfield House with Dell, Ross and Genna. Lorene and Tinmore were expected for dinner. No one was eager for Tinmore's company, but he was the price they would gladly pay to have Lorene with them.

Only Edmund could not be with them, which was a shame, but it was for a very happy reason. His wife, Marc's sister, was about to deliver a child in two or three months.

Other than Edmund being gone, it would almost be like it used to be.

Only better.

Because Genna was married to Ross.

People actually called her the Marchioness of Rossdale. It made her giggle.

In the hall of Summerfield House this Christmas Day, Genna hugged Lord Penford—Dell—the man responsible for this lovely day. 'Have I thanked you for inviting us all for Christmas, Cousin?'

'A dozen or so times, Genna.' Dell extricated himself from her grasp and turned to the others, who were all divesting themselves of topcoats, hats and gloves. 'I've asked the servants to have some wassail for us in the drawing room and something to eat.'

'Excellent!' Marc offered Tess his arm.

Before they had a chance to leave the hall, though, there was a knock on the door. The two footmen were already laden with coats and such, so Ross opened it.

'Lady Tinmore!' he exclaimed.

'Lorene,' she corrected, stepping inside. 'I did not expect to see you attending the door.'

He leaned his head outside before closing it.

'Lorene!' Genna ran over to her and gave her a buss on the cheek. 'Let us get those wet things off you. How did you get so full of snow?'

'I walked,' she said.

'Walked?'

'You are alone?' Ross asked. 'Where is Tinmore?'

Dell helped her off with her cloak.

'Tinmore refused to attend,' she said. 'I do not think he wished to be among my family. He tried to keep me from coming. Refused me the carriage, so I walked.'

'Goodness,' Tess said. 'Was he very angry that you defied him?'

Lorene shrugged. 'Quite. But I wanted to spend Christmas with my sisters. So I came anyway.'

'Good for you!' Genna said. 'You stood up to him.'

'We will see how good it is when I return home.' Lorene laughed.

'I do not know about the rest of you, but I am in great need of wassail,' Marc said.

'As am I,' Ross agreed.

* * *

The Summerfield sisters had a lovely afternoon together and a lovely dinner with the men most important to them. Afterwards, they all sat around the yule fire, exchanging gifts, Dell gave Lorene some piano music. He gave Tess and Genna trinkets from the house. Tess and Marc gave everyone books. Like the previous year, Genna gave them paintings she'd done. She'd painted scenes of Summerfield House, parts of the house or estate that had been special to each of her sisters. She gave a miniature of herself to Ross and one of Tess to Marc. She'd done one of Lorene for Tinmore, as well, as she had the year before. At least this one would not be thrown on the floor. Dell offered to hang it in Summerfield House instead. For Dell she framed an oil painting of the landscape around Summerfield House, showing the house in the distance.

'It is not a Turner,' Genna said, 'but I have improved since last year.'

'I do not know what the devil a Turner is,' Dell said, 'but this is quite good, I'd say.'

'It is very good,' Ross said. 'I may want to borrow it and get it accepted in the Royal Academy Exhibition.'

'I have a gift,' Tess spoke up excitedly. 'It is mostly a gift for Marc.' He took her hand and her gaze swept all of them. 'I am going to have a baby!'

'Another baby!' Genna cried. 'First Edmund, now you.'

'Lovely news,' Lorene said, rising to give her sister a kiss on the cheek.

Ross took a small wrapped box out of his pocket. 'I thought of giving Genna oil paints and watercolours, but those are her tools. She must always have what she needs. So I got this.'

He handed Genna the box and she opened it. It was a lovely diamond pendant. 'Oh, it is beautiful! I must wear it. Put it on me, Ross.'

He fastened the clasp. His fingers were warm against the tender skin of her neck and, as always, they made her body come alive. But she could wait, because she wanted to spend this precious time with her sisters and these wonderful men who had been so good to them. She could also wait, because she knew Ross would be there for her every night. She'd sleep in his arms tonight in the bed she'd slept in as a young girl vowing to make her own way in the world.

She could have done it, too. She could have made a living with her painting, but she'd found something she wanted even more.

Ross.

As it got later, Tess was yawning and Marc insisted on having her retire for the night. Dell ordered his carriage for Lorene and offered to accompany her back to Tinmore Hall. Genna and Ross were left alone in the drawing room.

'I suppose we ought to go to bed, too.' She fingered her pendant. 'I believe I shall sleep in my diamond. I do not wish to take it off.'

Ross put his arm around her and kissed the back of her neck. 'I am delighted it pleases you.'

She turned around and hugged him close. 'We should go.'

'One moment.' Ross stepped away and took a candle from one of the tables. He went to the hidden door and opened it. 'Let's take the hidden passage.'

She giggled. 'Of course.'

By the light of his sole candle she led him expertly to the hidden stairs and up to her bedchamber.

'The door is here.' She extended her hand to push the door open.

He seized her hand. 'Not so hasty.' He blew out the candle and the only light came through slits where the doors were. 'I want to do something I wished to do a year ago.'

'What did you wish to do?'

'This.' He pulled her into an embrace and placed his lips upon hers.

She could have stayed like this with him for ever.

* * * * *

BORN TO SCANDAL

To my sister Judy, my first and forever friend.

Chapter One

⁓⁓⁓

Mayfair—May 1816

The Marquess of Brentmore walked out of the library of his London town house and wandered into the drawing room.

He'd agreed to consider his cousin's scheme. What the devil had he been thinking?

He strode to the window and gave a fierce tug at the brocade curtains. Why hang heavy curtains when London offered precious little sunlight as it was? One of many English follies. What he would give for one fine Irish day.

At times like this, when restlessness plagued him, his thoughts always turned to Ireland. He could never entirely banish his early years from his mind, no matter how hard his English grandfather, the old marquess, had tried to have it beat out of him.

He stared out the window, forcing his mind back to the weather. The sky looked more grey than usual. More rain coming, no doubt.

A young woman paced in Cavendish Square across the street. Something about her caught his eye and captured his attention.

He could not look away.

She brimmed with emotion and seemed to be struggling to contain it. He felt it as acutely as if those emotions also resonated inside him, as if he again waged a battle with a fiery temperament. The Irish inside him, the old marquess always told him.

Were his thoughts to always travel back to those days?

Better to attend to the pretty miss in the square.

What was she doing there all alone, looking as unsettled as he felt? She stirred him in a way the countless *ton*'s daughters who attended the Season's balls and musicales failed to do. Foolish girls, who gazed at him hopefully until their mamas steered them away, whispering about his *reputation*.

Was it his disastrous first marriage those mothers objected to? he wondered. Or was it the taint of his Irish blood? The title of marquess did not make up for either one.

He did not want any of it. Not the Season. Not the marriage mart, certainly, no matter what his cousin said. He'd done that once and look where it had led him. No, he had no wish to be stirred by any woman, not even a glimpse of one, pacing across the street. He had work to do.

He pushed away from the window, but, at that same moment, she turned and the expression of anxious anticipation on her face cut straight to his heart.

He could see her eyes were large and wide, even from this distance. Her lips looked as if kissed by roses. Dark auburn hair peeked from her trim bonnet and the blue muslin of her skirt fluttered in the rising winds, showing a glimpse of her slim ankles.

He took in a quick breath.

She gleamed with expectation. Passion. Hope. Fear. She roused him straight from his heart to his loins, something not easily done, certainly not since Eunice soured all women for him.

Was she waiting for someone? A man? Was this to be some forbidden tryst?

Brent bit down on a stab of envy. Once he would have yearned to have such a young lady flouting respectability…to meet him.

He spun away from the window, dropping the brocade curtain again to block out the tempting sight of her.

What foolishness. Having endured a marriage from hell, he well knew how easily passion could lead to misery.

Brent marched back to the library and the piles of paper on his desk. He riffled through his correspondence. With one hand he lifted a letter and re-read the news from Brentmore. Parker, his man of business, was there taking matters well in hand.

The children's elderly governess had died suddenly. Parker had been there and was able to attend to her affairs. He'd seen to her funeral and burial, but, damnation—how much were two young children supposed to endure?

First their mother's death…now their governess?

Brent rubbed his face.

His children had suffered too much in their young lives. Perhaps his cousin was right. Perhaps it was time for him to consider marrying again. Eunice had been dead a year and the children needed a mother to watch over their care, to handle matters about governesses and such, to make certain their lives were worry-free.

Brent knew nothing of children. Eunice had taken charge of them and resented his interference. He'd been a virtual stranger to them. His brief visits to the children since Eunice's death had been almost a formality. The governess always assured him she had the children under excellent control. Who was Brent to question her years of experience? When he'd been a boy, the old marquess had left him in the care of rather harsh tutors and then sent him off to school. He hardly saw the man until he'd returned from his Grand Tour. From what he could tell, other peers were similarly uninvolved in the care of their children.

Brent pressed his fingers against the smooth dark wood of his desk. He always felt sick inside when thinking of his children and how they would suffer for the sins of their parents. Better to go back to the drawing-room window and pine over a passionate young woman awaiting her paramour, than agonise over what he could not change.

There was a knock. Davies, his butler, opened the door a crack. 'Pardon, your lordship. A Miss Hill to see you. Says she has an appointment.'

His mind went blank. An appointment?

Ah, yes. Sometimes luck actually shone on him. At White's last night, he'd overheard someone saying he had a governess to fob off on someone. No longer needed her and wanted to settle her elsewhere as soon as possible. Brent told the fellow—who had it been?—to send the woman to him today. He wanted this problem of the children quickly solved, even if he had no clue what to look for in a prospective governess.

'Send her in.' Brent put down the letter and sat behind his desk.

'Miss Hill, m'lord,' Davies announced.

A soft feminine voice murmured, 'My lord.'

Brent raised his eyes and every sensation in his body flared.

Standing before him was the passionate young lady he'd spied in the square. She took two steps towards him, close enough for him to catch the faint scent of lavender and to see that her large, wide eyes were startlingly blue and even more vibrant than the blue of her most ungoverness-like dress. Fringed with long curling dark lashes, those eyes gazed at him with the same hope and fear he'd witnessed from the window.

Up close she did not disappoint. With skin as smooth and flawless as a Canova statue, she bloomed with youth. Her rose-coloured lips were endearingly moist. Worst of all, her obvious nervousness piqued tender feelings inside him, a much greater danger to him than his body's baser response.

'Anna Hill, sir.' She made a small curtsy.

His gaze seemed unable to break away from how gracefully she moved, the expectant brightness in her eyes, the rise and fall of her chest.

She was no governess. That was apparent with a glance. She was quality, some society daughter all dressed up to impress.

She lifted her chin in a show of bravado and he broke his gaze, lowering it to the papers on his desk.

'This will not do at all, miss.' Whatever her game —attempting to compromise him into marriage or some other foolish idea—he was not playing. 'You may leave.'

She did not move.

He glanced at her again and waved her away with his fingers. 'I said you may leave.'

Two spots of red tinted her cheeks.

Damnation. He did not want to care about upsetting her.

She lifted herself to a dignified height and walked haughtily to the door. Yes, she was definitely quality.

As she turned the latch and opened the door a crack, he spoke again. 'Let this be a lesson to you, Miss Hill.'

She whirled around, arching one brow. 'A lesson, sir?'

Brent rose and impulsively walked towards her, closing the distance in a few long strides. She stood her ground, fixing her eyes on his approaching form. He put his hand on the door, whether to close it or force it open, he did not know. It brought him inches from her.

But she suddenly seemed small and vulnerable.

'You would not have gained entry, but for the fact that I was expecting a woman applying for the position of governess.' He deliberately flicked his gaze down to her breast, to intimidate her and teach her how dangerous being alone with a man could be. 'You are no governess.'

She, however, did not flinch. 'How would you know, sir, when you are not civil enough to hear my qualifications?'

Qualifications? Ha!

He touched her shoulder, rubbing his finger lightly over the cloth of her pelisse. 'You do not dress like a governess.'

She pulled her shoulder away. 'I do not know who you think I am, sir, but I have come to enquire about the position of governess. I concede I do not yet have the wardrobe of a governess.' Her lovely blue eyes flashed with fleeting pain. 'My clothes are provided by Lady Charlotte, for whom I act as companion.'

He shook his head in confusion. 'Lady Charlotte?'

She lowered her gaze. 'Earl Lawton's daughter.'

That's who it was! Brent felt like slapping his forehead. Lord Lawton had set up this interview. Good God. *This* was the governess.

It was her turn to look confused. 'Did Lord Lawton not explain my situation?'

Brent had consumed a lot of brandy that night. He did not remember much of what Lawton explained, only that there was a governess when he needed one.

'You tell me, Miss Hill.' He pushed the door shut and stepped back a more respectable distance.

She averted her gaze. 'I have been Lady Charlotte's companion. Now that she is launched in society, my services are no longer needed.'

He turned sceptical again. 'Companion, Miss Hill? You look as if you just stepped out of the schoolroom and are in need of a chaperone yourself.'

Her chin rose. 'I was Lady Charlotte's *companion*, not her chaperone. I—I've been her companion since we were children. The situation was...' she paused as if searching for the right words '...unusual.'

He folded his arms across his chest. 'Explain it to me.'

Her eyes sparked with annoyance, but she also looked on her guard. 'I was raised with Lady Charlotte. She was an only child and extremely timid. She needed a companion. To take the place of an older sister, so to speak.' She locked her gaze with his. 'I also must tell you that I was— am—the daughter of Lord Lawton's servants. My mother is a laundress and my father a groom.'

Brent shrugged. His lineage was nearly as undesirable. His mother had been as poor as an Irish woman could be. Brent had spent his early years on his Irish grandfather's tenant farm in Culleen.

Until his English grandfather took him away. An uncle he'd not known existed died and suddenly Brent was heir to a title he'd known nothing of and sent to a land he'd considered the enemy's.

'I was raised as a lady,' Miss Hill went on. 'I studied the same lessons as Lady Charlotte. Learned everything she learned.' She reached in the pocket of her pelisse and withdrew a paper. She handed it to him. 'I have written it out.'

His fingers grazed hers as he took the paper. He noticed that her glove was carefully mended.

He pretended to read, then glanced back at her. His bare fingers still registered the soft texture of her glove. 'My apologies, Miss Hill.'

She straightened her spine, as imperious as a lady patroness of Almack's.

Her neck, so erect and slim, begged for his fingers to measure its length. In fact, his fingers wished to continue lower to the swell of her breasts—

'Why do you regard me so?' Her voice quivered slightly.

Good God, he'd been contemplating seduction.

Why did this beauty wish to bury herself in the thankless job of governess? Surely she knew the perils that befell a young woman in the employ of the wealthy and privileged. A governess had neither the protection of the other servants, nor that of society. She would be prey for any man who wished to seduce her.

He shut his eyes and turned to the bookshelves, fingering the bindings. 'My apologies once more, Miss Hill. I fail to understand how a young woman of your—' he turned back to her, involuntarily flicking another full-length gaze '—particular disposition would seek the position of governess.'

Her eyebrows rose in a look of superiority. 'Do you doubt my ability to perform the task?'

He admired her bravery much more than was prudent. 'You are very young.'

Seating himself on a chair by the library window, he stretched out his legs and crossed them at the ankle.

Her chin lifted again. 'My youth is an asset, Lord Brentmore.'

He frowned. 'Precisely how old are you?'

She pursed her lips. 'I am twenty.'

'So old as that.' He spoke with sarcasm.

She took a step towards him. 'My youth shall lend energy to the education of my charges.'

He tapped on the arm of the chair. The previous governess had been ancient. Retaining her had been a terrible error. Would hiring one so young also be a mistake?

'I shall understand the children better,' she went on. 'I well recall the mischief of young children.'

He narrowed his eyes. 'I do not need a governess who would join them in mischief.'

'I would not!' His insinuation obviously irritated her. 'I am a most sober young lady.'

He stood and moved close to her again, close enough for his skin to warm from the proximity.

'Tell me more, Miss Hill.' His voice turned low.

She backed away, her hand fluttering to her hair, trying to brush a tendril off her cheek. 'I know I am not a lady, precisely, but I was trained in the same way. I received every advantage....' Her voice trailed off.

Curse him. He needed to keep his distance.

She took another breath. 'There is another reason to engage me, sir.'

'Pray tell,' he said.

She looked him in the eye. 'I have an acute appreciation of learning, my lord. My unique situation——that of one who would never otherwise be so educated——makes me appreciate the advantage. It has opened the world to me.' She swept her arm towards the walls covered with leather-bound books. 'I would show your children the world.'

For the first time, her face filled with sincere pleasure. It touched something deep within him, something he needed to keep buried. 'You would create a bluestocking.'

'Indeed not,' she snapped. 'I would create a lady.' She pointed to the paper she'd handed him. 'I learned all the feminine arts. Stitchery, watercolours, the pianoforte. Manners and comportment and dancing, as well.' She jabbed her finger at her list. 'I also have skills in mathematics and Latin, so I am well able to help prepare a boy for Eton...' Her voice trailed off as if she feared she'd said too much. Her eyes pleaded. 'I would please you, my lord. I am certain I would.'

He forced his gaze downwards, as hungry as a starving man for some of that youthful passion. Lawd. He was only thirty-three, but, at this moment, he felt like Methuselah.

The children deserved a proper education. A proper upbringing. He tapped a finger against his leg.

More than that, his children deserved some joy. The children were innocents, even if they embodied all his failures and mistakes. Let this governess—this breath of spring air—be a gift to them.

What's more, she would be in a household where no man would take advantage of her. It was not as if he would be tempted. He hated Brentmore Hall and spent as little time there as possible.

He allowed his gaze to wander along the bookshelves, less dangerous than looking again into those hopeful eyes.

'You need not attire yourself in drab greys,' he finally said. It would be a shame to conceal all that loveliness under high necklines and long sleeves. 'Your present wardrobe should suffice.'

'I do not understand.' Her voice turned breathy. 'Do you mean—I have the position?'

He swallowed. 'Yes, Miss Hill. You have the position.'

She gasped. 'My lord! You will not regret this, I assure you.'

Her relief was palpable and the smile that broke out on her face made his insides clench.

He cleared his throat. 'You will make yourself ready to assume your duties within the week.'

Her eyes glittered with sudden tears, and his arms flinched with an impulse to hold her and reassure her that all would be well, that she had nothing to worry about.

'I will be ready, sir.' Even her voice rasped with emotion.

He had to glance away. 'I will send word to Lord Lawton that I have hired you.'

Anna blinked away relieved tears furious at herself for allowing her emotions to overrun her at this important moment. She wanted—needed—to remain strong or risk the chance that this marquess would again change his mind.

She'd not imagined him to be so formidable, nor so tall. And young. She'd thought he'd be like the gentlemen who called upon Lord and Lady Lawton, shorter than herself, with rounded bellies, and at least ten years older than the marquess. His eyes, as dark as the hair that curled at the nape of his neck and framed his face, unnerved her. Her legs trembled each time he looked at her with those disquieting eyes. Especially when he dismissed her without even allowing her to speak. At that moment she'd been sure all was lost.

What would she have done? Lord Lawton had made it clear there were limits to the assistance he'd render to help her find employment. And there was no one else she could turn to in London. Her parents and all the other people she knew were back at Lawton.

But the marquess had hired her! Even after she'd lost her temper with him. Even after that speech of hers about her esteem of learning.

Hopefully her love of learning would be enough to make her a governess, because she possessed no other qualifications for the job.

'Well.' She struggled for what to say next. 'Excellent.'

His brows lowered again.

Oh, my. What if he changed his mind?

She cleared her throat, groping for an idea of what a

governess ought to ask. 'May I ask about the children? How many will be in my charge and—and to whom do I answer regarding their care?'

That sounded sufficiently like a governess.

He frowned, as if her question vexed him. 'Two, only.'

She tried a smile. 'Their ages?'

He averted his gaze. 'My son is about seven. My... daughter, five.'

'Lovely ages.' Two children did not sound terribly daunting, especially two so young. 'And are they at Brentmore Hall?'

She and Charlotte had looked in the *Topography of Great Britain* and an old volume of *Debrett's* in the Lawtons' library to learn about this marquess. They knew the marquess's wife died a little over a year ago, but all else they discovered was that the marquess's manor house, Brentmore Hall, was in Essex.

'Of course they are at Brentmore,' he snapped. 'Where else would they be?'

Did that question offend him? Conversing with him was like walking on eggs.

He paced like a panther, a huge wild cat she and Charlotte saw once at the Tower of London. That black cat had prowled its cage, back and forth, back and forth, lethally dangerous and yearning to escape.

This marquess's hair was as dark as a panther's. As were his eyes. When he moved, it was as if he, too, wished to break free.

In any event, there was no call for him to growl at her.

'I do not know where the children *should* be,' she said in her haughty voice. 'That was the point of my asking. I also wish to know where I am to live.'

He waved a hand. 'Forgive me once more, Miss Hill. I am unaccustomed to interviewing governesses.'

She lifted a brow.

He pressed his lips together before speaking. 'The previous governess passed away suddenly.'

She gasped. 'Passed away? Your poor children!' First their mother, then their governess? She felt a wave of tenderness for them. It seemed a lot for two little children to bear.

He stared at her again and some emotion flitted through those black eyes. Precisely what emotion, she could not tell.

'How are they managing?' she asked.

'Managing?' He seemed surprised at her question. 'Tolerably well, Parker says.'

'Parker?'

'My man of business,' he explained. 'Fortunately he happened to be at Brentmore and has taken care of everything.'

'You have not seen the children?' How appalling.

His eyes narrowed. 'Not since this happened. Not for a few months.'

She clamped her mouth shut. It seemed the only way to control it. Charlotte's governess used to tell Anna to mind her tongue and never forget her station. It had always confused her, because she was also supposed to show Charlotte how to speak up and be bold.

She changed the subject. 'Will I answer to your man of business, then?'

Oh, dear. Did he hear the disapproval in her tone?

'You will answer to me.' He fixed his panther eyes on her again. 'In daily matters you will be in total charge of the children. You will decide their needs and their care. The other servants will defer to you in matters regarding them.'

Her eyes widened.

His expression turned stern. 'If you are not up to the task, tell me now, Miss Hill.'

She could still lose this position.

She took a breath. 'I am up to the task, my lord. I merely felt it wise to know the extent of my responsibility.'

He held her captive with his eyes, which turned unexpectedly sad. 'Provide my children what they need. Make them happy.'

For a moment it was as if a mask dropped from his face and she glimpsed a man in agony.

This glimpse shook her more than the pacing panther.

'I shall try my best,' she whispered.

'We are done, Miss Hill. I will send word to you when you are to leave for Brentmore.' He turned away and prowled to the door.

She remembered to curtsy, but he did not see her. He left the room and a moment later the butler appeared to escort her to the hall. Once in the hall, the butler walked her to the door and opened it.

She was about to step across the threshold when the marquess's voice stopped her. 'Do not leave.' He stood on the marble staircase, looking down on her.

Her anxiety returned. Perhaps he had reconsidered.

'It is raining,' he said.

The rain was pouring in sheets outside.

'I do not mind the rain,' she assured him.

'You will be soaked within minutes.' He descended the stairs and walked directly towards her.

Her fingers fluttered. 'It is of no consequence.'

'I will call my carriage for you.' The marquess gestured towards the open door.

Her hand flew to her throat. 'That is much too much trouble, sir. If you insist, I will borrow an umbrella—'

He cut her off. 'An umbrella will be useless.' Again he

stared at her and did not speak right away. 'I must go out. Very soon.'

The butler made a surprised sound.

The marquess shot him a sharp glance and turned his panther gaze back to Anna. 'Wait a few moments. I will drop you off on my way.'

Ride with him in the carriage? Enter the panther cage? She could not refuse. He all but demanded it.

She curtsied again. 'Thank you, sir. It is beyond generous of you.'

'Shall the young lady wait in the drawing room, my lord?' the butler asked, closing the door.

'Yes.' Lord Brentmore turned back to the stairs.

'Very good, sir.' The butler bowed curtly.

He led Anna to a beautifully furnished drawing room on the same level as the hall. Its brocade-upholstered sofas and crystal and porcelain spoke of opulence. One wall held a huge family portrait from a generation ago. A Gainsborough? It certainly appeared to be. She and Charlotte had seen engravings of Gainsborough's portraits.

There was even a fire lit in the room, taking away the early spring chill.

'Do sit, Miss Hill,' the butler intoned.

She lowered herself into a chair by the fire and listened to the ticking of the mantel clock as she waited.

Twenty minutes later Brent was informed that the carriage waited outside. He donned his topcoat and hat, and had Davies collect Miss Hill.

He was putting on his gloves when Davies led Miss Hill back to the hall. Brent nodded to her and Davies escorted her to the door where footmen waited with umbrellas. One walked her to the carriage and helped her inside.

When Brent climbed in, she had taken the backward-facing seat, which meant he could not avoid watching her the whole trip.

She sat with graceful poise, her hands folded in her lap.

The carriage started moving.

He ought to engage her in polite conversation but, in such intimate quarters, he could not trust what might escape his mouth.

Finally it was she who spoke. 'This is kind of you, sir. I am certain it takes you out of your way.'

He shrugged. 'Not too far out of the way.'

Lord Lawton's town house was on Mount Street, not more than a mile from Cavendish Square.

While the carriage crossed the distance, she looked out the window, but glanced his way occasionally. He could not keep his eyes off her, although he tried. When she caught him gazing at her, she smiled politely. He pined to see that genuine smile, the one that burst from her when she realised he had hired her.

The carriage reached Mount Street and stopped at the Lawton town house. One of the marquess's footmen put the stairs down and opened the door, his umbrella ready to shelter her. The footman assisted her from the carriage.

She turned back to Brent. 'Thank you again, my lord. I will await word from you when I should leave for Essex.'

He inclined his head. 'I will see you are informed as soon as possible.'

'I shall be ready.' She smiled again, a hint of her sunshine in this one. 'Good day, sir.'

He watched as the footman escorted Miss Hill to the door of the Lawtons' town house. Even hurrying through the rain, she made an alluring picture. He watched until she disappeared behind the town house door.

He groaned.

It was a good thing she'd be on her way to Brentmore in a few days.

The coachman knocked at the window. Brent leaned forwards to open it.

'Where to next, sir?' the man asked.

'Home,' Brent said.

'Home?' His coachman probably thought Brent was addled.

And the man would be dead accurate if he did.

Brent had ordered his carriage, his coachman, footmen and horses out in the pouring rain. All to carry a governess one mile.

He was addled all right.

'Home,' he repeated and leaned back against the leather seat.

Anna glimpsed Lord Brentmore's carriage pulling away through the crack of the town house door.

Rogers, the Lawton footman attending the hall, bent forwards to see as well. 'Fancy carriage.'

'Indeed.' Anna's emotions could not be more in a muddle. 'Imagine riding in it with a marquess.'

'So, what happened with your interview?' Rogers asked.

She tried to smile. 'He hired me. I am going to be a governess.'

Rogers closed the door. 'Do I congratulate you?'

The position of governess was not an enviable one. A governess existed somewhere between servant and family, but was a part of neither. It was a rank to which Anna was very accustomed, though. Her unique situation as Charlotte's companion made her too educated and refined to fit in with the servants, but she never, ever, could be considered family. She belonged...nowhere.

She took a breath. 'Congratulate me.'

At least she would not wind up alone and penniless on the London streets.

Tears threatened suddenly, so Anna rushed up the stairs to her room, which once had been a maid's room attached to Charlotte's bedchamber. Charlotte and her mother would still be out making calls. Anna had time to compose herself.

She removed her gloves, hat and pelisse and tossed them on a chair. She flopped down on the small cot that was her bed and covered her face with her hands.

It had been only two days ago that Lord Lawton informed her it was no longer desirable to have her act as Charlotte's companion. She was uncertain why. Perhaps it was because she had danced with some young gentlemen at a recent party? She'd thought it would have been rude to refuse. That was, however, the last social engagement she'd attended. Charlotte had henceforth gone on her own with only the company of one or both of her parents.

She'd not frozen or become mute as everyone feared. Charlotte had conquered her timidity, as Anna always knew she could.

Anna's days as companion had always been numbered. Charlotte was expected to make an excellent match and marry well. When that time came, Anna's place in Charlotte's life would have been lost. Anna had always assumed she'd return to Lawton House when Charlotte no longer needed her. She thought some useful role would be found for her. Lord Lawton, however, made it very clear he and Lady Lawton were terminating her services altogether.

What had she done to displease them so?

She'd never expected nor aspired to their affection, but she'd expected to be treated as a loyal servant.

At least Lord Lawton had troubled himself enough to arrange the interview with Lord Brentmore. For that she should be grateful. Instead her emotions were consumed with the idea of losing the only home she'd ever known and being separated from all she knew and cared about. Her mother. Her father.

Charlotte.

Especially Charlotte. She was closer to Charlotte than to anyone else, even her mother.

Her chin trembled.

She put her fist to her mouth and fought for control of her emotions.

This was not a banishment, even though that was precisely how it felt. It was a natural progression of change, nothing more. It had been her folly not to anticipate its possibility. She must remain strong and fearless. Being strong and fearless were precisely the qualities that had led to her becoming Charlotte's companion in the first place, a circumstance she could never regret.

She'd told Lord Brentmore the truth when she'd said her education opened up the world for her. She could not imagine not knowing about geography, philosophy, mathematics. She'd learned Latin and French. Painting. Dancing. Needlework. There was no end to all the wonderful things she'd learned at Charlotte's side. No matter what happened to her, no one could ever take away all she'd learned.

She sat up and thrust her unhappiness aside. How bad could it be to become a governess to two small children in a country house that was very likely similar to Lawton House? And as a governess, she would have an excuse to continue to study and read.

The door to Charlotte's bedchamber opened. 'Anna?'

Anna rose from her bed and walked to the doorway that separated her little room from Charlotte's. 'I am here.' She smiled at this young woman with whom she felt as close as a sister. 'How were your calls?'

Charlotte grinned, showing the pretty dimple in her cheek. 'Very tolerable. I made myself join the conversation and soon I was not even thinking about it.'

Anna crossed the room and gave her a hug. 'That is marvellous. Did you also enjoy yourself?'

Charlotte nodded, her blonde curls bobbing. 'I did! Very much.' She pulled Anna over to the chairs by the window. 'But you must tell me about your interview!'

Anna sobered. 'I am hired. I start within a week.'

Charlotte jumped out of her chair, looking stricken. 'No!'

'It is true.' Anna watched Charlotte sit again. 'But it is a good thing, Charlotte.'

Lines of worry creased Charlotte's brow. 'Maybe you should not take the first position offered you. I've heard things. People talk as if there is something wrong about Lord Brentmore. Something about his past.'

'It does not matter.' Anna took her hands. 'I cannot afford to refuse. I have nothing to recommend me. I am very fortunate the marquess agreed to hire me.'

'Why did he hire you, then?' Her tone turned petulant. 'If you have nothing to recommend you?'

'I believe he was in urgent need of a governess.' She squeezed her friend's hands.

Charlotte lips pursed. 'You sound as if you met the man.'

'It was he who interviewed me.'

Charlotte's eyes grew wide. 'What was he like? Was he as grand as a marquess should be?'

The image of the panther, restless and dangerous, returned. 'He was formidable, but I doubt I shall have to encounter him much. I will be at Brentmore Hall with his children.'

'So far away?' Charlotte cried.

Far away from all she knew.

Charlotte's lip trembled. 'I am telling Mama I will refuse all invitations. I'm going to spend every second of this week with you. It is all we have left!'

The prospect of being separated from Charlotte tore Anna apart inside. This bond between the two of them, borne of sharing a childhood together, was about to be shattered. They could never again be together like they had been before.

Not even for this last week.

Chapter Two

Only three days later Anna was again riding in Lord Brentmore's carriage, this time travelling alone to Essex, a long day's ride from London.

The countryside and villages passed before her eyes, becoming indistinguishable as the day wore on. From one blink of an eye to the next, her life had changed and each mile brought her closer to something new and unknown. With each bump in the road, she fought a rabble of butterflies in her stomach.

'This is an adventure,' she said out loud. 'An adventure.'

Such an adventure would test her mettle, certainly. She'd often acted braver than she felt, because that was what was expected of her as Charlotte's companion. She must do so again here. At Charlotte's side she'd tackled each new lesson, mastered each new skill. This should be no different. Except this time she had no instructor guiding her, no friend looking up to her. This time she was alone.

The sun dipped low in the sky when the carriage approached an arched gate of red brick. Atop the gate was a huge clock upon which were written the words *Audaces Fortuna Juvat*.

'Fortune favours the bold,' she murmured.

She laughed. Fortune certainly put her in a position to be bold.

She girded herself as the carriage passed through the gate and a huge Tudor manor house came into view. Also made of red brick, it rose three storeys and had a multitude of chimneys and windows reflecting the setting sun. Two large wings flanked a centre court with a circular drive that led to a huge wooden door where the carriage stopped.

The coachman opened the window beneath his seat. 'Brentmore Hall, miss.'

Her nerves fluttered anew. 'Thank you, sir.'

She gathered up her reticule and the basket she'd carried with her. A footman appeared at the carriage door to help her out. As she stepped on to the gravel, the huge wooden door opened and a man and woman emerged.

The man, dressed as a gentleman and of about forty years of age, strode towards her. 'Miss Hill?' He extended his hand. 'Welcome to Brentmore Hall. I am Mr Parker, Lord Brentmore's man of business.'

She shook his hand and summoned the training in comportment she'd received at Charlotte's side. 'A pleasure to meet you, sir.'

A gust of wind blew her skirts. She held her hat on her head.

Mr Parker turned to the woman, who was more simply dressed. 'Allow me to present Mrs Tippen, the housekeeper here.'

The woman perfectly looked the part of housekeeper with grey hair peeking out from a pristinely white cap and quick assessing eyes.

Anna extended her hand. 'A pleasure, Mrs Tippen. How kind of you to greet me.'

The woman's face was devoid of expression. She hesitated before shaking Anna's hand. 'You are young.'

She stiffened at the housekeeper's clear disapproval, but summoned a smile. 'I assure you, Mrs Tippen. I am old enough.'

The housekeeper frowned.

Mr Parker stepped forwards. 'The previous governess was of a more advanced age.' He gestured towards the door. 'Shall we go inside? The footmen will see to your trunk and boxes.'

The trunk and boxes contained all her worldly belongings, sent from Lawton to London so that she could carry them with her.

Anna entered a large hall with grey marble floors and wainscoted walls. A line of flags hung high above her head. A larger-than-life portrait of a man with long, curly, blond locks, dressed in gold brocade, filled one wall and one of a woman in a voluminous silk dress faced it on the other wall. The hall smelled of beeswax from the burning branches of candles and the polish of the wood.

Intended to be majestic, Anna supposed, the hall seemed oppressive. Too dark. Too ancient.

So unlike Lawton House, full of light and colour.

Another man crossed the floor and Mr Parker spoke. 'Ah, here is Mr Tippen, Lord Brentmore's butler.'

This butler was as stern-faced as the housekeeper. His wife?

'Mr Tippen,' Mr Parker went on, 'this is Miss Hill, the new governess.'

The butler nodded. 'We have been expecting you.'

Mrs Tippen spoke, her face still devoid of expression. 'You'll be weary. Come with me to your room and then dinner.'

'What about meeting the children?' Her whole reason to be here.

'Asleep. Or nearly so,' Mrs Tippen said.

'Did they not expect to see me?' She would hate to fail them on her first day.

'We did not tell them,' Mr Parker said.

'You did not tell them I was coming today?' Should the children not have a warning that their new governess was arriving?

'We thought it best not to tell them anything at all.' Mr Parker inclined his head in an ingratiating manner. 'Go ahead and refresh yourself. I will see you for dinner.'

Anna had no choice but to follow Mrs Tippen up the winding mahogany staircase.

Was she to be another surprise to the children, then? Had they not received too many surprises already, with the death of their mother a year ago and now the death of their governess?

She followed the housekeeper up two flights of stairs. 'Your room is this way.' She turned down one of the wings, stopping at a door and stepping aside for Anna to enter.

The room was panelled in the same dark wood as the entrance hall and stairway. It was furnished with a four-poster bed, a chest of drawers, chairs and a small table by the window, and a dressing table. Compared to Charlotte's bedchamber, it was modest, but would be comfortable if it were not so dark. Even the fire in the fireplace and an oil lamp burning did not banish an aura of gloom.

Had this been the previous governess's room? Anna wondered. Had the woman died here?

She decided she'd rather not know. 'This is a nice room.'

Mrs Tippen seemed unmoved by her compliment. 'There is fresh water in the pitcher and towels for you. Your trunk will be brought up forthwith.'

'Where are the children's rooms?' Anna asked.

'Down the hallway,' a young woman answered as she entered the room. 'This whole wing is the children's wing.'

The housekeeper walked out without bothering to introduce Anna to this new person. The newcomer was a servant, obviously, from the white apron she wore and the cap covering her red hair. She appeared to be only a few years older than Anna and had the sturdy good looks of so many of the country women of Lawton.

Anna felt a wave of homesickness.

The servant strode towards her with a smile on her face. 'I'm Eppy, the children's nurse. Well, I'm really a maid, but since I take care of the children, I call myself a nurse.'

'I am pleased to meet you.' Anna extended her hand. 'I am Anna Hill.'

'I'm sure I'm more pleased than you are.' The nurse laughed. 'I am also to act as *your* maid, so what can I do to assist you?' She turned towards a sound in the hallway. 'Oh, that will be your trunk now. You must be eager to change out of your travel clothes.'

Two footmen carried in her belongings, nodded to her and left.

Anna removed the key of her trunk from her reticule. 'I must change. I am expected for dinner.'

The maid took the key and unlocked the trunk. While Anna removed her travelling dress and washed the dirt of the road off her skin, the maid chattered on about how lovely the clothing was that she unpacked for Anna, the gowns which once were Charlotte's. Eventually Eppy found one gown without too many wrinkles that would be suitable for dinner.

Anna always felt a sense of irony about having a servant attend her, the daughter of servants, but she'd been accustomed to the assistance of a Charlotte's maid. As Charlotte's companion, she'd received nearly the same services as Charlotte herself, to show the timid girl that there was nothing to fear. That had been her main task—showing Charlotte there was nothing to fear.

Eppy helped Anna into her dress.

'Are the children really sleeping?' Anna asked. It was nearing eight in the evening according to the clock in the room.

'Last I checked,' Eppy replied good-naturedly. At least the maid was cheerful, unlike Mr and Mrs Tippen.

'Have the children truly not been told I was coming?' Anna straightened the front of her dress.

The maid tied her laces. 'That was Mr Parker's idea. Goodness knows what he was thinkin'.'

Indeed. The children should have been told. Charlotte always adjusted better when warned of something new.

Anna herself would have preferred to be warned in advance that the future she'd expected for herself would be snatched away from her.

After Charlotte married, she'd thought she'd return to Lawton House and eventually also would encounter someone who wanted to marry her. A scholarly man, perhaps, a man who would value an educated wife. They'd have children, she'd hoped, to whom she could pass on all that she'd learned.

Now she did not dare to look into her future. She did not dare dream. She knew now that nothing could ever be certain.

She sat down at the dressing table and pulled pins from her hair. 'Can you tell me about the children?' she asked the maid. 'I know nothing. Not even their names, actually.' Lord Brentmore had never mentioned their names.

'Well—' Eppy continued to unpack her trunk '—the boy is Cal—Earl of Calmount, if you want to get fancy. Given name is John, in case you need it. He is the older at

seven years and a quiet little thing. Next is little Dory—
Lady Dorothea, that is. Not quiet at all.'

'And she is five years old?' Anna remembered.

'That she is, miss.' Eppy placed some folded articles of
clothing in a bureau drawer.

Anna repinned her hair. 'It must have been difficult for
them to lose their governess.'

The maid shrugged. 'Mrs Sykes was sickly for a while.
You'll be a nice change for the little ones.'

She hoped so.

She stood and smoothed out the skirt of her dress. 'I am
supposed to dine with Mr Parker. Will there be someone
downstairs to show me the way?'

Eppy closed the drawer. 'One of the footmen will be
attending the hall. I expect you'll eat in the dining room.
That is where Mr Parker is served.'

The maid accompanied her out in the hall. She pointed
down the long hallway of the wing. 'I have been sleeping
in the room at the very end of the hall. The children are
two doors down from you here. Come knock on my door
if you need help before you retire.'

Anna walked down the stairs to the entrance hall. As
Eppy had said, a footman was there to escort her to the
dining room.

Mr Parker stood when she walked in the room. 'Ah,
there you are. I hope everything was to your liking.'

As if she were free to complain. 'It was.'

Two places were set at the end of a long table, across
from each other, leaving the head of the table, with its
larger chair, empty. Lord Brentmore's seat, obviously.

Mr Parker helped her into her seat and signalled to another waiting footman. 'We shall be served in a moment.
May I pour you some wine?'

'Certainly.' She glanced about the room, as wainscoted

as the rest of the house she'd seen. Were there any rooms with plastered walls and colourful wall coverings? The only attempt at brightness in this room was a huge tapestry that covered the wall behind the table's head. Its faded colours told the story of a hunt that must have taken place at least two centuries ago. The sideboard held gleaming silver serving dishes, which, she suspected, would not be used to serve a man of business and a governess.

Mr Parker raised his glass. 'Here is to Brentmore, your new home.'

It was hard to imagine this place, both grand and dismal, ever feeling like home. Home was Lawton House. And the small cottage she sometimes shared with her parents.

'To Brentmore,' she murmured.

A footman brought in a tureen of soup and served them.

Mr Parker tasted the soup and nodded his approval. Anna ought to be starving after her day of travel with only quick meals at posting inns, but sipping the soup was more formality than famish.

'Tomorrow before I leave I will make certain Mrs Tippen knows you need a tour of the house and grounds.' He took another spoonful.

She looked up at him. 'Before you leave? You are leaving tomorrow?'

He nodded. 'Lord Brentmore wishes me to return to town as soon as possible.'

Did Lord Brentmore not feel the children needed some transition? Even if Mr Parker did not involve himself in their care, he must be a familiar figure to them.

She pursed her lips. 'I suppose the marquess's needs are greater than the children's.'

His spoon stopped in mid-air. 'The children? The children do not need me here. Oh, no, no, no. All I've done is

see to the former governess's burial. She had no family to
speak of, so it was entirely up to me. The nurse takes care
of the children.' He cocked his head. 'You met her, I hope.
She was to have presented herself to you.'

'She did.' She frowned. 'Have you had nothing to do
with the children at all? Did you not speak with them and
tell them that you were attending to the burial?'

His brows rose. 'Their nurse took care of that. I thought
it best not to disrupt their routine.'

Disrupt their routine? Their governess died, for goodness' sake. That was a disruption. She'd better say no more
about that, lest she really lose her temper.

The footman brought turbot for the next course.

'What can you tell me about the children?' Anna asked.

'Not a great deal.' Mr Parker dug his fork into the fish.
'I understand they are easy to manage.'

She needed to learn something about them. 'Their
mother died, did she not?'

He glanced down at his plate. 'Yes. A little over a year
ago. It happened here. A riding accident.'

'Here?' She swallowed. 'The children must have been
very affected.'

He took a bite. 'I suppose they were.'

Anna expelled an exasperated breath. This man knew
nothing of the children. 'Tell me about their mother. Did
you know her?'

He froze, then put down his fork. 'I cannot say I knew
her. She was...' He paused. 'Very beautiful.'

That told her nothing.

His voice stiffened. 'You should ask Lord Brentmore
about his wife. It is not my place to discuss such matters.'

She thought she was discussing Lady Brentmore and
her children. Not the lady's husband.

'Was Lord Brentmore here when his wife died?' She hoped so for the children's sake.

'He was abroad.' Mr Parker took another bite. 'Finishing up his diplomatic mission.' He followed with a sip of wine. 'He did travel back as soon as he could.'

That was something, at least. 'I did not realise he was involved in diplomacy.'

'During the war and Napoleon's first exile.' Mr Parker relaxed. 'Very hush-hush, you know.'

She had a sudden vision of the marquess moving through dark alleys, meeting dangerous men. 'He was away a great deal?'

'For very long periods. I managed his affairs for him and the estate business while he was absent.' He said this with a great deal of pride.

She supposed that the marquess's absence from his children might be forgiven while he performed the King's service. Perhaps she could not expect that every father show the same sort of devotion Lord Lawton lavished on Charlotte. Anna's father certainly never showed her much affection. He'd always resented her living with Charlotte in the House, she'd supposed.

But surely the marquess must see how painful it would be for his children to lose their mother and their governess. Why had the man not come to comfort them? Why had he sent his man of business instead?

She only hoped her woeful lack of experience would not cause the poor little ones more trouble and sadness.

For the rest of the meal, Anna fell back on the conversational skills she and Charlotte had practised to prepare for Charlotte's come out. Making pleasant conversation when one's nerves were all in disorder was an achievement, indeed.

* * *

By the last course, however, all she desired was solitude. 'Mr Parker, I wonder if you would excuse me. I am suddenly very fatigued. I believe I shall retire for the night.'

His expression turned solicitous. 'Of course you are fatigued. A day's carriage ride is vastly tiring.'

She rose from her chair and he stood, as well.

'In fact,' he went on, 'I will bid farewell to you now. I am leaving as soon as the sun rises.'

She extended her hand to shake his. 'I wish you a safe trip.'

She returned to her room and readied herself for bed without summoning Eppy to assist her. After washing up and changing into her nightdress, she extinguished the candles and sat for a long time in a chair, staring out the window overlooking extensive gardens, landscaped so naturally she wondered if they had been designed by Inigo Jones.

Beautiful, but unfamiliar.

She took a deep breath and forced her emotions to calm. She must accept what she could not change.

The next morning Anna woke to the sun shining in her window. She rose, stretched her arms and gazed out her window. The sky was clear blue and cloudless and the country air smelled every bit as wonderful as at home—at Lawton, she meant. This was home now.

When a maid entered to feed the fire in her fireplace, Anna introduced herself and asked the girl to have Eppy attend her when it was convenient.

A quarter-hour later, Eppy knocked on her door. 'Good morning, miss,' she said cheerfully. 'Are you ready for me?'

Anna had already washed and donned a gown. 'I just need a little assistance with the laces.'

'Certainly!' Eppy tightened her laces.

Anna looked over her shoulder. 'Are the children awake?'

'They are indeed, miss. Eating their breakfast in the nursery.' She tied a bow.

'I am anxious to make their acquaintance.' Best to jump in right away.

Eppy frowned. 'You are supposed to tour the house. Mrs Tippen was very clear about that.'

'Do the children know I am here?' she asked.

Eppy lowered her head. 'I told them. I could not keep it secret any more.'

'You did right, Eppy,' Anna told her. 'But I'll not keep them wondering another minute. The tour of the house can wait.'

She followed Eppy to the nursery.

'I've brought someone to meet you,' Eppy called out as she entered the room. She turned to the doorway. 'Your new governess.'

Anna put on a brave smile. 'Good morning! I am Miss Hill.'

All she saw at first were two small faces with wide eyes. Both sat ramrod straight in their chairs. The little boy was dark like his father; the girl so fair she looked like a pixie.

Anna approached slowly. 'I'll wager you did not expect a new governess today.'

The girl relaxed a bit, smiling tentatively.

Anna turned to Eppy. 'Will you do the introductions, Eppy? I should like to know these children.'

Eppy hurried over.

'Miss Hill, may I present Lord Calmount.' She squeezed his shoulder fondly. 'We call him Cal.'

'You call him Lord Cal,' the girl corrected.

Eppy grinned. 'That I do, because I'm your nurse.'

'Do you know what you wish me to call you?' Anna asked the boy.

His eyes remained fixed on her.

His sister answered. 'He likes Cal or Lord Cal.'

Anna smiled at both of them. 'Very well.'

Eppy put her hands on the girl's shoulders and shook her fondly. 'This little imp is Lady Dorothea—'

'Dory,' the little girl piped up.

'Dory,' Anna repeated. She looked at each one in turn. 'And Lord Cal. I am delighted to make your acquaintance.'

Lord Cal remained as stiff as before, but little Dory now squirmed in her chair.

'What plans did you have today,' Anna asked, 'if I had not arrived so suddenly?'

'Cal said you came last night,' Dory said. 'He peeked out the door and he said you were our new governess, but how he knew we were to have a new governess, I cannot say.' Her expression turned solemn. 'Our other one died.'

Anna matched her seriousness. 'I know that. That must have been dreadful for you.'

The girl nodded.

Anna sat in a chair opposite them. 'Lord Cal was very clever to learn of my arrival and to figure out who I was.'

A look of anxiety flashed through the boy's eyes.

She faced him directly. 'I greatly admire cleverness.'

She thought she saw surprise replace the anxiety in his eyes. Eppy had not been exaggerating about him being very quiet. Up close he appeared to be a miniature version of his father. The same eyes that bore into you. The sensitive mouth. The nearly imperceptible cleft in his chin.

The same austere expression.

She smiled at him. 'Lord Cal. You look a great deal like your father.'

He glanced away.

'Do you know our father?' Dory asked, eyes wide again. She acted as if her father was some mysterious legend she'd only heard about.

Anna turned to her. 'It was your father who decided that I should be your governess.'

The girl's eyes grew even wider. 'He did?'

'He did,' Anna said firmly. She pointed to their breakfast plates with remnants of bread crusts and jam. 'I see you are finishing your breakfast. I have not yet eaten my breakfast. I wanted to come meet you right away.' She also needed a tour of the house and grounds. 'I will leave you for a little while, but I have an idea, if you both should like it.'

Dory leaned forwards, all curiosity. Cal at least turned his gaze back to her.

'I must have a tour of the house and grounds and I wondered if you would come with me. I would love to see this lovely place with you.'

Dory popped up. 'We would!' She thought to check with her brother. 'Wouldn't we, Cal?'

The boy apparently gave his sister his approval, although its communication was imperceptible to Anna.

Proud of herself for thinking of bringing the children on the tour with her, Anna left them to go in search of her breakfast and the waiting Mrs Tippen.

The footman in the hall directed her to a parlour with a sideboard filled with food. Although the parlour had the same wainscoted walls as the rest of the house she had seen, it had a large window facing east. The room was aglow with sunshine. She selected an egg and bread and cheese, and poured herself a cup of tea.

No sooner had she started eating when a scowling Mrs Tippen entered the room. 'I expected you earlier.'

Mrs Tippen's disapproval continued, apparently. What could be the source of such antipathy? The woman did not even know her.

Anna understood the servant hierarchy in country houses, having grown up in one. She knew a housekeeper would consider herself second only to the butler in overseeing the servants, but a governess would not be under her control. Was that what Mrs Tippen resented?

Anna lifted her chin. 'Good morning, Mrs Tippen,' she said in as mild a tone as she could manage. 'If there was an urgency about touring the house, I was not informed of it. In any event, my duties are to the children. I needed to meet them right away.'

The woman sniffed. 'I have many responsibilities. I will not be kept waiting by a governess.'

Anna gave her a steady gaze. 'I grew up in a house much like this one and I am well aware of the housekeeper's responsibilities. I did not ask you to wait for me, however. It matters not to me when I see the house and grounds. Name me a time convenient to you—'

'A half-hour ago was convenient for me,' Mrs Tippen snapped.

Anna held up a hand. 'You will address me respectfully, Mrs Tippen. As I will address you.' Goodness. She sounded exactly like Lady Lawton reprimanding a servant. 'I will be ready in an hour for the house tour. If that will not do, name a time and I will accommodate you. We are done discussing this, however.'

Mrs Tippen turned on her heel and left the room.

Anna took a sip of tea and fought to dampen her anger. The last thing she desired was to be engaged in a battle. She was no threat to a housekeeper. She was no threat to anyone.

* * *

An hour later Anna and the children waited in the entrance hall. Anna half-hoped Mrs Tippen would not show. In that event, Anna had already decided she'd ask the children to show her the house. She wished she'd thought of that earlier. It would certainly be more enjoyable than enduring Mrs Tippen's company.

It was Mr Tippen, the butler, who presented himself, which was hardly better than his wife. Mr Tippen reminded Anna of an engraving she had once seen of Matthew Hopkins, the witch-hunter. Mr Tippen resembled him, with his long, narrow face and pointed chin. Put him in a capotain hat, cover his chin with a beard and the picture would be complete.

He frowned down on the children.

Anna spoke up in their defence. 'The children will accompany me on the tour, Mr Tippen.'

His nose rose higher. 'The marchioness preferred the children to stay in their wing.'

'The marchioness?' Anna was confused.

'Lady Brentmore.'

But Lady Brentmore was dead. How insensitive of him to mention her in front of the children.

Anna straightened. 'I am in complete charge of the children now, am I not?'

One corner of his mouth twitched. 'So Mr Parker informed us.'

'Well, then.' She smiled. 'Shall we get started?'

Lord Cal stared at the floor, looking as if he wished it would open up and swallow him.

Dory took Anna's hand and pulled her down to whisper in her ear. 'You were *insolent* to Mr Tippen!'

She whispered back, 'Not insolent.' What a big word for a five-year-old. 'I am in charge of you. Your father said so.'

Cal's head snapped up.

The little girl's eyes grew wide. 'He did?'

'He did,' Anna repeated.

Mr Tippen began the tour in the formal parlour where hung a portrait of the late marchioness, fair like her daughter, and beautiful, as Mr Parker had said. She looked regal and aloof, and also as if she could step out of the canvas and give them all a noble dressing down.

The children, poor dears, barely looked at the portrait.

Anna directed their attention to a portrait of their father on the opposite wall.

'This looks very like your father!' she exclaimed, mostly because their late mother's image obviously upset them. Lord Brentmore's portrait, though of him younger and leaner, perfectly conveyed his sternness, but there was also a sad yearning in his eyes that tugged at her heart. His son's eyes carried that same sadness, she realised, but the boy looked as if he'd given up yearning for anything. Anna's heart bled for the child. How could she help him? she wondered.

Lord Brentmore's voice came back to her. *Provide my children what they need. Make them happy.*

How could she make them happy?

As the tour continued Mr Tippen turned out to be a competent guide, able to explain the family connections in the myriad of portraits and other paintings all through the house. He proved knowledgeable about the furnishings and about the house's history, when parts of it were built and by which Lord Brentmore.

The children remained extraordinarily quiet, gaping at everything as if seeing it for the first time. How often had the children seen these rooms? Surely they had not been always confined to the nursery.

Mr Tippen, opening a door that led to the garden, seemed to read her mind. 'As you have seen, these rooms are filled with priceless family treasures, Miss Hill. They are not play areas. The children are not allowed in them—'

Anna stood her ground. 'If you are attempting to tell me how to manage the children, Mr Tippen, you would do better to be silent.'

Dory was holding Anna's hand. The little girl squeezed it and grinned up at her.

Anna grinned back. She was being *insolent* again.

She only hoped it did not make matters worse for all of them.

Chapter Three

Brent walked with his cousin up Bond Street, heading towards Somerset Street, where Baron Rolfe had taken rooms for the Season.

'I do not know why I let you talk me into this, Peter.'

Peter's grandfather had been the old marquess's younger brother, making Peter and Brent second cousins. The two of them were all that was left of the Caine family.

Besides Brent's children, that was.

'All I am asking of you is to meet her,' Peter responded.

They were to dine with Lord and Lady Rolfe, and, more importantly, Miss Susan Rolfe, their daughter.

Almost a month had gone by before Peter again broached the topic of Brent marrying again. Peter considered Miss Rolfe the perfect match for Brent.

The Rolfe estate bordered Peter's property and Peter had known this family his whole life, had practically lived in their pockets since his own parents passed away. Brent was slightly acquainted with Baron Rolfe, but he could not recall if he had ever met the man's wife or the daughter.

'You could not find a finer woman,' Peter insisted.

Yes. Yes. So Peter had said. Many times.

His cousin went on. 'You need marriage to a respectable woman. It will counteract the unfortunate scandal that surrounds you.'

Brent averted his gaze. This was exactly what Brent had told himself before his first marriage. Eunice, he'd thought, had been the epitome of a good match.

In the end she'd only compounded the scandal.

Peter glanced around, as if a passer-by might overhear him. 'There are those who still believe your blood is tainted because of your poor Irish mother. Some claim that is why Eunice was unfaithful.'

Brent's gaze snapped back.

His grandfather had hammered it into him that his blood was tainted by his mother, the daughter of a poor Irish tenant farmer. Brent could still hear Eunice's diatribe on the subject, which had indeed been her justification for blatant infidelity.

Brent remembered only a smiling face, warm arms encircling him and a sweet voice singing a lullaby. He felt the ache of a loss that was over a quarter-century old.

'Take care, Peter,' he shot back, his voice turning dark and dangerous.

His cousin merely returned a sympathetic look. 'You know I do not credit such things, but your children are bound to hear this same gossip some day, as well as stories of their mother. These will be heavy burdens for them to bear. You need to do something to counter them or they will grow up suffering the same taunts and cuts that you have suffered.'

Peter rarely talked so plainly.

Brent held his cousin's gaze. 'My one marriage certainly did nothing to increase my respectability.'

He'd stayed away from Eunice as much as possible for the children's sake. There was no reason the poor babes should hear them constantly shouting at each other.

He'd been completely besotted by Eunice from their first meeting. She'd been the Diamond of the Season, the daughter of a peer, the perfect match for a new marquess, and she'd accepted his suit.

After marriage, however, Brent learned it was his title and wealth that had value to her. The day he'd held their newborn son in his arms, thinking himself the most fortunate man in the world, Eunice had told him how happy she was that her duty was done. Now they were free to pursue other *interests*. After that her *interests*—her infidelities, that is—kept tongues wagging.

At least the war offered him ample opportunity to stay away from her.

Unfortunately, it had also kept him away from his son.

Brent consoled himself that most aristocrats had little to do with their children, instead hiring nurses, governesses and tutors, sending them away to schools and seeing them only at brief intervals until the children were old enough to be civilised, the way the old marquess had reared him. How he had spent his early years was considered strange—suckled by his own mother, cared for by his Irish grandfather in a one-room, windowless mud cabin.

Brent and Peter reached Oxford Street, a lifetime away from the land of Brent's birth.

He turned his attention back to the present. 'Peter, what makes you think another marriage would not make matters worse?'

In no way would Brent allow his heart to again become engaged as it had done with Eunice. It had cut to the core that she'd married the title and scorned the man.

Peter responded once they were on the other side of Oxford Street. 'Marry a woman of high moral character this time. A woman whose own reputation is unblemished —nd who can be trusted to be a faithful wife and attentive mother.' He glanced away and back. 'Miss Rolfe is all these things.'

Brent kept his eyes fixed on the pavement ahead. 'What makes you think Miss Rolfe will accept me?'

'Because you are a good man,' Peter said simply.

Brent rolled his eyes. 'You may be alone in believing that.'

'And because you could be such a help to her family.' The young man's tone was earnest.

At least it was out in the open this time. Miss Rolfe needed to marry into wealth. Her father was only a hair's breadth away from the River Tick, and the man had a huge family to support—two sons and two more daughters, all younger than Miss Rolfe. Brent's money was needed to save Rolfe from complete ruin.

'Ah, yes.' Brent nodded. 'My wealth is greatly desired.'

'By a worthy man,' Peter emphasised. 'The most important thing is Miss Rolfe will make a good mother to your children.'

His children. The only reason he'd consider this idea of marriage. Brent might not see his children frequently. He might not keep them at his side like his Irish grandfather kept him, but he wanted the best for them.

'Speaking of your children, how is the new governess working out?' Peter asked.

Brent welcomed the change in subject, although it pricked at his guilt even more. She'd sent him one letter shortly after her arrival at Brentmore, but he'd not written back to enquire further.

'Fairly well, last I heard.' Was the passionate Miss Hill making the children happy? He certainly hoped so.

Perhaps he would write to her tomorrow to ask if the children needed anything that he could provide. He had no clue as to what his children might need or desire. He'd

tried to keep their lives as quiet and comfortable and unchanged as he could, knowing firsthand how jarring too
much change could be. That was why he'd left them at
Brentmore Hall, to disrupt their peace as little as possible
with his presence.

Who could have guessed their old governess would die?
He'd not protected them at all from that trauma. How difficult for them that the woman's death to come so soon
after their mother's accident.

If a second marriage could accomplish all Peter said,
how could Brent refuse? If Miss Rolfe was indeed the
paragon Peter vowed she was, perhaps she could give the
children a better life.

He and Peter turned on to Somerset Street and knocked
upon Lord Rolfe's door. A footman opened the door and
a few minutes later led them to the drawing room and announced them to the Rolfes.

Baron Rolfe immediately crossed the room to greet
them. 'Lord Brentmore, it is a delight to have your company.' He shook Brent's hand. 'Peter, it is always good to
see you.' He turned to two ladies who stood behind him.
'Allow me to present you to my wife and daughter.'

The wife was a pleasant-looking woman, the sort whose
face just naturally smiled. She was soft spoken and gracious.

The daughter had a quiet sort of beauty. Her hair was a
nondescript brown, her eyes a pale blue, her features even.
There was nothing to object to in her. Brent gave her credit
for being remarkably composed in the face of being looked
over by a marquess as if she were a bauble in some shop.

'I am pleased to meet you, my lord.' She had a pleasant
voice, not musical, perhaps, but not grating. 'Peter has told
me so much about you.'

He hoped Peter had told her everything. He'd learned

the hard way it did not pay to assume she already knew. He'd assumed Eunice had known of his early life. After their marriage when she'd learned of it, she'd been shocked and appalled.

'I am pleased to meet you as well, Miss Rolfe.' He bowed.

He ought to say something witty or charming, but he was not trying to impress. If this idea of Peter's was to work, Miss Rolfe must know him as he was. There should be no illusions.

They sipped sherry as they waited for dinner to be served. Conversation was pleasant and amiable. Brent liked that these people were very fond of his cousin and were as comfortable as they were in his presence. He was supposed to be the family's salvation, after all, but they refrained from fawning over him and labouring to earn his regard.

The dinner proceeded in like manner. He was seated next to Miss Rolfe, which gave him an opportunity to share conversation with her alone. She, too, retained her poise, although she did shoot occasional glances to Peter, for his encouragement or approval, Brent supposed.

When dinner was done, Brent broke with the convention of the gentlemen remaining at the table for brandy and the ladies retiring to the drawing room.

'May I speak with Miss Rolfe alone?' he asked instead.

'Of course,' Lord Rolfe said.

Miss Rolfe glanced at Peter before saying, 'I would be delighted.'

Brent and Miss Rolfe returned to the drawing room.

She went to a cabinet and took out a decanter. 'My lord, would you like a glass of brandy as we speak?'

He was grateful. 'I would indeed.'

She poured his glass and settled herself on the sofa.

He chose a chair facing her. 'It is clear that Peter discussed this matter with you and your parents, as he did with me.'

She lowered her eyes. 'He did.'

'I need to know your thoughts on this.' She had to be fully on board with the scheme or he would not proceed.

She raised her head and gave him a direct look. 'It is a reality that I must marry well...' She paused. 'It is also a reality that my prospects to marry well are very slim. My dowry is very modest—'

He put up a hand. 'Money means nothing to me.'

She smiled. 'Actually, money means nothing to me, either. It is far more important to me to marry a good man.' Her gaze faltered. 'Peter—Peter assures me you are such a man.'

He glanced away. 'It is important to me that you realise precisely what you are agreeing to.'

'Peter was quite forthright.' Her expression turned serious. 'I know about your Irish parentage and your wife's infidelities. I also know that you keep your word and pay your creditors and fulfil your responsibilities to your tenants, your servants, and your country.'

He felt his cheeks warming. 'That is high praise.'

She lowered her lashes. 'It is what Peter told me.'

All Brent truly did was what any decent man should do. It seemed no great thing to him.

He changed the subject. 'What of children?'

Her cheeks turned pink. 'Our children?'

Lawd. He had not thought that far.

'You shall, of course, have children, if you wish it.' He could not contemplate bedding her, not at the moment. There was nothing about her to repulse, however. He could imagine becoming fond of her in time. 'What I meant was your feelings about my children. Are you willing to take charge of them and rear them as your own?'

Her hands fidgeted, twisting the fabric of her skirts. 'If you think they would accept me in that role.'

He had no idea. Sadly, his children were strangers to him.

She spoke more confidently. 'I am the eldest of five. I am certainly well used to the company of children. I would try my best for yours.'

The words of his new governess came back to him—*I would please you, my lord. I am certain I would*—spoken with a passion Miss Rolfe lacked.

Perhaps that was fortunate. Passion must not be a part of this decision.

'Do you have any questions for me?' he asked her.

She tilted her head in thought. 'I need your assurance that you will help my family, that you will help launch my brothers and sisters if my father is unable to do so. My father will repay you if he can—'

He waved a hand. 'I do not require repayment.'

'He will desire to, none the less.'

Brent had made enquiries about Lord Rolfe. His debts appeared to be honest ones—crop failures and such. His needs were a far cry from Eunice's father's incessant demands that Brent pay his gambling debts.

Brent shrugged. 'I am well able to assist your family in whatever way they require.'

'That is all I need,' she said, her voice low.

He stood. 'What I suggest, then, is that we see more of each other. To be certain this will suit us both. If you are free tomorrow, I will take you for a turn in Hyde Park.'

She rose as well. 'That would give me pleasure.'

Brent ignored the sick feeling inside him and tried to

sound cheerful. 'Shall we seek out your parents? And let Peter know his scheme might very well bear fruit?'

She blinked rapidly and he wondered if she was as comfortable with this idea as she let on.

'Yes,' she murmured. 'Let us tell my parents…and Peter.'

'We do not need a physician!' Anna was beyond furious.

Three weeks in her new position had also meant three weeks of battling Mrs Tippen, who seemed intent on keeping things exactly as her late marchioness had wanted them.

'I have sent for him and that is that.' Mrs Tippen gave her a triumphant glare. 'We cannot have you endangering the children like this.'

'Endangering!' Anna glared back. 'The boy was running. He fell and cut his chin on a rock. He has a cut, that is all!'

'That is all *you* think,' the housekeeper retorted. 'You are not a physician.'

'And you are not in charge of the children!' Anna retorted.

From all she'd heard this woman had never expressed concern when the children were kept virtual prisoners in the nursery, rarely going out of doors.

Anna glared at her. 'If you have something to say about them, you will say it to me. Is that clear?'

Mrs Tippen remained unrepentant. 'You may bet Lord Brentmore will hear about this.'

Anna leaned into the woman's face. '*You* may be assured Lord Brentmore will hear about this! He gave me the charge of the children, not you.'

Mrs Tippen smirked and made a mocking curtsy before striding away.

Anna bit her lip as she watched the woman. Would Lord Brentmore believe the housekeeper over her? What would he think if Mrs Tippen reported that the new governess behaved in a careless fashion and allowed his son to fall and injure himself?

She and the children had been playing a game of tag on the lawn when Lord Cal tripped and fell. It had frightened him more than anything. A small cut right on his chin produced enough blood to thoroughly alarm his sister. Dory wailed loudly enough to be heard in the next county.

Anna had to admit she'd been alarmed herself. She'd scooped him up and carried him back to the house, but a closer examination showed the injury to be quite minor. She wrapped him in bandages and told the children about men in India who wore turbans for hats. Soon he and Dory were looking in a book with engravings of India and calm had been restored.

Until two hours later when Mrs Tippen informed her that the physician had arrived.

Trying to damp down her anger, Anna strode to the drawing room where the doctor waited.

She entered the room. 'Doctor Stoke, I am Miss Hill. The children's new governess.'

He stood and nodded curtly. 'Miss Hill.' The man was shorter than Anna, stick-thin, with pinched features and a haughty air. 'Inform me of the injury, please.'

'I fear you've made an unnecessary trip.' She smiled apologetically. 'Lord Calmount fell outside and suffered a tiny cut to his chin.'

'A head injury?' The doctor's brows rose. 'Did the boy become insensible?'

'No, not at all,' she assured him. 'It was not a head in-

jury. Just a minor mishap, needing no more than a ban-
dage—'

He broke in. 'Are you certain he did not pass out? Were
you watching? A blow to the head can have dire consequences. Dire consequences.'

What had Tippen told him?

She gave the doctor a direct look. 'He did not pass out
and he did not suffer a blow to his head. I was right there
beside him. He fell and cut his chin on a rock.'

He responded with a sceptical expression. 'I must examine the boy immediately.'

'Certainly.'

She led Dr. Stoke up the stairs to the nursery wing.

'How old is the boy?' he asked as they walked.

He'd not asked the child's name, she noticed. 'Lord
Calmount is seven years old.'

She led him to the schoolroom where she'd left the children with Eppy to draw pictures of Indian men in turbans
in their sketch books.

Anna made certain she entered the room first. She approached Cal and spoke in a soft, calm voice. 'Lord Cal,
here is Doctor Stoke. Mrs Tippen sent for him to examine
your head so we may be certain it is only a very little cut.'

Cal gripped his pencil and glanced warily at the doctor.

'Hello, young man!' Doctor Stoke spoke with false
cheer. 'Let me see that head of yours.'

The doctor reached for his head and Cal shrank back.

'None of that now,' the doctor said sharply, pulling off
the bandages.

Cal panicked and pushed the man and soon was flailing with both fists and feet.

'No!' Dory caught her brother's fear and pulled on the
doctor's coat to get him off. 'Don't take his turban! He
wants to keep it!'

'Lord Cal! Dory! Stop it this instant!' She'd never seen them this way. She turned to Eppy. 'Take Dory out of here!'

Eppy carried a screaming Dory from the room.

Anna pulled the physician away and placed herself between him and Lord Cal. 'Cal, it is all right. The doctor will not hurt you. He wants to look at your cut and then we will make a new turban.'

Cal shook his head.

'Are you in pain?' Doctor Stoke demanded of the boy.

Cal, of course, did not answer. He pressed his hands against his chin.

It took a great deal of coaxing on Anna's part, but finally Cal allowed her to coax his fingers away and show the physician the cut. It had stopped bleeding and looked all right to Anna. She doubted it would even leave a scar.

The doctor then tried other examinations, like having the boy follow his finger as it moved side to side and up and down. Lord Cal refused. Cal also refused to answer any questions put to him, even those that could be answered with a nod of his head.

Doctor Stoke made no secret of his impatience with the boy. He finally gestured for Anna to leave the room with him.

'Come to the drawing room,' Anna said. 'We can speak more comfortably there.'

He was grim-faced as they walked to the drawing room, a room nearly as gloomy as the man himself.

Doctor Stoke stood stiffly as he faced Anna. 'How long has the boy been this way?'

'I think he was frightened,' she explained. 'It was a surprise to him that you came and he is not used to strangers.'

The physician pursed his lips disapprovingly. 'It was a mania.'

'A mania?' How ridiculous. 'It was a temper tantrum.'

He held up a halting hand. 'No. No. Definitely a disorder of the mind.'

'Nonsense!'

He steepled his fingers and tapped them against his mouth. 'I feel it my obligation to inform Lord Brentmore that his son is lapsing into lunacy. I've seen this happen before—'

'Lord Cal is not a lunatic!' she cried.

He tilted his head condescendingly. 'Ah, but you cannot deny the boy is prone to fits and is mute—'

'He is not mute!' she responded. 'He merely doesn't talk.'

The doctor smirked again. 'The very definition of mutism. I will write to the marquess this very day and inform him of this unfortunate circumstance. I will, of course, recommend the very best asylums. I know just the place. The child needs expert care.'

Anna's anxiety shot up. 'You will not write to Lord Brentmore!'

The doctor's mouth twisted in defiance.

She had to stop this! Who knew what Lord Brentmore would think if such a letter came his way?

She changed tactics. 'I mean, this is not something for a father to read in a letter. Lord Brentmore…Lord Brentmore is…is due to arrive here very soon. You should speak to him in person. Surely there is no harm for the boy to remain a few more days at home. We…we will watch him carefully.'

Doctor Stoke averted his gaze as if thinking.

'I—I am certain it would be a good thing to meet the marquess in person. He is bound to have questions only you can answer.'

The doctor turned back to her. 'Very well. I will wait.

Two weeks, no more. After two weeks I will summon the marquess myself.'

No sooner had the doctor left than Anna hurried to the library for pen and paper. She must write to Lord Brentmore immediately and convince him to come to Brentmore Hall.

Lord Cal was no lunatic! He was merely a frightened and timid boy who needed time to emerge from his shell. He was like Charlotte had been, although Lord Cal had no doting parents to support him. Lord Cal's parents had been anything but doting.

This time Lord Brentmore must not neglect his parental duty. He must come! Anna would show him his son was a normal little boy, albeit an unhappy one. He would see for himself his son was no lunatic.

She laboured to word her letter carefully.

After three tries, she composed the letter as well as she could. She ended it with: *You must come, Lord Brentmore. You must. Your son needs you.*

Four days passed, too soon to hear back from Lord Brentmore. If he answered her right away, his letter could arrive tomorrow. Meanwhile she would do what she'd been doing since the doctor's ridiculous call. Keep the children busy.

Today they were outside again, taking advantage of glorious blue skies and bright sunshine. The weather had been cool for early June, but today the sun felt deliciously warm.

Anna dressed the children in old clothes, old gloves and perched wide-brimmed straw hats on them. She marched them outside to a small square near the kitchen garden that the gardener had prepared for planting at her request.

She and Charlotte had loved planting seeds and watching them grow into beautiful flowers, so why would Lord

Cal and Dory not like such an activity as well? Besides, they had been so confined, it would be lovely for them to get a little dirty.

She made the whole enterprise a school lesson. In the school room they had read books about how plants grew from seeds. She'd discussed with the gardener what they might plant. He had suggested vegetables instead of flowers. Boys, he said, would value vegetables over flowers.

An excellent idea! Much more appealing to the practical Lord Cal, she was sure. Plus, eventually they could eat what they planted.

'We're going to plant peas and radishes and we are going to care for the plants until they are ready for eating,' Anna told the children as they walked towards the small plot of tilled earth.

As they reached the garden plot, a man stepped forwards. 'Good morning, miss.'

Anna smiled at him. 'This is your gardener, Mr Willis.' Mr Willis, a kindly man with children of his own, had proved a willing participant. 'Mr Willis, Lord Calmount and Lady Dory.'

Mr Willis had told her that he'd rarely even glimpsed the children up to now, even though he'd worked on the estate their whole lives.

Anna's anger burned at the thought of these children living as recluses. They'd been sheltered, clothed and fed, but not much more from what she could tell.

She had a theory about why Lord Cal had ceased speaking. It was not out of lunacy—he'd stopped speaking because no one but his sister had been there to listen to him.

'Are you ready for planting, then?' Mr Willis said.

'We are, sir,' Dory replied.

The gardener handed each of the children a small shovel. He showed them two wooden bowls.

Pointing to one, he said, 'These are the radish seeds.' He put one seed in each of their hands. 'See? It is brown and it looks a little like a pebble, does it not?'

'It does look like a tiny pebble!' Dory cried.

Cal placed his seed between his fingers and examined it up close.

Mr Willis put his hand out to collect the seeds, replacing them with two other ones. 'Now these seeds look a little different. Can you tell what they are?'

Cal looked at his seed and quickly put a smug expression on his face.

'They look like old peas!' Dory said.

The gardener stooped down to her level. 'That is because that is what they are. The peas you eat are really seeds.'

Soon Mr Willis had them digging troughs in the dirt with their shovels. Next he showed them how to plant the seeds, starting with one row of peas, alternating with one row of radishes.

Soon they were happily placing the seeds in the trough and carefully covering them with soil. Anna was pleased that Cal participated in the activity with enthusiasm. She gazed at him, so absorbed in his planting and looking for all the world like a normal boy.

He needed time, she was convinced. Would his father give him time or would he lock him away in an asylum? Who was she to know better what a boy needed than a trained physician?

But she did know.

Would Lord Brentmore see his son as she did? Would he trust her to bring the boy out of his bashfulness? She could do it, she knew. She'd done it for Charlotte.

Charlotte.

Sometimes she missed Charlotte so much it hurt. She

missed talking to her, confiding in her, laughing with her. There was no one here at Brentmore to talk to. Sometimes at night she wanted to weep out of loneliness.

And yet worse than the loneliness was the worry that Lord Brentmore would discharge her for being so brazen as to tell him and a physician what they should do. What would she do if she lost this lonely job?

Suddenly a shadow fell over her and a man's voice broke into her thoughts. 'Why are my children digging in the dirt?'

Mr Willis snapped to attention and the children froze.

Anna turned and faced an enraged Lord Brentmore.

'My lord.' She made her voice calm, though her legs trembled. 'We are engaged in a botany lesson. We are planting peas and radishes.'

The children dropped their seeds and scampered behind her skirts.

'My children will not dig in dirt.' His voice shook with an anger that mystified her. What was wrong with planting a garden?

'Let me explain,' she began in a mollifying tone. 'We would not wish to frighten the children, would we?'

His eyes flashed.

She must take care. 'This is a botany lesson. Your children are learning how plants grow. We've read about it in books and now we are going to see how seeds grow into food we can eat.'

He looked no less displeased.

Her own temper rose. 'Your children are engaged in a useful occupation out of doors, in the fresh air, and are wearing old clothes which can be laundered. How is it you object to this, my lord?'

From behind her she heard Dory gasp. She felt Cal's grip on her skirt.

Lord Brentmore's eyes held hers for a long moment and she half-feared he was going to strike her.

Still, she refused to look away. It was imperative that the children not feel that enjoying themselves in useful activity was wrong.

His eyes still glittered, but he took a step back. 'Carry on your lesson, then.' He continued to hold her gaze. 'Attend me when you are done, Miss Hill.'

Before she could reply, he turned on his heel and strode back into the house.

None of them moved until he was out of sight.

'Why is Papa angry?' Dory cried.

Anna crouched down and gave the little girl a hug. 'Oh, I think we surprised him, didn't we? He probably thought Mr Willis and I were making you and Cal work like field labourers!' She said this as if it were the funniest joke in the world. 'Come on, let us finish. Mr Willis has the rest of the gardens to tend to.'

Luckily they had almost completed the task. Only two lines required seeding. The joy that had been palpable a few minutes ago had fled, however. Their father had made it vanish.

Anna put her hand to her stomach, trying to calm herself. Here she wanted Lord Brentmore to be her ally in helping Cal, and now she had offended him for planting a garden.

Would she lose her position over a botany lesson, over finding an excuse to take the poor reclusive children out in the fine June air?

Chapter Four

As soon as Brent entered the house, Mrs Tippen was waiting for him. He'd already had an earful from her when he arrived just a few minutes before.

'Do you see what I mean, sir?' the housekeeper said. 'She gives the children free rein over the house, the garden, everywhere! Allows them to get dirty—'

This he did not need. Tippen and her husband had come from Eunice's father's estate and had been Eunice's abettors. He'd never liked either of them.

He leaned down, bringing them face to face. 'Tend to the house, woman, and keep your nose out of what does not concern you!'

She gasped and backed away.

He pushed past her and made his way to the hall where her husband was in attendance. 'Bring me some brandy!' he ordered. 'In the library.'

The library was about the only room in this house he could stomach. Eunice had possessed little desire to inhabit it, so the only ghost that lingered there was his grandfather's.

A footman soon appeared at the door with a bottle of brandy and a glass. Brent did not recognise him, but then he'd come to the house so rarely, he did not know half the servants. Eunice had replaced all his grandfather's old retainers.

Brent grabbed the bottle and glass from the man. 'Bring me another,' he ordered. 'Make that two. While I am here I want a bottle of brandy in the cabinet at all times.'

'Yes, m'lord,' the man said.

Brent poured himself a glassful and downed it in one gulp. He poured another.

An hour passed and still Miss Hill had not shown herself. Was the chit defying him? She would regret it if she were.

Brent paced the room, still attempting to calm himself. The sight of his son crouched down on the tilled soil had set him off.

He closed his eyes as memories washed over him. Digging hole after hole after hole, his stomach rumbling with hunger, his bare feet cold from the damp earth. He could still smell the soil, potatoes and manure. He rubbed his arms, his muscles again aching from the work.

By God, his son had looked exactly like him.

He poured another glass of brandy.

Where the devil was Miss Hill? He needed to have this out with her.

One more hour and two more glasses of brandy later, Miss Hill knocked at the door. 'My lord?'

He'd achieved a semblance of calm, but now his head swam from the drink.

She'd changed from the plain frock she'd worn in the garden to something soft and pink. Wisps of her auburn hair escaped from under a lace cap that framed her face and only made it appear more lovely.

By God, he did not want to be aroused by her! He was angry at her. What had he been thinking to come to this hated place?

He shook himself. His son. He'd come for his son.

'Come in, Miss Hill.' He straightened and hoped he would not sway.

She approached him, a wary smile on her face. 'Forgive my delay, sir. We finished the planting and a great deal of cleaning up was required.'

He narrowed his eyes. 'Because you allowed the children to wallow in dirt.'

Her chin rose. 'Getting dirty is all a part of planting, my lord.'

He closed the distance between them, coming so close the scent of her soap filled his nostrils. 'I know all about planting, Miss Hill.'

His first ten years of life had taught him.

She stepped back. 'Yes, well, perhaps then you can explain to me why planting peas and radishes in the kitchen garden made you so angry.'

She was questioning him? She needed to answer to him. 'Heed me, Miss Hill.' He glared at her. 'My son, my—children, are to be reared as a gentleman and lady, not as common serfs.'

She did not back down. 'It was a botany lesson.'

He held her gaze. 'It was demeaning.'

She looked incredulous. 'I do not think planting a garden and watching the plants grow could even remotely be demeaning.'

He slashed his hand through the air. 'My son does not need to know how to dig holes in order to become a gentleman.'

She countered, 'But as marquess some day, does he not need to know what effort goes into the crops his lands produce? What labour? What science? That was the intent of the lesson, my lord.'

He had no answer for that. He could only think of the back-breaking work of his childhood. 'He can read that in books.'

She bowed her head and fell silent, as if thinking how to proceed. He hoped she discovered it, because his brain felt too fuddled for conversation and his emotions too disordered to be trusted.

She walked over to the window and gazed out. The sun was near its brightest and it illuminated the air around her.

He swallowed.

She turned back to him, her arms crossed over her chest—her high, round breasts. 'We waste our time talking of this. I am so grateful you have come, and so quickly, too. You received my letter?'

'Yes.' He'd dropped everything to come to his son.

Her expression was earnest. 'Believe me, my lord, Lord Calmount is not demented. He is a normal little boy who is very timid and who has been very unhappy. He cannot be placed in an asylum. He cannot!'

No one would place his son in an asylum, of that Brent was resolved.

'He does not speak.' How could he, the boy's father, not know that the boy was mute? He knew the answer to that. He'd not been around long enough to notice. His brief visits had not included conversation.

'That is no reason for an asylum!' she cried. 'He is able to speak. He talks to his sister, but only to her. Doctor Stoke thinks this is some sort of insanity, but it is not, my lord. It is most assuredly not.'

It would be too cruel for the boy to suffer insanity on top of all the other strife he'd endured. From his mother.

And his father. 'You contradict the expertise of the doctor, Miss Hill?'

'I do. I know Calmount can improve in time.' She leaned closer. 'I told you that I was Lady Charlotte's companion. When she was Calmount's age, she was not terribly unlike him. Charlotte was excessively timid. Starting when I was a child myself, I became her companion to help bring her out of her shell. I am convinced that your son is merely timid, as well. I know he can be helped.' She spoke earnestly. 'But not by sending him away!'

He glanced away. 'How am I to believe you?' God knew he wanted to believe her.

She lifted her chin and her blue eyes glittered with anger. 'Perhaps if you spent some time with your son, you would see for yourself. It has not helped him that neither of his parents troubled themselves very much about his welfare.'

His attention snapped back to her. 'I was compelled to be away.'

'Because of the war?' She shook her head. 'The war has been over a year.'

The truth of that stung. He'd stayed away as much as possible this last year.

But he refused to be scolded by a mere governess.

He rose to his fullest height and glared down at her. 'Do you presume to judge me, Miss Hill?'

A look of anxiety filled her eyes. She put a hand on her forehead. 'Forgive me, my lord. I spoke too plainly.'

He sank into a chair, feeling suddenly weary. 'Sit, Miss Hill. Tell me about my son.'

She lowered herself in a chair facing him. 'I have heard him talking to his sister, so there is no disorder of speech. But he will not speak to anyone else. In fact, Dory will speak for him every chance she gets. He hears well and is alert to everything. He is very clever, actually. He reads. He can write sentences, but he never writes to communicate. Instead, he nods or shakes his head or uses gestures.'

The poor boy. 'Why is this?'

What had happened to him, to cause him not to speak?

She hesitated. 'I must speak plainly again.'

He waved a hand. 'Proceed.'

She took a breath. 'The noise and commotion of children has been unwanted in this household. I am given to understand that your wife insisted the children remain in the nursery wing and later, after her death, the policy was unchanged and might have suited the governess because by then she was in ill health.' She paused. 'I do not know if that is precisely true. I only know for certain that... some...some members of the staff dislike having the children out and about.'

Mrs Tippen, no doubt.

She continued and her tone was accusatory, 'I do not believe that is healthy for children. That is why I plan as many activities outside as I can contrive. Like planting a garden.'

Undoubtedly she blamed him for not countering his wife's excesses, not realising the governess could no longer do her job, not paying enough attention to how his servants attended to his children's care and well-being.

His own conscience battered him for the same reasons.

'What would you have me do?' he snapped in defensiveness, even though there was no defense for his neglect.

'Do not allow Lord Calmount to be placed in an asylum!'

He averted his gaze.

Her voice quieted, but still trembled with emotion. 'I

realise you are considering discharging me, but I beg you not to. Please give me a chance, for your children's sake. Do not listen to Dr Stoke. Give me a chance—' She broke off for a moment. 'Spend a little time with the children, at least? See for yourself. Observe your son for yourself. You will see what I see in him. I am certain of it.'

Her passionate defence of his son shook him to his depths. He was not considering discharging her. Quite the contrary. He thought her the children's salvation.

'How would I observe him?' he asked, his voice still sharper than he intended. 'I will not have him paraded before me.'

'I agree.' She leaned closer. 'Go to him. Join him in the nursery. Spend time with him. The children will be served dinner soon. Come share the meal with them.'

Share a meal with children? It was not something a marquess would do, at least not until children turned twelve or thirteen.

With the excess of brandy inside him, with his emotions so raw, could he even trust himself to sit with his children? It was hard enough to sit with Miss Hill.

But he'd dropped all his obligations in London to come to his son, to learn what had happened to the boy to make a physician declare him insane. To move heaven and earth to fix it.

He clenched his fist. 'Very well.'

She rose, walked to the door and waited for him.

He hoped he could cross the room without listing to one side or the other. When he managed to reach the doorway, the scent of lavender filled his nostrils and he remembered that first glimpse of her in the square outside his town house. She was no less beautiful now. No less passionate.

And he was no less aroused by her.

God help him.

* * *

Brent climbed the stairs behind Miss Hill. Her hips swayed seductively, while she kept up a discourse about the children, explaining the structure of their days. He hoped she would not ask him to recite the list back to her. At the moment there was not much staying in his brain beyond a reminder to keep his hands to himself.

When they approached the nursery door, Brent had a sudden attack of nerves. Ridiculous. These were children. They must respect and obey him.

Good God. Now he sounded like the old marquess, the English grandfather who'd despised him.

'Look who has come to eat dinner with us!' Miss Hill said brightly as she entered the room.

The two children were seated adjacent to each other at a small table upon which were four place settings.

'Papa!' Dory cried, jumping from her seat. 'Cal said it would be you. I said it would be Eppy.'

Cal stood as well, but, after sending an angry look at his sister, appeared as if he were facing the gallows.

'Oops!' The little girl covered her mouth with her hand. 'I must not speak unless spoken to.'

She was the image of Eunice, all bright blue eyes and blonde curls. It pained him to look upon her.

He approached one of the chairs. 'Well, then I must speak and say good afternoon. And thank you for inviting me to dinner.'

Those blues eyes grew wider. 'But we did not invite you!'

He had an impulse to leave.

She giggled. 'I suspect Miss Hill invited you, did she not?'

He glanced at Miss Hill. 'She did indeed invite me.'

'I did.' She smiled, but tossed him an uncertain look.

He noticed an extra place was set at the table. She had apparently been confident he would accept.

Brent also noticed that Cal's forehead was furrowed as if he was not believing any of this conviviality.

Brent cleared his throat. 'We may be seated.'

He waited for Miss Hill to sit and noticed Cal waited as well. At least someone had taught him manners.

'Sit down, Miss Hill!' Dory commanded as she flopped into her seat.

Miss Hill lowered herself more gracefully. 'I do hope you children kept the covers on the dishes.'

Dory sent a very guilty look in Cal's direction. Cal, whose seat was directly across from Brent's, was too busy trying not to look at his father. He slipped into his chair, as if wishing he could disappear.

Brent remembered the agony of being in the old marquess's presence, the sure knowledge that sooner or later he would do something to raise the man's ire. It pained him that his son looked exactly as he had once felt.

He was not like his English grandfather, no matter how hard the marquess tried to make him so. Half of the old man's rages were on that very subject. How Brent failed to live up to the old man's expectations. How very Irish Brent was.

From a corner of the room, a maid stepped forwards to remove the covers from the dishes, starting with Brent's. His plate was filled with a generous slices of ham and cheese and one thick slice of buttered bread.

'Do you know our nurse, Eppy, Papa?' Dory glanced at the maid.

Another unfamiliar servant, Brent thought. 'I do not believe so. Good afternoon, Eppy.'

Eppy's face turned red. She bobbed a curtsy. 'M'lord.'

She uncovered Miss Hill's plate and then the children's.

Their portions were smaller and the cheese on their plates showed definite signs of teeth marks.

So much for keeping the plates covered.

He glanced at Miss Hill, curious as to how she would rebuke them.

She merely returned an amused look. 'Who would like to say the blessing?'

Brent put down the fork he'd picked up.

Miss Hill's question was directed at Cal, who visibly shrank into himself.

Dory piped up. 'I will!'

Brent could not remember the last time he'd said a blessing before eating, but the brogue of his Irish grandfather returned to him—*Rath ón Rí a rinne an roinn...*

He no longer remembered what the words meant.

Little Dory straightened with great self-importance. 'Bless, O Lord, this food for thy use, and make us ever mindful of the wants and needs of others. Amen.' She spoke the words so fast they were nearly incomprehensible.

Miss Hill smiled at her. 'Very nicely done, Lady Dory.'

The little girl beamed.

She picked up her fork and stabbed down at a piece of ham. Cal merely moved his food from one side of his plate to the other.

Brent would learn nothing about his son if he did not address him. 'Calmount, Miss Hill tells me you can read.'

Cal's eyes rose and glanced at him.

'Cal likes reading,' Dory explained. 'He reads a lot.'

Brent turned back to Cal. 'What sorts of books do you like to read?'

The boy looked stricken.

'We read books about plants,' Dory piped up.

Miss Hill exchanged a knowing glance with Brent. Dory did indeed speak for her brother.

They ate in silence for a few moments, as if they'd all caught Calmount's inability to speak. It was unbearable. Worse still, Brent's head continued to swim and was starting to ache from too much brandy.

Miss Hill broke the silence. 'Shall we tell your father what we were planting in the garden today?' She pointedly looked at Calmount.

Dory rushed in to answer. 'We planted peas and radishes and Mr Willis told us just how to do it—' She launched into a detailed explanation of Mr Willis's instructions, glancing from time to time to her brother.

Brent tried to listen, but memories flooded him. His Irish grandfather's voice rang in his ears again, instructing him on how to plant the potatoes.

The man lived only four years after Brent was whisked away from him. Grandfather Byrne fought at the side of his kinsman, Billy Byrne, in the Irish Rebellion and was killed when Brent was fourteen. Brent read about it in a newspaper account.

The pain of that loss struck him anew and, for a moment, he could not breathe. Miss Hill kept up the conversation about the garden, but sent him a puzzled look. He blinked away the stinging in his eyes.

Had he stayed in Ireland, what would have been his fate? Would he have become an Irish rebel, too? Or would the others have shunned him because the blood of English nobility flowed through his veins? He'd long concluded he could belong in neither place. He belonged nowhere.

Dory's chatter filled the empty spaces. Brent tried watching his son, but that only intensified the boy's pain. And his own.

He wanted to spare his son pain. He wanted his son to be spared the suffering he'd endured. He wanted his son to feel he belonged wherever he was.

Clearly, he'd already failed.

'Papa? Papa?' Dory's tone mimicked her mother's.

'What is it?' he responded, trying not to sound vexed.

Dory gazed at him with her huge blue eyes. 'Why are you not angry at us now about the planting? You scolded us very severely when we were in the garden.'

Calmount looked alarmed and not very surreptitiously kicked his sister under the table. Dory kicked him back.

Brent took a bite of cheese and swallowed it, giving him time to compose himself. 'I was not angry at you.'

'At Miss Hill, then,' the child persisted. 'Why did you scold Miss Hill?'

He knew what the old marquess would have done had Brent spoken to him like that. Bitten his head off and spat it out.

He refused to respond in like manner. 'I —I was mistaken…'

Dory seemed even more emboldened. 'Miss Hill said you thought she had made us into field labourers.'

He glanced gratefully at Miss Hill. 'I did indeed.' It was an excuse a child would believe. 'I thought next she'd have you selling your wares at market.'

Miss Hill smiled and Dory burst into giggles. 'It was a *lesson*, silly! To teach us how things grow. She's been reading to us about it for days and days.'

He cut a piece of ham. 'So you are not to be planting my fields?'

Dory dissolved in more giggles. 'No!'

He could follow this tack. 'Has Miss Hill started reading to you about cleaning the stables? Will I see you raking out the hay and polishing the tack?'

Calmount looked very confused.

Dory turned to Miss Hill. 'May we read about stables? I like horses very much.'

Miss Hill laughed. 'Perhaps we can read about horses and visit the stables with your father's permission, but I have no plans to teach you to muck out a stable.'

'May we visit the stables and see the horses, Papa?' Dory fluttered her lashes, reminding him too much of her mother again.

'Not today.' His tone sounded sharper than he'd intended.

Calmount immediately stared down at his plate, looking stricken.

'Maybe tomorrow,' Brent added.

Maybe tomorrow he'd have more control over his emotions.

He stood. 'I must be going. I—I have some estate business to attend to.'

'Do not forget about tomorrow!' Dory said.

He nodded towards her and turned to Miss Hill. 'May I see you in the hallway for a moment?'

'Certainly.' She placed her napkin next to her plate and followed him from the room, closing the door behind her.

She immediately spoke. 'Do you see? It is as I described.'

He closed his eyes against the sight of her, so close, before nodding. 'He seems so…so sad and so frightened.'

'Yes!' Her voice brightened.

He forgot what he wanted to say to her and his head was throbbing. 'I—I have much to do today.' This was a lie. All he needed to do was recover from too much brandy, too much emotion and too many memories. 'I will spend more time with Calmount tomorrow. I'll—I'll arrange a visit to the stables.'

'That will certainly make Dory happy.' Her lovely smile faded quickly. 'But what of Doctor Stoke? Will you see him?'

He might throttle the physician if he met the man in person. 'A letter should suffice.'

Anna had no idea when Lord Brentmore would send for them to see the stables, but she made certain the children were ready bright and early, having Eppy dress them in clothing suitable for the out of doors.

'Will Papa take us to the stables like he promised?' Dory asked as soon as Anna entered the nursery.

She swept a stray curl off Dory's forehead. 'If he said he would, I am sure he will.'

His prompt arrival so soon after she had posted the letter to him had been as astonishing as his burst of temper upon his arrival. Truth was, she did not know what to expect from him. In any event, she must believe his concern for Lord Cal was genuine. At least he'd believed her about Cal and would not even listen to Doctor Stoke. That seemed a miracle in itself.

For the moment her job seemed secure as well, which was a great relief. She was becoming very fond of the children and confident in her duties towards them, but she was lonely. She missed her home at Lawton House and especially missed Charlotte. She expected no correspondence from her parents, who could not write, but why had Charlotte not responded to her letters? Had she been so easily forgotten?

She shook these questions out of her head and faced the children. 'We will start our lessons, as always. Your father will come when it is convenient for him.' She handed a slate to each of the children. 'Dory, you may practise the alphabet. Lord Cal, I want you to write a sentence about planting radishes.'

Dory squirmed in her chair and made several pointed glances at the door while she laboured with her ABCs.

Lord Cal quickly finished his sentence and put the slate down.

Anna picked it up and read aloud, 'Plant radish seeds three seeds to an inch in a trench that is one-half inch deep.' It was a verbatim quote from Mr Willis. 'Very good sentence, Cal.' She handed the slate back to him. 'Now write a sentence about planting peas.'

He wiped the slate with his cloth and bent over it with his piece of chalk.

Anna glanced at Dory's slate. The child was only on the letter D. Too busy watching the door.

A knock sounded and the door opened.

Lord Brentmore stepped inside. 'Good morning.'

The room seemed to fill with his presence and Anna's senses flashed into alert. She could not shake the image of a panther caged as she watched him move. The very air around him turned turbulent in a manner that she did not understand.

Cal had turned quickly back to his slate. Did the boy absorb the same impression of his father as Anna did?

Lady Dory, on the other hand, seemed oblivious.

'Papa!' The child jumped up from her chair and ran to him. 'Are we going to the stables now?'

Anna's heart beat faster. Would he be in a rage again? Or would he be kind?

His expression gave no sign. 'When Miss Hill says so.' He looked at Anna. 'I do not wish to interrupt your lessons.'

Dory's look was imploring.

Anna took a breath and made herself smile. 'Well, there is no sense doing lessons with this one.' She tweaked the girl's chin. 'She can think of nothing but horses.' Lord Cal was still riveted to his slate. 'Let me see if your son is near finishing his sentence about planting peas.'

Cal wrote hurriedly and handed her the slate, taking care not to look at anyone. Anna handed the slate to Lord Brentmore.

He read aloud, 'Plant peas every two inches in a trench two inches deep.'

Anna glanced at Lord Brentmore before putting her hand on Cal's shoulder. 'Another good sentence.'

Lord Brentmore looked at the slate again. 'Yes. A good sentence.'

Cal sat very still and stared at the table.

Dory skipped over. 'Cal is *excellent* at writing.'

'I can see that.' Lord Brentmore appeared uncomfortable and Anna had the strangest sense that it pained him to be in the presence of his children.

She clapped her hands. 'Let us get our hats and coats and gloves and we shall have our visit to the stables.'

Once they were outside, the children and Anna had to scamper quickly to keep up with Lord Brentmore's long-limbed stride. Did he not realise that children had short legs?

They crossed the lawn to a set of buildings made from the same stone as the house. The wide door of one of the buildings was open and the stable master awaited them.

'M'lord.' He pulled at his forelock.

'Good morning, Upsom,' Lord Brentmore said. 'We have come to see the stables.'

Anna waited to be introduced, but Lord Brentmore neglected that nicety.

She stepped forwards. 'I am Miss Hill, Upsom, the children's governess. We have not met before. And the children, of course, are Lord Calmount and Lady Dory.'

Upsom was almost as tall as Lord Brentmore and lanky, not at all like Anna's father, also a stableman, but shorter than herself and thick as a tree trunk. The smell of hay and horse, though, made her homesick for Lawton.

'Pleased to meet you, miss,' the man said. 'This stable is for the carriage horses and riding horses. The working horses are in a separate stable.'

They stepped inside. The stables were huge, more than double what Lawton possessed.

'But there are no horses!' cried Dory.

'The horses are not here, my lady,' Upsom said. 'They are all in the paddock.'

Dory looked crestfallen.

'We may go out to the paddock,' Lord Brentmore said.

'Yes!' Dory jumped up and down.

'Follow me, then.' Mr Upsom gestured towards the back of the stables.

In the paddock beyond the stables several horses grazed. Lord Brentmore whistled and a beautiful ink-black gelding trotted over to the fence.

'This is my horse.' Brentmore stroked the horse's muzzle.

'This is your horse?' Dory clambered up the fence for a closer look. 'Did you ride him here?'

'I did.'

'What is his name?' Dory asked.

'Luchar.'

Anna's brows rose. In an Irish myth she'd read, Luchar and his brothers killed their grandfather.

'May I pet him?' Dory begged.

Lord Brentmore hesitated a moment before lifting her up so she could reach the horse.

'Gently,' he said. 'Keep your hand away from his mouth.'

Anna glanced towards Cal, who held back. Cal's eyes were not looking at his father's horse, but at another horse

on the far side of the paddock, a majestic white horse galloping restlessly, back and forth.

She crouched down to Cal's level. 'What horse is that?'

He crossed his arms over his chest and bowed his head.

Anna touched his shoulder and left him. Walking to
Brentmore's side, she gestured to the white horse. 'Lord
Cal was watching that horse.'

'That was Mama's horse,' Dory piped up.

Brentmore put her back on the ground and averted his
gaze from the beautiful white horse.

Cal stood stiffly, clearly disturbed as well.

What was it about the horse that upset them all? Anna
had half a mind to ask little Dory. She was the only one
who talked.

Brentmore turned away from the horses. 'Do you children ride?'

Cal gave him a quick glance before withdrawing again.

Dory did not hesitate. 'No. We do not ride, but we would
like to ride above all things.'

'Upsom!' Brentmore called. 'Have my horse saddled.'
He turned to his son. 'Calmount, you are the oldest. You
will be first.'

The boy's eyes widened, but he looked engaged. Whatever had happened inside him when he saw the white horse
had disappeared.

Well done, Lord Brentmore, Anna thought.

When Luchar was saddled, Lord Brentmore lifted his
son on to the horse's back and mounted behind him. He
set a sedate pace, circling the paddock. Cal looked almost
peaceful as he sat in front of his father.

When it was Dory's turn, she could barely contain her
joy.

Anna smiled, liking Lord Brentmore very much at this
moment.

His reaction to the white horse caused her worry, though. She'd thought for a moment that he would explode in temper again.

The impending storm passed, though. This time.

Chapter Five

Brent could not sleep. The morning at the stables had disturbed him all day.

He did not know what gave greater distress—Calmount's suffering, Miss Hill's allure, or the memories evoked by the white horse.

And little Dory.

She was so like Eunice. In her looks. Her charm. She possessed that gift of easy speech that so eluded Calmount — and Brent himself, if he were truthful. Eunice had always known precisely what to say to get what she wanted.

Except, perhaps, that fateful day when she was thrown from her white horse in her mad dash to catch up with her departing lover. She fell on to the hard rocks and broke her neck. When the news reached him in Vienna, his immediate reaction had been relief.

God help him.

But his next thought had been of how badly he'd failed her by not being the man she'd believed him to be. She'd been unfaithful, to be sure, but she'd also been made very unhappy by her marriage to a man with the blood of an Irish peasant flowing in his veins. Not even the birth of their son had made up for it.

As soon as Brent had heard of her death he'd hurried back to Brentmore for the children's sakes, but, once there, had not a clue how he could assist them. He still did not know.

Did the children enjoy riding in the paddock? He hoped so. Certainly Dory had seemed to, but he could not tell about Calmount.

Afterwards he'd taken Luchar for a proper run around the estate, checking on the tenants' welfare and on the planting. Luckily everything seemed well. The cottages looked in good repair. His tenants seemed content. His fields were verdant with crops.

At least his wealth did some good. It provided a comfortable livelihood to many people.

All his wealth, his huge house, his vast estate, had not prevented his children from living in a small set of rooms, their lives even more confined than his poverty-stricken early life in Ireland.

Awash with guilt, he paced the second floor in his shirt-sleeves and bare feet, surrounded by the trappings of his wealth.

It had been Miss Hill who had freed them from their prison, apparently defying Mrs Tippen in the process. He was beginning to see he owed her a great deal, not the least of which was saving his son from an insane asylum.

Now that he could not sleep, he pined for her company, her mettle, her passion. He yearned to talk to her, confide in her, rouse her from her bed—

He stopped himself. Thinking of Miss Hill in bed was not a good idea.

He'd be better off fetching another bottle of brandy. He picked up a candle to light his way and walked out of the bedchamber to the stairway.

A cry came from above.

From the children's wing?

He hurried up the flight of stairs and stopped at the top to listen.

He heard it again.

'Nooooo!' came the cry.

Brent rushed towards the sound, which grew louder and louder.

'Nooo! Do not hit me! Do not hit me!'

He flung open the door to the room that had once been his childhood bedchamber. Calmount was sitting straight up in bed, flailing his arms, a look of terror on his face.

'No!' he shrieked.

Brent ran to his side and seized his arms. He tried to awaken him. 'Cal! It is a dream. Wake up! Wake up.'

Footsteps sounded in the hallway and Miss Hill rushed in, dressed in nightclothes, her auburn hair loose about her shoulders.

'What is it?' she cried.

'A nightmare. I cannot wake him.' Brent held the boy. 'Wake up, Cal. You are dreaming.'

Calmount's eyes suddenly focused on him. The child gasped and pulled away, scooting to the wall and cowering.

'Do not hit me!' he cried, awake this time.

And speaking!

'I will not hit you.' Brent reached for him. 'You've had a nightmare. That is all.'

The boy shrank away.

'I would never hurt you.' Brent wrapped the boy in his arms and held him close. 'It was only a dream.'

The boy stiffened. Brent felt his struggle, his terror, but finally Cal relaxed against him and his tears dampened Brent's shirt.

Miss Hill sat on the bed next to them, stroking the boy's

hair and murmuring, 'There. There. It will be all right now. You are safe now.'

Brent rocked the boy as Miss Hill's warm voice assured him, over and over, that he'd only been dreaming. Eventually Cal fell asleep again, an exhausted sleep.

Brent laid him down on the bed and tucked the blankets around him.

He turned to Miss Hill. 'Good God. What was that all about?'

She whispered, 'This has not happened before.'

'Yes, it has.' A voice came from the doorway. Dory stood in the threshold in her nightdress. 'Cal has bad dreams a lot.'

Miss Hill picked Dory up and held her.

'Do you know what the dreams are about?' Brent asked the girl.

She nodded. 'They are about Mama. About that bad time.'

'What bad time?' Brent did not want to leave Cal, but did not wish to wake him either. He gestured for them to step further away from Cal's bed.

Dory snuggled against Miss Hill's chest. 'That bad time. I did it, though, so you should kill me and not Cal.'

Kill her?

Brent felt as if the child had pierced him with a dagger. 'I'm not going to kill anyone.'

'Why would you say such a thing?' Miss Hill asked.

'Because Mama said that Papa would kill us for breaking anything, especially the big vase, but I broke it. I ran in the hallway and knocked it down. Cal said he did it and told me to hush. So he got the beating and not me.'

'Beating?' Brent felt the dagger twist.

'Mama gave Cal a terrible beating. She said he was a terrible boy, but it was really me who was bad.' The child's voice rose. 'And then...then...she hugged Cal and said she was sorry. She was unhappy, she said. And...and that she was only trying to protect Cal. That it was you who would kill him if you found out about the vase.' A sob escaped her lips. She fell into a fit of weeping.

Brent could not breathe. He'd never imagined that Eunice's unhappiness had been that acute. She'd always vowed her children were more precious to her than any jewel and that she could not bear to be parted from them. But she beat her son. Because of her unhappiness?

How much responsibility of this belonged to him?

Dory's weeping quieted.

'Dory,' Brent asked. 'Did this sort of thing happen often? That your mother hit Calmount?'

'She hit me, too.' She turned to him, her eyes glistening with tears. 'And then she hugged us. Mrs Sykes told us we must be very good around Mama. Not be noisy or bother her. Mrs Sykes said we should stay in the nursery.'

Brent felt sick inside.

'We must get you back to bed,' Miss Hill told Dory.

She tightened her arms around Miss Hill's neck. 'I don't want to go. I want to stay with Cal.'

'Let her stay,' Brent said. 'I do not want Cal to be alone.'

Miss Hill carried her to the bed and tucked her in. 'You come to me if he has another bad dream.'

'He won't.' Dory yawned. 'They always stop if I stay with him.'

Brent fetched the candle and walked out of the room behind Miss Hill.

When they were in the hallway, he stopped her. 'Will you come with me? I am in great need of a drink.'

She hesitated for a moment, but nodded.

They walked side by side to the library, which still had

coals glowing in the grate. He placed the candle on a table and added a few chunks of coal to the fire.

'Please sit, Miss Hill.' He gestured to one of the large comfortable chairs facing the fireplace. He retrieved a bottle from a cabinet nearby, glad he'd instructed the footman to keep it stocked. He lifted the bottle. 'It is brandy. Would you care for a glass?'

She nodded. 'Yes. I believe I am in great need of drink, too.'

He poured her glass first and handed it to her, his fingers grazing hers as she took it. He poured himself a glass, downed it and poured himself another before lowering himself in the chair adjacent to hers.

'What you must think of me.' He could not face her. 'I must tell you that I knew nothing of Eunice's treatment of the children.'

She looked unconvinced.

He took a gulp from his glass. 'I thought she was devoted to them.'

She took a small sip from her glass.

He gave a dry laugh. 'I'm astonished you do not ring a peal over my head. Chastise me for not being around enough to know that my son and his sister were in the hands of a monster.'

She faced him. 'It is not my place—'

He lifted a finger. 'Ah, but you thought it, all the same.'

She looked away. 'It should not matter to you what a governess thinks.'

He fixed his gaze on her. 'It matters what you think.'

She looked as if she was considering whether to answer. She met his eye. 'I think it was convenient for you to stay away.'

He bowed his head.

She was right, of course. He didn't look too carefully at

his children because he wanted to stay away. From them. From Eunice. From this house and its memories.

He took another gulp and refilled his glass. 'What do you know of me, Miss Hill?'

She blinked. 'Nothing.'

'I am surprised Lord Lawton did not warn you.' The earl ought to have told her. 'I am half-Irish. Did you know that?'

She shook her head.

'My wife did not know it when I married her. She thought she was marrying an English marquess.' He rubbed his forehead. 'It never occurred to me that she did not know. Or perhaps I did not wish to consider that possibility. I was quite smitten...' He glanced at her. 'I did not wish to lose her, but I did that anyway.' He stared into his brandy. 'I knew she was unhappy. Her efforts to seek comfort elsewhere led to great scandal.' He downed his glass. 'And great conflict between the two of us. When I was with her there was turmoil. The opportunity offered itself to work for Lord Castlereagh on the Continent. I seized it. It seemed the perfect solution. I thought it would make her happy.'

The expression on her face gave him no idea of her reaction to this story.

He turned away again. 'Over the better part of three years, my visits to Brentmore were brief. I thought my wife's unhappiness was confined to the times I was present. I...I had no idea...'

She took a sip of her drink. 'You see the problems now, my lord. It is now you who must change.'

He rose from the chair and took out another bottle. 'What can I do? Except feel responsible for all the misery the children have endured?'

He could feel her eyes following him.

'If your neglect was responsible, as you say, then taking charge of making it better is what you must do.'

His gaze snapped back to her. 'Taking charge?' His head swam and his legs seemed unsteady, but he made it back to his chair. 'I must take charge.'

'Do not think of the past.' Her tone was soothing, as it had been when she murmured to his son. 'You cannot change what is past.'

Did she really believe he could atone for his past neglect? He would not know where to begin.

He gazed at her, at her long flowing hair, the thin layers of cloth that covered her naked body. He yearned for the comfort of her arms just like when she had held Dory.

He lifted his gaze. 'Will you help me, Anna Hill? I do not know what to do.'

The intensity of Lord Brentmore's gaze shook Anna. She'd watched him drink glass after glass of brandy, knowing he was trying to dull his pain. When he rose to fetch a second bottle, though, she could see he was quite inebriated.

'Anna,' he repeated. 'Such a pretty name. So much prettier than Miss Hill.'

Her face grew hot. No one had ever spoken her name like that before.

'Anna,' he repeated, then turned away, running a hand through his thick dark hair. He returned to his chair. 'Forgive me. We were talking about the children. You were going to tell me what to do.'

She sipped her drink, surprised that the brown liquid felt so warm in her chest. This had been her first taste of brandy.

She must say something quickly or he might speak her name in that deep, velvet voice again. 'I think you spend time with them. Let them become accustomed to you and you accustomed to them. Then you will know better what to do.'

That sounded wiser than she felt.

Since she arrived at Brentmore, she'd been sure that the children needed to be free of the nursery, free to run and shout and play. She knew that Lord Cal's muteness could improve, as Charlotte's bashfulness had improved. But what she did not know—and what she could not allow Lord Brentmore to guess—was if she was even a passable governess. Perhaps she'd helped only because the children's situation had been so dire anyone would have helped.

Now Lord Brentmore was relying on her to help him. The children's fate seemed squarely on her shoulders.

Not even for the children's sake should she be sitting in a dark room, so late at night, in her nightdress and robe, sipping brandy with a man who spoke her name in that disturbing way. She'd never been with any man like this, not even her father, but then her father rarely spent more than a few minutes in her company.

Something besides the children was vibrating between this powerful marquess and herself, something that made her think of him as man, not merely her employer.

He rubbed his hand back and forth on the arm of his chair and she felt it as if he touched her own bare skin.

'I must stay at Brentmore, then.' His words slurred.

He stood. So suddenly she jumped in surprise.

He crouched down in front of the fireplace and poked at the coals. Sparks scattered, brightening the room momentarily. 'I despise this house and have done since I was a child. Eunice wanted to be here, but even living here did not make her happy. There is nothing but unhappiness here.' He threw down the poker and it clanged like a bell against the stone hearth. 'From my grandfather to Eunice. Unhappy memories.'

He turned back and loomed over her, taut with pain. 'I do not want to stay here.'

She felt small in the shadow of this man who'd turned suddenly forbidding.

'Perhaps—' She swallowed. 'Perhaps this is a time when you must not do what you want, but what the children need.'

He dropped into his chair again and downed yet another glass of brandy. 'The children. I wanted to give them an easy life. Every advantage. Nothing like—' He broke off to pour more brandy.

She was afraid to speak.

Lord Brentmore buried his face in his hands. His shoulders shook and, in spite of her fear, Anna's heart went out to him. Without thinking, she left her chair and came to his side. She pulled his hands away from his face and made him look at her. 'Do not despair,' she said. 'It will come to rights, my lord. You will see.'

He rose and his arms went around her, pulling her flush against him. He buried his head in her shoulder. She felt the warmth of his skin through the thin fabric of his shirt, the steady beating of his heart, the prickly texture of his beard.

But his pain shook her most of all.

She held him close and murmured to him, trying to soothe him the way she had tried to soothe Lord Cal. Could she make everything turn out right, as she was promising?

He eventually relaxed, as Lord Cal had relaxed.

His hold on her loosened and she drew away. 'I think you should go to bed, my lord.'

His eyes darkened and he did not answer her. Another sensation flashed through her, one she could not identify.

Not fear. Not pity. Something else. She felt as out of breath as if she'd run a mile.

He seized her hand and wrapped his fingers around hers.

She pulled her fingers from his grip and held his arm to steady him. Picking up the candle, she urged him to walk with her to the stairway. They climbed together, Lord Brentmore gripping the banister. He led her to his bed-chamber, a room she'd only glimpsed during that first tour of the house. She intended to leave him at the door, but he pulled her in the room and took her in his arms again.

'Stay with me, Anna,' he whispered in her ear. 'Do not leave me. I have no wish to be alone.'

His hand slid down the length of her body and pressed her *derrière*. She felt the bulge of his manhood beneath his trousers.

She gasped, almost dropping the candle.

It was the drink causing him to behave so. And his un-happiness. He was not in control of his mind or his urges.

Her head was clear, however. So why did she not push him away? Why so wantonly allow his hands to move over her body, sparking sensations she'd never known possible?

Why was his invitation so difficult to resist?

'Of course I will stay,' she murmured. 'Let us get you to your bed.'

She placed the candle on a nearby table and let him lean on her as she walked him to his bed, its covers rumpled and disordered as if abandoned after a fitful sleep. He climbed into the bed and reached for her.

'In a moment, my lord,' she managed.

His fingers twisted locks of her hair, causing even more disturbing new sensations. He pulled her towards him and placed his lips upon hers.

Her first kiss from a man.

And such a kiss. Dizzying in its intensity. His lips were warm, firm. Wanting. Coaxing her to part her lips. His tongue touched hers, tasted her, savoured her as if she were some exotic delicacy. He tasted of brandy and heat and her body ached with new urges. Carnal urges.

With difficulty she broke off. 'Settle yourself under the covers, my lord.'

'Join me,' he rasped as he slid himself under the covers.

'I will.' She tucked the blankets around him the way she had done for the children. 'Close your eyes. I'll be only a moment or two. I must blow out the candle.'

'Candle,' he murmured, pulling on the sash of her robe.

She stepped away and her sash slipped off, but she did not dare pull it from his grip. Instead she waited, watching him by the light of the candle. He lay still, her sash in his hand. In a moment his breathing turned even.

She picked up the candle and backed towards the door. Still he did not move. She quietly crossed the threshold and pulled the door closed as she stepped into the hallway.

As quickly as she could, she returned to the stairway and made her way to the second floor. Before returning to her own bed, she peeked in at the children, snuggled together and sleeping peacefully.

She might have lain with Lord Brentmore as close, his strong arms encircling her, but nothing about lying with him would be peaceful. Her heart pounded in her chest as she returned to her room. Her senses still flared with the memory of his body against hers, his lips tasting hers.

But she climbed into her bed alone.

Brent woke to the sound of rain pattering the windows and a servant tending to the fire in his fireplace. He found a sash in his hand.

Miss Hill's sash.

The events of the previous night came back in a muddle. He remembered being unable to sleep. Remembered hearing Cal cry out in a nightmare. Remembered hearing of the abuse the children suffered out of Eunice's unhappiness.

The rest was confusion. He could recall drinking brandy in the library, confessing to Miss Hill his mistakes. His devastating mistakes.

Why was her sash in his hand?

He vaguely recalled the feel of her hair through his fingers, her soft skin under his hands, the taste of the soft recesses of her mouth.

Lawd. Had he seduced her?

He quickly hid the sash under the covers so the servant would not see, not that this sort of thing could ever be kept secret in a country house. As a boy, he always knew which of the maids his grandfather took to his bed. Poor women. They'd hardly been in a position to refuse.

Had Miss Hill presumed the same? That she must do as he asked or be tossed out on her ear?

Even in his misery and his drink-soaked mind, he'd noticed how beautiful she'd looked with her hair loose about her and her robe tightly cinched at her waist. He remembered that.

He balled the sash into his hand. He also remembered calling her Anna.

Anna. She could no longer be Miss Hill to him, but he hoped it was not because he'd forced an intimacy upon her that was beyond all that was respectable.

The servant left the room and Brent shook the memory of Anna from his brain.

He climbed out of bed.

He was still in his shirt-sleeves and trousers, but that meant nothing, only that perhaps he'd not taken the time to undress before slaking his need. Lawd, was he truly to add seducing the children's governess to his many sins?

His head pounded like the very devil. In two days' time he'd twice imbibed to the point of inebriation. It was not like him at all. It was this house. Brentmore Hall brought out the worst in him.

He quickly washed and shaved and dressed without summoning the footman who'd assumed duties as valet. He stuffed the sash into his pocket and made his way to the breakfast room where a pot of hot tea and a sideboard filled with food awaited him.

Mr Tippen stepped into the room. 'Do you require anything, m'lord?'

'No.' Brent's stomach roiled at the smell of kippers. He reached for the tea pot.

The butler turned to leave.

'Wait.' Brent stopped him. 'Do you know if the children are awake? Have they been served breakfast?' He did not dare ask if their governess had yet risen from her bed.

'I am sure I do not know, m'lord,' Tippen replied, acting as if the question was beneath him.

The prig.

'Find out for me,' Brent ordered. 'If they have not eaten breakfast, I want them to eat here. In this room. With their governess.'

He needed to see them, to assure himself that the night that had disturbed him so had not scarred them even more.

And he needed to see Anna.

Tippen gave him a disapproving look, but bowed. 'Very good, m'lord.'

A few minutes later a footman appeared with more place settings. 'Mr Tippen said I was to tell his lordship that the children will be eating with you as you desired.'

'Thank you—' He did not know the footman's name.

'Wyatt, m'lordship,' the footman offered.

'Wyatt.' Another task to forge for himself, Brent thought. Learn the servants' names.

Wyatt retreated to a corner of the room while Brent finished a second cup of tea. The door opened and Anna— Miss Hill—entered, the children behind her.

Brent stood. 'Good morning.' He caught her eye, but her expression revealed nothing.

'Are we being punished?' Dory asked, somewhat defiantly.

'Punished?' Had he done something last night to give the child that impression? 'No. I wanted your company, that is all.'

'Oh.' The little girl slid into a chair. The table top came up to her chin.

Anna turned to the footman. 'Wyatt, I believe Lady Dory could use a fat pillow to sit upon.'

'I'll attend to it, miss.' He left the room.

She did not look at Brent, but said, 'Please sit, my lord.' She addressed the children. 'Come see what is on the sideboard for you to eat.'

Dory scooted off the chair and decisively made her choices. Cal tentatively pointed to what he wanted.

By the time they settled back at the table, Dory had her pillow.

Anna again spoke to Brent. 'Shall I fix you a plate, my lord?'

Was her tone sharp? Wounded? He could not tell for certain. 'Some bread and butter, perhaps.' Definitely no kippers.

When she placed the plate in front of him, he finally caught her gaze. 'Do I owe you an apology, Miss Hill?'

Her face flushed. 'You are not obligated to me, my lord.'

What did that mean? He still did not know and could

not ask for clarification in front of the children. He ought to have summoned her alone, perhaps. But he'd wanted to see the children, too.

She fixed her own plate last. When she finally seated herself and they all commenced eating, no one talked. Brent remembered countless mornings seated with his grandfather in this very room, with nothing but oppressive silence. With Eunice, the silence had been fraught with her undisguised disdain for everything about him.

He hated that his children were left to imagine what was unspoken.

He turned to Dory. 'Why did you think coming here was a punishment?'

Her blue eyes looked up at him over her jam and toasted bread. 'Because we woke you up. We *disturbed* your sleep.'

Brent could hear Eunice in those words. He glanced at Cal, who watched them both warily.

Brent leaned towards him. 'You had a nightmare last night. Do you remember waking up from it?'

The boy very slightly shook his head.

Brent was heartened. This was at least communication between them. Other than the boy's words during and after the nightmare, that was. 'Dory told us you dream about your mother. Do you remember dreaming about your mother last night?'

Cal paled and shook his head again.

Brent deliberately attended to his food, buttering his piece of bread. 'I've heard your mother said I would kill you children if you broke anything—a vase—anything.' He pretended to look absorbed in spreading the butter. 'She was very mistaken. I do not kill children for breaking things, nor do I hit them for it. I was a boy once, too, and boys and girls break things sometimes.'

He glanced at Anna, to see her assessment of this little speech.

She gave him an approving look.

It encouraged him. 'I do not kill children under any circumstance and I cannot think of one reason to hit children either. If I had not been busy with the war, I would have forbidden your mother from hitting, as well. She was wrong to do so. Apparently even she recognised that fact and regretted her actions.'

Dory's eyes were wide as saucers and colour returned to Cal's face.

Lawd, he hoped he chose the right thing to say.

Dory's brows lowered and she tilted her head. 'Are you going back to war?'

Cal rolled his eyes at her question. He knew about the war, Brent realised.

Brent winked at him, then took a bite of his bread, chewed and swallowed, trying to make this conversation as easy as possible for them. 'The war is over.'

He wanted to say to them that he would stay for a while at Brentmore, that he would give them more rides on his horse and share more meals with them. But he did not know if what he had done the night before might make his presence here impossible. He needed Anna to tell him.

There were countless reasons not to stay. Financial matters mostly, although his man of business could take charge of most of those. Parliament was still in session, but he could still work behind the scenes, if he wished. Miss Rolfe—

Good God. Had he betrayed Miss Rolfe, as well as seducing the governess? He was a betrothed man and he'd be no better than Eunice had been if he would bed one woman while committed to another.

But perhaps he had not dishonoured himself. He must

find out. Even if he had not, his absence was bound to disturb the Rolfes. He ought to write his cousin and ask him to explain his abrupt absence to Miss Rolfe and her father. Brent was perfectly willing to immediately settle some money on Lord Rolfe if the man needed it right away, so there was no reason to set a quick date for the wedding. Peter ought to be able to reassure the Rolfes and inform Brent what they required.

Brent wanted to stay with the children and help them if he could. It all depended on Anna.

Dory blinked her long-lashed eyes at him. 'If you are not going back to war, will you take us for a ride on your horse?'

She reminded him of Eunice again. He tried not to frown, instead gesturing towards the window. 'Not in the rain, Dory.'

'You will have lessons today,' Anna broke in. She slid Brent what seemed to him a wary glance. 'Unless you have other plans for them, my lord.'

She was being cautious with him.

'Not at the moment.' He met her eye. 'I would speak with you first, Miss Hill.'

She lowered her gaze. 'As you wish.'

Brent took a sip of tea and stood. 'I will see you in the library when you have finished breakfast.'

Before he left the room he turned back and saw his son staring at him with an expression of discomfort and confusion that mirrored precisely what Brent felt inside.

Chapter Six

Brent paced the library. It seemed he was always waiting on this governess. Were not those in his employ supposed to be at his beck and call?

He pressed his fingers against his temples. It did him no credit to be churlish, especially since her primary concern must be the children.

And he had very likely seduced her. She would be in no hurry to see him, certainly.

He paced and watched the clock for a good forty-five minutes before there was a light knock on the door.

She entered. 'I am sorry to keep you waiting, my lord.' Her voice sounded calm. 'The children needed to be started on their lessons.'

He strode straight for her and placed the sash in her hand. 'I need to know what happened last night.'

She lifted her gaze from her sash and responded quietly. 'Nothing happened, my lord.'

His irritation flashed. This would get them nowhere.

'Do not tell me that.' He gestured to the sash. 'Something happened.'

'*Nothing* happened,' she repeated more emphatically.

She stood her ground, but her gaze faltered, betraying her.

He leaned closer. 'Speak plainly, Anna. I need to know if I seduced you last night. If I compromised you. I need to know what is required of me.'

'Required of you?' She looked surprised.

'Do not play games with me,' he snapped, but immediately lifted an apologetic hand and lowered his voice. 'You must know I cannot marry you—'

A wounded look flashed across her face, so quickly he thought he might have imagined it. She lifted her chin. 'Of course you cannot *marry* me. I am a governess and base born, as well.'

He stiffened. That was not what he meant. He meant he was betrothed to Miss Rolfe, but somehow, with no date set and no banns read, it still seemed unreal. Until he knew for certain that Miss Rolfe wished their betrothal to be generally known, he spoke of it to no one. For him to break off the betrothal would be a serious breach of gentlemanly behaviour. Miss Rolfe might do so, however.

'I must marry without scandal,' he said instead.

Her posture stiffened. 'Of course you must, but why say this to me? What does it matter if you compromised a governess or not?'

Brent had no wish to explain that his behaviour towards her did matter a great deal, but that, if he'd indeed taken her to bed, he could not avoid wronging someone. Her or Miss Rolfe. He needed for her to tell him what he'd done to her and then he would know what impossible decision he must make.

He fixed her with a steady stare. 'Tell me what happened last night.'

She waved a dismissive hand. 'You embraced me. You kissed me. That is all. You had a great deal to drink…'

'That does not explain the sash in my bed,' he persisted.

She drew in a quick breath. 'I—I helped you into bed.'

He pressed on. 'And did you share the bed with me?'

'I did not.'

He drew close to her again. 'You are not telling all.'

Her eyes filled with pain. 'Very well, I will tell you.' She lowered her gaze. 'You asked me into your bed. I made an excuse to extinguish the candle. As I stepped away, you pulled off my sash. I knew you had consumed too much brandy. I knew you would easily fall asleep. I thought it prudent not to retrieve my sash. I waited until I was certain you were sleeping and I left the room.'

He closed his eyes and felt sick with self-loathing.

At least she'd had her wits about her.

She went on, 'So you see, nothing happened.'

'A great deal happened.' A few drinks of brandy and he acted upon the attraction to her that had been present from his first glimpse. 'I do not know how to apologise to you.'

Her cheeks flushed with colour. 'All I wish to know is if I still have employment.'

His brows rose. 'Of course you have employment.' Did she think he'd disrupt the children's lives again? Punish her for his transgression?

Her posture relaxed and her expression turned to one of relief.

She straightened again, as if recouping her dignity. 'Then we have nothing left to discuss. I will return to the children.'

She turned to leave.

'Wait.' He seized her arm. 'We cannot pretend what happened did not occur.'

'We cannot change it either,' she countered.

He released her and stepped away. 'Perhaps it is best that I return to London.'

'Leave?' Her voice rose and her eyes shot daggers at him. 'Leave your children? Do not use me as an excuse to neglect them. If you have no wish to help them, then, indeed, go back to the pleasures of London. Forget them as you have done before—'

'Enough!' He closed the distance between them again. 'You forget your place!' He sounded just like the old marquess.

She did not back down, none the less. Instead, she looked directly into his eyes. 'Last night you lamented the damage done your children by your absence. Now you seize upon the slimmest excuse to leave them again.'

His gaze was entrapped by her blue eyes, so clear, so forthright and brave. Before he realised it, his hands had rested on her shoulders, drawing her even closer to him. A memory, foggy and blurred, returned. He remembered kissing her...

He stepped back, jarred at how easily his own behaviour turned scandalous. 'See, Anna—Miss Hill—how easily I might compromise you again?'

Under the intensity of his gaze and her skin still tingling from his touch, Anna's limbs trembled. Ever since she first entered the library, she'd been a mass of quivering fear inside and now all her bravado was failing her.

She'd thought it her greatest talent, pretending to be calm and fearless even when shaking with fear inside. She'd honed the skill for Charlotte's sake, but with the marquess, she needed her pretence of courage for her own sake. She'd done well until he touched her and come so close she could feel his breath on her face.

She'd done so well she'd scolded the man who employed

her. How foolhardy could that be? She needed this position. She had nothing else.

But she was correct that he needed to be here as well. His children needed him to stay. They needed to know there was someone who loved them, someone to whom their welfare was important. Someone who, unlike herself, was not paid to love them.

To not be loved by anyone was a terrible loneliness.

Perhaps that was why her senses begged for the marquess's touch, why her body wished so much that he would wrap her in his arms, why she had come so close to sharing his bed. She yearned for the illusion that someone loved her. She'd seemed of very little importance to her mother, none at all to her father and Charlotte seemed to have forgotten her.

Her heart pounded when she looked up in his eyes. She wanted to tell him to compromise her all he wished, anything to keep her from feeling so alone.

'That is why I need to return to London,' he murmured.

Anna forced herself to take a deep breath. She tensed her muscles and gave him a steady look. 'No, my lord. We must see to your children's needs and behave as we ought.' She curled her fingers into a fist.

His expression was pained. 'I want to stay. I want to mend the damage of the past and give the children the life they deserve, but—'

'Then you must stay with them. Certainly you are able to exert self-control…about…about the other.' As she must do, as well, Anna ought to add.

'You are correct, as I suspect you often are, Miss Hill.' His jaw set. 'There will be no repeat of my improper behaviour, I promise. I will do nothing to bring scandal upon you or upon this house.'

'Then you will stay?'

He nodded. 'I will stay.'

Two weeks passed and Lord Brentmore spent part of every day in the company of his children. He started the day having breakfast with them. He spent time with them in the school room. He took them riding on his horse. He even helped them tend their peas and radishes. He never asked anything of them. Never raised his voice.

Anna's esteem for him grew, but that made it only more difficult to be in his presence. Luckily they were never alone together for more than a few moments. The children or the servants or other workers were always present or nearby. What had passed between them that night did not disappear, however. Her senses heightened whenever he was near. She caught herself gazing at him far too often, but he also gazed at her. Sometimes their eyes caught and the colour rose in his face. She knew he was responding to her as a man responds to a woman. Everything about him captivated her. The easy way he sat upon his horse. His deep voice. His rare laugh.

Nights were often worse. The marquess now slept in a room near where the children slept, so he would be near if Cal had a nightmare. It meant he was also near to where Anna slept—or tried to sleep. Each night she tossed and turned and remembered the feel of his arms around her, the press of his lips against hers.

Her regard for him increased even more when he took another bold step.

He removed all visible reminders of his late wife.

The marchioness's portrait was crated and sent to the attic. Her stunning white horse was sold. Her belongings were removed from her bedchamber to be stored away. Most of her clothing was given away.

Most surprising of all, the marquess rid the house of Mr and Mrs Tippen. He pensioned them off and sent them away, presumably to return to the marchioness's home county from whence they had come. The gardener's sister, Mrs Willis, who'd been a senior housemaid in Brentmore Hall, became the new housekeeper. Wyatt, the footman, was promoted to butler.

A stunning number of changes in so brief a time.

One thing had not changed, though. Lord Cal still did not speak. But he was not totally unimproved. He smiled sometimes and was more free with his nods of the head or his hand gestures. Anna was very encouraged.

Lord Brentmore no longer shared dinner with Cal and Dory. Rather he insisted Anna dine with him so they had time to discuss the children and make plans for them. Dining together, with the footmen coming in the room and out, provided a safe place for them to be together without the temptation of those urges simmering beneath. Most of the time they talked about the children, but sometimes it became natural for them to converse on other topics. The social or political issues of the day. Their personal lives.

Anna shared a little about her growing up at Lawton House. Lord Brentmore told her of his activities during the war. He'd been a spy, slipping into France to receive messages from informants and passing on information to those working against Napoleon.

Dinner became Anna's favourite time of the day, a time for the sort of camaraderie she'd missed so desperately since losing Charlotte's company. It was all the more special because her companion was the marquess. The more he shared with her, the more Anna began to know the man and the more difficult he was to resist.

When she left the dinner table, however, Lord Brentmore remained behind. If he had once knocked upon her bedroom door, she did not know what choices she might make.

This morning he was not in the breakfast room when she and the children entered. Instead there was a folded piece of paper at Anna's seat.

'What does it say?' asked Dory before Anna even had a chance to read the words.

'A lady is not so rude as to ask what is in a letter that may not concern her at all,' Anna scolded in good humour. The spirit that was so appealing in the five-year-old would quickly be seen as ill mannered if Anna did not succeed in dampening it. 'It is addressed to all of us, so I will tell you. It is from your father.' She quickly read the note. 'He will not be joining us this morning, but expects to see us mid-day, when he will have a surprise.'

'A surprise!' Dory's eyes lit up.

As did Lord Cal's.

'What is the surprise?' Dory asked.

Anna laughed. 'It would not be a surprise if he told us what it was.'

Word came in the early afternoon, summoning them to the stables and telling them to be dressed for riding.

'Papa is taking us riding this afternoon,' Lady Dory guessed as they walked the pathway to the stables. 'That is why he wanted us dressed for it. That's the surprise, isn't it, Miss Hill?'

'I do not know.' Anna turned to her brother. 'Do you think that is the surprise, Lord Cal?' She and Lord Brentmore agreed to seize any opportunity to ask him to communicate.

The boy shrugged his shoulders, but clearly he was excited about what they would find. Anna's heart swelled. Cal was anticipating something good happening to him.

With the stables in sight, the children broke into a run.

'Slow down!' Anna called to them, but they were not listening.

When she reached the stable door, Mr Upsom was there, trying to fend off two excited children.

But he had a grin on his face. 'His lordship said to meet him in the paddock.'

She grabbed the children's hands to keep them in tow as they walked through the stable to the paddock on the other side.

Lord Brentmore stood inside the paddock. In his hands were the reins of a black pony and a brown one.

Dory let out a shriek and pulled away. *'Ponies!'*

Cal was right behind her, and Anna thought she heard him cry aloud.

Lord Brentmore flashed a smile.

'Ponies!' Dory cried again. 'You brought ponies!'

Both children climbed through the fence.

Anna stayed on the other side. 'My lord, what have you done here?'

He smiled directly at Anna. 'I conceived an idea.'

He handed the reins to a stable lad and stepped forwards to halt the children's mad dash. 'Not so hasty. An explanation is needed.'

'May we pet the ponies?' Dory took no heed of him and tried to scamper past him.

He caught her arm.

'Lady Dory!' Anna said sharply. 'Mind your father this instant!'

Her brother grabbed her and pulled her back, whispering something into her ear that made her stand still.

Lord Brentmore crouched down to their level. 'These ponies *might* be yours. You *might* learn to ride them—'

'They are our ponies?' Dory cried.

'*Might* be,' her father corrected. 'But there is a stipulation involved.'

Dory's brow furrowed. 'What is a *stipulation*?'

'A condition that must be satisfied,' Anna offered. 'Something you must do first.'

'That is correct.' Lord Brentmore took Dory's hand. 'You may pet the brown pony while I speak first with your brother, but heed Samuel here. He will hold the reins.'

She suddenly hesitated, looking back at Cal as if reluctant to leave his side, but the pony was too tempting. She approached it carefully, but finally stroked its neck.

Lord Brentmore took the reins of the black pony and walked it over to Cal.

He crouched down again to the boy's level. 'Would you like this pony, Cal? Would you like him to be yours to ride?'

Cal enthusiastically nodded his head.

'When I was a boy,' his father said, 'I was taught that I must perform a task in order to get something that I wanted, so I have a task I want you to perform.'

Cal looked a bit wary.

His father continued. 'It is time for you to get used to talking again—'

'Cal talks,' Dory broke in.

'Dory!' Anna scolded.

Her father turned to her. 'The task you must perform, Dory, is to stop speaking for your brother. I will explain about that in a minute.' He addressed his son again. 'Do not be concerned. You may get used to speaking a little at a time, but I must see you trying. Do you understand?'

The boy nodded again, solemnly this time.

'If you give me your word that you will practise talking again, this pony will be yours. You may name him and I will teach you to ride him.' Lord Brentmore looked directly in the boy's eyes. 'But you must give me your word. A gentleman always keeps his word. Can you do this? Do you wish to do this?'

Cal nodded again.

'Will you give me your word?'

Cal nodded.

'No.' Lord Brentmore lowered his voice. 'To give your word, a gentleman must say it aloud. It is a rule. Will you give me your word?'

Anna held her breath.

Barely audible, she heard Lord Cal whisper, 'Yes.'

Tears sprang to her eyes.

Lord Brentmore exchanged a glance with her and she sensed that he shared her emotions. His plan would work. Lord Cal would begin to talk again.

Later when they were all walking back from the stables, the children ran ahead.

'Did you see Cal?' she said to Lord Brentmore. 'He leaned forwards and spoke to the pony! This is marvellous, my lord. Whatever gave you the idea?'

He showed some pleasure at her compliment. 'I merely thought about what I wanted most at his age.'

She smiled. 'And did you receive your pony?'

He shook his head, his expression sobering. 'No. My Irish grandfather could barely put food on the table. But I would have done anything to have had one.'

That day of the ponies was just the beginning of more enjoyable days passing quickly. The weather was a great deal cooler than a normal summer, but the children still spent much of their time out of doors, learning to ride, taking walks, tending the garden. They picked their first crop of radishes and put trellises up to support the grow-ing pea vines.

Riding became the children's favourite activity and their skill on horseback quickly improved. It helped that their fa-ther had chosen two very mild-mannered, tolerant ponies. Lord Brentmore found a horse in the stable for Anna and sometimes the four of them would ride together, exploring the marquess's vast lands. The marquess often took Cal alone to ride over the estate while Anna and Dory made games of learning to serve tea or sew dresses for her dolls.

Lord Cal started talking again, bit by bit, although rarely without being spoken to first and always with as few words as possible. He was making the effort, though, and Anna believed it was because his father had made his home a comfortable place.

It seemed as if everything about Brentmore Hall had changed. The dark wainscoting stopped looking so bleak and maids might be caught humming while they worked. The footmen and other workers performed their tasks cheerfully.

It felt as if someone had taken a bucket and washed away all the gloom that had been there before.

It was all due to Lord Brentmore, Anna knew. He made the summer as idyllic a one as Anna had ever experienced. The pain of being thrust out of the only home she knew and banished from the only people she'd cared about faded with the joys of a summer without stress, spent with a man whose companionship she relished and with children she'd grown to love as if they were her own.

She still battled the surge of excitement inside her when Brentmore was near, but she supposed he had mastered any attraction he might once have felt towards her. His manner with her was always gentlemanly, even convivial, as if he was more friend than employer.

And he'd moved back to his own bedchamber.

This morning promised to be another sunny day. She and Lord Brentmore sat in the breakfast room with the children, encouraging Cal to speak by discussing plans for the day.

'What would you like to do today?' Lord Brentmore asked him.

Cal hesitated, as he always did before speaking. 'Ride.'

'May we ride to the village?' Dory piped up. 'We should like to go to the village.' She clamped her hand over her mouth. 'I mean, *I* would like to go to the village.'

Anna lifted a finger. 'Lady Dory, your father was speaking to your brother. Wait until you are addressed.'

'Yes, Miss Hill.' The girl lowered her head.

Lord Brentmore's gaze passed quickly over Dory. He turned back to his son. 'Where would you like to ride, Cal?'

Cal glanced from his sister to his father, a hint of mischief on his face. 'To the village.'

No doubt he and his sister had discussed the matter ahead of time.

'Your sister is not ready to ride to the village yet,' their father replied. 'There is too much commotion. Too many people and wagons. So we must pick some other place to ride or some other way to go to the village. What say you?'

Cal appeared to mull this over. 'Both?' he asked in a hopeful tone.

His father laughed. 'Perhaps.' He turned to Anna. 'How does that suit you, Miss Hill?'

'I believe I will forgo the riding, if I might.' All this activity left her with little time to sort out the nursery, mend her clothes and plan lessons. 'But a trip to the village—'

The butler entered the room. 'Your newspaper and mail, m'lord.'

Lord Brentmore took them from the tray. 'Thank you, Wyatt.' He set the paper aside and looked through the mail, opening one envelope.

A letter fell from it. He picked it up. 'It is for you, Miss Hill. It must have been mailed to London by mistake.'

'For me?' Who would send her a letter besides Charlotte? Charlotte knew she was not in London.

'It is from Lawton House.' He handed it to her.

'From Lawton?' Her anxiety rose.

Anna quickly broke the seal. She felt the blood drain from her face as she read.

'What is it?' Lord Brentmore asked, sounding concerned.

The children grew very quiet.

'It—it is from our housekeeper at Lawton.' Her heart pounded in her chest. 'My—my mother is very ill. Very ill indeed.' A fever and an affliction of the lungs, she'd written. 'This was sent days ago.' She handed the letter to him.

'You must go to her,' he said.

She shook her head. 'How can I? The children. My duty here—'

He looked up from the letter and captured her gaze. 'You must go.' He turned to the children. 'We will manage without Miss Hill, will we not?'

Cal sat wide-eyed, staring from his father to Anna.

'No!' Dory's voice rose in panic. 'I do not want Miss Hill to leave us!'

Lord Brentmore gave her a dampening look. 'None of that, now. We must not be selfish. Miss Hill's mother is ill and she must tend to her.' His tone turned reassuring.

'Besides, Miss Hill will only be gone a few days. Until her mother is recovered.'

Dory blinked. 'She will come back?'

Anna left her chair to gather Dory into her arms and hold her close. 'Of course I will come back, my little pet. Do not fear.'

'Do you wish to leave today?' Lord Brentmore asked.

Things were moving so fast. 'I do not see how I can.' She gave Dory a kiss on the cheek and returned her to her chair. 'I must make arrangements. Check the coaching schedules—'

He raised a hand. 'Nonsense. You do not need a public coach. Not when I have a number of carriages to offer. Leave those arrangements to me. If you wish to be in Lawton before dark, it can be done.'

Her throat tightened. 'How can I ever thank you?'

His gaze held hers. 'It is the least I can do, when I owe you so much.'

Chapter Seven

Anna excused herself from the breakfast table and went in search of Mrs Willis to inform the housekeeper of her impending absence.

The housekeeper gave her a warm hug and admonished her against excessive worrying. 'It will help nothing, my dear. You must save your strength for the care of your mother.'

They discussed the menus for the children and other issues about their care.

'You are not to worry over the little ones, either, Miss Hill,' the woman said. 'They are doing splendidly under your care and their father's. We are all astonished at the change in them. I promise you, we will keep up your good work.'

'Thank you.' Anna thought she might weep at the kind words. 'I think Eppy can handle them. And Lord Brentmore, of course. I believe they could be placed entirely in his care, actually. He is so good with them.'

'That he is, my dear,' the woman agreed. 'He is changed, as well, thanks to you. He is like a new man.'

Thanks to her? Surely any governess with good sense would have acted as she had. Perhaps better.

Anna hurried to the nursery wing to find Eppy, who also enfolded her in her arms when hearing of her mother's illness.

'I am sorry to leave you with more work,' Anna said.

Eppy patted Anna's back. 'Now, now. You must go to your mother. Besides, the children are a pleasure now. Not ever so sad and skittish as before. It is an easy thing to take care of them.'

Anna was not so secure that the children would be no trouble. She would, after all, be one more person leaving them. The very idea of it was bound to upset them.

Eppy helped her pack and the two women discussed the children's care while they folded Anna's clothing and gathered the items she would need, placing them in her portmanteau.

She carried it down to the hall herself.

Mr Wyatt awaited her there. 'Cook packed a basket for you and his lordship sent all the instructions to Mr Upsom to have you driven in the chaise. It should be here directly.'

'Where are the children?' And Lord Brentmore?

He averted his gaze as he took the portmanteau from her and opened the door. 'With his lordship.'

Would she not have the chance to say goodbye to them?

She felt a stab of pain, disappointed in Lord Brentmore for the first time since he'd agreed to stay with the children. Did he not think it important that she say goodbye to them?

Did he not think it important for him to say goodbye to her?

She stepped outside and watched the chaise make its way towards the front entrance, one of the stable lads driving. Wyatt placed her portmanteau in a compartment behind the seat and helped her into the small carriage.

'I hope you mother recovers quickly,' Mr Wyatt said, handing her the basket. 'Come back to us soon.'

She squeezed the man's hand. 'Thank you, Mr Wyatt.'

But it was not the butler's good wishes she longed for.

She felt as bereft as when she'd left Lord Lawton's London town house. At least Charlotte had made a point to say goodbye to her. She blinked away tears as the chaise made its way down the drive towards the arched gate.

When it passed through the gate, the driver brought the horses to a stop. He jumped down.

'Why are we stopping?' she asked.

The man gestured with his thumb. 'You are getting a new driver.'

A man emerged from the shadows, followed by two children.

Anna climbed down from the carriage and the children ran into her arms.

She kissed them both. 'I thought I would have to leave you without saying goodbye.'

Dory grinned. 'It was Papa's idea!'

She glanced at Lord Brentmore. He was not dressed at all like a gentleman. In fact, her coachman was better dressed. 'Lord Brentmore?'

He climbed into the chaise. 'I am going to drive you to Lawton House.'

Her old driver was grinning. 'Do not fret, miss. I'll see the children back to the house, safe and sound.'

'Papa gave you a surprise!' Dory cried.

He certainly had. She could barely grasp it.

'Bid these children farewell!' He took the ribbons in his hands. 'We must be off.'

Anna kissed the children again and hugged them for good measure. 'I will return as soon as I am able. You mind Eppy, now. She will take care of you.'

'We'll be good!' Dory said.

Cal hugged her again. 'I—I hope your mother recovers.'

It was the longest sentence he'd spoken yet.

She held him tightly. 'Thank you, Lord Cal. I will miss you both so very much.'

She handed them over to the old driver and climbed back in the chaise.

Lord Brentmore flicked the ribbons and the horses started off again. He waved to the children, who enthusiastically waved back.

Anna leaned out the side of the chaise and called back to them, 'I'll return soon.'

When they reached the road, Anna turned to him. 'Lord Brentmore?'

He gave her a quick glance. 'The children will be well cared for. And I'll drive back tomorrow.'

'But look at you!' She took in his linen shirt, brown coat and trousers.

He shrugged. 'A costume that proved useful in the war.'

She was still not comprehending.

'If the Marquess of Brentmore drove the governess to an earl's estate, there might be gossip, but if Egan Byrne drives you, no one will credit it.'

'Egan Byrne?' Her brows rose.

'My name,' he explained. 'And my Irish grandfather's surname.'

'But someone might recognise you.' What if Lord Lawton saw him? 'What will they think?'

He dipped his chin like the lowest of servants. 'Don't you worry now, miss.' His accent turned to a lilt. 'No one will be noticing an Irish stable lad. I'll be quiet as a mouse and you'll be the only one knowin' the truth of it.'

She doubted such a man, even if dressed as a workman, could avoid notice.

He spoke in his own voice again. 'But you must remember to call me *Egan* and not *my lord*.'

She swallowed. 'But why would you do this?'

His expression turned solemn. 'I thought you might need the company of a friend.'

Tears stung her eyes.

This was a folly of the highest order.

Brent trained his eyes on the road, although that did not prevent him from being acutely aware of the woman seated beside him. He felt her tension. Her worry. And also the brushing of her arm against his when the road turned rough.

He must be mad to put himself in her company like this. His intense attraction to her had never abated. She was a constant allure, cause of a daily battle against an urge to lose himself in all that warmth and beauty. Knowing her better, seeing her kindness to his children, feeling her sadness, made it all the more difficult.

She never complained, but he caught snatches of how lonely life was for her, in how she spoke of her childhood, or in the fact that she never received letters even though she wrote them. The letter informing her of her mother's illness had been her first since coming to Brentmore Hall.

He'd had a bad feeling about that letter and could not send her off on the trip alone.

Her worry that someone would recognise him was unfounded. He'd learned as a boy how to make himself invisible—much like Cal had done. Or to make himself into someone else. He possessed a talent for mimicking accents, originally honed from a desire to rid himself of his Irish accent and avoid the taunting and teasing of his schoolmates. When he learned French, his French accent became nearly as flawless as his English one. During the war, no one in France had suspected an English marquess had been spying on them.

He'd slip in and out of Lawton as easily.

The chaise hit a rut and he reflexively threw an arm across Anna to keep her from falling.

'I beg your pardon.' He quickly removed his hand. Any time he touched her, it aroused his senses.

She glanced at him. 'I am not likely to complain about anything you do, my lord.'

God help him. If she only knew how many sleepless nights he'd suffered, thinking of marching into her bedchamber and slaking his need for her. It made it more difficult to know she would not refuse him. The idea that he could be the man to awaken her sensuality was more torture.

'Egan,' he said.

'What?' she looked puzzled.

'You called me *my lord* again. Practise saying *Egan*.'

If only he were Egan Byrne and not the Marquess of Brentmore. Then he would not be betrothed to a baron's daughter and no one would lend scandal to anything he did. No one would care.

'Egan,' she repeated. On her lips his name sounded as if murmured between bed linens.

This manner of thinking would not do at all. Better to change its direction. 'This is not the most comfortable of roads.' Perhaps inane small talk would help.

'Again, I shall not complain,' she assured him. 'If not for your kindness, I could be squeezed into a post-chaise with travellers who eat a great deal of garlic and transport cheese.'

'And bathe but once a year,' he added.

She almost smiled and his heart gladdened, relishing any moment of easy camaraderie between them.

'You have spared me such a fate,' she said, although her eyes quickly filled with pain and worry.

He wanted to ease it. 'Your mother could be recovered by the time we arrive, you know. Is she susceptible to inflammation of the lungs?' He feared worse, of course. Life was fragile.

'She is never sick.' She bit her lip. 'That is why I worry. Our housekeeper would not contact me if she thought this a trifling thing.'

Illness was never a trifling thing. Brent had a flash of memory of his mother, lying abed, the sound of her breathing as loud as a fireplace bellows.

A wave of grief washed over him.

He tightened his grip on the reins. 'Do not give up hope, Miss Hill.'

He rarely thought of his mother, but when he did, the yearning for her returned fullfold, even after twenty-five years. He never spoke of her. Whenever the old marquess had spoken of her, he'd called her *that Irish whore*.

Anna's voice pulled him out of his reverie. 'I was never close to my mother, you know. I was always with Charlotte. Weeks could go by and I would not even see her.' Her voice cracked. 'I want to see her again.'

He put his hand over hers.

As they rode towards Lawton, she talked about her life there, about growing up neither servant nor family, but something in between. She'd become close to the Lawton daughter, but separate from her as well, never truly accepted in her social circles.

Brent knew all about not being accepted. He'd never been accepted, not by his grandfather, his schoolmates, his contemporaries.

Or his wife. How bitter a pill that had been. He'd believed she'd loved him.

At least when he married this next time, he'd know the woman did not love him.

Brent flicked the reins and drove as hard and fast as he dared.

They changed horses frequently at the coaching inns and did not pause for much more than a quick look at *Cary's Itinerary* or to pay at the toll gates. They ate from the basket Cook packed for them rather than wait for food at the inns.

By the time the light was waning in the sky, Brent's arms ached from holding the reins and from the bumps in the road. Anna looked more fatigued by the hour. Their fast pace had paid dividends, though. There was still plenty of daylight left when they finally passed a road sign indicating Lawton was near and soon a tall church spire rose in the sky.

'The village!' Anna cried.

Anna examined each building as they passed through the village. Committing it to memory, perhaps? Would he recognise any part of his Irish village? he wondered.

This village had nothing to distinguish itself from dozens of other English villages. Stone houses with steep slate roofs. A coaching inn. A smithy. Shops.

'Lawton House is not far,' she said as they left the village and the main road behind.

Brent felt her tension grow.

Suddenly a vista opened, revealing a majestic country house set in manicured lawns and flowering gardens. Constructed of the same grey stone as the village buildings, it was a hodgepodge of additions and wings, as if the various Earls of Lawton were seized with a compulsion to build every half-century or so.

This was the place Anna had spent nearly her whole

life, the home she lost when Lord Lawton so abruptly terminated her services. She leaned forwards in the chaise as if in a hurry to be among familiar surroundings, familiar people.

Her mother.

The sight of Brentmore Hall always plummeted him into depression.

Brent turned the chaise on to the long gravel drive leading to the house. 'Do I leave you off at the house?'

'Yes. Our housekeeper said Mama was being cared for in the house.' Her brows knit. 'Unless you want me to go with you to the stables.'

He waved a hand and put on his Irish accent. 'Do not go concerning yourself about me, now. I'm not a marquess, a'tall. Just a simple stable lad who can find his way.'

He drove her to the servants' entrance and watched her enter quickly, hating to leave her alone.

He shook his head. What a ridiculous notion. She would not be alone. She'd be among people she'd known her whole life.

He drove the chaise towards the stables.

As he neared, a man stepped out into the stable yard. 'And who might you be?'

He touched the brim of his hat. 'From Brentmore Hall. I brought Miss Hill to visit her mother, you see.'

The man's face fell. 'She's come?'

'Miss Hill?' Brent pretended to be confused. 'Yes. Come to see her mother, she has.'

The man dropped his head in his hands for a moment, then seemed to recover. He gestured to Brent. 'Well, climb down. Do you stay?'

'The night at least,' he responded. 'I'm to await her instructions.'

The stableman called to some other grooms and tasked

them with unhitching the horses and seeing to their care. Brent removed Anna's portmanteau and the kitchen basket. He was shown to a place to sit and given a draught of ale.

After a few moments the man who'd greeted him in the yard walked over to him again. 'Are you hungry? You can probably beg some food from Cook, if you've a mind to.'

He wanted to see what was happening to Anna.

'Food would be welcome, for sure.' He touched his stomach and tried not to look too eager.

The stableman gestured for him to follow. 'I'll show you the way.'

He knew the way, but a visiting worker would not argue with anyone who might be above him in station.

As they walked the man spoke, more to himself than to Brent. 'She should have come sooner.'

'Sooner?' Brent repeated.

The man stopped and gazed blankly into the distance. 'Her mother...' He paused and lowered his head. 'Her mother is dead. Buried yesterday.'

Brent's insides clenched. They were too late.

'Miss Hill will be grieved, indeed,' he said in a low voice.

The man's expression turned bleak. 'She was my wife.'

'You are Miss Hill's father, then?' Brent asked.

'In a manner of speaking,' the man replied.

Brent's brows rose. What the devil did that mean?

It was not a visiting stableman's place to ask questions, though.

He followed Mr Hill to the tradesman's entrance, which opened into a long corridor with doors to the other rooms. The sound of voices and clanging pots signalled that the kitchen was somewhere ahead.

Mr Hill escorted him to the servants' hall.

Anna was there, seated at the long table, surrounded

by the housekeeper and maids, all trying to comfort her. Her expression was desolate and her eyes red from crying.

'I heard you'd come,' Anna's father said.

She looked up. 'Papa.'

The maids made way for him, but he did not approach her. 'They told you about your mother.'

That was obvious.

She caught sight of Brent, her silent communication of grief as clear as if she'd shouted aloud. To her father she said, 'How do you fare, Papa?'

He did not answer. 'Your room is ready at the cottage. Mrs Jordan expected you days ago.' He glanced at the housekeeper, who must be Mrs Jordan.

Mrs Jordan explained, 'The letter went astray.'

Mr Hill shrugged. He inclined his head towards Brent. 'Anna's coachman is hungry.'

Brent supposed that was an introduction. Or a changing of the subject.

Mrs Jordan turned her attention to Brent. 'I expect you would like some food, then?'

'His—his name is...Egan,' Anna volunteered.

'Egan.' Mrs Jordan patted the table. 'Sit down and we'll bring you a plate of food.' She snapped her fingers at one of the maids. 'Mary, find something for the man to eat.'

Brent took the nearest chair, trying not to watch Anna too obviously. It pained him to see her so disconsolate.

Her father moved towards the door. 'Your things will be at the cottage.'

She nodded. 'Thank you, Papa.'

Brent frowned. Hill was so cold to her. He reminded Brent of the old marquess.

The girl brought food for Brent and tea for Anna. Servants drifted in and out of the room, completing their duties for the day or stopping to give Anna their condolences.

For a moment they were alone in the room. 'Anna?' he murmured, forgetting to address her formally.

She looked pale and desolate. 'I feel like I cannot breathe.'

He wanted to hold her in his arms and comfort her the way he comforted Cal after his nightmares. He moved to a chair across the table from her and reached over to squeeze her hand.

'Let yourself cry,' he murmured. 'It will help.'

Although, as a boy, he'd learned quickly never to cry.

She blinked rapidly and gripped his hand.

Someone approached and she quickly released him. 'Are you finished eating?' she asked.

'Yes.' His plate was nearly empty, but he'd tasted none of the food.

'We should go, then. We are in the way here.' She stood. 'Wait a moment while I stop in the kitchen to tell them.'

When she returned and they left the house, he said, 'I'll walk you to your father's cottage.'

She did not refuse.

'I—I cannot believe she is gone,' she said after a time.

He steadied her with his arm.

When they reached the cottage, she rapped on the door before opening it. 'I am here, Papa.'

Inside the cottage, the room was dark, with only the glow of the fireplace for light. Brent caught a strong whiff of gin.

Her father rose from a chair by the hearth. 'Well, come in, then.' His tone was sharp and his words slurred.

Brent waited in the doorway, uneasy at leaving her.

'Come have a drink, you,' Hill called to Brent.

'Don't mind if I do,' he said in his coachman's voice. He'd stay as long as she needed him to.

* * *

Anna gave up any hope of sharing her grief with her father. She had never seen him drunk like this. It frightened her.

He gestured with his arm. 'You sit for a while, *daughter*.' This last word was bitterly said.

Anna sat.

He filled a glass for Lord Brentmore, some of the liquid splashing over the sides from his unsteady hand.

'You should have come earlier.' Her father shook a finger at her.

'I waited for Egan to eat, Papa,' she explained.

He wiped the air with his hand. 'Don't mean that. Mean for your mother.'

'I could not.' That was the worst of it. Tears stung her eyes. She'd not arrived in time.

Her father stared into the fire. 'There was no one at her funeral, you know. No one to put her in the ground.' He turned his gaze on her. 'Why didn't you come? Too busy tending that lord's brats?'

Her gaze flashed over to Lord Brentmore.

He answered for her. 'She came as soon as she received the letter.' His Irish accent faded. 'Which was this morning.'

Her father made another dismissive gesture and took a swig directly from the bottle.

Anna glanced away and, her eyes now accustomed to the room's darkness, saw dishes left on tables, clothing scattered on the floor, bottles everywhere.

She stood. 'I'll just tidy a bit.'

She lit one of the lamps and moved around the room, picking up empty bottles.

Her father took no notice. 'Rankles me,' he said. 'After all her mother did. All those years.'

Anna only half-listened to him. She carried the bottles to the bin by the sink, which was full of unwashed dishes.

Her father kept talking. 'She tolerated me. Nothing more. What chance did I have? A man who mucks out stables and comes home smelling of horse?' He swivelled around to Anna and pointed his finger at her. 'And the daughter. No better.'

All her life she'd wanted her father to love her. He never did.

Lord Brentmore rose and walked over to her. 'How can I help?'

His nearness was a comfort. She was grateful he'd remained. 'I would not ask you.'

'I know you would not ask,' he countered. 'I am offering.'

She picked up a bucket. 'Would you bring me some water? The pump is outside.'

He nodded.

She collected more plates, bowls and spoons from around the room and placed them in the basin. She could not properly wash the dishes without boiling some water on the hearth, but that meant crossing in front of her father. She did not wish to risk disturbing him. The dishes would keep until morning.

Lord Brentmore returned with the water bucket. She took it from him and poured water in the basin to soak the dishes.

'What is next?' he asked.

'That is more than enough, my lo— *Egan*.' She gave a grateful smile.

He did not return to his chair, but stood aside, his arms folded across his chest.

She moved through the room, picking up clothing and

clutter from the floor. She paused near the chair where Lord Brentmore had been sitting. His glass was still full.

Her father, still rambling, reached for it and downed the gin as if it had been water. 'Cursed man,' he cried. 'You'd think *he* would come. After all those years—'

Anna's brow creased.

Her father went on, 'He owed it to her to come put her in the ground.'

Of whom was he speaking? 'Papa?'

He lifted his head to look at her. 'You know. Don't pretend you don't know what I'm talking about.'

She shook her head. 'Indeed I do not. Are you speaking of Mama?'

A bark of a laugh burst from him. 'Of course I am speaking of your cursed mother.' He jabbed his finger into his chest. '*My* wife!'

Brentmore walked up behind her, a silent support.

'Do not be profane when speaking of Mama,' she scolded.

The man half-rose from his chair. 'I'll speak of her any way I like. She was *my* wife. Not his.' He jabbed his chest again.

'Mr Hill.' Lord Brentmore spoke without accent in a low, firm voice. 'Heed what you say. Your daughter is already overwrought with grief.'

Her father sprang to his feet. 'Heed what I say? Ha!'

Lord Brentmore pulled her behind him, placing himself between her and her father. 'Enough, sir!' he ordered.

A puzzled look crossed her father's face, but that was the only indication he noticed the coach driver now spoke like a marquess.

Her father sank back in his chair and covered his face with his hands. 'He ought to have come. He ought to have shown his respects.'

'Who, Papa?' Anna asked.

His bleary eyes caught hers. 'His lordship.'

'Lord Lawton?' She gaped at her father. 'You are not making any sense. Why expect Lord Lawton to come? Mama was only a laundress.'

Her father gave her a disgusted look. 'There you go, pretending you do not know.'

Her anxiety rose. 'Know what?'

Lord Brentmore put a hand on her arm.

Her father lifted Lord Brentmore's empty glass and peered into it as if it might be hiding more gin. 'Why d'you think you were chosen to be the companion?'

He was changing the subject.

Her father pointed to her. 'He could not have you reared to be a servant, could he?'

Lord Brentmore's grip on her arm tightened.

'Papa.' Her heart pounded. 'Speak plainly.'

'*Papa,*' he mocked her. 'I'm not your *papa*, girl, and I don't ever again have to say I am.'

She felt the blood drain from her face. 'Are you saying... Lord Lawton?'

He slapped the arm of the chair. 'See? You knew it all the time. His *lordship* sired you. Not me. Not me.'

Her head spun and inside she shouted, *No. No. No.*

Her father—the man she'd thought was her father—continued talking. 'She used to work in the house, y'know. An upstairs maid and the prettiest thing you ever did see. Caught *his* eye and every chance he got he tumbled between the sheets with her.' He stared into the fire. 'Then she was increasing. Made her ladyship furious when she found out. Sent her out of the house, but only far as the laundry because he wouldn't let her go. He had a plan, you see.' He sighed. 'His lordship came to me. How would I like a cottage? he says. More pay, he says. All I had to do was marry her.' He laughed, a dry mirthless sound. 'I was as young as she was. I thought she'd fancy me after a time, but it was always him.'

He glanced at her. 'She made him promise. Raise you to be a lady, not a servant. Wouldn't bed him 'til he agreed.' He rose from the chair and staggered to a corner where he rummaged until he found another bottle. 'Then his legitimate daughter turned out to be a mousy little thing and he sent you to teach her some backbone, not that her ladyship ever liked that.' He laughed again. 'You know all this. Everyone knows this.'

She'd never suspected.

No wonder this man had never loved her. No wonder Charlotte's mother had always been cold to her.

But Lord Lawton never showed her any favour. None at all.

'Does Charlotte know?' Was Anna the only one who didn't know?

He waved a hand again. 'The twit? Not at all.' He rose from his chair again, swaying as he tried to take a step. 'Thing is, he should have come. Should have come before she died. Should have come to put her in the ground!' He took a step and reached out to steady himself on the back of the chair.

He missed and collapsed to the floor.

'Papa!' she cried.

Lord Brentmore rushed over to examine him. He looked back at her. 'He's just passed out from the gin.'

She backed off. 'I—I can't believe—'

Lord Brentmore lifted him from under his arms and managed to hoist him over his shoulder. 'Where's his bed?'

She led him into the room he'd shared with her mother, to the bed that her mother probably shared with Lord Lawton as well.

Lord Brentmore dropped him on to the bed like a sack of flour. He started immediately to snore.

What was she to call him now? Even in her head she could not say he was her father.

Brentmore took her arm. 'Come.'

As soon as he closed the door behind them, the enormity of her mother's death and her father's disclosure fell on her. It was like being pummelled with fists.

She clutched her stomach and closed her eyes.

Lord Brentmore enfolded her in his arms. He held her tight against him. The strength of his arms encircling her, the warmth of his body, the steady beating of his heart, held her together.

But the pain remained. 'I have nothing now,' she cried against his chest. 'Nothing.'

'Anna, you are exhausted,' he murmured. 'Go to bed. Tomorrow will be better.'

She shook her head. 'Nothing could be worse than today.'

'That is right.' He released her, but brushed her hair away from her face with his fingers. 'Nothing will be worse than today.'

He picked her up, surprising her so much she was speechless. 'Where is your bed?'

She pointed.

It soothed her to be absolved of the need to walk. He carried her into the little room she'd rarely slept in as a child and lowered her on to her bed.

'Goodnight, Anna.' He started to walk away.

She jumped off the bed and seized the cloth of his coat. 'Don't leave me, please. I—I don't want to be alone! I don't think I can stand to be alone.'

'I will stay right outside your door,' he assured her.

'No. I will still be alone.' She was sounding irrational,

but she could not stop herself. 'Stay with me, my lord. Here. Hold me. Please.'

He stared down at her, his eyes darkening. 'Very well,' he murmured. 'I will stay.'

Brent held her all night. Both of them remained fully dressed, but he shared her tiny bed with her.

He could not say that no thought of making love to her crossed his mind, but she was in too much pain for him to take advantage of her and he cared about her too much.

He watched her sleep, savouring the sight of her pretty face, even though it was still pinched with pain. Sleep had not come easy for her.

Nor for him, but eventually he had dozed off and on until dawn illuminated the room.

Anna murmured something in her sleep and moved from her back to her side, cuddling against Brent.

He tried to remain very still.

The door suddenly burst open, banging against the wall with a report as loud as a musket.

Anna's eyes flew open and she sat up.

Brent vaulted from the bed.

Mr Hill stood in the doorway. 'Harlot!' he shouted. 'Just like your mother!' He advanced on her, rage and disgust on his face. 'Tumbling into bed with the likes of this.' He gestured to Brent. 'At least your mother bedded an earl. At least she got something for it.'

Brent blocked Hill's way and seized his arm. 'You, sir, are leaving.' He forced the man out of the room.

'How dare you put your hands on me! You scum!' Hill tried to break free of Brent's grasp, to no avail.

'Now you listen to me.' Brent forced the man against a wall. 'She's done nothing to deserve your words. You were cruel and drunk and I could not leave her alone with the likes of you. Her mother died, man! And all you cared to do was hurt her.'

Hill gaped at him. 'I thought you were Irish.'

Brent leaned into his face. 'I am more Irish than is safe for you.' He continued to glare at the man. 'Now tell me why you dared enter her room.'

Hill cowered. 'I—I wanted to see if she was there.'

He tightened his grip. 'Do you believe me when I say I am able to get you fired from your job?'

Hill's eyes widened and he nodded.

'Then say nothing of this. You created this situation. You will not make her pay for it by sullying her good name.' He shoved the man towards the door. 'Now go and make some use of yourself in the stable.'

Hill rushed out of the cottage. Brent turned away and saw Anna standing in the doorway of her room.

'He will tell them.' Her voice trembled. 'I will be the talk of the household.'

Brent raised his brows. 'Shall I have him fired, then?'

She shook her head. 'It does not matter. I will never come back here.' She glanced away. 'Would you take me home, my lord? To Brentmore, I mean. I do not want to stay here.'

He crossed the room, as drawn to her as he'd been that first glimpse of her. Only now he knew her. And cared for her.

He lifted his hand to touch her, but dropped it again. 'We can leave right away.'

Chapter Eight

While Lord Brentmore stopped at the stables to have the horses hitched to the chaise, Anna walked over to the house to say goodbye.

'You mustn't go!' Mrs Jordan cried. 'It looks like rain outside.'

The maids chimed in, 'Stay longer, Anna. You just arrived.'

'I—I must get back to the children.' Anna explained. 'It is a very good position and I do not want to lose it.'

The maids nodded. They all knew the value of good employment.

Mrs Jordan sighed. 'Well, go if you must.' She turned and bellowed to one of the maids, 'Mary! Pack up some food for Anna and that nice coachman of hers.'

Would they gossip about her after she had left? Her father—the man she knew as her father—would certainly lose no time in passing the word that he'd found her in bed with her coachman. *Blood will tell,* they would likely say. *At least her mother bedded an earl.*

Mary placed the box of food in her hands and Mrs Jordan and the maids hugged her goodbye. Anna knew she would never see any of them again. Once they tired of the gossip, would they ever think of her? She did not know.

She walked to the servants' door, past rooms once familiar to her. She knew she would never walk past them again.

She had an impulse to run up to Charlotte's room. To see it once more. To see the schoolroom. The library. The music room. All the lovely places she and Charlotte had passed their days. She wanted to run in the gardens again where they had picked flowers or played hide and seek.

She squared her shoulders and kept walking to the outside door.

She'd had the privilege of growing up here because her mother bedded the earl. What she'd believed was a beautiful opportunity now seemed soiled and tarnished.

When she stepped outside, Lord Brentmore was there, waiting in the chaise. He'd secured her portmanteau under the seat. She placed the food into the basket she'd brought from Brentmore and left the box by the door. No part of Lawton House would come with her.

Lord Brentmore helped her into her seat. 'How are you faring?'

She steeled herself against the grief of all she had lost. Her mother. Her home. Her very identity. 'I will fare well.'

His glance was sceptical before he signalled the horses to be on their way.

She made herself not look back. The life she'd missed so acutely had never truly existed. When they passed through the village, she kept her eyes resolutely on the road. Once the village was behind them, all that was once familiar to her was behind her. Lost to her for ever.

Anna's gaze was captured by a leaf caught in a whirlwind ahead of them. The leaf rose and fell at the whim of the wind. She felt like its kin.

* * *

After they passed through a tollgate, the road was nearly empty of traffic. Lord Brentmore gave the horses their heads.

Without looking at her, he spoke. 'Did I ever tell you about Ireland?'

He was attempting to distract her from her grief. His kindness made tears prick her eyes.

She tried to keep her voice steady. 'You lived there once.'

'I was born there.' He turned his gaze back to the road. 'My father's regiment was stationed in Ireland and somehow my father met my mother and married her. My mother was the daughter of a poor Irish tenant farmer and was as common as they come. The poorest of the poor. The old marquess—my father's father—disowned my father for marrying her. Cut him off without a penny and never spoke to him again.'

'Because he married a commoner.' She was a commoner who had aristocratic blood in her veins. How ironic was that?

'Yes.' He looked away. 'My father died soon after and my mother and I lived with my Irish grandfather. I was barely out of leading strings when she, too, died.'

This distraction was only increasing her pain. Her heart ached at his loss.

He continued. 'Even as a small boy I worked the farm with my grandfather.' He glanced at her. 'Seeing you and the children in the kitchen garden that day brought that memory back.'

She could not look into his eyes.

He fell silent.

Keep talking, please! she wanted to beg. His voice seemed all that was keeping her together.

'How did you come to England?' she asked.

'An uncle I did not know existed—my father's older brother—died,' he said. 'The old marquess needed an heir and thus came looking for me. Up until that time, I thought I was Egan Byrne. I knew nothing of my real name, Egan Caine, and nothing of my father being English. I was suddenly the heir and the old marquess took me from Ireland and brought me to Brentmore Hall. I was ten.'

'Was that a good circumstance?' she asked.

He shrugged. 'At the time I did not think so, but it was good in that I had food to eat, clothing to wear and a fire to keep me warm.' He glanced at her. 'What I want you to know is that I remember that time in Ireland with a clarity that sometimes escapes me when I'm trying to recall what happened yesterday.' His Irish accent slipped into his speech. 'And I mostly remember the happy parts.'

She understood. 'So I will remember the happy times at Lawton?'

He gave the briefest of nods. 'The memories will be with you always.'

She wished she could believe she would some day remember Lawton without thinking of how her life was conceived and how the education she held so dear had been exacted. It seemed impossible.

'You have not spoken of happy times, though,' she accused. 'You tell of suffering and grief.'

'Only to show the contrast,' he explained. 'Those events are like shadows. What I remember most clearly is sitting near the fireplace in the cabin with my grandfather, while he told story after story of the fairies or silkies or pookas. Or walking at his side through the potato fields.' He shook his head. 'I know it rained a great deal, but I only remember the sunny days. Like one day when I worried my *daideó* by running all the way to the sea. Must have been three or four miles.'

'Your *daideó*?'

'My grandfather.'

'What happened to him?' she asked.

'He fought with Billy Byrne in the 1798 Rebellion and was killed at the Battle of Arklow.' His voice turned hard. 'I read of it in the newspapers when I was at school.'

She gasped and felt the pain of his memory as if it had been her own.

She stole a glance at him, needing now to distract him as he had tried to distract her. 'You should tell Dory and Cal your grandfather's Irish stories.'

'Never!' He looked appalled. 'The less they know about their Irish blood, the better.'

'You cannot mean that!'

'Indeed I do,' he said with emotion. 'I'll not have them suffer the taunts and cuts that were my lot. The less they know of their Irish blood, the better. They must think themselves the privileged children of a marquess. Nothing else.'

She'd merely pictured the children sitting on his lap listening to the stories, as she'd pictured he had sat on his grandfather's lap. It would be something she never had.

'Tell me the stories,' she said to him, lest she dwell on fathers who cared nothing for her. 'I want to hear about fairies and silkies and pookas.'

So he filled her ears with tales of mischievous little people, of fearsome horses with yellow eyes and fantastic creatures that shed their skins to become human.

As the day passed, the overcast sky turned grey and soon rain pattered the top of the chaise, getting thicker and thicker as the miles went by. When it started to pour as hard as it had done that first day she'd met the marquess, he pulled into an inn.

'We must wait out the rain,' he told her.

They left the horses and chaise to the care of the ostlers and ran through the rain to the door of the inn.

Inside it was noisy and crowded with other travellers taking shelter from the storm.

He found a space for her in a corner. 'Wait here. I'll speak to the innkeeper and see what is available.'

She watched him disappear behind the other people waiting out the rain and her anxiety rose, as if, without him, she might blow away like the leaf she'd watched on the road. The buzzing of all the voices filled her ears and mixed with the clatter of more carriages arriving.

There were all sorts of travellers stranded here. Gentlemen. Tradesmen. Workmen of all types. She saw a woman holding a little girl's hand and she remembered how her mother's hand felt holding hers. Tears threatened again and she searched the crowd for Lord Brentmore.

It seemed an eternity until he came back.

'There are no private parlours and no rooms,' he said over the din. 'We can wait in the public room, though. I arranged for a bench near the fire. It is somewhat private.'

She nodded and took his arm. He led her through the people into the tavern, more crowded than the anteroom. The scent of ale and meat and unwashed people assaulted her nostrils. Their combined voices were like beating drums and every inch of the space seemed filled.

Except for a small bench and table near the fire. 'How did you manage this?'

'I told them you were my wife.' His gaze caught hers for a fleeting moment. 'And that you were not well.' He settled her in the seat. 'And, of course, I paid well for the men sitting here to move.'

She could not help but smile.

He sat next to her. 'They were happy with the coin and we have a warm place to sit and take away the damp from our clothes.'

A moment later a harried tavern maid brought hot cider and bowls of mutton stew. Lord Brentmore pressed a coin in the woman's hand and her countenance brightened considerably. Anna ate and drank by rote, but soon she was warm inside and out and a lassitude washed over her.

'It has been a long time since I've spent more than a few minutes in a crowded tavern,' Lord Brentmore remarked. 'I fear we will be here for a while.'

'I am sorry, my lord.' If it were not for her, he would not have had to endure this discomfort.

He leaned to her ear. 'I am Egan Byrne here. Better we not command undue attention.'

She nodded.

'And I do not mind it,' he added. 'We are reasonably comfortable here.'

She was more than comfortable. She belonged nowhere and to no one, so there was some comfort in anonymity, in being the fictional Mrs Byrne.

She stole a glance at him and wondered why she'd ever felt he was formidable. Merely her employer, he'd extended himself as a friend.

But she could not think of him only as a friend. Her father—the man she'd thought was her father—had not been entirely incorrect. In her heart she was a harlot, as much as her mother had been. If she did not feel dead inside at this moment, she had no doubt that her desire for Lord Brentmore would be raging inside her.

Now it was even more crucial that she control it. How long would she remain in his employ if she came to his bed? She could not depend upon him to keep her around as Lord Lawton had her mother.

Brentmore slipped his arm across her shoulders and nestled her against him. 'Rest, Anna,' he murmured.

His embrace felt more a shelter than the roof over her head, but it was as much an illusion as the rest of her life had been. She shuddered in pain and he held her tighter.

If only he really were Egan Byrne and she...his wife.

She felt wonderful in his arms. A peace came over Brent that made no sense at all in the midst of this simple tavern awash in all forms of humanity. No one cared who they were here. He could hold her without worry of censure or gossip.

Best of all, the sheer numbers of eyes prevented his more dangerous temptations from coming to the fore. Still, he would have forgone even the pleasure of holding her if he could have procured a comfortable room for her.

The last traveller who'd entered the tavern loudly declared it was 'raining stair rods' outside. A downpour, he meant, apparently.

In the crowd he spotted two gentlemen known to him. No matter. He blended so well with the rest of the ordinary people, those acquaintances would never notice him. They might gaze at Anna, though, whose beauty had turned melancholic from her shock and grief.

He pulled his cap down to shade more of his face, just in case.

Anna straightened. 'What is it?'

'Some men I know,' he replied. 'But do not fear. They've entered a private parlour.' He tipped his hat back again.

'You will not wish to be seen with me,' she commented.

He put his arm around her again. 'I merely wish to avoid explaining why I'm dressed as a coachman.'

'I wish you were a coachman,' she said, so quietly he barely heard her.

So did he. How free he might be. Free to look upon her not as the marquess who employed her, but as a man.

'I would make love to you, then,' she added.

Could she see into his mind? 'Anna—'

She hurried on. 'I want to. It has been hard not to.' She averted her gaze.

She was overwrought and how could she not be after the day she'd endured?

'You should not talk of this,' he said.

She lifted her chin defiantly, reminding him of that first interview with her. 'You want me, too, my lord. You would bed me if I permitted. That is a man's way, is it not? That is why daughters like Charlotte are chaperoned. If they were alone, they might permit men to bed them.'

There was truth in that. The daughters of earls were protected, but not so much from their own urges, but those of men who thought only of their own pleasure.

Lawton ought to have protected Anna. She was his daughter, as well. Damned man! He should have cared for her, not sent her off to fend for herself. He knew what could happen to unprotected governesses.

She took a deep breath. 'I thought there was something wrong with me, but now I see I am just like my mother.'

He turned so he could face her directly. 'Lawton seduced your mother, Anna.'

Her lovely brows rose. 'Or did she seduce him? She was given a cottage to live in and her daughter was educated. That was much more than other servants received.'

He shook his head. 'He should have given your mother an independent means. Set her up in a nice house.'

She placed her hand on his arm. 'She would not have known how to run her own house.'

'He should have acknowledged you at the very least,' he insisted.

Her voice turned low again. 'I expect he did not care.' She stared into flames licking a large log in the fireplace. 'It all makes sense now, though, does it not, why I want so much to bed you? I am like my mother.'

'Enough talking like this.' He gathered her in his arms again. 'You are upset and tired. Try to rest.'

If only he were not a marquess. He'd not have to worry about damage to the children because of him. He'd not be betrothed to a baron's daughter. It would not matter who he married. He'd be free...

He looked down into her face. Her eyes were closed and her expression was composed. She slept and he was free to relish the sight of her.

If he were indeed Egan Byrne he'd be free....

Chapter Nine

Anna had remained cosseted in the warmth of Lord Brentmore's arms the whole night. When morning dawned full of sunshine, the tavern began to empty of its travellers, but they tarried by silent agreement as if reluctant to return to the old routines, the old identities.

Over an unhurried breakfast, Anna searched the marquess's face for any hint he would address the loose words she'd spoken the night before. She felt her cheeks burn merely from thinking of what she'd said to him in her grief and despair.

Yet it was a reality she must accept within herself. She was her mother's daughter, yearning for carnal pleasure just as her mother must have done with Lord Lawton.

Her real father.

If only she could talk to her mother about such yearning, discover why her mother chose to carry on a long affair with his lordship. Ask her why she'd hidden the truth from her daughter all these years.

Grief threatened to overwhelm her. She tried relentlessly to push it away. She was more fortunate than most women. She had employment. She had a lovely place to live. She had an education. And books. The library at Brentmore was filled with books.

She lifted her gaze to the man who sat across from her at the table.

She had a friend, as well as an employer, in Lord Brentmore. Likely back at Brentmore, they would return to their previous routine and the friendship would be as buried as her desire for him must be.

She pretended to eat with appetite and forced herself to talk of the trip ahead.

No more tears. No more feeling sorry for herself. Her mother was gone. Her life was what it was.

Her consolation must be the children for as long as they needed her.

After they'd eaten, Lord Brentmore asked, 'Are you ready to depart?'

She nodded.

Soon they were back in the chaise and on the road.

Anna confined her conversation with Lord Brentmore to topics involving the children. Their needs. Their activities. Ways to make their lives secure and happy.

By early afternoon they reached the inn where Lord Brentmore's team of horses awaited him. His team was hitched to the chaise again, marking the last leg of the journey. Soon they reached the outskirts of the marquess's estate. When the house came into view, Anna felt relief.

'Lawd, I hate this place,' Brentmore said at the same time.

It disheartened her. 'Why? It is where your children are.'

He nodded. 'It is also where my unhappiest memories live.'

She squared her shoulders. 'Do not think of the past. Only the future. Only what is ahead.'

He covered her hand with his and his expression turned grim.

When they reached the arch, Lord Brentmore halted the chaise.

'Why are we stopping?' she asked.

He turned to her, and his eyes darkened. 'To say goodbye.'

'Are you getting off here?' She could not drive the chaise.

A ghost of a smile flitted across his face. 'No, but Egan Byrne is saying goodbye.'

He leaned over to her and kissed her cheek.

She gasped and turned her head, offering him her lips and trembling with need to taste him again.

He indulged her, softly pressing his mouth to hers, but carefully holding back and enabling her to bank the passion that flared through her.

When he moved away again, she released a breath.

'Back to being the marquess and the governess,' he murmured.

She squeezed her hands together, to keep from clasping his. 'I cannot thank you enough, my lord, for coming with me.'

He bent down and kissed her cheek again, but said nothing. He flicked the ribbons and the horses passed under the arch.

They came closer and closer to the house and suddenly Anna's grief intensified. She'd just suffered another loss, the loss of a friend named Egan Byrne.

When they pulled up to the front door, it opened and two footmen emerged to attend to them. After they alighted, Cal and Dory burst through the doorway.

Dory vaulted into her father's arms. 'Papa! You are home!'

He hesitated before fully accepting Dory's embrace. Cal stopped a short distance away as if his shyness had grabbed hold of him and held him back.

'Miss Hill!' Dory cried and reached out for Anna.

Lord Brentmore handed the little girl into Anna's arms and Anna fussed over her while the marquess approached his son, drawing him into a huge hug. 'My boy, I missed you.'

Cal wound his arms around his father's neck. 'Me, too,' he said.

His father hugged the boy tighter.

'Cal talked to Eppy and to Wyatt, too, while you were gone,' Dory informed them.

'Isn't that fine!' Anna exclaimed, realising how genuinely she'd missed the children. 'And what mischief did you get into while we were gone?'

Dory giggled. 'Nothing.' Her brother actually smiled. She whispered to Anna. 'Cal caught a toad and put it in Eppy's pocket!'

'That is mischief, indeed!' And a marvellous change for him.

'Don't tell Papa!' Dory whispered loud enough for her father to hear.

Anna put Dory down and hugged Cal. 'What a prankster you are,' she said quietly.

One of the footmen retrieved her portmanteau and the basket, the other took the horses and chaise to the stables.

'Let us go inside,' Lord Brentmore said.

Dory reached up for him to carry her and Anna took Cal's hand.

As they entered the hall, Cal gestured for her to bend down. He moved his mouth before finally forcing the words out. 'Is your mother better?'

A wave of grief engulfed her. 'No, Lord Cal. She was too sick. She died.'

The boy's expression turned solemn. 'Mine did, too.'

Anna crouched down and hugged him, tears pricking her eyes. 'I know.'

As the days went on, they returned to their previous routine and the children thrived. Cal spoke more and more, and Dory calmed down and became less vigilant and protective of her brother. Their former confinement made them hungry for new experiences. There was nothing they would not try and they soaked up information like sponges.

For Anna, though, everything seemed slightly askew. During the day she often felt as if she were standing beside herself, watching what she was doing, what she was saying, what she was hearing. She often declined riding with Lord Brentmore and the children and Lord Brentmore spent more time at his correspondence and estate business.

In the evening, she and Lord Brentmore still dined together and still discussed the children, but always Anna sensed the tension between them, borne of all they did not say.

Anna tried to convince herself that everything was as it should be, that she would soon be content again, but at times a restlessness overtook her that was nearly as unbearable as her grief. Sleep was nearly impossible. When slumber finally came, she dreamed she was running and running until she reached the sea.

Just as he said he had done as a child in Ireland.

The happy memories he'd promised her never came and her desire for him never abated. At times she feared she would go mad if he did not touch her. If he did happen to touch her, she felt the touch in every part of her. That was enough to drive her insane.

Perhaps she should be locked away as a maniac in Doctor Stoke's asylum.

She was merely masquerading as sane, although she was reasonably certain no one could perceive her struggle. She could teach her lessons while her mind wandered back to Lawton or to the library below where Lord Brentmore wrote his letters. She could converse at dinner about the children, share anecdotes about them, make plans for them, while remembering the meals she and the marquess shared in the inn. She could bid him goodnight after dinner and confess to be sleepy when she knew she would stare at the ceiling for hours.

This night her thoughts turned to the future and all she could see was more bleakness and loss. He would not stay at Brentmore Hall for ever. Eventually he would return to London and take his place again in society. His visits here would become shorter and less frequent. She'd be alone.

Anna got out of bed and paced the room, hoping to tire herself.

It did not work.

She must train herself to think of him only as an employer, nothing more. She must distract herself. Fill her mind with something other than how he smiled, how he moved, how his lips had felt against hers.

This was ridiculous! She snatched a candle from the table and rushed out of the room, without bothering to put on her slippers or wrap a robe around her. She padded her way down the hallway to the stairs, headed for the library. Books had filled her imagination as a child—perhaps they could fill her mind now and crowd him out.

She wanted a book about some faraway place where people unlike herself lived lives totally different from her own. Perhaps the marquess's library had *Captain Cook's*

Voyages Around The World, which would certainly fit the bill.

No. She had a better idea. She really did not wish to read. She wished to sleep. A glass of Lord Brentmore's brandy might bring her sleep. Perhaps he would not mind just one glassful missing. Perhaps he would not even notice.

Somewhere in the house a clock struck two, its chime echoing in the silence and making her jump. The library door was ajar and inside the room the coals in the fireplace still glowed.

She crossed the room and placed her candle on the cabinet, which was kept stocked with brandy. She opened the cabinet door and took out a bottle and a glass. She poured a full glass and quickly drank it down, almost choking from its warmth.

'Anna?' A voice came from the sofa in front of the fire.

Lord Brentmore's voice.

She almost dropped the glass.

He sat up. He was in his shirt-sleeves. His coat, waistcoat, and neckcloth were tossed on a nearby chair. 'What are you doing?'

There was no sense lying. He'd caught her in her theft. 'Drinking brandy. I could not sleep and I thought brandy would help.' Servants were discharged for stealing spirits from their employers.

He rubbed his face. 'Brandy rarely helps.' He peered at her. 'I thought you said you were tired tonight.'

She was tired to the point of exhaustion. 'I was. I am. But I cannot sleep.'

He groaned. 'And I fell asleep on the sofa. We are like bookends, facing opposite ways.'

His analogy was apt, she thought. Together they held things in place, but were never meant to meet. To touch.

'I—I know this looks like theft.' Her hand shook. He could end her employment. 'I was feeling quite desperate.'

With a dismissive wave of his hand, he stood. 'You are welcome to what I have.' He walked over to her. 'But what is amiss?'

'Nothing is amiss,' she replied. 'I cannot sleep.'

'It is not like you.' He felt her forehead. 'You are not warm.'

She was now. His touch enflamed her.

His gaze swept down her body and his hand slipped to her shoulder. 'What keeps you awake?'

Her limbs felt like melting candle wax under his fingers and his gaze. 'I—I do not know.'

'Or you will not say?' He put his arm around her. 'Come. Sit with me. Tell me. Pretend I am Egan Byrne. Tell me what makes it so difficult to sleep.'

He sat her down on the couch and leaned her against him. She could feel the heat of him through the thin fabric of her nightdress and his shirt. She wanted to discover what his bare skin felt like beneath his shirt.

'Talk to me, Anna,' he murmured.

What could she say that he would believe? She could not say the truth.

That she ached for him, although she'd confessed that very thing to him at the inn.

'At—at night thoughts consume me. About my mother. About Lawton. About all of it. About being alone now.' She did think about such things…and more.

He held her tighter. 'You are not alone.'

His words and his arms were meant to comfort, but they only tortured. She yearned for more and knew she could not have it.

She drew away. 'You could dismiss me for taking the

brandy. That is how precarious my life is. What would happen to me then? I have nowhere to go. No one to help me.'

'I do not begrudge you the brandy.' His expression was sincere. 'You are safe here, Anna. You are wanted here.'

She wiped a loose lock of hair off her face. 'I do not mean to complain. Or to feel sorry for myself. Please do not pay me any mind.' She tried to rise, but he seized her hand and pulled her back on to the sofa.

'Anna.' He stroked her arm. 'What can I do to ease your worry?'

'Nothing, my lord,' she said, trying to remain composed. 'It is the lot of a governess.'

He turned her to face him. 'You know you are more than a governess.'

His lips were perilously close. His body was warm and hard-muscled. The scent of him filled her nostrils, so male, so pleasant, so unique to him alone. She yearned to join with him.

Wrenching herself away, she cried, 'I—I must go.'

She ran from the library.

Chapter Ten

'**A**nna!' Brent ran after her.

When she reached the second floor, he caught her by the arm and made her face him.

'What is wrong?' He gave her a shake.

She tried to pull away. 'Sometimes—sometimes I cannot forget all that I feel.'

He could not forget, as well. Travelling with her had changed something in him, made him wish to be a mere man, not a marquess. It had been a long time since he'd yearned to turn away the trappings of his title and strip himself down to mere flesh and bone.

He put his arms around her and held her close, wanting to comfort her, wanting her to comfort him. It was like a match to tinder. Her arms encircled his neck and through the thin fabric of her nightdress he felt the roundness of her breasts, the curve of her body, the special place that fired his senses. His hands travelled to her narrow waist and he pressed her pelvis against his, drowning in desire.

She tilted her face to his and he took possession of her lips, this time indulging in the full taste of her. Her tongue immediately sought his. She tasted like brandy.

He lifted her into his arms and carried her to his bedchamber, taking her to his bed. She was as willing as any woman could be, as lost in the passion as he was.

He tore his shirt off and lay with her on the bed, their legs tangling as his hands explored her and his mouth revelled in her kisses.

What harm could it do to make love with her? They both wanted it. And he would be good to her. He wanted to be a man with her, to join his body to hers, to bring them both to physical release.

What harm if they continued?

His hand slipped between her legs, to that place where pleasure could explode. She moved against his hand and his craving surged.

They could have many nights of pleasure until—

Until he married.

He stilled and moved away from her.

'No, do not stop,' she rasped. 'I want this.'

He took her face in his hands. 'I cannot.'

He ought to tell her that the Marquess of Brentmore was soon to make a respectable marriage, but this seemed the worst possible time and, when he was with her, he wanted to pretend his fiancée did not exist.

Her expression showed all the anguish he felt inside. 'Why?'

'You could have a child,' he managed.

Her eyes widened. 'Like my mother,' she whispered.

He climbed off the bed, found his shirt and put it back on.

He ran a hand through his hair. 'God knows I want to make love to you, Anna, but it would be wrong. It would change things between us.'

She pressed her fingers to her temples. 'What are we to do, then?'

'Not this.' He shook his head. 'We must take care. I promise, I will not do this again.'

'I am not certain that is what I want,' she said in a quiet tone.

He glanced at her. 'I know it is not what I want, but what I must do.'

'Things are changed between us anyway.' She gave him an intent look. 'I feel as if a door has opened that I cannot close, no matter how hard I try.'

He returned her gaze. 'I am sorry, Anna.'

She looked away and was silent.

If she were in society, he would be duty bound to marry her for behaving in such an ungentlemanly manner. But she was not in society. And there was no one—no father who cared about her—to insist he wed her.

That thought made him ache for her, her vulnerability, her aloneness.

If he made love to her, he would have to marry her—how could he live with himself otherwise? He could just imagine the scandal of it. Jilting Miss Rolfe to marry a governess with a background as scandalous as his own.

His children would suffer the consequences if he behaved dishonourably.

'We must think of the children,' he said. 'I want what is best for them.'

She nodded and climbed off the bed, raising herself to her full height. 'I have behaved abominably tonight. I hope you will forgive me for it.'

Before he could compose a response, she walked out of the room.

The next day they behaved as mere employer and governess, maintaining a distance between them that was as distressing as it was necessary. Having come so close to making love to her, Brent's desire surged stronger than ever, but she had been correct. Things had already changed between them.

If that were not enough, London beckoned. Parker had any number of matters to which Brent must attend. And he had letters from Members of Parliament who wished him to return. Even though it was August, they were still in session.

All these he could ignore, but today letters arrived from both Peter and Baron Rolfe, begging him to return to London and make final plans for the marriage. Matters were becoming urgent for Lord Rolfe.

He needed to return.

It seemed too soon to leave the children.

Or Anna.

Rain and chill kept them all indoors and the confinement did nothing to relieve Brent's unease. He wandered through the house, winding up in the gallery, gazing at portraits of ancestors stretching back to the sixteenth century. Men with pointed beards and embroidered jerkins. Women in lace ruffs. It was difficult for Brent to believe that their blood flowed in his veins. After all these years, he still felt as if he were in a foreign land.

Wyatt found him. 'Ah, there you are, m'lord.' The butler stood at the far end of the gallery and his voice echoed. 'Dinner is served.'

'Thank you, Wyatt,' Brent said.

By the time Brent reached the beginning of the gallery where Wyatt had stood, the butler had disappeared from the hallway. When he reached the dining room, Anna was already seated.

'I am sorry to keep you waiting,' he said. 'I lost track of time.'

She smiled politely. 'Mr Wyatt said he'd had difficulty finding you.'

Brent sat. 'I was in the gallery.'

'The gallery,' she repeated in a perfunctory tone.

'With my ancestors.'

The footman served the soup almost immediately and Brent asked about the children's lessons.

Anna responded in dutiful detail about what they had done on that rainy day. 'I hope we can go outside tomorrow,' she added. 'Both of them were very unsettled.'

'As was I,' he said, pained at how stilted their conversation was.

She dipped her spoon into the soup. 'If it continues to rain tomorrow, I will move to the music room and give them dancing lessons.'

He looked up from his bowl. 'If it rains tomorrow, I may join you.'

She caught his gaze. 'I would like that.'

Their gazes held.

She glanced away. 'And the children will love having you.'

When the second course came, he looked down at his plate. 'I tackled my pile of letters today.'

'Was there any news?' she asked, polite again.

'Parliament is still in session.'

'Is it?' she asked without real interest.

'Mr Parker has amassed a number of matters I must address.' He glanced over at her.

She stared at him.

He glanced away. 'I need to go to London.' When he returned his gaze to her, she'd gone pale.

'The children will miss you.'

He felt the emotions behind her words and reached over to her. He pulled back, remembering that touching made things worse for both of them. 'Will it do harm to leave, do you think? Is it too soon?'

She put down her fork and turned her face towards him. 'You must leave us some time, my lord.'

The inevitability of that statement depressed him. These weeks had given him more peace than any other time he could remember. With Anna he felt more himself than anywhere else.

The conversation between the two of them virtually ended at this point, even though Anna asked him dutiful questions about his need to go to London and he provided dutiful answers while they finished the meal.

He still did not tell her about his betrothal. When he was with her, it seemed too unreal to speak of. Besides, their emotions were still too raw after they'd nearly made love the night before.

'When will you leave?' she asked finally as the dishes were removed and his brandy was poured.

'In a couple of days, I suppose.' He stared into the liquid in his glass and remembered her in the library. Nearly naked. Hair flowing about her shoulders.

She stood. 'Well. I will bid you goodnight, my lord.'

He stood as well. 'Goodnight, Anna.'

As she walked towards the door, he was seized with a desire to call her back. 'Anna, wait!'

She turned to him.

He walked towards her. 'Come with me.'

Her face coloured. 'My lord,' she whispered.

Without thinking he put his hand on her arm and spoke in a low voice. 'I meant you and the children should come with me to London.' Why had he not thought of this before? 'It will only be for a few weeks. There is much we can show Cal and Dory in London.'

She looked wary. 'I do not know.'

'We could take them places. Astley's, for one. Dory would love the horses at Astley's. We can have new clothes made for them. They need new clothes. It will be a good experience for them.' He held his breath, waiting for her response.

She regarded him with solemn eyes. 'Very well, my lord. We will go to London.'

A few days later they made the trip to London. Lord Brentmore rode his horse. Anna rode in his carriage with his children and Eppy.

It was a difficult trip. Cal and Dory had never travelled further than the village. They were both giddy with excitement as well as unused to the rigours of riding in a coach all day. To break up the day, their father allowed them to take turns riding on Luchar with him, but that only temporarily amused them. By the time the carriage pulled up to Lord Brentmore's town house, the children—and Anna—were exhausted.

The door opened to the familiar hall where Anna took the first step into a new chapter of her life. Little did she know that day how thoroughly the previous chapters would be closed to her.

Brentmore entered first, but stood just inside the door waiting for Anna, who had taken the children by the hand.

Mr Parker stepped forwards. He'd obviously been awaiting their arrival. 'My lord.' He bowed to the marquess. 'Good to have you back. I've taken the liberty of having Cook prepare a meal for us. With your permission, we can discuss some of the more pressing matters that await your attention.'

Lord Brentwood shot a glance Anna's way and returned to his man of business with a stern glare. 'Have your manners gone begging, Parker?'

Mr Parker looked puzzled, then realised what his employer meant. 'Oh, I beg your pardon.' His apology was directed at Brentmore. He turned to Anna. 'Good day, Miss Hill.'

'Good day,' she replied, noting that he paid no attention at all to the children who hid behind her skirts as soon as they'd seen him.

Lord Brentmore spoke again. 'I am not prepared to discuss business at dinner, Parker. Come back in the morning.'

Mr Parker looked as if he'd been slapped in the face. 'My lord, there are one or two things that I believe cannot wait, even for tomorrow.'

Lord Brentmore did not relent. 'Well, since you have invited yourself to dinner, we may talk about this afterwards, but I have no intention of boring Miss Hill with tedious business, not when she has spent the day riding in the carriage with two small children.'

'Miss Hill?' Mr Parker's brows rose into his forehead.

Clearly it had never occurred to Mr Parker that she would dine with the marquess.

And she was too weary to put up with not being welcome. 'My lord, if you do not mind, I would like to dine with the children. They are in a place that is new to them. I want to be certain they are comfortable.'

Lord Brentmore's brows knitted. 'Are you certain?'

'With your permission,' she responded.

He turned to Mr Parker. 'Very well, Parker. It will be as you wish.'

'May we see our rooms?' Anna asked.

'Certainly.' Lord Brentmore turned to his butler, who had just re-entered the house and closed the door behind him. 'Davies! Find someone to show Miss Hill and the children to their rooms.'

At that moment a grey-haired portly woman bustled in from the servants' entrance. 'My lord! I've this minute learned you'd arrived.'

'Ah, Mrs Jones.' The marquess nodded towards her. 'Allow me to present you to Miss Hill, the children's governess, and Eppy, the children's nurse. Mrs Jones is the housekeeper here. You did not meet her before, I believe.'

'That is correct,' Anna replied. 'How very glad I am to meet you now, Mrs Jones.'

The housekeeper's smile was friendly. She leaned down to peek behind Anna. 'And who is that hiding behind you?'

Anna brought the children forward. 'This is Lord Calmount and his sister, Lady Dory.'

The housekeeper put her hands on her hips. 'Well, what a treat to have you here. We've fixed up a set of rooms for you that I hope you will like.'

Lord Brentmore came over to the children. 'Go with Mrs Jones to see your rooms. We'll have your trunks and your dinner sent up to you.' He glanced at the butler. 'Is that not right, Davies?'

'The trunks are being carried up as we speak and Cook has planned a special meal for the young ones.'

'Excellent.' Brentmore turned to Anna. 'Is there anything we've forgotten?'

'Not that I can think of,' she replied, although she was really too fatigued to think at all.

'Then you children can be on your way.' He gave Cal a reassuring squeeze of the shoulder.

'I want Miss Hill and Eppy to come, too!' Dory whined.

Lord Brentmore crouched down to her. 'Of course they will come with you. And Miss Hill said she would eat dinner with you tonight. That will be a treat, will it not?'

'I want you to eat dinner with us, too, Papa,' Dory whimpered.

He patted her arm. 'I cannot, but I will come up later to say goodnight.'

She popped her thumb into her mouth and Anna did not bother to tell her to take it out.

She also did not trouble herself to say goodnight to Mr Parker.

They followed Mrs Jones up to the third floor.

'We've set up one room as the school room and another for the children to sleep in. There is a small room for Eppy and another for you, Miss Hill. I hope that sounds satisfactory.'

'I am certain it will do very nicely,' Anna replied. 'I think Lord Cal and Lady Dory will be happier in the same room. Everything will seem strange to them.'

Mrs Jones smiled. 'That is what his lordship told us.'

'His lordship?'

Mrs Jones nodded. 'The marquess wrote very specific instructions. You are also to have a maid attend you. I will send her to you after we settle you in.'

'How very kind of him.' Although his kindness made everything more difficult. How unfortunate he was not the stern, fearsome man she had first met in this house. It would be so much easier to dislike him.

She shook herself. Of course it was preferable for him to be kind, especially for the children. She was simply much too fatigued.

Their rooms were satisfactory, but the school room was sparse. Anna had packed the children's slates and chalk, their sketchpads and some books, but she doubted it would be enough to amuse them.

Their dinner consisted of roast beef and plum pudding, with wafers for dessert and a hot milk posset when the children were ready for sleeping.

As he had promised, Lord Brentmore came to wish

the children a goodnight. He tucked the covers around them and kissed them each on the forehead. Hid tenderness made Anna's heart ache.

Making them promise to sleep well, he started to leave the room, but whispered to Anna, 'May I see you a moment?'

She nodded and hurriedly said her own goodnights to the children. 'You know which room is mine and which is Eppy's, so come fetch us if you need anything during the night.'

She walked out of the room to where Lord Brentmore waited. The hallway was narrow, placing her much closer to him than she would wish.

'How are they, do you think?' he asked her.

'Dory is much subdued and Cal has not said a word, not even to his sister,' she told him. 'But most likely that is from sheer weariness.'

He frowned. 'Did I make a mistake to have you come with me?'

Perhaps it would have been better to leave them all in the country. Perhaps accustoming herself to his absence was better done sooner than later.

But she could not speak to him of that. 'If I am able to keep the children occupied, it should be satisfactory, but there is nothing here in the house to occupy the children.'

His brows rose. 'I meant you—but, never mind. What do you mean, nothing in the house?'

'No toys. No blocks to build with. No games or puzzles. No dolls or toy soldiers.'

He rubbed his neck. 'Toys. How could I not think of that? We will remedy that first thing tomorrow.'

She nodded.

He gazed at her longer than was comfortable. 'But, Anna, how do you fare?' He extended his hand as if to touch her, but withdrew it again. 'Was the trip too much for you?'

She must look a fright. Not that it mattered so very much. She could not bear to see admiration in his eyes.

'I need rest, is all,' she managed.

He still looked concerned. 'I must return to Mr Parker. Will you be all right here? Will you ask the servants for anything you need?'

She nodded. 'Goodnight, my lord.' Her tone was more curt than she'd meant it to be.

She turned to leave, but he caught her arm. Instantly, her senses flared in response. She faced him and the yearning she'd worked so hard to conquer returned as strong as ever.

He must have felt it, too, because he held on to her arm and moved closer, but caught himself and released her.

'I wish to apologise for Mr Parker's rudeness to you,' he said. 'That was badly done of him.'

She touched her arm where he had held it. 'I am a governess. I did not expect more from him.'

'I do,' he responded hotly. 'In any event, you and I may dine together tomorrow.'

She inclined her head. 'As you wish.'

He searched her face. 'Anna,' he whispered, his tone aching.

She looked away. 'Goodnight, my lord,' she murmured and hurried into her room.

Chapter Eleven

The next morning after breakfast, Brent took Anna and the children to Noah's Ark, Mr Hamley's toy store on High Holborn Street.

When they stepped inside, Dory gasped. 'I have never seen anything so wonderful!'

Who could blame her? The toy store was a children's wonderland. From floor to ceiling toys filled the shelves. One whole wall honoured the store's name with its sets of Noah's Arks of various sizes and designs. Another shelf was filled with dolls. Another section held spinning tops and balls and other outdoor toys.

Cal was silent, but as wide-eyed as his sister. Even Brent was not indifferent to the sight. At Cal's age he would have been amazed that such toys existed. He remembered amusing himself for hours with the clay marbles his *daideó* made for him.

Where were they? he wondered. He'd hidden them from the old marquess and managed to bring them to England with him, but, over the years, he'd lost track of where he'd hidden them.

Brent glanced at Anna, but her expression was impossible to decipher. Was she thinking of the toys of her childhood as well? Surely Lord and Lady Lawton would have indulged their daughter with dolls and tea sets and all sorts of toys that little girls liked. Perhaps Anna only played with toys that were never to be hers.

Anna followed Dory over to the display of dolls, more than the child could count.

Some were made of painted wood. Others were made of wax and appeared so real Brent was certain they were about to open their mouths and demand to be fed. On the floor in front of the shelf was a huge doll's house, complete with miniature furniture so detailed one could imagine shrinking and living there in great comfort. Anna crouched down with Dory and pointed to the small doll family, the mother and father in the parlour, the children in the nursery with their governess.

He walked over to where Dory and Anna stood.

'Would you like a doll house, Dory?' he asked.

The little girl sighed. 'Oh, yes!'

'Should I purchase it for her?' he asked Anna. 'Is it suitable?'

She glanced at him. 'I believe she adores it.'

He would purchase it, if for no other reason than that Anna approved of it.

He turned. 'Shopkeeper!'

The gentleman behind the counter signalled for a clerk to assist the woman he'd been helping. He quickly approached Lord Brentmore. 'Your lordship? How may I serve you?'

It always surprised Brent how shopkeepers knew he was titled. Did the man spy the crest on his carriage through the shop window? Or was there some other clue?

'I want this doll house and everything in it,' he told the man. 'Packed up and delivered to me by this afternoon, if possible.'

The shopkeeper's face lit up. 'With pleasure, sir!' His expression turned shrewd. 'There are other sets of dolls that may be added. Would you like to see them?'

'What sorts of dolls?' Dory piped up.

'A set of servants, sir. A dog and cat.'

She looked beseechingly at her father and became the image of her mother.

Brent's enjoyment was shaken.

'Include all the dolls,' he said, turning away so Dory—and Anna—would not see his mood so abruptly change.

He turned to Cal, who seemed frozen in place, looking from one display to another. The boy, like Brent at that age, had never seen such toys, Brent realised.

He put a hand on Cal's shoulder. 'What shall we find for you, Cal?' He glanced to the shopkeeper. 'What special toys do you have for my son?'

'Well.' The man wrung his hands in eagerness. 'We've just received a set of tin soldiers from France. Made by Mignot. The finest I've ever seen. It is a Waterloo set, my lord.'

Brent felt Cal tremble with eagerness.

'Let us see it,' he said.

'It is still in boxes in the back, my lord. Give me a moment.' The man rushed off.

Brentmore looked at his son. 'Do you want to see the Waterloo soldiers, Cal?'

Cal nodded.

Brent crouched down to his level. 'Will you say it out loud for me?' he asked gently.

'Y-yes,' Cal uttered.

Brent squeezed his shoulder and glanced towards Anna, who stared at them both.

Once she would have smiled at Cal's effort.

'What else should we buy?' he asked her.

Anna looked around the shop. 'Puzzles? Spinning tops?'

'Choose whatever you like,' Brent would purchase whatever she liked, heedless of cost.

The woman who'd been passed on to the clerk completed her purchases and left. They were the only customers in the shop.

The clerk approached them. 'May I assist, sir?'

'May we see that Noah's Ark, please?' Anna pointed to the largest wooden ark on one of the shelves.

'This is quite good quality,' the clerk said. 'Finest wood and paint.'

The ark was cleverly designed to act as a box for the pairs of animals in the set, about fifty in number and including Noah and his wife.

Dory skipped over. 'Oh, look at that Noah's Ark!'

The shopkeeper emerged from the back room. 'Here is a part of the Waterloo set, my lord.' He placed a box on the counter and brought out a replica of a French soldier and a British dragoon. Cal touched it with a finger.

'These are finely done. Very lifelike,' Brent remarked.

'Were you there, my lord?' the shopkeeper asked.

Brent placed the tin soldier back in the man's hand. 'Not as a soldier.' He'd been deep in clandestine work then, though, gathering information to send back to Wellington. He turned to Cal. 'Should we buy it for you?'

'Yes.' The boy responded without hesitation. 'Th-thank you.'

'Send it with the doll's house,' Brent told the shopkeeper.

They walked around the shop and added spellicans and dominoes, battledore and shuttlecocks, dissected puzzles and spinning tops, skittles and a fine set of marbles, small gems compared to the ones Brent had loved.

The shopkeeper appeared to be in ecstasy as he made a tally of all the purchases.

Dory pulled on Brent's coat. 'Papa, may I please have a doll?'

Her request was tentative so that, this time, she was very unlike her mother.

He felt a pang of tenderness towards her. 'Of course you may.'

Anna went with her to the doll shelf where Dory chose, not any of the finely made porcelain or wax dolls, but a simple wooden one, with hair painted yellow, eyes blue, and wearing a simple frock covered with an apron.

'Not one of the fancy ones, Dory?' Brent asked her.

Dory shook her head. 'This doll needs me.' She looked up at him. 'Please, Papa? This doll?'

He nodded, unable to speak. Perhaps she was not like Eunice at all.

Cal carried a toy sword over to Brent and asked just as tentatively as Dory had, 'Papa? May I?'

Brent's voice turned thick. 'Yes, Cal. You may.' He swallowed the lump in his throat. 'What else do we need?'

Cal looked up at him. 'Blocks?'

The clerk added a fine set of blocks to the pile of purchases and Brent asked that everything be delivered to Cavendish Square that very day. He allowed Cal to carry his toy sword with him and Dory held on to her doll as if her life depended on it.

Anna glanced at him and he fancied she felt as he did: that these children deserved this indulgence. They'd been nearly as deprived as he until she came into their lives.

'Do you approve?' he asked her.

Her eyes were warm. 'Very much,' she said.

Brent felt that erotic pull between them, even in the

middle of the toy store. Good God. He needed more distraction.

When they left the toy store and climbed into the carriage again, he instructed the coachman to take them to
Berkeley Square.

'How would you like some ices?' he asked the children.
'I feel a great need for something sweet.'

Cal gave him a puzzled look.

'What are ices?' Dory asked.

These children had never tasted ices? Brent's guilt
rushed back.

Anna explained, 'Ices are sweet and cold and delicious
treats.'

Gunter's Confectionery on Berkeley Square was one
of the few places that a gentleman might properly escort
an unmarried woman. A marquess, his children and their
governess would raise no one's eyebrows.

Brent instructed the coachman to pick them up in a
half-hour. Dory carried her doll and Cal his sword, both
promising not to disturb anything with them.

As soon as they opened the door, the scent of sugar,
spice and fruit enveloped them. The shop was filled with
display cases of marzipan made in the shapes of colourful fruits.

'Oh, look!' cried Dory, peering into the cases. 'What
are they?'

'They are sweets,' Anna explained.

Dory looked at her father. 'May we buy some? They
are so pretty!'

'Yes, we may.' He gave her a serious look. 'But it is for
a special treat. Not for all the time.'

She nodded solemnly.

He glanced at Anna and wondered how often she'd had
sweets like this. Had Lord and Lady Lawton favoured her

in even that small way or had she been forced to watch her half-sister eat them alone?

He ordered pistachio ices for all of them, including Anna, and a box of the marzipan.

As Dory and Cal quietly examined every confection in the cases, Brent leaned over to Anna. 'It pains me how much of childhood they've never seen. I want to make it up to them all at once.'

She looked up at him, her lovely blue eyes filled with understanding. 'You are doing very well, my lord.'

To his surprise she touched his arm, a light, fleeting touch, but one that he felt deep within him.

Lawd, he wanted to take away all her suffering, as well, but he had caused part of the sadness that now wrapped around her like a cloak.

The Gunter's waiter bowed and handed him the box of sweets. 'If your lordship wishes, you may wait in the Square and I will bring your ices as soon as they are ready.'

Anna took the box. 'I will carry it, my lord.'

Brent called to the children, 'Come. Let's wait outside.'

As they walked to the shop door, it opened and in walked the two people Brent most wished to delay encountering.

His cousin and Miss Rolfe.

'Brent!' His cousin Peter broke into a surprised grin. 'You are in town!'

'We arrived yesterday.' He intended to send word to Peter and Lord Rolfe later this afternoon. He nodded to Miss Rolfe. 'Good day, Miss Rolfe.'

'Good day, Lord Brentmore.' She appeared reticent and why should she not be? He'd left her abruptly and taxed his cousin to make his excuses.

Peter crouched down. 'Do not tell me this is Calmount and Dorothea! They are so grown.'

Dory appeared willing to accept the attention of this new person, but Cal stepped back.

'Yes.' Brent was glad to turn his attention away from Miss Rolfe. 'Children, this is my cousin, who last saw you when you were babies.'

'At their christenings!' Peter smiled at them.

Why had he not told Anna of Miss Rolfe?

He knew why. When he was with Anna, he wished to pretend Miss Rolfe did not exist.

'Say "How do you do," children,' Anna told them.

Brent felt sick inside.

Dory curtsied and parroted, 'How do you do.'

Cal nodded, but did not speak. Instead the boy looked as if he'd sensed his father's discomfort.

Brent had no choice but to continue the introductions. 'Peter. Miss Rolfe. May I present Miss Hill, the children's governess.' He turned to Anna. 'This is my cousin, Mr Caine, and Miss Rolfe...' he paused '...my fiancée.'

Anna felt as if she had no air to breathe, no control of her muscles.

She forced herself to curtsy. 'How do you do, Mr Cain. Miss Rolfe.' She quickly turned her attention to the children. 'Come, let us go to the Square. Give your father a chance to visit.'

The children did not hesitate to accompany her. She hoped that Lord Brentmore's...companions did not guess that she needed to flee.

From him.

They found a bench with a view of the teashop door and sat.

'What is a fiancée?' Dory asked, clutching her doll to her chest.

Anna should not be compelled to tell the children their

father planned to remarry. 'Oh, a special friend. I am certain your father can explain it better.'

Cal gave her a searching look, as if he knew her suffering.

She picked at the string that tied the box closed. 'Shall we peek in the box and see what treats the waiter gave us?'

They complied, but Anna believed they were merely helping her to calm down.

Of course he should marry again. Widowed men remarried, especially if they carried a title and had only one son to inherit. He did not owe her any explanation of his private life. She was merely a governess, after all.

But could he not have told her of this fiancée before she showed him her heart and desire?

She glanced up and spied him crossing the road. The waiter—and his cousin and fiancée—followed him. He looked directly at her.

She closed the box and tied its string. 'Your father is coming with the ices.'

'I'm not hungry now,' Dory said.

'Well—' Anna spoke in a firm voice '—your father has been very generous today and we will be very polite and eat what is offered to us. Can you agree?'

They both nodded.

Lord Brentmore's gaze remain fixed on her until he was within a few feet of them, then he seemed to force a smile for the children. 'Here are your ices.'

The children placed their toys on the bench and the waiter served them. They dutifully dipped their spoons in and had their first taste of ices.

'This is delicious!' Dory said too brightly.

Cal nodded.

Miss Rolfe and Mr Caine joined them, taking their own ices from the waiter's tray.

Anna stood. 'Miss Rolfe may sit here,' she said quietly to Lord Brentmore.

'Anna—' he began.

She did not give him a chance to say more. She walked behind the bench and stood by a tree as Miss Rolfe took her place.

A place that had never truly been Anna's.

It seemed an eternity before the carriage returned. Anna let Lord Brentmore gather the children to leave. She joined them at the carriage while the children were climbing in.

The marquess extended a hand to assist her. She avoided looking at him. He gripped her hand. 'Anna, I will not be accompanying you. My cousin wishes me to call upon Lord Rolfe.' He gave her an entreating look. 'I have been remiss...'

She finally looked at him directly, but she could not speak.

'Please tell Davies I expect to return in time for dinner.'

She climbed inside.

'Papa isn't coming with us,' Dory said.

Anna hugged her. 'Yes, he told me. He is going to visit more friends. We will see him later.'

She talked about all the toys that would be delivered and what enjoyment would come from playing with them and, by the time they pulled up to the town-house door on Cavendish Square, some of the children's excitement was restored.

Dory ran to show Eppy her doll and to tell her about all the toys her papa had purchased. Cal walked up the stairs with Anna, his sword gripped in his hand.

When they reached Anna's door, he pulled on her hand. She leaned down. 'What is it, Cal?'

He lifted his sword. 'I can protect you with my sword.'

She threw her arms around him and held him close. 'Yes, you can, Cal.'

He looked so much like his father, it was as though his sword pierced her heart.

Lord Brentmore did not come home for dinner. He sent word of his absence at the last minute, when the table was already set. Rather than put the servants to more trouble, Anna dined alone at the big, unfamiliar table meant to seat at least a dozen people.

It merely made her mood more desolate.

All afternoon she had held her pain inside her and pretended nothing was amiss. Luckily the children had the toys to delight them. Anna tried to get caught up in their excitement as they unpacked the several crates that arrived. The crates stirred much curiosity. The footmen wished to see the Waterloo soldiers, and the maids were agog over the doll house.

Even in her misery, Anna realised this was a more relaxed and happy household than Brentmore Hall. Perhaps nothing would entirely erase the unhappiness of that place. She shuddered that she might spend years there.

Would the new marchioness be in residence there often? Or would she and the marquess spend most of their time in London? Would Lord Brentmore abandon the care of the children to his new wife? Would both she and the children lose him entirely?

How would Anna bear up under such changes? It was likely that she would be required to answer to the new marchioness and would lose her say over the children. Had she not lost enough already?

Most painful of all, how was Anna to endure the knowledge that Miss Rolfe would share Lord Brentmore's bed?

There was nothing to object to in Miss Rolfe, truth

be told. Her eyes were kind and she'd tried to engage the children in conversation as they ate their ices. She'd been gentle with Cal. Her clothes were not extravagant. Her light brown hair was simply dressed and all but covered with her bonnet. She was shorter than Anna, about as tall as Charlotte, whose height the comportment tutor insisted gentlemen preferred.

By the time Anna had finished dinner, she'd erected walls around her pain. It had been her foolishness that had caused her to become infatuated with a marquess, the weakness like her mother's to wish to seduce him.

She was strong. She could overcome loneliness and need. She'd merely forgotten what her father—Mr Hill, she meant—always said to her. That she was not a lady, no matter how many ladylike airs she adopted, and that she should never expect to be treated as one.

'I had forgotten that, Papa,' she said aloud to the empty room. 'But I shan't forget it any more.'

After leaving the dining room, Anna checked on the children. Both were sound asleep in their beds. Dory still held her doll in her arms. Cal slept with his sword. She kissed their smooth, untroubled foreheads and tucked the covers around each of them.

Anna retreated to her room, and allowed the maid to assist her in readying herself for bed. She let the maid's chatter wash over her. The girl went on about all the toys his lordship purchased today and how delighted the children had been and how enjoyable it must have been to pick out whatever they wanted at the toy shop.

When the maid finally bid her goodnight, Anna stood in the centre of the room, her arms around herself in a vain attempt at self-comfort. Tears threatened, but she refused to give in to them. Instead she paced the room, scolding herself for romantic fantasies, forcing herself to return to the strong, sanguine person she'd once been as Charlotte's companion. Back then she'd never expected anything for the morrow, never made plans, just happily accepted what came her way.

She walked to the window that overlooked the street and faced Cavendish Square. The long summer day had finally given way to night and the silence and darkness was broken only by the occasional carriage, with its lamps lighting the way.

It was time for her to accept who she was and where she belonged—somewhere in between Charlotte's world and her mother's, but not part of either.

She would purge herself of that carnal awareness of Lord Brentmore and learn to regard him, not as a lover, not as a friend, but as her employer.

'I'll not weaken again,' she vowed.

Chapter Twelve

Brent and his cousin Peter climbed into Brent's carriage after spending an afternoon and evening with Baron Rolfe and his wife and daughter. It had not been Brent's plan. He'd planned to make a quick call on the baron, reassure him that all was well, make an appointment for a later time and return to his children—and Anna.

He'd forgotten how affable the Rolfes were and how dependent they were on him for the survival of the baron's estate and for the well-being of the baron's children. He'd forgotten how thoroughly duty to others ruled the time of a marquess.

So he'd stayed with the Rolfes the afternoon, remained for dinner, and for tea afterwards.

'It was good of you to spend the evening, Brent,' his cousin said as soon as he was settled in the rear-facing seat of the carriage. 'Lord and Lady Rolfe were nearly at their wit's end when they had little word from you for so many weeks.'

'I'd not intended them to worry.' He'd actually given the Rolfes little thought when he was at Brentmore. 'The children were in great need of my attention.'

'The new governess summoned you, you said.' Peter

leaned back on the seat, clearly wanting Brent to tell him more.

There was little detail Brent wished to provide, even to his cousin. That a physician declared his son insane? That the children had been like prisoners in their rooms? That he had formed this unusual and at times ungentlemanly attachment to their governess?

That he had treated her very shabbily this day?

He rubbed his face. 'It was fortunate that she summoned me. The children were more troubled over their mother's death and the death of the old governess than I had been led to believe. Parker, it turned out, was not a very good reporter on the children's welfare.'

'And the governess was?' Peter added.

'She made all the difference.' And look how he repaid her. Hurting her, over and over.

'She's quite stunning,' Peter said. 'I'd not expected that.'

Stunning was a good description. Not the perfection of feminine beauty, but none the less so lovely it was difficult to look away.

'Quite stunning,' Brent agreed, keeping his tone even.

'How is that for you?' Peter persisted.

'How is what for me?' Brent played dumb.

'That your governess is a beauty.'

Brent made himself shrug. 'That would be to no purpose if she were not excellent with the children.' Where would his children be without her?

Peter's expression turned sceptical.

Brent ignored it. Instead he launched a counter-attack. 'You said you would explain my continued absence to Baron Rolfe and his daughter. Did you not do that?'

'Of course I did!' Peter looked offended. 'But Rolfe is insecure. He needs funds quickly.'

'So I learned.' The baron had humbled himself, both in

his recent letter and in his conversation with Brent this day, disclosing how desperate he was. 'I'll settle some money on him now. Parker can arrange it tomorrow.'

'That is good of you,' Peter murmured. 'I hope he accepts it.'

'Why wouldn't he?'

Peter glanced away. 'He's a proud man. He might think it is charity. You are not yet married to Susan—Miss Rolfe, I mean. You have not made an announcement or set a date.'

'I am not ready.' He frowned. 'The children are not ready.'

Brent knew Peter was right. He was being unfair to these good people to keep them in limbo, but he was not ready to marry.

Peter persisted. 'Do you not think it wise for the children to see Miss Rolfe as their mother as soon as possible?'

'No.' His tone was firm, but his reasons elusive. Why wait?

He wanted more time, like their time together during the summer. He wanted to help his son heal. He wanted to love Dory for herself.

And he wanted more time alone with Anna, as dangerous that was to them both.

Peter gave him a direct stare. 'Forgive me speaking my mind, Brent. But it is this attitude that creates the Rolfes' insecurity. I'll not have you trifle with these people. They are more than friends to me—'

Brent halted this speech with a raised hand. 'I have no wish to trifle with anyone. And certainly no wish to cause scandal. I've come to London to set everything straight, as you asked me to. Do not expect me to do so within a matter of hours.' He lowered his voice. 'Miss Rolfe must understand my children take precedence over everything. I intend to spend a great deal of time with them in London.

I will make an announcement and set a date for the wedding when I feel it is right for the children. If she cannot accept that, then perhaps she ought to cry off.'

The carriage stopped and both men glanced out the windows. They had reached Peter's rooms.

Peter rose to leave. 'Very well, Brent. I suspect there are several who will think this attention to your children very odd, but I see much to commend in it. I will explain it to Miss Rolfe.'

He climbed out and the carriage moved again, heading back to Cavendish Square.

Brent's thoughts immediately turned to Anna.

He relived the shock on her face when he introduced her to Miss Rolfe and was filled with guilt and regret.

No one was more deserving of happiness than Anna. Brent despised those people in her life who had so callously caused her pain.

And he suffered from the knowledge that he was one of them.

As Anna stood at the window another carriage approached, but this carriage stopped in front of the town house and discharged its passenger.

Lord Brentmore.

His appearance was no more than a dark silhouette, but that familiar thrill erupted inside her. She was glad she was on the third floor, far away from him.

She walked over to her bed and stared at the pillows. She was too restless to climb in and burrow under the covers. The brief glimpse of him was enough to set her insides fluttering like butterflies. She pressed her palm against her stomach and tried to still them.

There was a knock on her door, causing her to jump.

She crossed the room and put her lips near the door,

pausing before saying, 'Who is it?' She knew very well who it was.

'It is Brent.'

Why did he use a familiar address? She'd never called him Brent...although she had called him Egan.

'Will you open the door, Anna? I need to speak to you.' His tone was pleading.

She opened the door wide. No point in being tentative. She lifted her chin. 'Yes, my lord?'

'I owe you an apology—' he began.

She held up a hand. 'No, you do not, my lord.'

'I ought to have told you about my betrothal—'

She shook her head. 'I am governess to your children. I am in your employ. You do not owe me anything but wages.'

His cheek stiffened.

'I was surprised,' she went on. 'I admit that, but I quickly realised how inappropriate that was for someone of my station.' Oh, she was managing this so well!

'Stop it, Anna!' His stepped inside and closed the door behind him.

Anna's heart beat faster.

He stood inches from her. 'I ought to have told you long ago about Miss Rolfe, because you know very well there is something more between us than governess and employer. I feel it now as I felt it the first day, when I spied you pacing back and forth in the square outside this house. It is what led us to overstep the proper bounds.' His breathing accelerated. 'It is what led us to almost make love.'

All she had to do was take one step forwards and she could be in his arms; she could feel his lips against hers. She wanted his hands to stroke her body. She wanted him to touch her, to arouse her and to show her at last what it meant to be a woman.

She forced herself to stand her ground.

He ran a hand through his hair and turned away. 'God help me, I want to make love to you right now—'

'Do not say so,' she rasped.

He raised a hand. 'I know we cannot. I will not. I will not dishonour you. I cannot dishonour her.'

She turned her cheek as if he had struck her.

He seized her arms. 'Do you not see, Anna? I cannot treat you as Lawton did your mother.'

She raised her eyes, full of pain and worry. 'What do you do then? Do you send me away?'

Lord Lawton—her father—had sent her away.

His brows knitted. 'Do you wish to leave?'

Her chest ached. 'If you wish me to, I have no choice.'

He dropped his hands and swung away. 'I want you to raise my children. I want them to know you will be there for them every day, but—but you are not trapped here, Anna. If you wish to leave I will help you in every way I can.'

She folded her arms around her. 'Who would hire me? You ought not to have hired me. I know nothing of being a governess.'

He gave her an intent look. 'You knew better than anyone what Cal needed. What both the children still need. You loved them. They feel secure with you. I want nothing to change that.'

She stared at him. 'Marrying Miss Rolfe will change things.'

He gave her no argument.

She straightened. 'So we are to ignore this—this passion between us for the sake of the children?'

'We must,' he said in a low voice.

She went on. 'There must be no pretence of a friendship between us. We must be governess and employer. Nothing more.'

He nodded and made a gesture of surrender. His face turned solemn. 'I agree, but you must know, Anna, that I am still your friend ready to help you in any way, at any time.'

Did he not know that his kindness was the sharpest dagger he plunged into her flesh?

He raised his hand and drew a finger lightly down her cheek. 'Goodnight, Anna.'

He slipped out of the room and Anna touched her cheek.

Would their bargain make matters better for her or worse?

The next morning Brent entered the dining room to find Parker seated there, sipping a cup of tea.

'What the devil are you doing here?' Brent barked.

Parker rose to his feet. 'I came early, my lord. There is much correspondence to pore through and since you were not available yesterday, I thought you might wish to get started as soon as possible.'

'I can give you an hour this morning, no more.' Brent poured his tea and sat. 'I am taking the children to see the menagerie at the Tower.' Not that he owed his man of business an explanation.

'The children?' Parker's brows rose. 'But you spent the day with them yesterday.'

'I will spend part of each day with them, not that it is any of your concern.' He lifted the teacup to his mouth and sipped. 'By the way, I should tell you that I eat breakfast with the children. The governess will bring them any time now. You may fix yourself a plate and wait for me in the library.'

'Wait for you?' Parker seemed shocked.

Brent nodded. 'There is something I want you to arrange for me. A transfer of funds to Baron Rolfe.'

'Baron Rolfe?'

Parker knew nothing about his betrothal. 'I'll explain later. Go on with you.'

Parker rose and hurriedly put some bread and ham on his plate. 'Begging your pardon, sir, but I am astonished that you allow the children in the dining room.'

Parker was a confirmed bachelor who had even less need for children than he had for women. It was obvious to Brent now that Parker knew nothing of the children's needs.

He gave the man of business his coolest stare. 'I am astonished you would question my personal family affairs.'

Parker stiffened, then bowed, plate in hand. 'It will not happen again, my lord.'

'Thank you.' Brent took another sip of tea. 'You may ask Davies to bring you some tea.'

Almost immediately after Parker left, Anna and the children came in, Cal carrying his sword, Dory, her doll.

Brent caught Anna's eye briefly and smiled. She smiled back. It was a tentative smile at best, but then so had his been. But it was enough to encourage him that they could do this, help the children in spite of what hummed between them.

'Papa!' Dory ran over to give him a kiss.

He kissed her back, disarmed in spite of the memories of her mother that she evoked.

He left his chair to give Cal a hug. 'How are you this morning? Did you sleep well?'

Cal nodded.

Anna spoke up. 'As well as a boy could who slept with his sword.'

Brent ran his finger down the wooden blade of the toy

sword. 'A knight must be ready at all times to defend the castle. Is that not so, Cal?'

Cal made a face. 'Not a knight. An officer.'

'An officer?' Brent felt a pang of tenderness every time Cal spoke. 'In the war, I suppose.'

Cal nodded and then caught himself. 'Yes.'

Dory thrust her doll at Brent. 'I slept with my doll, Papa.'

'So you did, Dory.' He obligingly admired the doll. 'Did she sleep well?'

Dory's expression turned serious. 'She did not make any noise all night long.'

As they'd been afraid to do while Eunice has been alive.

Anna clapped her hands. 'Put the toys aside now, as you promised, and come tell me what you wish to eat this morning.'

The breakfast was as calm and pleasant as Brent could expect. So why did he feel a tug of regret, as if he'd lost something he would never get back?

After breakfast, Brent met with Parker, then took the children to the Tower to see the animals. Kings had kept their menageries of exotic animals there for centuries, and now visitors could pay to see them.

The trip was an unqualified failure. Although seeing the porcupine and zebra were met with cries of delight, the stench was so oppressive that Dory spent the entire time holding her nose. When they came upon the lions and tigers and other wild cats, the children stood silent. The big cats paced back and forth in their cages, always looking through the bars as if yearning to be free.

Brent understood why the sight of the caged animals disturbed the children. They'd been caged, too, until recently.

He less understood why Anna's gaze was riveted to the panther cage.

'Shall we go?' he asked.

'Yes,' Cal said.

Dory, her fingers still pinching her nose, nodded.

Anna took one last glance at the panther. 'As you wish.'

She engaged the children as before, but spoke to him only when necessary. He mourned the loss of their easy camaraderie.

When they waited for the carriage outside the Tower walls, Brent looked back at the imposing stone structure and leaned towards Anna. 'I should not have brought them here, to see a prison and caged animals.'

'Perhaps not,' she responded noncommittally.

'The panther seemed to captivate you,' he tried again.

'The panther,' she repeated absently, but she did not explain.

The children were delighted to return to the town house and to the abundance of toys waiting for them upstairs. They barely noticed when Mr Parker immediately begged for their father's attention on an urgent matter.

Anna was left with nothing to occupy her, though. She had no wish to impose lessons on the children after the depressing outing to the Tower, but she could not bear to be confined like the cats in their cages.

No matter her good intentions or her promises, it had been agony to be in Lord Brentmore's presence.

'My lord. If you please, I do need to speak with you,' Mr Parker said in a clipped voice.

The marquess crouched down to the children. 'I will try to come upstairs later.' He gave them hugs.

'Please, my lord. Come to the library.' Mr Parker was full of anxious impatience.

Lord Brentmore glanced at Anna before turning to follow Mr Parker.

She spoke up. 'My lord, may I have some time off? Eppy can keep an eye on the children.'

He turned back to her and she saw in his eyes the heat of passion they were trying so hard to ignore. 'Of course you may, Anna,' he said in a low voice.

The children ran up the stairs and Anna started to follow them, to make certain they were settled in before she left.

'One moment, Anna,' Lord Brentmore called to her.

He left Mr Parker and walked back to her. She waited for him on the first step, her heart racing at his approach. When he reached her, her face was even with his and their eyes connected.

Without looking away, he took her hand and placed several coins in her palm. 'Buy something for yourself, Anna. A book. A hat. Anything that pleases you.'

Another dagger of kindness. 'Thank you, my lord,' she murmured.

He held her gaze. 'Do not linger past two o'clock.'

'I will not.'

Men loitered on Bond Street and around the shops after two. Respectable women did not visit the shops at that hour.

He closed her fingers over the coins and squeezed her hand before releasing it and walking swiftly away.

Clutching the coins, warm from his hand, Anna climbed the stairway to tell Eppy and the children that she was going out. The children were already busy playing, Cal with his soldiers, Dory with the doll house.

'I'll keep a good eye on them, never you fear,' Eppy said.

As she walked away from Eppy, Anna finally looked in her hand.

He had given her five pounds! Never in her whole life had she possessed five pounds of her own. Goodness! Her salary for the whole year was only thirty pounds. She could buy a whole wall full of books for five pounds.

She put two pounds away with her other savings and carried the other three coins in her reticule. A few moments later she was walking towards New Bond Street. The weather was still cool for August, even as noon approached. She was glad she'd worn her spencer.

She walked past linen drapers and haberdashers, confectioners and watchmakers, shops she and Charlotte had visited when they'd first arrived in London. It seemed such a long time ago, not merely months.

She stopped in Griffin and Son to purchase a new pair of gloves and some hosiery. She peeked in the jewellery shops and admired glittering necklaces and bracelets, the sorts of items a gentleman might give a lady. As a betrothal gift, perhaps.

She quickly turned away.

At the stationers, she purchased new sketchbooks for the children and, on a whim, a journal, pen and ink for herself. She opened her heart to the simple pleasure of having money to spend and lovely things to purchase with it.

Her main intent was to visit Hatchard's Bookshop on Piccadilly to pick out a book for her very own. Once inside the shop, however, she could find nothing she wanted. A few short months ago, any book would have been a delight and all of them would have interested her. Now her mind seemed too restless to read.

She walked along the street to Jermyn Street and entered the Floris perfumery.

A clerk dressed almost as finely as a gentleman looked up from behind the counter. 'May I be of assistance, miss?'

'I would like a scent. Something new.'

This was frivolous indeed. She'd never purchased perfumery before, although she'd helped Charlotte make selections. Anna considered herself fortunate to have the lavender water she and Charlotte made themselves.

He sniffed. 'You wear lavender. An excellent scent, I agree, but for a young lady such as yourself, we have mixed something special.'

He placed a drop of scent on a piece of paper and lifted it to her nose.

It smelled light and floral, like being in a garden surrounded by flowers. 'Rose, obviously. And iris?' she guessed.

'Very good, miss, with a hint of jasmine.'

It was a lovely scent. 'Yes, that is perfect. I will have it. And some French-milled soap, please.' She might as well indulge herself completely.

'Would you like the scent in a throwaway? An *étui*? Or a larger bottle?'

Who knew when she might have another chance to spend without worry? A throwaway was a mere sample. An *etui* would be gone in a matter of weeks, even if she conserved it.

'A larger bottle,' she responded.

He showed her a range of pretty bottles. She selected one and paid him a pound. He returned her change on a velvet tray.

She'd never truly realised the power money gave a person. It was freeing to purchase whatever one desired. No wonder wealthy aristocrats spent great amounts on unnecessary things. It almost restored her to her old self. Happy and content.

She left the shop smiling as a lady and gentleman were preparing to enter.

'You!' the lady exclaimed.

Lord and Lady Lawton. She'd never dreamed they would be in London. Not in August. The plan had been for them to be in Brighton for the summer.

Anna curtsied. 'My lord. My lady.' She could not look at them. Could not look at Lord Lawton. Her father.

'What are you doing in London?' Lady Lawton demanded.

Anna reverted to old habits, saying or doing nothing to provoke Lady Lawton. 'My duties as governess.'

Her ladyship sniffed. 'As governess? What governess comes to London?'

Anna, eyes downcast, replied as if this were not a rhetorical question, 'I do not know, ma'am.'

But she glanced up at Lord Lawton, who did not look upon her any differently than he'd always done. With little interest. It suddenly infuriated her.

She straightened and looked him in the eye. 'I presume you were informed of my mother's death?'

His face turned red.

Lady Lawton said, 'Yes. Our condolences.' She made an annoyed gesture.

The poor woman. Made to endure seeing her husband's bastard child every day, the constant companion of her cherished daughter. Anna pitied her.

Her ire was confined to Lord Lawton. 'Did you attend the funeral, my lord?' She knew he had not.

He could not look at her. 'Impossible. Too busy.'

'A pity,' said Anna, 'after all her service to you.'

Lady Lawton made a shocked sound and Lord Lawton actually looked at Anna, as if seeing her for the first time. He now realised she knew who he really was, she was convinced.

Anna curtsied again. 'I am delaying your visit to the shop. Good day. Please give my regards to Charlotte.'

She walked away without waiting for permission to take her leave.

Perhaps she would tell of this meeting when she and Lord Brentmore dined this evening. He was the only one who could appreciate her small triumph.

Or maybe she would say nothing of it. It felt too much like a return to their previous intimacy.

It turned out she did not have to make the choice. Lord Brentmore had been summoned to his club to discuss some Parliamentary matter. Davies conveyed his apologies to her. He would dine at the club and be home late.

'I believe I will have dinner with the children, then,' Anna told the butler.

She did not want to be alone with her thoughts, with her loneliness.

This was merely a sample of what life would be like. His life would be among the *ton* and with his wife. At best she would see him with the children. She might not even be able to consult with him about the children. Likely she would report to his new marchioness. She would never be able to share her small triumphs and trials with him, and she had no one else to tell.

Chapter Thirteen

The next day Brent saw the children and Anna briefly at breakfast and heard all about how they played with the new toys. Brent promised Cal he would help him set up the soldiers and show him how the real battle unfolded, but he did not know when he could manage it.

Parker commanded much of his time out of necessity. One of his estates had been badly managed and there was much to be done to rectify the problems. Brent could not postpone addressing these issues because his tenants' lives depended upon his actions.

No sooner had Parker left the library than Davies entered. 'You have a caller, m'lord.'

It was early for callers. 'Who is it?'

Davies handed him the calling card. 'Mr Kenneth Yates, m'lord.'

Brent's gaze flew up. 'What the devil does he want?'

Davies—and everyone else—knew precisely who Kenneth Yates was—the man Eunice was chasing when she suffered the fatal fall from her horse.

'He did not tell me the purpose of his visit, m'lord,' Davies replied.

Brent rubbed his face. He might as well get this over

with. If Yates was back in the country, it would be only a matter of time before he would have to confront him. Better the first time be in private.

Brent rose. 'Send him in, Davies. I will see him here.'

A moment later Davies announced him. 'Mr Kenneth Yates, m'lord.'

Yates entered the room and the door closed behind him. He and Brent stared at each other before either of them spoke.

Yates finally said, 'Thank you for seeing me, Brent.'

The two men had known each other in school. Yates had been younger than Brent, but a decent sort of boy, not one to bully or ridicule. It made his betrayal with Eunice more surprising and doubly painful.

'I had not heard you were back,' Brent remarked. 'Where had you been? The Colonies?'

Yates tried a tentative smile. 'They prefer to call it America.'

Not that it mattered to Brent what the Americans called their country. 'Why did you come here, Yates?'

'To offer you my apology.'

It was a simple answer, but the reason to apologise was more complex. 'Why should I accept it?'

Yates drew a nervous breath. 'I cannot say whether you should or should not accept anything I say. I came to explain.'

'What good will that do?' He walked over to the window. 'What is done is done.'

If he hoped Yates would take the hint and leave, he was mistaken. Why had the man not remained in the Colonies?

Yates continued, 'It took me this year to understand what role I played in what happened. If I told you that I'd loved her, I am not certain now that would be the truth. I do know that my character was such that I could not resist her. She was captivating and I was weak. That might be the whole of it.'

How well Brent knew that Eunice could be captivating. She'd also possessed such exacting standards that she could never accept the truth about the maternal side of her husband's family.

'Are you asking for my forgiveness?' Brent countered, his tone sharp.

Yates's eyes widened. 'No. Not at all. But I could not return to London without attempting this conversation with you.'

Brent wished the man had never returned. His presence would only cause more talk and remind Brent of painful memories.

'There is only one thing I wish to know.' He glared at Yates. 'Do you intend to cause me more trouble? Or more trouble for my family?'

Yates took a step forwards. 'Believe me, Brent. I give you my word as a gentleman. I came here to assure you that I will not cause you or your family any trouble. Society will never know what you and I both know.'

Brent felt his anger flash. 'If you break your word I will destroy you. Do I make myself clear? There are innocents I will not have hurt.'

Yates held his gaze with a steady determination. 'I would rather die than have anyone hurt further by my follies.'

Brent believed him. He turned his head away in thought. 'If we are seen as feuding, it will cause gossip. If we are cordial, people will soon pay us no heed.'

Yates nodded. 'I could not agree more. I will not assume such behaviour changes your personal feelings about me, but I wish you to know my esteem of you is genuine. Eunice and I have got what we deserved. My punishment is to live with my mistakes and regrets, but you have done nothing wrong.'

Brent knew that statement to be false. He had wronged his children. Abandoned them to suffer Eunice's unhappiness. He had vowed to amend his ways. Perhaps he could believe Yates capable of the same thing.

'Well!' Yates expelled a tense breath. 'I will not trouble you more. I have said all I needed to say. I bid you good day, Brent. Thank you for seeing me.'

He turned and walked to the door.

When he opened it, Brent said, 'It took courage to face me, Yates. I wish you a good day, as well.'

The tension in Yates's face eased. He bowed and walked out of the library.

Anna and the children burst into the hall just as a gentleman was leaving. The children ran into him.

'Children! Take care!' Anna cried, pulling them out of the man's way. 'Go upstairs and wash your hands and faces.'

They ran for the stairway.

'And do not run!' she cried, tossing the man a look of dismay.

He watched the children scamper up the stairs.

'Forgive me, sir,' she said to him. 'I thought a walk would deplete them of energy. Obviously it had the opposite effect.'

He blinked and dragged his gaze away from where the children had been. 'They have grown since I saw them last.'

'Oh?' she smiled. 'You know Lord Brentmore's children?'

He looked rueful. 'I have seen them before...' His voice

faded, then he seemed to collect himself. 'I am remiss. Allow me to present myself. I am Mr Yates.'

'A friend of the family?' she asked. There was something in his manner. Something unspoken.

'No.' He looked sad. 'Someone known to Lord Brentmore. I have newly returned to town and have paid my respects.'

She extended her hand. 'I am Miss Hill, the children's governess.'

He shook it. 'I remembered the governess as a lady with grey hair.'

He had seen Mrs Sykes? 'I am the new governess.' She suddenly felt uneasy about saying too much, not knowing who this man was, after all. 'Where were you that you have returned to town?'

'I— I spent a year in America,' he responded.

'America?' She forgot her reticence. 'I have read a great deal about America. The savages. The bison and bears. In fact, yesterday we saw a grizzly bear at the Tower.'

'You took the children to the Tower?' he asked.

She wished she had not mentioned it. She stepped back. 'I am keeping you from wherever you need to be. I bid you good day, sir.'

'Good day, Miss Hill.' He bowed.

Davies appeared in the hall. 'Did I hear Mr Yates leave?'

She nodded. 'Who is he? He seemed to know the family.'

Davies came close to her ear. 'Do not tell Lord Brentmore I said so, but he is the man with whom the marchioness had a long affair. It is said he broke it off and that is why she rode after him and fell from her horse.'

Her eyes widened. 'Why did he come here?'

Davies was clearly eager to discuss this. 'That is a puzzle. He wished to speak to his lordship, is all I know.'

'He said he came to pay his respects,' Anna shared.

'That is odd, indeed.' Davies seemed to catch himself. 'But I have said too much already. One must not gossip.'

'I will say nothing, Davies,' she assured him.

Lord Brentmore walked into the hall. 'Did he leave, Davies?'

'He did, m'lord.' Davies slid a glance to Anna, who started to climb the stairs.

Lord Brentmore spoke to her. 'How are you, Anna?'

'Very well, my lord.' She lowered her gaze and tried to dampen her response to him.

'Where are the children?' he asked.

'Washing up. We just came in from a walk.'

He frowned. 'I've seen so little of them.'

'They will be playing with the toys.'

He looked regretful. 'I wish I could spend some time with them. I have an appointment at Coutts and then I'm engaged to meet my cousin.'

It seemed each day took him further away.

He added, 'I plan to return for dinner, though.'

She glanced towards the butler. 'Discuss it with Davies. It is better for me and for the servants if I dine with the children.'

He looked disappointed. 'I suppose I deserve that. I have cancelled out on you each night since we've been here.'

She raised her eyes to his. 'London has changed things.'

As the days passed by Anna and the children adapted to this new routine. Lord Brentmore continued to share breakfast with his children, but any other time spent with them was snatched from his busy schedule. An hour here or there to show Cal with the tin soldiers some part of the Waterloo battle. A few minutes to see how Dory had rearranged her doll house. Quick instruction in fencing for them both, because Dory would not be left out of something so exciting and fun. Anna was never alone with him.

She resumed giving the children their lessons and did her best to devise outings for them, some enjoyable, some not. They were measured and fitted for new clothes, something that delighted Dory, but not her brother. They took walks around Mayfair and played with the ball and skittles in the Square or in the small garden behind the town house. She took them to the Egyptian Hall to see Napoleon's carriage and other artifacts from Waterloo. They visited the shops and had ices from Gunter's again, but it was not Anna's favourite place, reminding her of Miss Rolfe.

Lord Brentmore never spoke of Miss Rolfe to Anna. Never mentioned if the social events he attended at night were in her company. Never told Anna when the marriage date was planned so she would know when her life was about to change again.

Her outing with the children for this day was Hyde Park. They would spend a couple of hours there exploring its paths until the fashionable hour was upon them and the society carriages began circling the park. She and Charlotte had once sneaked into the park to witness this event. Anna remembered reassuring Charlotte that some day Charlotte would be riding in a gentleman's carriage, dressed in finery as lovely as any of the ladies they'd seen.

The children, dressed and ready for the park, were fidgeting in the hall, impatiently waiting for Anna to finish pulling on her gloves and tying her bonnet.

The door opened and Lord Brentmore walked in. The children ran to him for hugs.

'Where are you off to?' he asked Cal.

Cal hesitated, but said, 'Hyde Park.'

'Indeed? What will you do there?' he asked.

'Play,' replied Cal, lifting up his sword.

'I have never been to Hyde Park,' piped up Dory. 'I do believe Hortense will like it.'

'Hortense?' Her father's brows rose.

'My doll.' Dory was still trying out different names for her doll.

Lord Brentmore glanced over at Anna. 'Do you mind if I accompany you?'

Her stomach clenched. 'If you desire it.'

A few minutes later they were on their way. The children skipped ahead and Lord Brentmore fell in step with Anna.

'How are they faring?' he asked her.

'They seem happy enough,' she responded.

'And you?' His gaze was too penetrating.

She paused before answering, 'Well enough, my lord.'

He glanced around. 'This reminds me of our walks at Brentmore.'

She darted a look at him. 'Except for the town houses and the carriages and other pedestrians.' And the tension between them.

'There is that,' he agreed. His voice lowered. 'I miss our time at Brentmore.'

She took several steps before responding. 'I suppose you will never have much time to spend there.'

They entered the park at Grosvenor Gate. The afternoon was so fine that there were several other people strolling through the park.

When they came upon an expanse of grass, Dory asked, 'May we run, Papa?'

Lord Brentmore answered, 'You may, but stay in our sight.'

Dory squealed in delight and she and Cal took off.

'Mind that sword!' Anna cried to Cal. He could fall on it and injure himself.

Cal didn't fall. Anna was forced to walk at Lord Brentmore's side, so reminiscent of more carefree days. At least the children were happy.

May it last for them, she silently prayed.

Lord Brentmore's arm brushed against hers, setting off memories of more tender touches. Was he happy? she wondered. She could not tell and would not ask.

'Anna,' he spoke. 'I have been meaning to tell you that I've seen Lord Lawton in town. The family are spending the summer here.'

'I know,' she said.

'You know?' He sounded surprised.

'I saw him at the shops.' She offered no more detail and he asked for none.

They walked on in silence.

Finally, Lord Brentmore murmured, 'Anna.'

She glanced at him and their gazes caught for a moment. His eyes darkened and filled with yearning. As did hers, she suspected.

They had almost reached the other side of the grassy area and the children ran back to them.

Cal tapped his father on the arm. 'May we walk to the Serpentine, sir? Anna said we might feed the ducks.'

Lord Brentmore touched the boy's cheek. 'Of course, but you must walk.'

Both Cal and Dory nodded and skipped ahead.

'You thought of feeding the ducks?' Brentmore asked Anna.

'Davies suggested it,' she answered. 'Cook gave us some bread.'

When they reached the water, Anna pulled from her pocket the pieces of bread wrapped in a napkin. She handed a piece to each child and instructed them on how to tear off bits and throw them to the ducks. Soon a flock of ducks surrounded them, quacking for more.

When they finished the bread they continued their walk, turning on a footpath heading toward The Ring, a circle of trees planted during the reign of Charles I.

From the carriage road a voice called, 'Lord Brentmore! Yoo hoo! Brentmore!'

He glanced behind them. There was a curricle stopped on the road and an older woman waved her handkerchief at them.

'I must greet them,' he said, turning back.

Anna watched him approach the curricle. A younger woman leaned forwards.

Miss Rolfe.

Anna swung away and walked quickly to catch up to the children. She let them go a far enough distance that she could not see the curricle. 'Dory! Cal! We must wait for your father.'

She saw a group of people approaching from the other direction and guided the children to a patch of grass nearby, so they would not be in the way.

The grass was dotted with patches of clover. 'See if you can find a four-leaf clover,' she suggested. 'It will bring good luck.' And keep them occupied.

Good luck was lost to her, she imagined. The children, however, took to the task with much enthusiasm.

The people, a woman and two gentlemen, came closer. Anna turned her back to them, making herself as inconspicuous as a governess ought to be. She heard their footsteps coming near.

'Anna?' The woman hurried up to her. 'Anna!'

It was Charlotte.

Her dear friend—her half-sister—gave her a hug. 'I did

not know you were in London!' She glanced towards the children. 'Are those your charges? They are darling! But tell me why you are here. Why did you not tell me you were in London? Why have you not written to me?'

Charlotte did not receive her letters? Obviously her mother and their father had not shown Charlotte Anna's letters or told her of seeing Anna at the scent shop. But what good would it do Charlotte to know those things? 'Perhaps my letters were lost. I—I have been kept very busy.'

'With those two?' Charlotte gave them a fond look. 'They appear to be no trouble at all.' She turned to the two men who were accompanying her. 'But let me present you.' She gestured for them to come closer. 'Anna, this is Lord Ventry and Mr Norton. Gentlemen, this is my very dearest friend, Miss Hill.'

Their brows rose and their gazes darted to the children.

Charlotte went on, 'Miss Hill is the governess to Lord Brentmore's children.'

'Lord Brentmore?' Mr Norton's brows rose. 'Pleased to meet you.'

Lord Vestry inclined his head. 'I tell you, my governess looked nothing like you. I might have spent more time with my lessons if she had.'

Charlotte threaded her arm through Anna's. 'Isn't she beautiful? She quite puts me in the shade.'

Mr Norton smiled diplomatically. 'Together you make a very pretty picture indeed.'

Charlotte turned back to Anna. 'Lord Vestry and Mr Norton both called upon me at the same time to take a ride in the park, but it is such a beautiful day I suggested we walk instead.' She leaned into Anna's ear and whispered, 'I believe they are both suitors.'

Another gentleman walking on the path approached. He caught Anna's eye and tipped his hat. 'Good day, Miss Hill.'

'Mr Yates,' she responded.

He slowed when he caught sight of the children. 'I see you have gone for another walk.'

'Yes, indeed,' she replied.

He seemed to notice Charlotte and his expression changed. 'Good day, miss. Forgive my intrusion,' he said in a low voice.

The other two men jostled each other and whispered something.

Charlotte stepped forwards. Her manner towards her escorts had been cordial, but for Mr Yates her colour heightened and her voice became breathy. 'You did not intrude, sir.'

Anna had no choice but to introduce them. 'May I present Mr Yates to you, Charlotte.' She turned to Mr Yates. 'This is Lady Charlotte, Lord Lawton's daughter.'

Yates extended his hand and Charlotte grasped it. Neither seemed inclined to let go, but Charlotte finally collected herself. 'Anna is my dearest friend, Mr Yates,' she explained. 'I have not seen her for weeks and did not even know she was in London.'

'So this is a reunion,' he said.

Charlotte pressed her cheek against Anna's. 'A very welcome one.' She released Anna and looked into her face. 'But now we may see each other! Surely Lord Brentmore gives you time off. You can come call on me.'

She could not tell Charlotte how unwelcome she would be. 'I cannot, Charlotte. I have to care for the children.'

'But not in the evenings, surely! I know! You must come to our ball. Mama and Papa are giving a ball next week. It will not be a huge ball because there are not that many people in London, not as many as during the Season.' She turned to her companions. 'Gentlemen, Miss Hill should come to my ball, should she not?'

Mr Norton nodded. 'I should like that very much, indeed.'

'A lovely lady such as you would be welcome,' Lord Vestry added.

But a governess who was the natural daughter of the lord of the house would not be at all welcome. 'It is not my place to attend—' she began.

Charlotte cut her off. 'Nonsense! You are my dearest friend. You have always been with me.' She turned to Mr Yates and her tone grew softer. 'And will you come, too, Mr Yates? We need more gentlemen.'

He bowed. 'I would be honoured.'

Brent walked quickly to catch up with Anna and the children. He'd have to leave them again and the idea depressed him. He did not wish to see Anna's face—or the faces of the children—when he told them.

He found her surrounded by three gentlemen and another lady. At least two of the men whose faces he could see were smiling at Anna.

He quickened his step.

'Anna!' he called out, when he was in hearing distance. 'What is this?'

She turned to him and stepped away from her companions. 'Lady Charlotte, my lord.' She sounded upset. 'We met by chance.'

That did not explain the cadre of men around her. One of the men turned and nodded to him.

Yates.

What was he doing here?

'Where are the children?' Brent demanded. Had she forgotten them? Let them run off?

She pointed to where the children sat in the grass, absorbed in something or another.

'They are looking for four-leaf clovers,' she explained in a cautious voice. 'I have been watching them.'

Lady Charlotte left the group and came to Anna's side. 'Lord Brentmore?' She smiled. 'Forgive me for stealing a moment of Anna's time. I have not seen her in so long.' This woman had been a child plagued with shyness? 'Oh, dear. We have not been introduced.'

Anna made the introductions.

'And do you know these gentlemen?' Lady Charlotte asked, gesturing to her entourage.

'Mr Yates and I are acquainted,' Brent said.

One of the other gentlemen elbowed the other. Obviously they knew the gossip, even though they looked as if they'd just been breeched.

'Good to see you, Brent,' Yates said.

Lady Charlotte presented the young gentlemen to Brent, who merely nodded to them.

He turned to Anna. 'I would speak with you for a moment.' He took her aside. 'Lord and Lady Rolfe desire me to take a turn around the park with them.' He refrained from mentioning Miss Rolfe to her.

She stiffened almost imperceptibly. 'Will you tell the children or shall I?'

'I will tell them.' He felt consumed with guilt, although it should be the most natural thing in the world to spend time with one's fiancée and her parents. 'Do you feel comfortable walking home alone with the children?'

Her chin rose. 'If you wish it, how can I object?'

If this had been a fencing match, her hit would have earned a point. He nodded and walked off to tell the children.

'Papa!' Dory cried when she saw him. 'We are looking for lucky four-leaf clovers.'

He smiled at them. 'And have you found any?'

Cal looked at him. 'No.'

'Well, you will have to make your own good luck.' He tried to sound cheerful. 'I came over to tell you I am going to say goodbye to you here.'

'Why?' Dory asked.

'Did you see the people in the carriage? I walked back to talk with them?'

The children both nodded.

'Well, they want me to ride in their carriage, and because I have not seen them in a long time—' almost a week at least '—I need to go with them now.'

Dory's eyes widened. 'Will you come back?'

Another wounding question. Did she think he would leave them? 'Of course I will come back, I will see you later, before you go to bed.'

'Oh.' She relaxed. 'Then goodbye, Papa.'

'Goodbye,' Cal added.

When he walked back to Anna, Yates stood with her. 'Brent, I was on my way to my town house, but, if you like, I am at liberty to escort your governess and the children home.'

The young gentlemen were watching this exchange intently.

Brent raised his voice a little. 'Thank you, Yates. That is good of you.' He glanced at Anna. 'I will see the children later at home.'

She did not respond.

Anna watched Lord Brentmore walk away. It seemed as if she'd been ripped to shreds and casually discarded, even though she had no right to feel that way, merely because he'd chosen to spend time with his fiancée.

'Will you walk with us, Miss Hill?' Mr Norton asked.

She'd forgotten about Mr Norton and Lord Ventry and anyone else. 'I must get the children home.'

'Oh, Anna!' Charlotte came over and hugged her again. 'I will see you soon, when you come to our ball. Promise me you will come?'

What reason would Charlotte accept? 'I did not bring a gown with me.'

Charlotte waved that excuse away. 'We can fix that.'

'No, Charlotte. I simply must say no.' She turned away. 'And now I need to get back to my duties.'

'Very well.' Charlotte sounded disappointed. 'But we must see each other. I have so much to tell you. And I want to hear all about being Lord Brentmore's governess.'

Lord Ventry and Mr Norton exchanged glances, but she could not worry about what they thought of Lord Brentmore.

And there was too much Anna could not tell Charlotte. That they were sisters. That their father cared nothing for Anna or Anna's mother. That Anna was more like her mother than she could ever have guessed. That she wanted to be Lord Brentmore's lover as well as his children's governess. That another woman—and his scruples—prevented it.

'Perhaps if I have a day off,' she prevaricated.

'Lady Charlotte,' Lord Ventry called, 'shall we be on our way?'

'I have to go.' Charlotte gave her another swift hug, then hurried over to her companions.

Anna joined the children. 'Shall we walk some more?' she asked. 'Mr Yates is going to walk with us, is that not nice of him?'

'We didn't find any clovers.' Dory picked up her doll and popped her thumb into her mouth.

Anna gently pulled her thumb out again. 'Come on.' She took Dory's hand. Cal rose and walked with them.

Mr Yates stood waiting for them. 'If we continue past The Ring there will be a foot path leading directly to the Cumberland Gate. That will be the fastest way out.'

They passed The Ring, Mr Yates walking a little behind Anna, Anna holding each child's hand.

Dory dawdled, forcing Anna to pull her along. She was losing patience. 'Dory, faster, please.'

The little girl walked slower.

'She is tired,' Mr Yates said in a low tone.

'She's had a busy day.' Anna released Cal's hand and picked up Dory. 'Oh, she is heavy.'

Cal walked slowly, as well, hitting his sword on the path as he went.

Anna's arms and back quickly began to ache.

Mr Yates stopped her. 'Allow me to carry the child.'

'Thank you, Mr Yates.' Anna handed Dory to Mr Yates.

He turned his head to ask the little girl, 'Do you mind if I carry you, Lady Dory?' His voice was low and tremulous.

Why this emotion from him? she wondered.

'I do not mind,' Dory whimpered.

Both Mr Yates and Dory turned their faces to Anna.

She stifled a gasp.

Looking back at her were two identical pairs of eyes. There was also a very similar shape of the chin.

'Oh, Mr Yates!' she exclaimed breathlessly.

This man was Dory's father. Not Lord Brentmore. She was certain of it.

He shook his head as if to silence her.

Dory twisted around and laid her head on his shoulder. He closed his eyes as if savouring the moment.

There was nothing to do but be on their way. Anna bent down to Cal, who'd sat down on the path to rest. 'Come on, Lord Cal. Time to start moving again.'

The boy took her hand.

Anna's own turmoil was momentarily forgotten. She could not think of anything but the secret she'd discovered. Did Lord Brentmore know? She could say nothing while with the children, but she must know more.

They walked in virtual silence back to the town house. Once when she exchanged a glance with Mr Yates, his eyes appeared moist.

Finally they arrived at the town house and were admitted into the hall by Davies, whose brows almost disappeared into his forehead.

'She is sleeping,' Mr Yates whispered.

Cal already was plodding up the stairs.

'Davies, would you be so good as to carry Lady Dory up to Eppy? I want to thank Mr Yates before he must leave.'

Davies reached for the little girl. 'Where is his lordship?'

Of course, he would not know. 'He—he encountered some friends and went with them.'

Davies frowned as Yates transferred Dory to him.

Anna gestured for Mr Yates to follow her to the drawing room right off the hall.

'You have guessed?' Yates said as soon as she closed the door. He sounded anxious and resigned.

She met his eye. 'That you are her father? Yes, indeed.'

He leaned towards her. 'You must say nothing of this. Nothing. Ever! Do you understand me?'

She did not flinch. Instead she looked askance. 'Does Lord Brentmore know?'

'He knows.' Yates's eyes flashed. 'With Eunice dead,

he and I are the only ones who know.' He glanced down. 'And now you.'

She peered at him suspiciously. 'Is this why you are back? Because of Dory?'

Had not this child's life been shaken enough?

'No!' He turned away. 'I came back to make amends. And because I cannot neglect my estate and business matters any longer. I did not know the child would be here in London. I never guessed...' His voice trailed off wistfully.

He swung back to Anna. 'But I will not allow her to be hurt. Do you hear? She must never know. Never! If you do anything to shatter her secure life, I will take my revenge on you and you will regret it.'

He loved the girl, she realised.

'You have nothing to fear from me, sir!' She, too, loved Dory. 'I want what is best for her.'

'Then she must grow up as Brentmore's daughter. She is his daughter in the eyes of the law. Do not ever tell her otherwise.'

Keep the truth from her, like the truth of Anna's paternity had been kept from her? One should always know the truth, should they not?

Would she have been happier not knowing the truth about her mother's character, her father's true identity? Would she have preferred to believe she had only one father who didn't love her?

Dory, apparently, had two fathers who loved her very much.

'I give you my word, Mr Yates.' She stared directly in his eyes. 'You must give me your word that you will never cause trouble for Dory. Ever.'

He looked solemn. 'That has been my vow since I learned of her existence. It will never change.'

'Then we are settled.' She blew out a breath. 'And I

must thank you very sincerely for escorting the children and me, and for assisting me with Dory.'

'It was my privilege.' His eyes filled with pain. 'It may well be my only opportunity to hold her.'

She touched his hand in a sympathetic gesture. 'Oh, Mr Yates.'

She walked with him to the hall. 'Thank you again, sir. And good day to you.'

He nodded. 'Good day to you, too, Miss Hill.' He placed his hat on his head and opened the door, but turned back to Anna. 'Miss Hill, if—if she should ever need anything, if she is ever in trouble, will you tell me, so I may help?'

His words touched her heart. 'Yes, I will,' she promised.

Chapter Fourteen

Brent did not see Anna when he managed to return to the town house. He stopped by the room set up as the nursery, but she was not there.

Eppy was with the children.

'Where is Miss Hill?' Brent asked her.

The woman smiled. 'Taking a much-needed break, m'lord. Had a bit too much walking in the park, if you ask me.'

'Is she ill?' He would feel a complete cad if he'd left her when she'd been ill.

'No.' The nurse laughed. 'A fair bit weary, though.' She gestured to the children. 'These two scamps had a good nap and are full of beans.'

'We are not, Eppy!' Dory giggled. 'We have not eaten any beans!'

She and Cal had built an arrangement with blocks, putting the blocks side by side in a huge circle on the table and criss-crossing the circle with other lines of blocks. In one corner was a small looking glass. Two ducks from the Noah's Ark were placed on the glass.

'What is this, Cal?' he asked.

Dory put her hand over her mouth.

Cal finally answered, 'Hyde Park.'

'I can see it!' Brent exclaimed. 'The perimeter.' He pointed to the circle of blocks. 'The paths.' These were the criss-crossing blocks. 'And the Serpentine.' The looking glass. 'What else will you put in?'

Cal took a long thin block and set it on its end. 'Trees.'

Brent picked up a similar block. 'May I plant a tree?'

Cal nodded.

'I want to plant trees!' Dory cried.

Cal handed her some blocks.

Brent spent a pleasant half-hour with his children, building their replica of Hyde Park.

Dory ran to her doll house and brought back the doll family. 'This is Papa and Miss Hill and you and me,' she said to Cal.

She did not add any other dolls to the park.

A clock struck the hour and Brent realised he was late. He still had to change his clothes and meet Peter at White's. From there they would go to Lord Rolfe's to dine and attend a musicale together. He would come home too late to see Anna.

It unsettled him.

He wanted to see her, although he could not explain to her why he'd chosen to go with the Rolfes rather than stay with her and the children. He could not explain to himself why he did not tell her Miss Rolfe was in the carriage with her parents. He'd hoped to hear something from her about Yates. Had he behaved well with her and the children? Had Brent's trust been misplaced?

Mostly, Brent just wanted to see her.

Much more than he wanted to spend the evening with Miss Rolfe, her parents and his cousin.

The evening turned out to be pleasant, with nothing for Brent to complain of, except perhaps that he'd wished he were elsewhere.

The musicale had fine music—a skilled string quartet and a clear-voiced soprano—but it was torture to sit through it all, when his mind wandered back to his town house, his children. Anna.

At a pause in the music, Miss Rolfe leaned over and asked him, 'Are you feeling unwell, sir?' Her concern was genuine.

He shook his head. 'I am perfectly well. The music merely gives me too much time to think.'

Her brow wrinkled. 'Are you troubled?'

She was the sort of woman one could talk to and be guaranteed an understanding ear, but how could he confide in her?

He made a dismissive gesture. 'A business matter intrudes. It is nothing.'

'Perhaps Peter can help you,' she suggested. 'He is very clever at business.'

'That he is,' Brent agreed, although his cousin was not clever enough to accept the financial help Brent offered him. 'An excellent idea, Miss Rolfe.'

The music began again and he had no need to continue the conversation.

At the next break, refreshments were served in another room. Brent acted the suitor and fixed Miss Rolfe's plate for her. When he walked back to the buffet to fix his own plate, Lady Charlotte stopped him.

'Lord Brentmore! How delightful to see you here.' She seemed to have deliberately sought him out. 'Do you remember me? I met you in the park today.'

'Yes, Lady Charlotte, I remember you.' It was not likely he would forget in a matter of hours.

She boldly put her arm through his. 'Do you mind if I speak with you on a matter of importance?'

He glanced back at the table where Miss Rolfe and her

parents sat. Peter seemed to be entertaining them very well. 'Of course.'

They stepped away from the refreshment table.

'As you must know, I am a very dear friend of Anna's—Miss Hill,' she began.

'I have heard her say so.'

That made her smile. 'Well, I want her to come to our ball next week and she refuses, because she must stay with the children, she says.'

He doubted that was the reason. 'She is very conscientious.'

'She is. I agree.' She took a breath. 'But I have a very special reason for her to come to the ball.'

'What is that?' he asked politely.

'Forgive me for saying so, but I do not think Anna should be a governess. I believe she can make a very respectable match if she is able to mix in society a little.' Her eyes twinkled. 'Why, the one entertainment she did attend with me, she was a great success! She had all sorts of gentlemen seeking to be introduced.'

A picture of Anna surrounded by Yates and those other two puppies flashed into his mind, as well as the rush of jealousy he felt upon seeing them gaze upon her.

Charlotte went on. 'I know she cannot reach so high as to a man with a title, but perhaps a younger son or some such.'

'You think she can marry?'

'I think she *should* marry! Do not you?' Charlotte seized his arm. 'Will you help me? I know it means losing a governess, but Anna is so lovely and so ladylike, she deserves to have a house of her own and children of her own.'

He had never thought that Anna might aspire to a respectable marriage, home and children.

The idea depressed him. 'What would you have me do?'

'Bring her to my ball!' she exclaimed. 'If you tell her she must attend, she will have to do it, because you are her employer.'

He frowned. 'What of your parents? Will they wish her to be included?'

She grew thoughtful. 'I dare say not, but they could not complain if a marquess escorted her. They will invite you, certainly. They do not expect you will come, but if you do attend, it will be a coup for them.'

Brent was not so certain of that. Perhaps Lord Lawton had considered him good enough to hire his bastard daughter as a governess, but would he truly want the scandalous Marquess of Brentmore to attend his ball?

Charlotte looked towards the table where Miss Rolfe sat. 'Your friends are invited. I know the Rolfes plan to attend, actually. Your cousin was invited, as well. Town is so thin of company, they have expanded the invitation list to include gentlemen who will certainly be suitable for Anna.'

Was Lady Charlotte including his cousin in that list? That idea disturbed him. 'You said she has already refused.'

Her eyes implored. 'You can command her to come. Please say you will do it. If you have any regard for Anna, please say you will do it.'

Was he so selfish he would prevent her any chance to attract a suitor? He could offer her nothing but the lonely and thankless job of governess. No, her happiness must be considered.

'I will try, Lady Charlotte. That is all I can promise.'

She almost jumped up and down. 'I knew you would see it my way!'

'I must get back to my party,' he said, although the night had just become even more depressing.

'Me, too.' She smiled.

As he walked her back to the buffet table, he could not help but say, 'Lady Charlotte, I was under the impression from Miss Hill that you suffered from bashfulness.'

Her eyes widened. 'Oh, I do. I am horribly bashful!'

'Then how was it you could speak with me, with such little introduction?'

She grinned. 'When I am afraid, I merely pretend I am Anna and then I can be brave. I am pretending now and, I assure you, my stomach is full of butterflies.'

He nodded, admiring her courage for her friend's sake—no, her half-sister's sake, but Charlotte did not know that. 'You must never feel afraid to speak with me, Lady Charlotte. Your courage on behalf of Anna has won my admiration.'

Brent dropped a few pieces of cheese on to his plate and walked back to the table where Peter and the Rolfes sat.

Miss Rolfe smiled at him. 'That took you a long time.'

'My apologies.' He lowered himself into the chair. 'I saw someone with whom I needed to speak.'

'How nice for you,' she said.

At least he did not have to explain himself to Miss Rolfe. It was another of her virtues, to not care enough to question whatever he said.

Later when Brent and Peter were in the carriage on the way home, Peter chastised him. 'That was not well done of you, Brent, to leave Susan for Lady Charlotte. Not well done of you at all. I thought you wished to avoid gossip.'

'Heed who you are talking to, Peter.' Brent's head already pained him. 'I will conduct my own affairs.'

'*Affairs* is a good term for it, Brent,' Peter shot back. 'You make the appearance of courting other women while saying you are betrothed to Susan—Miss Rolfe. You are using her ill.'

He glared at his cousin. 'My conversation with Lady Charlotte was about a matter that does not concern you. If Miss Rolfe objects to my speaking to her, let her tell me. I will discuss it with her. Not you.'

'I cannot leave this alone,' Peter went on. 'You are not behaving like a betrothed man. It is an insult to Miss Rolfe and her family.'

Brent was not about to let his cousin continue. 'Enough!' he shouted. 'This was your idea, Peter. I went along because it suited my needs, but I'll not have you scolding me as if I were the veriest schoolboy. I can walk away from the whole matter, if I choose, and I might if I have to listen to you talk like this.'

Peter looked alarmed. 'You would not cry off! That would be the ruin of her reputation and the ruin of her family.'

A woman might cry off without censure, but if a man broke a betrothal, the woman was looked upon as damaged goods. Brent's threat was empty. He could not do that to a decent woman like Miss Rolfe. He also did not want her family's ruin to be on his conscience.

He'd had his fill of his cousin's lectures, however. 'If you do not stop plaguing me about this, I may indeed cry off.'

Peter backed off. 'Very well. Very well.' He was blessedly silent for a while, but started in again. 'There was something else I wanted to say.'

'Good God, Peter! You do not know when to stop.' Brent crossed his arms over his chest.

'It is a small matter, but I need to say it.' He looked as if he might burst if he did not speak.

Brent gestured for him to continue.

'Well, it is a matter of reciprocity,' he began.

'Reciprocity?' What the devil?

'You have dined at the Rolfes' several times, but you have never invited them to dine with you. It does not seem polite.'

Brent could not believe his ears. 'You want me to plan a dinner party now?'

'You would not have to do the planning. Turn it over to your servants. Or, better yet, have your governess plan the dinner party. She's been trained as a lady, you said. She should know how to hold a dinner party.'

Ask Anna to plan a party for his fiancée? That would be cruel indeed.

'It need not be an elaborate dinner party,' Peter said. 'Merely a family one, with Miss Rolfe and her parents.'

'And you, of course,' Brent added sarcastically.

'I would be delighted to come.' He seemed to miss the sarcasm. 'It would be a good time for Miss Rolfe to become acquainted with your governess.'

Have Anna dine with them?

He did see the logic in Peter's idea, though. Anna and Miss Rolfe needed to be known to each other if they were eventually going to work together on the children's behalf.

Unless he found a way to marry Anna off, like Lady Charlotte suggested.

Another dismal thought.

Two days later Lord Brentmore requested a moment to speak to Anna. She left the children in the nursery and attended him in the library, where he'd been ensconced with Mr Parker all morning.

Mr Parker, she was pleased to see, was gone. 'You wished to see me, my lord?'

He smiled, but it was not the easy, relaxed smile of their early days together. 'Ah, thank you for coming, Anna.' He rose and walked out from behind his desk. 'Shall we sit in the chairs by the window?'

She complied.

She'd seen little of him the past two days by her own design, at breakfast and in passing. She'd not been alone with him at all. They'd not talked about that day in Hyde Park or anything else, for that matter.

He looked tired and worn. And distant.

'What did you wish to see me about?' she asked, wanting to rid herself of the suspense. There could be little he would say to her that she would wish to hear.

A sad look came over his face, but only fleetingly. 'I need to beg a favour from you.'

'A favour?'

He took a breath. 'I am having a small dinner party tonight and I want you to attend.'

'Me?'

She'd known of the dinner party, even though he had not mentioned it. There were few things that happened in a house that were not known to everyone in it. She knew the guest list. His cousin. Lord and Lady Rolfe. His fiancée.

'Whatever for?'

It was going to be difficult enough to know the dinner was taking place. She'd planned to stay up in her room and hope the sounds of conversation and laughter did not reach her ears.

'Miss Rolfe is attending and I think it is an opportunity for you to become acquainted.' His voice turned low. 'You must some time, you realise.'

She averted her gaze. 'I do realise that, but I assumed it would not take place on a social occasion.'

'It is more a family dinner,' he explained. 'And I think it odd not to include you.'

She lifted her chin. 'Which explains why you waited until the day of the party to tell me.'

His eyes flashed. 'I did so because I knew you would have this reaction.'

'What reaction is that?' she shot back.

'This—' He searched for the word. 'Hesitancy.'

'I hesitate because it is not my place to dine with you and your guests.' To watch him interact with Miss Rolfe would be so difficult. She was simply not ready for it.

'A governess certainly can be part of a family dinner,' he countered. 'I want you there, Anna.'

She straightened. 'Are you ordering me as my employer?'

Those words hurt him, she could see. 'If you wish to put it that way.' He stood and paced in the space in front of the chairs. 'Anna, I want you there. It is important to me.' He paused and looked down at her. 'But it is your choice.'

What did it matter? It was only one evening. She rose from her chair, but did not realise that doing so put her perilously close to him. Her senses hummed with the proximity.

'I will attend, if that is your wish,' she said in a quiet voice.

'Anna.' He reached for her, but withdrew his arm.

She could not bear it if he touched her, but she also could not resist looking into his eyes.

His eyes darkened in response. 'Anna,' he murmured again.

He stepped back. 'They will arrive at eight and we will dine at nine. I presume you have a suitable gown?'

'Yes.' She had brought one passable dress with her.

He smiled again. 'Excellent. It is kind of you to agree to this, when I know you do not wish it.'

She did not smile in return. 'I will manage, my lord.'

* * *

That afternoon as Brent walked back from St. James's Street, he encountered Yates, walking in the same direction. After exchanging greetings, they wound up walking together.

Yates looked burdened.

'Are you in some difficulty, Yates?' Brent asked.

Yates looked surprised. 'Does it show? Forgive me, Brent. It is nothing of consequence. A tangle with my investments right when I need some ready cash for the estate.' He smiled ruefully. 'And I just had to let my man of business go.'

'It sounds like something of consequence indeed,' Brent commented. 'Is there some way I can help?'

Yates gaped at him. 'Brent, you are the last person I would prevail upon for help.'

Brent agreed. 'Yes. It is unlikely for me to offer.'

In some ways he felt a kinship with Yates. They'd both hurt Eunice irreparably.

Brent went on. 'I have another unlikely idea to offer. Come to dinner tonight. I am having a very small party. Just my cousin and Lord and Lady Rolfe. And their daughter. I am to marry her, you might as well know.'

'Marry?' he cried. 'Did I miss this announcement?'

Brent shook his head. 'We have not formally announced it.'

Yates responded, 'I should not intrude on your dinner party.'

Brent frowned. 'It would be a good thing for you to attend. Undoubtedly the Rolfes know of our—our previous relationship. It will reassure them that the scandal about us is gone.'

Yates looked sceptical.

'Besides, my cousin and Mr Rolfe might have some

ideas about how to untangle your financial difficulties.'
He added, 'You will not be the only person outside the
family. Miss Hill will be attending as well.'

'Then perhaps I will attend.' Yates glanced at Brent. 'I
mean, I would be honoured to attend.'

Chapter Fifteen

Anna's maid and Eppy both became quite excited that she would be attending this dinner. She had packed one good dress, but it was a rather plain white muslin. Eppy found some dusty pink ribbon and white lace, goodness knew from where, and worked all day at embellishing the gown. The maid made a special effort to arrange her hair, threading some of the ribbon through her tresses. Anna added the very lightest tint of pink to her lips and wore her new gloves and stockings. She dabbed her new scent on her neck and in the peek of *décolletage* the neckline of her dress revealed.

The three women surveyed the result in a full-length mirror.

The peek of lace softened the neckline and sleeves, and the ribbon encircled the empire waist and draped into a bow whose tails fell nearly to the gown's hem.

Eppy declared, 'You look the very image of a fashion print!'

Anna hoped that was true. She was usually not so vain, but this night she wanted her appearance to compare favourably with Miss Rolfe's. Anna knew that Miss Rolfe

came close to the perfect image of feminine beauty and
Anna did not, but she at least wanted to look her very best.

She surveyed herself. 'It wants jewellery of some sort,
but I suppose a governess is not expected to own jewellery.'

'You look every bit like a lady,' insisted the maid.

The clock struck the quarter-hour. Anna was running
late.

An attack of nerves hit her and she pressed her hand
against her stomach. 'I should go now. Thank you both
very much.'

'Lord Brentmore will be dazzled.' Eppy grinned.

Anna had to admit that was what she wanted most—to
dazzle Lord Brentmore.

It was not at all admirable of her to wish to command
his attention. She should, by rights, dress to blend into
the woodwork, as Lady Lawton always insisted she do
and as the daughter of a laundress ought. Half her blood,
however, was aristocratic and, just this once, she wanted
to show that part of her.

With butterflies still fluttering inside her, she walked
down the stairs and entered the drawing room.

Two gentlemen turned.

'Mr Yates!' Anna exclaimed.

He stepped forwards. 'It is good to see you again, Miss
Hill. I trust you are well.'

'Yes, I am,' she responded. 'I did not know you would
be here.'

The other gentleman in the room was, of course, Lord
Brentmore. 'I invited him this afternoon.'

She felt Lord Brentmore's eyes flick over her, but his
expression gave away nothing of his opinion of her appearance.

Mr Yates was more forthright. 'May I say you are in
excellent looks this evening, Miss Hill.'

'I hope I will do.' She slid a glance to Lord Brentmore.

The marquess turned his back. 'May I pour you a glass of port, Anna?' he asked.

She was tempted to use port to calm her nerves. 'I will wait for the other ladies, I believe.' She turned to a chair in the corner. 'Please continue your conversation. I do not wish to intrude.'

'You do not intrude, Anna,' Lord Brentmore said, an edge of annoyance in his voice. He took a sip of his port.

'How do the children fare?' Yates asked her.

She could tell he tried to keep his voice neutral. 'Very well, thank you.'

'Have you taken more walks in Hyde Park?'

She could tell he had chosen his words carefully and that he yearned to ask her more, but could not with Lord Brentmore present.

She wanted to give Yates something of the happenings of his daughter's life. 'We have been busy with dressmakers and tailors.' She inclined her head to Lord Brentmore. 'Their father has generously wished them to be fitted for entire new wardrobes.'

'How nice for them,' Yates said in a polite voice.

'I dare say they detested the task,' Lord Brentmore added.

She wondered why he had invited this man, but because she was not supposed to know who Yates was, she could never ask.

'Have you called upon Lady Charlotte?' Yates asked her.

He would have overheard her entire conversation with Charlotte.

She lowered her voice. 'I have not the opportunity.'

Brentmore walked over, taking Yates's empty glass from him. 'Did she wish you to call, Anna?'

She lifted her gaze to him. 'She asked, but I cannot call upon her.'

Brentmore returned to the side table and filled Yates's glass. He walked back to hand it to him.

'How are you acquainted with Lady Charlotte?' Yates asked her.

'I was her companion before becoming governess to Lord Brentmore's children.' She hoped he did not ask for more explanation than that.

He did not. 'Will you attend her ball?' he asked instead.

'No,' she murmured.

'You should attend, Anna.' Lord Brentmore still sounded annoyed with her.

She faced him. 'You know I cannot.'

She caught Yates looking from her to Brentmore.

Davies came to the door. 'Lord and Lady Rolfe, Miss Rolfe, Mr Caine.'

Lord Brentmore crossed the room to greet them. 'Welcome,' he said.

Anna remained where she was, as did Yates. She braced herself to witness Brentmore's manner towards Miss Rolfe.

He bowed to her and to her mother and shook hands with her father and his cousin. Miss Rolfe curtsied.

As the group exchanged more pleasantries, Yates remarked to Anna, 'One wonders about this betrothal. It came as a surprise to me.'

And to Anna, of course.

When the greetings were done, Lord Brentmore glanced over at Anna.

She and Yates joined them.

Anna was presented to Lord and Lady Rolfe.

'You are known to Miss Rolfe and my cousin,' Lord Brentmore added.

Anna curtsied. 'How do you do, Miss Rolfe?'

'I am so pleased to see you again,' Miss Rolfe said, sounding very genuine.

When Brentmore introduced Mr Yates to Lord and Lady Rolfe, Anna saw the shock of recognition on their faces. They knew who Mr Yates was to the marquess.

Poor Mr Yates. He saw their expressions as well.

Lady Rolfe led her daughter around the room, remarking at the décor, and probably thinking that it would all be her daughter's one day. The gentlemen busied themselves with more port.

Anna stepped back, out of the way, convinced more than ever that she did not belong in this party.

Lady Rolfe finished her survey of the room. She addressed Lord Brentmore, 'Brentmore, my dear, I would love a tour of the house.'

'Mama!' Miss Rolfe turned a bright shade of pink. 'You mustn't ask.'

Brentmore said, 'I ought to have offered. Of course, you will be curious about the house. I don't like to leave the gentlemen....' His voice trailed off. He directed his gaze at Anna. 'Would you take the ladies on a tour of the house while there is still some daylight, Anna?'

She stiffened, but replied, 'As you wish, my lord.'

She led them out the door and started the tour with Lord Brentmore's library on this level, trying hard not to recall her encounters with him in the room.

After the library she said, 'Let us go to the first floor. You will see the dining room later.'

They climbed the stairs and she showed them the two large drawing rooms there. 'There is a folding door that, when opened, doubles the size.'

'Perfect for a ball, Susan,' Lady Rolfe remarked to her daughter.

Anna waited near the door while Lady Rolfe completed

her inspection. She next showed them a cosier sitting room behind the other two rooms.

She took them next to the second floor. 'There are two bedrooms on this level.' She gestured to one closed door. 'That is Lord Brentmore's bedchamber.' She opened a second door. 'This room was once the marchioness's.'

Lady Rolfe entered the room eagerly. Her daughter merely stepped inside.

'Is there a connecting door between the two bedchambers?' Lady Rolfe asked.

Anna felt sharp pain inside her. 'I do not know, ma'am.'

She showed them the dressing rooms and the lady's maid's room, as well.

She merely pointed to the third floor. 'There are five bedrooms on that level, currently being used as the nursery, for the children, their nurse and me.'

'The children must be sleeping,' Miss Rolfe said in a kind voice.

'Yes. If you will forgive me, I'd prefer not to take you up there and risk waking them.' She also did not want them looking into her room.

'I agree,' Miss Rolfe said.

They walked down the stairs again to the ground level. 'The kitchen and the servants' rooms are below, of course.'

They returned to the gentlemen.

'Did you make a full inventory, my dear?' Lord Rolfe asked his wife.

She smiled. 'It was very helpful to see where our daughter will some day be in residence.'

Miss Rolfe turned to Anna. 'Will you sit with me, Miss Hill?'

'Of course.' How could she refuse?

'Tell me about the children,' Miss Rolfe requested. 'I know so little of them.'

Lord Brentmore apparently did not discuss the children's troubles with his fiancée. Anna was certainly not going to be the one to talk of Cal and Dory's difficulties.

'They are very clever.' Anna talked about their lessons, matters that would likely be expected of a governess.

Finally Davies announced the dinner. Anna was surprised to see that Lord and Lady Rolfe were seated at each side of Lord Brentmore, who headed the table. Miss Rolfe sat next to her father and Mr Caine sat next to her. Mr Yates was placed next to Lady Rolfe and Anna next to him.

Lady Rolfe did not seem to have much to say to Mr Yates, and, across the table, Miss Rolfe and Brentmore's cousin seemed to have a great deal to talk about together and with Lord Rolfe. Yates and Anna were left with each other.

It was an excruciatingly long dinner.

Anna's attention could not help but be drawn to Miss Rolfe. It was a puzzle. She and Lord Brentmore were little more than cordial to each other, but, seated next to his cousin, Miss Rolfe seemed to blossom.

At one point, Yates bent to her ear. 'Do you make the same observation as I do?'

She watched more intently before responding, 'They are clearly attached.'

'Very attached, would you not say?' he added.

'But, then, why——?' She did not need to complete her thought.

Mr Yates explained, 'Word is that Rolfe is in financial distress. His daughter needs to make a good match to a generous and wealthy man. Mr Caine owns property, but his finances are only marginally better than Rolfe's.'

She peered at him. 'How do you know this?'

He gave a sad smile. 'Word gets around. The end of

the war has left many of us struggling, and this summer's crops are not doing well with all this cold weather.'

The weather was part of the reason so many of the *ton* were still in London in August.

Anna glanced from Miss Rolfe to Lord Brentmore. His gaze caught hers. He continued to appear displeased with her. It baffled her. She'd come to his party and made the best of it. What had she done to displease him?

'The web becomes more tangled as we speak,' said Mr Yates.

Brent held Anna's gaze for a moment. Was she deliberately seeking Yates's attention, or was it merely because they were seated together? He wished he had paid more attention to Davies's question of where to seat everyone.

He wished he had not invited Yates.

It had seemed like a good idea at the time, but now it felt like a repeat of history. Except Anna was not Eunice and not obligated to keep any wedding vows.

If she had been Eunice, then undoubtedly the flirtation would have been a deliberate ploy to shame and embarrass her husband. How many times had he watched Eunice initiate a seduction right in front of his eyes, all the while appearing as if she merely was engaging in conversation?

Anna's face, however, showed nothing of Eunice's contempt. She looked confused and hurt.

Perhaps he should be wary of Yates. Was the man deliberately seeking out Anna, and, if so, was Yates trying to wound him further?

Brent forced his eyes away and asked Lord Rolfe a question.

When the man launched into a loquacious response, Brent's gaze wandered back to Anna.

He had to admit she looked beautiful this evening with

her upswept curls and unadorned dress, like a statue of Aphrodite he'd once seen in his travels. She'd so taken his breath away when she'd entered the drawing room that he'd had to look away.

The last course was finished and it was time for the ladies to retire and the gentlemen to remain for brandy.

Anna, her head held high, left the room with Miss Rolfe and her mother. Brent had not thought the evening through in enough detail to realise Anna would be left with the two ladies. He felt guilty for making her do what she so clearly did not wish to do, but he still believed he was right. She and Miss Rolfe needed to become accustomed to each other.

Miss Rolfe. More reason for him to feel guilty. He'd hardly spoken to her all evening. He must make certain to rectify that.

Peter, Lord Rolfe and Yates were talking about the financial stresses of the times.

'I do not know what we would do without the Corn Laws,' Lord Rolfe said. 'If Great Britain were to import foreign grain, it would be the end of me, I'll tell you that.'

'It has caused a great deal of unrest,' Yates commented.

People were hungry, Brent thought, remembering long days in Ireland when he and his grandfather had not enough to eat.

He let the discussion wash over him, without debating either side of the issue. His fortune could weather these difficult times. He and his children would never want for anything and he could still afford to help those most unfortunate.

And men like Lord Rolfe, who had indeed accepted the money Brent transferred to him.

They finished their brandy and Peter suggested they return to the women.

When they walked out of the dining room, Yates fell into step with Brent. 'You were quite quiet during the discussion, Brent. Is there anything amiss?'

Brent was taken aback. 'I didn't realise. No, nothing is amiss.' He did not realise his preoccupation showed, he meant.

'I hope you do not regret inviting me,' Yates said.

'Why would you think so?' Brent asked.

'I noticed you looking my way from time to time.' Yates slid him a glance. 'Or perhaps it was Miss Hill who concerned you.'

'Concerned me?' Yates saw too much, Brent thought. 'I think it was more a case of my rethinking the seating arrangement.'

'Putting me near the Rolfes would have proved awkward,' Yates responded. 'They seem uncomfortable conversing with me.'

'I am sorry for it.' Brent slowed his pace as he and Yates crossed the hall. 'I still think it is a good idea to be seen together. If we can forget the conflict between us, the *ton* will soon forget, as well, but if we continue to feud, we keep the talk alive.'

'I hope you are right,' Yates said. 'But perhaps this private party of yours was not the best place to start.'

'It was for me,' Brent told him. 'I need to get used to seeing you without animosity.'

They entered the drawing room and Brent saw right away that Anna was seated in a chair adjacent to the sofa where Miss Rolfe and her mother sat. Her back was to him. Miss Rolfe was busy pouring tea for Peter and laughed at something he said.

He and Yates walked over to them.

Anna rose. 'You may have my seat, my lord,' she said to him. 'I am certain you wish to sit next to Miss Rolfe.'

It was where he ought to sit.

'You do not have to move, Anna.'

But she moved anyway, her skirt catching in her legs, showing their shape beneath the thin muslin. Brent felt a flash of arousal. He quickly turned away, taking a moment to dampen his desires before his body betrayed him.

He sat in the chair Anna vacated for him. It was still warm from her. He watched Anna withdraw.

Miss Rolfe switched her attention from Peter to Brent. 'Let me say, Lord Brentmore, that the food this evening has been superb. As has the company.'

'Thank you,' he responded. 'I am glad to have pleased you.'

She smiled.

He glanced away. 'Did you and your mother find something to converse about with Miss Hill?'

'The children, of course,' she replied. 'And Mother had several questions about how many servants you keep, if the meals are always so well prepared, if the house runs smoothly.'

'That is fine,' he said.

He wished he had discussed with Anna what to say about the children. Miss Rolfe did not need to know about Cal's affliction, nor about the abuse the children had suffered. There was so much he had not considered.

He glanced over at Anna. Yates engaged her in conversation.

'Is Mr Yates her suitor?' Miss Rolfe inclined her head in their direction.

'I beg your pardon?'

She turned to him. 'I thought perhaps Mr Yates was Miss Hill's suitor. I thought perhaps that is why they were included.'

'Miss Hill attends so you can become acquainted with her as the children's governess.' His tone was clipped.

'Of course,' she said mildly. 'But I thought perhaps Mr Yates was here because of her.'

'Do you know who Mr Yates is?' he asked.

She lowered her gaze. 'Peter told me. That is why I am trying to make sense of why he is here.'

It seemed too much effort to explain to Miss Rolfe the strategy behind inviting Yates. 'I have known him since my school days and, no matter what has happened, I hold no ill will towards him.'

She gave him a placid look. 'That is very commendable.'

Lady Rolfe broke into the conversation. 'Are you attending Lord Lawton's ball next week, Brentmore? We are attending, are we not, my dear?'

Her husband replied, 'We are indeed.'

'And you are attending, too, Peter. Is that not right?' she went on.

'I would never pass up an opportunity to attend a ball,' his cousin said.

Lady Lawton twisted back to Brent. 'Will you come? It promises to be a fine ball, as fine as if it were during the Season.'

'Perhaps,' Brent replied, adding, 'I have been asked to escort Miss Hill to the ball.'

'What!' Lady Rolfe's voice rose in shock.

Anna looked alarmed.

'I spoke with Lady Charlotte at the musicale the other night,' he explained. 'She asked me to bring Anna. They—they grew up together.'

'Oh, they grew up together.' Lady Rolfe looked relieved. 'You would be doing a kindness, in other words.'

Miss Rolfe glanced at Yates. 'Are you attending, sir?'

'I was invited.' He did not explain more.

She looked over at Anna. 'You must come, Miss Hill. It will be a delightful party.'

Brent watched Anna's expression. He could see in her eyes the hurt and anger, an anger he deserved. What possessed him to inform her of Charlotte's request in this manner? Was he punishing her for talking to Yates? Or for looking so lovely he could not take his eyes off her?

Whatever it was, it did him no credit.

How could he profess to be her friend when he treated her so shabbily?

'What say you?' Miss Rolfe pressed.

Brent watched Anna lift her chin, a gesture he now knew well. 'It is kind of Lady Charlotte to wish to include me and kind of Lord Brentmore to be willing to escort me.' She kept her eyes directly on Brent. 'But I will not attend the ball.'

Miss Rolfe said, 'I do hope you change your mind.'

Brent walked his guests to the hall and bid them goodnight. Anna waited outside the drawing room. When the door closed behind them, she crossed the hall and started up the stairs.

He hurried after her. 'A moment, please, Anna.'

She whirled on him right on the staircase. 'Do not speak to me, my lord. I am much too angry.' She lifted her skirts and doubled her pace.

He caught up with her again on the first floor. 'We must talk.'

He seized her arm and pulled her into the nearest room, lit only by light from the streets. Below them carriage lamps blazed while the Rolfes settled into Brent's carriage, which would take them to their rooms on Somerset Street.

Anna struggled against his grip. 'Release me, sir!'

'No. Not until you promise to listen to me.' This was becoming more unreasonable by the second, but he could not stop himself. He backed her against the wall between the two windows.

She suddenly stilled. 'Very well. Say what you wish to say, so I may go!'

What words could he say? He hardly knew.

'I am sorry, Anna,' was all he could manage.

'Sorry?' she cried. 'This is how you show you are sorry? By bullying me and putting your hands on me?'

He let his hands slip down her arms. 'I could not let you go to bed before letting you know how wrong I was. I should not have told you about Lady Charlotte in front of them all. I do not know why I did it.'

He heard the carriage drive off. The room plunged into darkness.

She went on. 'I did not want to attend your dinner party in the first place and then suddenly I must take your lady guests on a tour, as if I was their hostess and this was my house. But that was not enough, was it, my lord? You obviously withheld from me your conspiracy with Charlotte. You, of all people, know why I do not wish to go to that ball. You should have supported my wishes with Charlotte, and told me that she had spoken to you. Instead, you blather about it with people who are strangers to me.' Her voice cracked. 'I do not need this treatment, my lord. I do not deserve it.'

'You are right. You are right.' He cared about her. Why had he deliberately hurt her? 'Anna, I do not know why I did any of it. I only know I could not have a dinner party and leave you sitting alone in your room. And, then, you looked so very beautiful and Yates paid you such particular attention—'

'That was another thing. You did not do that poor man a

favour by inviting him. Who else was he to converse with? Your cousin and the Rolfes made no effort to include him. Or you. You left him to me.'

Had he done so? Had he handed her to Yates, as if she were another course for dinner?

No, she was wrong. He might have acted on impulse inviting her, inviting Yates, but she had played her part in this.

'What of you, Anna?' he countered. 'You knew you were included to become acquainted with Miss Rolfe, but you treated her more as a rival than the prospective marchioness—'

'A rival!' Her voice rose. 'How can you say such a thing?'

'How?' He placed his palms on the wall, caging her between his arms. 'Tell me you did not deliberately dress to be alluring.'

She gasped.

He was so close to her that he felt her breath. She was only a shadow in the dark room, but her allure was stronger than ever.

'Roses,' he murmured. 'You smell of roses.' An intoxicating scent, he decided. 'That is a new scent for you. Tell me you did not choose that scent tonight for a deliberate reason. Was that for me?'

She rose up in defiance. 'Does it work?'

By God, it worked very effectively.

He placed his hands at her waist and lowered his lips on to hers.

Her arms twined around his neck and he pressed her hard against him, as she hungrily kissed him back.

'No!' She pushed on his chest.

He regained his senses, if not his tongue. 'Is that what you hoped for, Anna?'

He backed away, wishing he could take those words back.

She shot back at him, 'Is that what *you* hoped for, my lord? Are you trying to prove to me how like my mother I am? I need no proof, my lord. It was I who told you so.' She took a breath and her voice dipped low and tremulous. 'Well, I will not *be* my mother. Do you understand? I choose not to be her.'

'Anna—' he began, but what could he say?

In the dim light he could see she rubbed her arms. 'If I had some place to go, some place with someone who knew me and would take me in, I would be gone from here!' She advanced on him, only to push at his chest again. 'I have no one and you know it. You, of all people, know it and still you take advantage!'

She shoved him one more time and rushed past him out the door. He heard her footsteps running up the stairs.

Chapter Sixteen

By the next morning Anna realised she must do something to determine her own fate. Always she'd accepted whatever others decided for her, provided for her.

And what they denied her.

She no longer had to do that. She could choose to leave Lord Brentmore's employ, if she wished it. She could investigate agencies in London and she had a little money, thanks to his generosity.

She'd counted her money—over five pounds. She could live on that amount for a time.

Although, what would she do if a position did not present itself?

When she entered the children's room, though, her resolve fizzled.

Dory greeted her with a hug and a kiss, as enthusiastically as if she'd thought she'd never see her governess again.

Cal grinned at her and said, 'Good morning, Miss Hill.'

She gave him a hug and a kiss as well.

Anna loved these children. She wanted to stay with them. She wanted to cosset them and protect them and never see them hurt again. Surely it would hurt them if she left.

'Do we have to go to the dressmaker today?' Dory asked in an exasperated tone.

'I thought you liked the dressmaker,' Anna said to her.

The child made a face. 'The first time, I did.'

Anna smiled at her. 'No, we do not have to go to the dressmaker today. Today we will have lessons and then, if you have worked very hard at them, perhaps an outing.'

'Will Papa come with us?' Dory asked hopefully.

'Papa will be busy, Dory,' Cal said. 'A marquess has much to do.'

'He didn't have much to do at Brentmore!' Dory whimpered. 'I want to go back there. I miss my pony. I want to go home.'

Home. To Brentmore Hall. There she would be free to love the children without distraction.

She gathered Cal and Dory together and hugged them both. 'Perhaps we will not be in London too much longer.'

'Will I have to leave my doll house and Hortense?' Dory asked.

'No, silly,' Cal said. 'Papa will allow us to take the toys home.'

Cal was assured of his father's devotion. That was a good sign. The children would adjust to not seeing him daily.

As she must do.

Anna resolved to talk to Lord Brentmore today. She would tell him to send them back to Brentmore.

As she and the children walked down to the dining room, Anna's improved spirits flagged. Facing him was the hard part.

His kiss of the night before haunted her. She'd pushed him away, but really yearned for more.

Lord Brentmore was not in the dining room. Would he not show? What would be worse—to see him this morning or have him avoid her?

She fixed the plates and she and the children were settled in their chairs when he finally entered.

'Papa!' Dory jumped from her chair to hug his legs.

'Good morning, Papa,' Cal said.

He smiled at his son and kissed Dory on the top of her head.

His gaze turned to Anna. 'Good morning, Anna.'

Her heartbeat accelerated. 'Good morning, my lord.'

He looked as if he'd not slept at all and, in spite of herself, her sympathy went out to him. He'd not been wrong to accuse her of dressing to attract him, to compete with Miss Rolfe. Miss Rolfe had been cordial to her, even friendly, you might say. It had been Anna who'd wrestled with her emotions.

Lord Brentmore selected his food from the sideboard and sat, chatting with the children who were delighted to respond. Anna alone perceived his sadness.

'Papa, will you take us on an outing today?' Dory asked. 'Miss Hill says we may go on an outing after lessons. No more fittings.'

He seemed to gaze at Dory intently. Did he struggle with the knowledge that she was not his child? Did he see Yates when he looked at her? Lord Brentmore had always been more reticent in his response to the girl. Now his behaviour made sense. Now his genuine devotion to the child made Anna ache in empathy with him.

He smiled at Dory. 'Perhaps I can break away for a little while.'

'Take us to Horse Guards to see the horses?' Cal asked.

'Perhaps not today.' He ruffled Cal's hair and his tone

was almost mournful. 'But maybe soon I can take you to see the Guards exercising the horses.'

Anna felt responsible for his misery. No doubt they must be parted.

The marquess finished his breakfast more quickly than usual. 'I must go, children. I will try to get back this afternoon.' He stood.

Anna also rose to her feet. 'May I speak with you a moment, my lord?'

He hesitated before finally nodding. 'In the library?'

'May we go up and play?' Cal asked.

'Of course you may,' Anna said.

The children scampered out of the room and up the stairs. Anna walked a little behind Lord Brentmore across the hall to the library.

'Cal is talking so well today,' she remarked, although she forced out the words.

'Remarkably well,' he agreed, but in a flat voice.

He opened the door to the library.

Anna heard a voice from within. 'Good morning, my lord. I have some papers for you to sign.'

Lord Brentmore turned to Anna. 'Mr Parker.' He gestured to the drawing room. 'We may talk in there.' To Mr Parker, he said, 'I'll return in a moment.'

'But, my lord——' Parker implored.

Anna entered the room where she and the marquess had created such unhappiness for each other the night before.

As soon as he stepped inside and closed the door, he said, 'What is it, Anna?'

She feared any apology she attempted would come to the same end as his had done the night before. Best they pretend none of it happened.

'I want to take the children back to Brentmore,' she said simply.

* * *

Brent's muscles relaxed. He'd been prepared to hear her say she was leaving for good.

'I cannot leave London for a few more weeks at least,' he told her. 'We can go back for harvest.'

'No.' She gave him a steady look. 'I want to take the children back now.' She lowered her voice. 'I think it will be for the best.'

He turned away and walked to the window, looking out on to the square where he'd first set eyes on her. To be here without her and the children? It would be desolate.

As he'd lain sleepless in his bed last night, he'd formulated another plan. To help her find a happy life for herself with a husband and children of her own, a family with whom she truly could belong.

He swung back to her. 'I want the children with me.'

She looked about to protest.

He raised a hand. 'But I am willing to compromise.'

'How?' She peered at him with suspicion.

'Stay a few more days, at least,' he said. 'Attend the Lawton ball—'

'Attend the Lawton ball!' The colour rose in her face.

'After the ball you and the children may go back to Brentmore.'

Her eyes flashed. 'Why must I attend the ball? Why would you put me through such an ordeal?'

So she could see how easily she would attract suitors and perhaps attract a man who would be good to her.

No matter how depressing that thought was to him, it was the least he could do to repay her for all she'd done for him and the children.

'It does not have to be an ordeal, Anna. You might enjoy yourself.' He did not need to tell her why he was doing this. 'Your friend wishes you to come.'

'My sister, you mean.'

'Very well. Your sister.' He met her defiant gaze. 'If Lord Lawton had any decency in him, he would have raised you to be a lady who attends balls.'

She glanced away. 'It is ridiculous to require me to attend a ball in order to take your children back to Brentmore.'

He remained firm. 'That is my stipulation.'

She whirled around and left the room.

Brent pressed his fingers against his temples.

He'd done it. He'd set it up so Lady Charlotte could attempt her matchmaking. Unlike last night, he still must stand aside and not interfere, not sabotage. Perhaps if he and his children were very lucky, she'd choose them over a life of her own.

He walked slowly back to the library.

As soon as he walked into the room, Parker pounced. 'My lord, we really must go through these papers. You mustn't allow anything—or anyone—interfere.'

That set Brent's teeth on edge. He crossed the room and sat behind the desk. 'Who is it interferes with what I wish to do?'

Parker put down the inch-thick stack of paper he'd been gripping and faced him. 'If I may speak plain, sir, it is that governess. She is always luring you away from your business matters for one triviality or another—'

Brent glared at him. 'Take care, Parker.'

His man of business did not heed the warning. Instead, he picked up the papers again and swung them through the air as he spoke. 'I mean, it just is not done! She has you acting the nursemaid. You! A marquess!'

'Enough!' Brent rose from his chair. 'You forget your place, sir.' He stood face to face with the man. 'What I do, how I spend my time, who I spend it with, is not the sort of business to which you are paid to attend.' His anger was perilously close to exploding. 'Heed what I say. Discussion of my children or their governess is prohibited to you.'

Parker continued. 'She has changed you! She is pulling your strings as if you were a marionette. You cannot see it.'

Brent leaned forwards, his fists on the desk. 'That is it, Parker.' He lowered his voice to a growl. 'Leave now. Come back in a week's time and I will have a letter of recommendation for you and you will be paid for the year.'

'You are discharging me?' Parker eyes grew wide with shock. 'You cannot! We are in the midst of all this work.'

'I can and I did and I am not above tossing you out on your ear, as well.' He gave Parker his sternest look. 'Go now if you want any pay at all.'

'But—' Parker sputtered.

'Go!' Brent bellowed.

Parker dropped the papers and ran out.

Anna and Dory sat in a sunny spot in Anna's room, sewing. When Eppy had searched for the trim for Anna's dinner dress, she'd discovered a trunk with a sewing basket and scraps of fabric, lace and ribbon. Anna told Dory they might make new dresses for her doll with this treasure trove, and Dory was so excited about the prospect she willingly gave up an outing to the Horse Guards with her father and brother.

It suited Anna to miss that outing as well.

Dory had chosen a scrap of white muslin and pink ribbon for the first dress. 'Hortense will look as pretty as you,' Dory said.

First Anna showed Dory how to make simple stitches. She gave the child a scrap of linen on which to practise while she sewed the replica of her dinner dress. With every stab of the needle she saw Lord Brentmore's face in her mind.

She looked over at Dory. 'Keep your fingers away from the point of the needle.'

Dory was unusually quiet and intent on her stitches. 'I like sewing very much,' she said.

Anna could not help but smile. How could she ever have considered leaving these children?

There was a knock on her door.

Davies opened it and stuck his head in. 'Miss Hill, Miss Rolfe has called and requests a moment of your time.'

'Miss Rolfe? For me?' What could she possibly want?

'For you. She did not ask for his lordship.' He sounded as surprised as she. 'She is waiting in the drawing room.'

Anna set aside her sewing and stood. 'Would you find Eppy and have her come stay with Dory?'

'Very good.' Davies left.

'Dory, I'll be back soon. Eppy can help you sew while I see this caller.'

'Papa's fiancée,' Dory said without looking up from her sewing.

Anna took off her cap and the apron that covered her dress and quickly tidied her hair, all the while realising she wanted to appear at her best in front of this woman, just as Lord Brentmore had accused.

When Anna entered the drawing room, Miss Rolfe stood staring at the same Gainsborough portrait that had captured Anna's attention that first day.

She turned and smiled. 'Miss Hill, how kind of you to see me.'

'Miss Rolfe.' Anna curtsied. 'Please do sit down. Shall I have Davies bring some tea?'

'Oh, no, please do not go to such trouble for me.' Miss

Rolfe lowered herself on to the same sofa on which she sat the previous night.

'It is no trouble to serve you.' Anna was still puzzled by her presence. 'You will, after all, become the marchioness.'

The young woman brushed a curl off her forehead. 'I suppose you are correct, but I still would prefer not to have tea.'

'As you wish.' Anna sat in the adjacent chair.

Miss Rolfe smiled nervously. 'You are probably wondering why I am here.'

'I am certain you will tell me.' Anna could not help but try to put her at ease; she was so obviously troubled.

'I—I came to ask you something…' She placed her hand over her chest as if to try to calm herself.

What would cause a future marchioness to be nervous about speaking to a governess?

Anna waited.

Miss Rolfe tried again. 'My mother made a comment upon which I have pondered all night.'

'A comment?' She tried to sound encouraging.

'She said it half in jest, but it troubled me.'

Simply come out with it, Anna wanted to say. 'What was it?'

The young woman took a breath. 'She—she said that you and the marquess did not talk to each other like any employer and governess she'd ever known. It made me wonder—wonder if there was more to your relationship with the marquess than that.'

Anna's own nerves flared. 'More to our relationship?' She must answer this very carefully. 'The marquess acted as a friend to me on the occasion of my mother's death, but—but there is nothing more.' Nothing spoken—nothing acted upon. At least not fully acted upon, not fully disclosed.

'You are not lovers?' Miss Rolfe blurted out.

Anna lowered her gaze. 'We are not lovers.' Merely a hair's breadth from being lovers.

Miss Rolfe's face screwed up in anxiety. 'Because I am very desirous of making my marriage a good one. I—I should need to know if—if the marquess had other interests. I would hate to act the jealous wife.'

Anna gaped at her. 'You would tolerate such a thing?'

The young woman lifted a shoulder. 'What else can a wife do?'

Anna's brows knitted. 'May I ask, is this marriage a love match for you?'

Miss Rolfe's expression lost its tension. 'Oh, no, but Lord Brentmore understands that. Marrying me suits his need for a respectable wife and it suits me because his money saves my father from ruin and provides for the futures of my sisters and brothers.'

A marriage of convenience.

The young woman went on. 'It is all very civilised. Peter assures me his cousin is a fine man and I will be treated very well by him.'

'He is a fine man,' Anna murmured. She peered at Miss Rolfe. 'In this marriage would you also take lovers?'

She looked shocked. 'Oh, no. I cannot even imagine it.'

'Not even with your Peter?' Anna spoke in a low voice.

Miss Rolfe turned bright red. 'Peter? Why would you say such a thing?'

Anna spoke quietly. 'I noticed the way you looked at each other.'

Miss Rolfe, appearing alarmed, reached over and gripped Anna's arm. 'Do not tell the marquess, please!'

'I will not,' Anna assured her.

Miss Rolfe released her and expelled a relieved breath.

Anna went on. 'How do you see this, marrying Lord

Brentmore and being in love with his cousin?' If Miss Rolfe knew how to accomplish such a thing, perhaps she could teach Anna.

The young woman lowered her head into her hands. 'He—Peter—is going to move to the Continent. He says it will cost him less to live there, so it is a good thing for him.' She raised her head and her eyes filled with tears. 'You see, Peter has no money. Marrying him is out of the question. I—I do not care for myself whether we have money, but I'll not have the ruin of my whole family on my conscience.'

Anna felt sick. She might be able to bear it if Lord Brentmore made a marriage that brought him happiness and devotion, but this sounded dreadful.

Miss Rolfe took out a lace-edged handkerchief from her reticule. She dabbed at her eyes. 'It—it makes it all easier to know you and Brent are not lovers. I confess, I did not know how I would do, knowing such a thing and acting the good wife. I—I must be a good wife to him. He is the salvation of my family.'

And Miss Rolfe, apparently, was the sacrificial lamb.

A memory flew into Anna's mind. Her mother greeting Lord Lawton at the cottage door, telling Anna to hurry back to the house and to Charlotte.

Would this be Anna and Brentmore at Brentmore Hall some day? Snatching passionate encounters with each other, all the while knowing his wife suffered for it? Could they really resist it when their passion was as alive and as powerful as Miss Rolfe's for Peter?

Anna glanced towards the drawing-room door. What a deplorable muddle and who would be right in the middle of it?

The children.

Chapter Seventeen

Anna bided her time the few days before the ball and before she and the children could return to Brentmore Hall. She and Lord Brentmore existed in an uneasy peace that was every bit as painful as their volatile confrontations. She kept Miss Rolfe's visit from him, but it haunted her every hour.

Charlotte sent over a ball gown, complete with matching shoes, gloves and shawl. Anna recognised it as one of Charlotte's outfits of the last Season. Only a few short months ago, Anna had helped Charlotte select its design for the modiste. The gown, a pale blue silk with a sheer overskirt, was adorned with fabric flowers on the bodice and hem. Anna instructed Eppy to remove the flowers. A governess ought not to wear such a fancy dress.

When the night of the ball finally arrived, Eppy and Anna's maid helped Anna dress, just as they had for Lord Brentmore's dinner party. While they were putting the final polish on her appearance, Davies knocked on her bedroom door.

He bore a jewellery box. 'Lord Brentmore said you are to select whatever you wish from this box. The jewels belonged to the marchioness.'

When the women opened the box, they gasped. Diamonds, rubies, emeralds were all thrown in a jumble that glittered in the lamplight. Most of the necklaces, bracelets and earrings were much too opulent for Anna's station, but she found a blue sapphire pendant surrounded by seed pearls and hung on a delicate gold chain that would do. Digging further into the jewellery box, they pulled out teardrop pearl earrings to match.

Once Anna would have been delighted to dress for a ball. She and Charlotte had attended many near Lawton, where everyone knew precisely who she was. This night, though, brought Anna no joy. She did not aspire to dazzle anyone, merely to be presentable enough not to embarrass Lord Brentmore or Charlotte. All she really wished was to blend into the wallpaper.

But Eppy and the maid had other ideas. They'd visited Ackermann's and looked through the fashion prints in *La Belle Assemblée*. They aspired to make her as fashionable as possible.

'I'll defy any of those society ladies to hold a candle to you!' the maid said, pinning one of the fabric flowers into her hair.

'You are a picture!' Eppy agreed.

Anna thanked them, but hoped Lord Brentmore would not think she was attempting to look alluring.

Davies knocked at the door again. 'His lordship is waiting, Miss Hill. The carriage is here.'

'I am coming.' She hugged her maid and Eppy and hurried down the stairs.

He stood at the bottom, leaning against the banister.

Her breath caught.

He looked exceptionally handsome in his superbly fitting formal wear. His black coat, set against the pristinely white linen of his shirt and neckcloth, merely enhanced the impression.

His eyes followed her as she descended and her heart beat wildly.

'I am sorry to keep you waiting,' she said, walking past him to the door.

As she reached the door it was opened by a footman. She passed through to the outside and to the carriage, where another footman waited to assist her inside. She did not look back to see if Lord Brentmore followed, but she felt him behind her.

Inside the carriage, they faced each other as they had that first day when he'd given her a ride in the rain. It was no easier to converse with him this night than it had been that day.

When they pulled up to the Lawton town house, he said, 'If Charlotte wants you here, you will be welcome, Anna.'

Her gaze flew to his face. She knew her father did not welcome her.

The carriage door opened and a footman put down the steps.

When Anna reached out her hand for him to assist her, the footman grinned. 'Why, it is Anna! How'd you do, Anna!'

'Hello, Rogers,' she responded. 'I hope you are well.'

'Quite well.' His smile vanished when Lord Brentmore emerged. He resumed his formal role.

Lord Brentmore did not offer his arm, nor would Anna have taken it if he had. After what Miss Rolfe had suspected, she wished to be careful what impression she gave.

They entered the town house, where another footman greeted Anna and took their things. As they walked up the stairs to the ballroom, she felt an attack of nerves.

'Steady, Anna,' Lord Brentmore murmured.

The butler gave her a wink before stepping in the room and announcing, 'Lord Brentmore and Miss Hill.'

The chatter ceased for a moment and Anna suffered the gaze of many eyes upon her, followed by a hum of whispers. Lord and Lady Lawton stood to the side greeting guests, displeasure written all over their faces.

She felt Lord Brentmore's hand on her elbow. They approached the Lawtons together.

'Anna, this is not well done of you!' Lady Lawton glared.

'See here—' Lord Lawton huffed.

Lord Brentmore faced them both. 'Your daughter invited Miss Hill and begged me to bring her. It is the sole reason I attend.' His voice sounded dangerous. 'You will be civil to her or answer to me.'

'Anna, you should have known better,' Lady Lawton cried, as if the marquess had said nothing. 'No matter what Charlotte wanted you to do.'

Anna stood tall. 'I did know better, my lady. But Lord Brentmore insisted I attend and, since I am in his employ, what other choice did I have?' She turned to Lord Lawton. 'I would have nowhere to turn if I did not have the position he provides me.'

Lord Lawton flushed.

At that moment, Charlotte rushed over in a flurry of skirts. 'Anna! You came!' She gave Anna a quick hug and smiled at Lord Brentmore. 'I knew I could rely on you, sir!' She took Anna's hand. 'Come. There are so many gentlemen I should like to meet you.'

The names and faces of the gentlemen to whom Anna was introduced blurred after a while. Lord Vestry and Mr Norton, the men she'd met at Hyde Park, were among many others. This was not at all how Anna had wished to pass the time at the ball. She'd planned to find a chair near a big plant and wait out the entire thing.

She caught Charlotte between gentlemen for a brief mo- moment. 'Charlotte, you must stop pushing me off on these poor gentlemen.'

Charlotte squeezed her hand. 'Never! I intend to find one who will fall madly in love with you and then you shall no longer need to be a governess.'

Anna felt the blood drain from her face. Was that what this was about? Was Lord Brentmore in on the scheme?

She scanned the room and found him. He stood with Miss Rolfe, who was at that moment speaking to Peter Caine. Brentmore looked burdened. His gaze slid to her and held for a moment before he lowered his head and eventually turned away.

Anna felt a wave of sadness for him. She was not the only one who suffered.

'Oh, Anna!' Charlotte took a deep breath and pressed her hand against her stomach. 'I feel all tied in knots in- side. How am I doing? Am I talking too much? I feel like I am, like people are watching me. All I wish to do is run up to my room and hide.'

Anna fell into her familiar role. 'You are doing splen- didly. You are the very picture of a lively and delightful hostess.'

'I am just pretending, Anna.' She released a long breath.

Anna knew Charlotte could very easily freeze up when she started talking like this. Anna did what she'd always done: distracted her. 'Are there any of these gentlemen who particularly interest you, Charlotte?'

Charlotte surveyed the room. 'There is one man… But I do not see him yet.' She shot a glance over to Lord Ves- try and Mr Norton. 'Not those two, though. They are so childish.'

Lord Vestry and Mr Norton were whispering together like two dowagers with nothing to do but gossip. They caught Anna looking at them and quickly turned away.

The musicians began tuning their instruments.

'The dancing should begin soon,' Charlotte said. 'It is so much easier to dance and not talk.' She peered at Anna. 'Tell me you will dance.'

Anna shook her head. 'I should not—'

Charlotte pressed her arm. 'Oh, please say you will dance.'

Anna sighed. 'Very well. If anyone asks me.'

Charlotte gripped her arm harder. 'Oh, look. Here comes Mr Yates.'

Mr Yates walked up to them and bowed. 'Good evening, Lady Charlotte. Miss Hill.'

Charlotte smiled at him. 'I am so glad you came. Did—did you have any difficulty? I gave strict instructions that you were to be admitted.'

'No difficulty at all.'

One of Charlotte's gentlemen guests came to claim her for the first dance and she excused herself.

Mr Yates turned to Anna. 'So you are here after all.'

She nodded. 'Very unhappily.' She stole a glance towards Lord Brentmore. 'Very unhappily, indeed.'

Brent's gaze continued to seek out Anna. He was almost resigned to it, although he hoped it was not obvious to anyone else. Certainly in his party—Peter, Miss Rolfe and her parents—no one seemed to take notice.

She could not have looked more beautiful. Her gown flowed around her like water. Its blue colour brought out the blue in her eyes, so vividly that in the carriage he'd had to look out the window to avoid staring at her.

He watched her dance, her grace and her flowing skirts

making it seem as if she floated on the air rather than be attached to this earth.

He was also aware that other men noticed her, too. Perhaps Charlotte's plan for Anna would reach fruition. How could any man resist her?

That thought depressed him even more than watching Yates speak with her.

Lady Charlotte rarely left her side, except to dance, and after each set, quickly returned to her. Would the young woman want to know she and Anna were sisters?

After one set in which Yates danced with Anna, Charlotte dragged them all to where Brent stood with his cousin and the Rolfes.

'I do hope you are enjoying yourselves,' Charlotte said.

While the others were speaking—except for Anna, who looked distracted—Charlotte whispered to Brent. 'I do think she is a success, do you not, sir?'

'You are doing an excellent job of ensuring it, Lady Charlotte,' he responded.

In fact, as the night had gone on, Anna seemed to be gaining more approving glances from the men in the room.

The next set began. 'Let us all dance!' Charlotte insisted.

Brent glanced at Anna, who looked away. He asked Miss Rolfe to dance. Yates secured Lady Charlotte and Peter politely asked Anna.

The dance required groups of three couples to perform the figures. They began by facing each other in a line, ladies on one side, men on the other. They crossed and turned as the dance dictated, its music slow and sinuous. As Brent crossed the line and met Anna in the middle, their gazes caught. When they joined hands and danced in a circle, he clasped her hand. He could not say how any of the others moved or what expressions their faces held. It was, to him, as if he danced only with Anna.

God help him. He was to marry a woman who could occupy only fleeting thoughts in his brain, while Anna consumed all of him.

Finally the dance was over and he could try to break the spell that always seemed to weave itself around him when she was near.

He was only partially successful. He still could only make a pretence at conversation with others, when, all the while, he watched her.

She became more and more upset, he noticed. Something had happened, something that made her look like the caged animals at the Tower, as if she could do nothing but pace the cage and long for escape.

She broke away from Charlotte with some whispered excuse and made her way out of the ballroom. Brent followed her, determined to discover what had suddenly gone so wrong.

Other ladies walked in the direction of the retiring room, but Anna turned the opposite way, towards what Brent supposed would be the servants' staircase. He hurried after her, found the door and opened it.

She stood on the landing and whirled around when he entered the staircase.

He closed the door behind him. 'What is it, Anna? What is wrong?'

She hugged herself and rocked on her heels as if trying to soothe herself. 'May we leave now?' she asked. 'I really wish to leave now.'

He stepped towards her and seized her shoulders, trying to make her look at him. 'What is it? What happened?'

She kept her gaze averted.

He was puzzled. 'You have been dancing. You have received plenty of attention—'

'Attention,' she repeated sarcastically.

'Lady Charlotte meant for you to be such a success that you would have gentlemen proposing to you on the spot.'

'Proposing?' Her eyes looked wild. 'Not precisely.'

'Tell me, Anna.'

She met his eye. 'So you were in on Charlotte's scheme? Were you also in support of the idea that I needed to be married off?'

He frowned. 'You take this all wrong,' he snapped. 'Do you not see that marriage would be the best thing for you? You would have a home of your own, children of your own, something that is yours, not your employer's.'

Her eyes shot daggers at him. 'My whole life I have been manoeuvred and manipulated with others deciding what I should do. Now you, too, are deciding for me.' She leaned forwards. 'Do you wish to hear about the proposals I have had this night, Lord Brentmore? Because I have had many.'

'You have received proposals? Of marriage?' He felt sick inside. He would lose her after all.

'Oh, the proposals I've received are not of marriage.' She lifted her chin. 'It seems that Lord Vestry and Mr Norton have it on good authority that you and I are lovers and that when you marry Miss Rolfe, I will need a new protector.'

'No.' He felt as if punched in the stomach.

Gossip. Scandal. It followed him in spite of his efforts to avoid it. And now it wounded Anna.

She swung around and gripped the banister. 'I am sick to death of this! It becomes worse and worse. I find out I am not who I think I am, but I quite easily could become what they accuse me of. Even if I do nothing more to earn that reputation, I will somehow stand between you and your wife, because you and I—' She did not finish that thought. 'I will be honest,' she continued, her voice more composed. 'What is between us will not disappear.' She glanced away. 'What is between your cousin and Miss Rolfe will not disappear either, no matter how many miles he puts between them.'

'What the devil are you talking about?'

She clapped her hands against her head. 'Never mind! I'll not stay, do you understand? I'm leaving! I'll walk back to Cavendish Square if I must.'

She whirled around and ran down the stairs, her skirts flying, her shoes beating a frantic tattoo.

He ran after her, but by the time he reached the floor below, her footsteps were silenced and she was gone.

He rushed to the first door he saw, but was disoriented momentarily when he walked through. He emerged into the hall.

'Did she run through here?' he demanded of the footmen attending the hall.

'Who?' one asked.

He didn't pause to explain. He ran out of the town house and looked in both directions, but he could not see her. The streets were not safe for a woman alone.

He seized hold of one of the outside footmen. 'What direction did she go?'

The man pointed.

Brent shouted to him, 'Find my coachman and have him find us or go home.'

He ran off.

Anna ran as fast as her legs and ball slippers could carry her. She wished she could run all the way to the sea, like

Lord Brentmore had done as a child, anything to escape the disorder that had become her life.

She was like her mother, in love with the lord and more than willing to bed him. There was no use denying it to herself. The rumours those young gentlemen had contrived were based on something, a glimmer of the truth the men had gleaned from the way she and Brentmore looked at each other, perhaps. The sparks of attraction between them were so strong she would not be surprised if they were visible.

She could no longer talk herself into believing that she and Lord Brentmore could learn to resist each other. It was only a matter of time before they would fall in bed together.

She must be like his cousin and put distance between them. She must leave, no matter that she would be leaving the children—the poor children! She must go and trust that he would help the children to recover from her loss.

She reached Grosvenor Square and leaned against the wrought-iron fence, to catch her breath.

She heard footsteps ringing against the cobbles of the street behind her and knew it was him. She turned and he emerged from the darkness. She watched him stop and scan the area, and knew the instant he saw her. He rushed directly for her.

When he reached her, he gripped her arms. 'Are you mad? You put yourself in danger, running off alone.'

'I am alone,' she countered. 'Why pretend otherwise?'

'Enough of that nonsense.' He shook her. 'You have me.'

The sound of carriage broke into the silence of the street. 'That will be our coachman.' He dragged her into the street and waved to the man, who stopped the horses.

Lord Brentmore picked her up and carried her to the carriage. He lifted her inside and climbed in after her. 'Home,' he called to the coachman.

He sat next to her, but she slid quickly over to the far side of the carriage.

'Do not say more,' she cried. 'I know it was foolish to run, but I had to get away. I still have to get away.'

He seized her wrist. 'No more running. We face this now.'

'I have faced it, my lord,' she said. 'Nothing will change as long as we are together.'

He touched her face. 'No more of this. Call me Brent or Egan. Call me who I am, not my title.'

She turned her head away.

He moved closer to her and drew her into his arms, settling her against him, as he had done in the inn's tavern. 'I am sorry for the talk about you and me. I wish I could stop it. Nothing stops gossip but time. Protesting it only makes it worse.'

'The gossip is correct,' she said. 'We have not made love, but we both know I am too much like my mother—willing to take what I can and ignore the consequences.'

'Was your mother beautiful?' he asked.

She was too tired to ponder why he was asking. 'Very beautiful.'

He went on. 'Was she passionate?'

'I suppose so.' She shrugged.

He planted a kiss on her temple. 'Then you must be like your mother.'

She tilted her head. His lips were close, very close.

She slowly raised her lips to his, touching them lightly, tasting them with the tip of her tongue. She felt his body tense.

'Anna,' he rasped.

And took possession of her with his mouth.

She dug her fingers in his hair and indulged in the kiss while her body erupted in flames.

His hand cupped her breast and she longed to remove her gown, all her clothing and to finally feel his skin against hers. She yearned to finally learn the pleasures of joining with him.

This time there was no stopping. She wanted him, urgently wanted him. Before she left him, she wanted to know the glory of making love with him.

The carriage stopped. They were home.

Chapter Eighteen

Brent lifted her from the carriage and held her hand tightly in his as they hurried to the door.

A sleepy footman gave them entry. If he was surprised that Brent did not have his hat and Anna did not have her wrap, he did not say.

Brent and Anna walked past him, up the stairs. When they reached the second floor, Brent lifted her into his arms and carried her into his room, glad he'd told his valet not to wait up for him. The light from the fireplace cast the room in a soft glow, enough to see by. He carried her to the bed and set her down, kissing her again, a kiss of promise.

He pulled off her shoes and, kicking off his own, shrugged out of his coat and waistcoat.

She presented her back to him and he quickly undid the line of buttons there. She immediately lifted the dress over her head and waited for him to untie the laces of her corset. Then she spun around and watched as he rid himself of his shirt, breeches and stockings.

He had not considered that this was most likely her first view of a real naked man, but she was game. Her gaze flicked over him with approval and pleasure as she removed her stockings. He climbed on the bed next to her.

'I'll be gentle with you,' he assured her as he slid his hand over the soft thin fabric of her chemise.

She pulled the flowers out of her hair and used her fingers to comb out the tangles. 'I do not know if that is what I wish or not.'

She rubbed her fingers over the muscles on his back and he thought his senses would soar to the heavens. He edged her chemise up and she raised her arms so he could pull it off.

He gazed at her, becoming even more aroused to finally drink in the sight of her full breasts, dark-rose nipples, narrow waist and the dark hair at the apex of her legs. His eyes wandered back up the length of her.

He touched the necklace she wore.

'Should I take it off?' she asked.

'No need.' Odd that she should have selected that piece. His wife had looked at it and thrown it on the floor, uttering, 'Cheap trinket.'

Her brow creased. 'What is wrong? Do I disappoint?'

He knew now that the pendant, so perfectly matching her eyes, had always been meant for her. 'You could never disappoint,' he told her. He peered into her eyes. 'Are you certain of this, Anna?'

'Very certain,' she murmured. 'Show me. Show me, Egan, how loving you feels.'

His name on her lips, a name no one else spoke, made his heart swell. He loved her, he realised. There would be no going back if he consummated that love.

He'd find some way to make it all right, to face the scandal, to show the children how to surmount it.

He wanted to rush to that moment of no return. It was the place he wanted to be, a place they both belonged, the inevitable result of that first glimpse of her. He wanted all of her, wanted to feel himself inside her, wanted to feel her pleasure vibrate around him.

He whispered to her, 'Do not be alarmed. I am going to touch you. To prepare you.'

He slid his hand between her legs and gently stroked the part of her that was the key to her pleasure.

She gasped and arched her back, moving against his hand as she would soon move against his body.

'Never dreamed of this,' she managed.

'Neither did I,' he rasped. He'd never dreamed making love could feel like this. So important. So momentous. So right.

He withdrew his hand and rose over her. She smiled at him, a sensuous smile that stoked his masculine pride.

His body wanted to plunge into her and take his pleasure in a wild frenzy, but his heart wanted to make this first time as easy and pleasant for her as possible.

He forced himself to enter her slowly, a little at a time, giving her body a chance to adapt to him. She moved against him so that he slipped in easily.

He thought of the dance they'd briefly shared earlier, of the music and the rhythm, of moving closer and away. He moved now as if to the music, a dance that belonged to the two of them alone.

The music's tempo increased and he moved faster. She kept perfect pace, building his need little by little, extending the glory of her warmth enveloping him. A slow sensuous pleasure unlike he'd ever had before.

Anna was the first woman he'd cared enough to draw out the experience. No rushing to give the woman pleasure and take his own.

Anna made a compelling sound and he crossed the boundary between thought and sensation. His body took over and quickened the pace, building the need higher and higher.

She cried out and writhed beneath him, her climax coming in waves that pushed him over the edge. His seed exploded within her in an ecstasy of release. Together they reached the peak of sensation, the ultimate of pleasure.

And just as quickly the languor wended though him. Brent's bones seemed to melt like candle wax. He collapsed atop her and slid to the side, lying on his back, trying to make his arms and legs work again.

'No wonder,' she murmured.

'No wonder what?' he asked.

She turned her head and looked into his eyes. 'No wonder my mother wanted this.'

He caressed her cheek. 'Anna, believe me. This is more than what your mother ever had.'

To prove his point, as soon as his body recovered, he made love to her again.

And a third time, before he fell into a deep, contented sleep.

Anna rose from Brent's bed when the first peek of dawn appeared in the windows. She slipped on her chemise and gathered the rest of her clothing. With it bundled in her arms she gazed back at him.

He looked like Cal in his repose, so boyish and untroubled.

Making love with him had altered her. She felt now that a part of him would live in her for ever. For this brief time—these three brief times—they'd truly become one.

She resisted the urge to kiss him now. He might wake and that would make everything more difficult.

She rushed out of the room and ran up to her bedchamber. She dressed quickly and sat at the window to write two letters: one to Brent and one to the children.

There was no going back after this night that they had shared. No longer could she pretend she could see him briefly and act as the mere governess of his children. Brent—Egan—she was certain would understand. He, after all, faced the same situation. How could he build a marriage if he wished to bed the governess and she, him?

It was the children she grieved for the most. They would not understand. Perhaps they would never understand, even when they grew older. They would merely feel abandoned once more.

She knew, though, that the unhappiness her presence would cause would also spill over to them. Leaving was the best thing she could do.

And was the hardest.

Truth was hard, but not as difficult as living a lie. Truth opened the heavens and brought clarity. She knew now that she would some day tell Charlotte the truth about their connection. She wished she could ensure that Dory, too, would know who she was some day.

But she would never have that chance.

She'd packed a portmanteau in anticipation of travelling back to Brentmore Hall, a place she would never see again. It made leaving easier, before anyone saw her.

She tiptoed down the stairs and slipped out the front door. She was headed to the one person last night whose proposal she could accept.

She headed to Mr Yates.

Brent woke to the door opening. The room was bright with sunlight and the bed was empty next to him.

His valet stuck his head in. 'Do you wish to rise yet, m'lord?'

He felt the bed linens next to him, remembering she had slept there. Clever of her to rise early. Had she gone to her own room before anyone could take notice?

'I'll get up,' he mumbled. 'What time is it?'

'A little after ten, sir,' the man said.

Brent groaned. He had probably missed breakfast with the children.

He dressed hurriedly and went straight upstairs to the nursery. Anna and the children would have started their lessons already.

As soon as he walked in the nursery, Dory ran up to him. 'Papa! Miss Hill is gone! She is gone! Will she come back?'

He glanced around the room. Cal sat with his head bowed and his arms wrapped around himself.

Eppy rose from a chair. 'She left some letters in her room.' She pushed past him and gestured for him to follow her. 'I left them right where they were,' she whispered. 'Her portmanteau is gone.'

He entered Anna's room and broke the seal of the one addressed to him.

He read:

Dearest Egan,

Last night with you was the loveliest time I have ever spent. It also shows me how wrong it would be for me to stay. I've struggled with this for a long time, but now I know I must make a decision. I must leave or the happiness of too many people will be impossible.

Remember, please, that I love you and the children and it breaks my heart to leave you, but it is the best thing.

Yours always, Anna

He crumpled the paper and cried aloud, 'No!'

He would not let her go. He opened the children's letter, which said only that she had to leave and that she loved them above all things.

'What do they say?' Eppy stood in the door.

'That she has left us.' He felt empty.

Eppy nodded and dabbed at her eyes with the corner of her apron. 'I was afraid she would do something like that. What will you do, m'lord?'

'Find her,' he said. 'Stay with the children, Eppy. Tell them I've gone to bring her back.'

There was only one place she could be.

He could walk the distance faster than he could have a horse or carriage ready. As it was he practically ran to the Lawtons' house.

Lord and Lady Lawton were still abed, but Charlotte agreed to see him.

He paced the drawing room until she walked in. 'Where is Anna?' he asked.

Her eyes widened. 'Is she missing? I—I know she left the ball early. Disappeared, really, but you did, too, so I thought—'

'Lady Charlotte.' He spoke in his severest voice. 'Is she here? I beg you to tell me if she is.'

'She is not here,' she cried earnestly. Her fist covered her mouth. 'Do you think she has met with an—an accident?'

'No.' Where was he to look from here? 'I think she left deliberately, but how and to where, I cannot guess.' He strode to the door. 'But I will find her.'

He walked to the hack stand nearest Cavendish Square to see if any of them had taken her somewhere. None had.

He checked at various coaching inns, also to no avail. Walking back, he thought over everything she had said to him the previous night.

Grasping at straws, he decided to call upon Yates. Perhaps she had said something to Yates the previous night that would provide some clue. Yates's London town house was on George Street, not far from Hanover Square.

'Mr Yates is not here,' his manservant said. 'He went out earlier. You are welcome to wait, but he did not say when he would return.'

'Tell him Lord Brentmore wishes to see him on an urgent matter.' What more could Brent do?

He started to leave, but turned back. 'Tell me. Did a lady call upon Mr Yates this morning? A pretty young lady with auburn hair and blue eyes?'

'Why, yes, my lord,' the man said. 'She carried a portmanteau and Mr Yates left with her. He has not come back since.'

Brent felt as if a shaft had run through him.

He'd believed in Yates. Trusted him that his former betrayal had been Eunice's doing. He'd more than extended the olive branch to the man and Yates had turned around and acted the libertine at the first opportunity.

Brent's anger escalated as he walked back to his town house. How big a fool could he be?

When he opened the town-house door and stepped into the hall, Davies hurried up to him. 'Mr Yates has been waiting for you, m'lord, for almost as long as you've been gone.'

Brent strode into the drawing room. 'Why are you here, Yates?' he growled. 'What tale did you tell Anna to get her to go to you?'

Yates held up a hand. 'Wait, Brent! I can imagine what you think, but let me explain.'

Brent folded his arms across his chest. 'Explain why you took her from here? From my children?'

Yates gave him a sympathetic look. 'From you, you mean.'

Brent started to protest.

Yates shook his head. 'I could see the two of you were besotted with each other, even though you are intent on marrying another woman who does not love you. I do not know what happened last night between you and Miss Hill, but I expect you could tell me.'

Brent glared at him. 'You said *you* would explain.'

Yates nodded. 'She came to me this morning needing a place to stay. I could not have her stay with me in London, so I sent her to my estate.'

The estate near Brentmore where he had carried on his affair with Eunice.

Brent peered at him. 'To what purpose?'

Yates stepped back and lowered his voice. 'Brent, I promised you that I had reformed and that I want to atone for what I did to you. I have not changed. Last night when I saw Miss Hill so distressed, I told her I would act as her friend, if she needed one.'

Exactly what Brent had done. Offered friendship, but Brent had known there was more between them than friendship.

Yates went on. 'This morning she arrived with a portmanteau, asking for help. I suspected something had occurred between the two of you, but I did not ask and she said nothing. Only that she needed a place to stay until she could rally.' He looked Brent in the eye. 'You could reach there before dark if you left now.'

Brent looked away. 'I cannot. I have matters to attend to here.'

Chapter Nineteen

It had been a mistake for Anna to go on the long walk she'd taken, but after two days, she'd been so restless, so disconsolate, that she'd needed exercise and country air.

What she had not needed was to climb a hill only to discover it looked down upon Brentmore Hall.

She could see the archway she had passed through when first arriving at Brentmore and where Brent had kissed her. A corner of the kitchen garden was visible. Were there still peas to be picked? she wondered. Would the children plant other vegetables without her? Beyond the house were the stables and paddocks where the children had ridden their ponies and where Cal had begun to speak.

The pain of their loss brought her to her knees and it was a long time before she could make herself rise and embark on the long walk back to Mr Yates's house, not as grand as Brentmore, but a comfortable, prosperous property.

His servants had been gracious to her. She did not know if they really believed she was the down-on-her-luck sister of an old school friend who had died in the war, but they certainly could tell merely by the shadows under her eyes that she was down on her luck.

She had not yet written letters to seek a new governess

position. The idea of taking care of children other than Cal and Dory was, at present, too difficult to contemplate. Perhaps she would seek a companion position instead. Or teach in a school.

She pressed a hand to her abdomen. If she was not with child, that was. It seemed impossible to her that such a night of loving could fail to produce a child. His child. Her heart fluttered merely to think of the joy of holding his baby in her arms.

Even though she would have no way to care for the child herself.

Most of the walk back, though, she thought of Brent. Would he find happiness with Miss Rolfe? Would she indeed transfer her affections from his cousin to him?

She knew Mr Yates would tell Brent where she was. A part of her had hoped he would come for her, but that was mere reverie. He would see the logic in her leaving. He would accept it.

But no on could take away that one glorious night with him.

She crossed the field and soon would be in sight of Mr Yates's house. She walked along the road that led to the village. It was fortunate there was no chance she would encounter Brent and the children at the village. Brent would remain in London for weeks, he'd said.

From behind her she heard a horse approach, moving fast. She stepped off the road so the horse and rider could pass.

Instead, she heard her name. 'Anna!'

She turned—and saw Brent, riding his horse Luchar towards her.

Breathing, thinking, feeling became impossible. All she could do was watch him, his coattails flying behind him, his strong thighs hugging the horse's sides.

He dismounted before the horse came fully to a halt.

'Anna!' he cried again, advancing on her.

'My lord,' she managed.

He held her arms. 'What did I tell you? No more *my lord*.'

'Are—are you and the children at Brentmore?' She must be meeting him on the road by chance, exactly what she feared, being so close to Brentmore Hall.

'We are.' His expression sobered. 'I came for you, Anna.'

She glanced away. 'I cannot, my lord—Brent—*Egan*.' Her voice lowered to a whisper when she spoke his given name. 'I cannot be your governess. Not after—after making love with you. You once said it would change things. It has.'

'It has changed things for me, too, Anna.' He released her. 'May I walk with you and tell you?'

'It is no use,' she said, feeling anew the agony over their situation.

'I will tell you anyway.' He held Luchar's reins in his hand and walked beside her. 'After you left and I was searching for you, I came up with the solution to everything.'

She pressed her hand against her abdomen again. 'I cannot be your mistress.'

'I do not want you to be my mistress, Anna.' He stopped and held her face in his hand. 'I love you. I love you like my Irish grandfather used to tell me my father loved my mother. My father gave up everything for her. I am giving up worrying what other people think, worrying that my children will suffer the taunts I received, worrying that they will not be able to handle themselves in the face of it. They have been through much worse than taunts and

slurs.' He made her look into her eyes. 'Do you comprehend what am I trying to say? I want to marry you.'

'Marry me!' Her heart pounded. 'A marquess cannot
marry the daughter of a laundress!'

'He can. Had my parents lived, my father would have
been a marquess married to the daughter of a tenant
farmer.' He paused. 'Besides, you are also the daughter
of an earl.'

She looked away. 'What of Miss Rolfe? And her family?
You will ruin her. Her whole family will suffer.'

'I fixed that.' He grinned. 'I paid all of Rolfe's debts and
I settled an amount of money and property on my cousin
so generous he can marry Miss Rolfe and take on helping
her brothers and sisters should they need it.'

Her eyes widened. 'That must have cost a fortune. You
would give away such a fortune for me?'

He grew serious again, 'You are worth twice that.'

She felt hope growing inside her, but she must not let it
flower. 'What of Miss Rolfe's reputation?'

'To marry my cousin, she was happy to be the one to
cry off. Her reputation will only bear a slight tarnish. It
will be forgotten in a fortnight.'

'But yours?' She was afraid to believe this. 'People are
already talking of us.'

'Let them talk.' He held her again and brought her face
close to his. 'I want you to be my wife. To be the mother
of my children. Cal and—and—Dory. And the babies we
will have together. We will be a proper family.'

He was offering her everything she'd never dared to
dream of. It meant she could share his bed every night,
wake up beside him every morning, give Cal and Dory
the love and security they deserved.

'What say you, Anna?' His brow creased in worry.

She broke into a smile. 'I say yes!'

He threw his arms around her and swung her around in joy. 'Come, Anna! Let us go home and tell our children the good news.'

* * * * *